I0576097

Edwin Winchester Stone

Rhode Island in the Rebellion

Volume 1

Edwin Winchester Stone

Rhode Island in the Rebellion
Volume 1

ISBN/EAN: 9783337380946

Printed in Europe, USA, Canada, Australia, Japan

Cover: Foto ©Andreas Hilbeck / pixelio.de

More available books at **www.hansebooks.com**

RHODE ISLAND

IN

THE REBELLION.

BY EDWIN W. STONE,

OF THE FIRST REGIMENT RHODE ISLAND LIGHT ARTILLERY.

PROVIDENCE:

GEORGE H. WHITNEY.

1864.

PREFACE.

A long preface is seldom read, and this shall be brief. It is right that the reader should know how the following letters came to be in print. The responsibility of the deed is less with the author than with many partial friends. They were written amid camp scenes and on the march, under circumstances unfavorable to literary composition, and were intended for private perusal alone. Portions of them appeared in the Providence Journal, and were received with a favor alike unexpected and gratifying. Numerous requests having been made that they should be gathered up as a Rhode Island contribution to the history of the War of the Rebellion, the author, with unaffected distrust of himself, has yielded to the judgment of others. At first, he designed to recast his correspondence, and give it the graver form of historic narrative, but time forbidding, he has exscinded unessential portions, added to it from parts "contraband" to the public at their date, and in notes drawn from official and other reliable sources, has given particulars of movements of which he was not an eye-witness. In the introduction is noted some points of great importance, viewed in their relations to subsequent events. In the Appendix will be found sketches of the Rhode Island infantry and cavalry regiments and batteries, besides other information that may hereafter be convenient for reference. The author has labored under the disadvantage of being unable to examine the sheets of his work until after they had passed through the press. Had it been otherwise, he might have pruned with more severity.

To General Edward C. Mauran grateful acknowledgments are due, for his courtesy in giving free access to the records of his office. Thanks are also tendered to Hon. John R. Bartlett, Rev. Dr. Barnas Sears, President of Brown University, Colonel William Goddard, Professor William Gammell, Rev. A. H. Clapp, Captain William E. Hamlin, United States Provost Marshal for the First Rhode Island Congressional District, and to officers of the army, for valuable materials furnished.

While the aim has been to show the honorable position of the State in an unhappy war, it has also been the design to present a comprehensive view of the consecutive campaigns of the Army of the Potomac, with the fortunes of which several of the Rhode Island regiments and most of the batteries have, for longer or shorter periods, been identified.

E. W. S.

HEAD-QUARTERS BATTERY C,

R. I. L. Artillery, November, 1863.

INDEX.

A.

Annandale, 37.
Alexandria, 38.
Andrew Sharpshooters, 61.
Army withdrawn from the Peninsula, 130.
Army, strength of, 132.
Ambulance Corps, 160, 165.
After the Battle, 153.
Arnold, Capt. Richard, 83.
Arnold, Capt. William A. 188, 239.
Arnold, Col. Job, 322, 330.
Arnold, Hon. Samuel G, (see Introduction,) 284.
Acquia Creek, 198.
Averill, Gen. 213, 240.
Allotment Commissioner, 226.
Allen, Lieut. C. wounded, 239; promoted to command of Battery H. [See Appendix]
Adams, Capt. Geo. W. 239.
Appendix, containing sketches of the Rhode Island Regiments of Infantry and Cavalry, and Batteries of Light Artillery; together with other matter of interest, 283.

B.

Battery A, 114, 188, 239, 266. [See Appendix.]
Battery B, 114, 188, 240, 266. [See Appendix.]
Battery C, 2, 7, 18, 22, 84, 93, 139, 159; fires the first gun at Yorktown, 45, 240, 259, 260; marches to Gettysburg, 261, 266, 276. [See Appendix.]

Battery D, R. I. L. Art. 17, 188.
Battery E, 58, 81, 114, 115, 142, 188, 238, 266. [See Appendix.]
Battery F, 38. [See Appendix.]
Battery G, 56, 58, 100, 188, 239, 266. [See Appendix.]
Battle of Bull Run, 140.
"   "   Antietam, 146.
"   "   South Mountain, 152.
"   "   Fredericksburg, 183.
"   "   Chancellorsville, 228.
"   "   Gettysburg, 264.
Butterfield, Gen. 268.
Barnes, Gen. 268.
Blanding, Colonel Christopher, 297-299.
Bucktail Sharpshooters, 12.
Burnside, Gen. 132, 328; expedition, 27, 149, 152; assumes command of Army of the Potomac, 177, 178; at Fredericksburg, 183, 197, 198; his second plan, 202; is relieved; takes a new command, 208.
Bethel, Great, 45
Berdan's Sharpshooters, 46, 60.
Buckley, Lieut. 57, 74, 92. 105, 112, 113, 188.
Bartlett, Capt. 56.
Bloodgood, Lieut. 188.
Buford, Gen. 240, 268.
Bucklyn, Lieut. John K., wounded, 267.
Battle of Williamsburg, 79.
"   "   West Point, 83.
"   "   Hanover Court House, 94.
"   "   New Bridge, 90.
"   "   Fair Oaks, 97.

A*

Battle of Five Oaks, 110.
"   "   Mechanicsville, 111.
"   "   Gaines's Mill, 112.
"   "   Malvern Hill, 115.
"   "   Chantilly, 142.
Black, Col. 62d Penn. 73; killed, 113.
Burges, Col. Tristam, wounded, 80.
Bathing, 90, 101.
Branch, Gen. 93.
Bitterness of Rebel Women, 105.
Boxes accumulated at Washington, 108.
Bowditch, Dr. Henry I. Plea for Ambulance System, 161.
Brewster, Col. W. R. 74
Brown, John, 157, 174.
Bissell, Col. 66.
Babbitt, Major, Jacob, wounded, 187.
Browne, Col. George H. 187. [See 12th regiment, Appendix.]
Bayard, Gen. killed, 191
Bliss, Col. at Fredericksburg, 187; commands 7th R. I. 327.
Birney, Gen. 188, 231.
Bates, Lieut. wounded, 235,
Bradford, Lieut. 235.
Brown, Lieut. T. F. 240.
Brown, Col. Nathaniel, death of, 300.
Berry, Gen. Hiram G. killed, 242.
Balloon excursion, 50, 69.
Bartlett, Secretary J. R. [See Introduction.]

C.
Christmas in Secessia, 14, 193.
Curtin, Gov. 17.
Cummings, Rev. Silas S. 301.
Curtis, Lieut. Colonel, killed, 313.
Cameron, Secretary, 17.
Centreville, works at, 33.
Campaign, original plan of, 39; approved by the President, 29.
Camps, arrangements of, 243.
Camp Winfield Scott, 51.
California Joe, 65, 101.
Contrabands, 69, 101.
Clark, Lieut. 74, 105, 113.
Cumberland Landing, 83.
Colored Population, 87.
Clay, Henry, birth place of, 95.
Casey, Gen. 98; his vindication, 101.
Cass, Col. wounded, 118.
Camp Randolph, march from, 145.
Coffin, Mr. diagram prepared by, 147, 150.
Curtis, Col. killed, 187.
Caldwell, Gen. wounded, 191.

Couch, Gen. succeeds Sumner, 200, 230.
Contrast between the North and South, 237.
Chittenden, Mrs. 219.
Clendenin, Col. 253.
Clark, Bishop, T. M. Speech of, 281, 289.
Church, Capt. Benj. killed, 298.
Clapp, Rev. A. H. 297. [See 10th Regiment in Appendix.]
Conclusion, 278-282.

D.
Drainsville, Battle of, 12, 17.
Donelson and Fort Henry taken, 23.
Davis, Jeff. inaugurated, 31, 85.
"   " misstatements of, 100, 216.
Dyer, Ex Gov. Elisha, 337, 341.
Disappointed feeling, 135.
Devens, Gen. 80, 135.
Dana, Gen. wounded, 154.
Douglass, Rev. Mr. seized, 173.
Doubleday, Gen. 186, 264, 268.
Douglas, Capt. William W. 321, 324.
Duffie, Col. 214. [See 1st R. I. Cavalry, Appendix.]
Delilah, a modern, 214.
Dennison, Rev. C. [See 1st R. I. Cavalry, Appendix.]

E.
Easton's Battery, 17.
Embarkation for Peninsula, 40.
Ellis, Dr. Thomas T. 119.
Embalming House, 128.
Expedition, Burnside, 307.

F.
Falls' Church, 7.
Foraging Expedition, 23, 24.
Faulkner's Opinion, 29.
Floyd and Pillow, 28.
Fairfax Court House, 35.
Fortress Monroe, 42.
Federal and Rebel losses, 121, 151, 157, 186, 187, 192.
Flies, a torment, 129.
Franklin, Gen. 83.
Ferris, Capt. Frank, 72.
Fales, Mrs. J. T. 221.
Fales, Corporal, H. B. death of, 222.
Fogliardi, Gen. 226.
Fiske, Lieut. 231.
Flyer, Corporal, 236.
Furloughs, form of, 217.
French, Gen. sword presented to, 254.

Funkstown, 276.
Field, Rev. Samuel W. See sketch 12th regiment.
Flanders, Rev. A. B. 304, 315.
Flag presentation at Newbern, 310, 321.

G.

General Assembly, thanks to Col. Sisson, 325; presentation to, 326.
Goddard, Col. William, 288. [See Introduction.]
Greene, Captain Joe, and his bugle, 38, 306, 321.
Guns, Meditations on 18; new do., 27, 159.
Griffin's Battery, 22.
Gove, Col. enters Yorktown, 73; killed, 113.
Griffin, Capt. 3, 46, 94, 116.
Gaines, Dr. a Secessionist, 105.
Gibbon, Gen. wounded, 191, 268.
Greenbacks, 226.
German Regiments, break of, 231, 241.
Gettysburg, description of, 264.
Graham, Gen. 268.
Great Britain, conduct of, 279
Goff, jr., Col. Nathan, 289, 292, 293.
Gould, Rev. J. B. 11th R. I. [See Appendix.]

H.

Hall, Rev. Edward H. 321.
Health of the Army, 26, 103, 127.
Hodges, Lt G. F. death of, 25.
Hampton, 44.
Heintzelman, Gen. opinion of, 53, 140.
Hooker, Gen. 77; opinion of, 53; wounded, 151; at Fredericksburg, 187, 190, 197, 210, 215, 231, 250.
Hazard, Capt. Jeffrey. [See batteries A and H, in Appendix.]
Hunt, Sergeant, horse shot, 116.
Hospital stores, 108.
Ham, George W. Jr., wounded, 114.
Harrison's Landing, 127.
Harrison's, Benjamin, Will,128.
Halleck, Gen. visit of, 131.
Harper's Ferry, loss of, 157.
Howard, Gen. 187, 229, 268.
Humphreys, Gen. 187,
Hazard, Capt. John G. 188, 232, 240, 266. [See battery B, App.]
Hoof rot, 182.
Hanna, Sergeant, killed, 240.
Howe, Gen., Festivity at camp of, 254.

Hunt, Gen. 268.
Hall, Rev. E. B. speech of, 288.

I.

Infernal Machines at Yorktown, 75,
Ives, Lieut Robert Hale mortally wounded, 150.
Ives, Captain T. P. [See Introduction.]
Is that Mother? 211.
Illinois Cavalry, 253.
Invasion of Pennsylvania, 253.

J.

Jameson, Major T. C. 321, 325.
Johnson, Lieut. D. 324.
Joinville, Prince opinion of, 52.
Jackson, Gen. killed, 191
Jillson Mrs. 219.
Jenkens, Charles wounded, 240.
Jencks, Major Henry C. 236.
Jastram, Lieut. Pardon S. 288.
Jackson, Gen. Stonewall mortally wounded, 242.

K.

Kidd's Mills, 90.
Kearney, Gen. 79, 99, 140; killed, 142.
Kane, Col. wounded, 12.
Keyes, Gen. 79, 82.
Kimball, Gen. 191.
Kelley, Lieut. Benjamin E. death of, 239.
Kelly, Corp. 236.
Kitchen, reform of, 249.
Kearny Cross, 252.
Kilpatrick, Gen. 268.
Knight, Paymaster Gen. Jabez C. 288.

L.

Lander, Gen. death of, 36.
Letters from Home, 66.
Lee Gen. 87,
Lee Gen. Wife of, 91; Invasion of Maryland, 156; Escapes into Virginia, 155, 237; Falsehoods, 275.
Lincoln, President, Visit, 126, 167, 191, 223.
Life in Camp, 181.
Lowe, Prof. 190.
Leave of absence, 215.
Lee, Lieut. 231.

M.

Manran, Gen. E. C. 310.
McCall's command, 12, 125.

McClellan, Gen. 13, 30, 32, 33, 36, 50, 91; narrow escape of, 81; general order of, 99; his line of movement, 171; relieved of his command, 177; general order of, 121; invested with Pope's command, 143.
Michigan 4th Vol., 13.
Mementos from Home, 21.
Martindale, Gen. 28.
Manassas evacuated, 33, 36.
Magruder, Gen. 34.
Mount Vernon, 41.
Monitor, The, 42.
Magruder's evacuation of Yorktown not voluntary, 74; Retreat from Williamsburg, 81.
Moies, Frederick T. killed, 210.
Merrimac, destruction of, 85.
McQuade, Col. 92, 93, 118.
Martin, Capt. 94.
Marshall, Col. and Secesh Sympathizer, 107.
McDowell, Gen. 132.
Morell, Gen. 93, 135, 144.
Mails, 141.
Meagher, Gen. wounded, 154, 191.
Mansfield, Gen. killed, 154.
Munroe, Captain, 3.
Miles, Col. 155; Surrenders Harper's Ferry, 175.
Meade, Gen. at Antietam, 149, 150; at Fredericksburg, 186, 197, 229; succeeds Gen. Hooker, 261; at Gettysburg, 265.
Milne, Lieut., 188; wounded, 266;
Mud is King, 209.
Marye's Heights, storming of, 232.
May, Patrick J. 210.
Merideth, Gen. 268.
Metcalf, Edwin Major, 298, 299.
Mason, Lieut. Charles F. [See batteries A and H, in Appendix.]
Monroe, Lt. Col. J. A. [See sketch Battery D, in Appendix.]

N.

News from England, 11.
New Year, 22, 194.
Newell, Dr. taken prisoner, 114.
Napoleon's method, 106.
Newton, Gen. 232, 235.
Nichols Sergt. 235.

O.

Owen, Capt. Charles D. 56, 58, 100, 188.
Old Church, 96.
Officers, how to distinguish, 248.

P.

Palmer, Gen. 324.
Pell, Lieut. Duncan C. 317, 320.
Pierce, Lieut. Henry R. killed, 319.
Providence Journal, 2.
Porter, Gen. Fitz John 5, 13, 141; relieved of his command, 182; balloon excursion, 50, 69.
Pierpont's E. Pluribus Unum, 15.
Plan of operations, 39.
Picket duty, 48.
Picket firing discountenanced, 58.
Picket anecdote of 59, 196, 224, 252.
Pensions, 67.
Paymasters, 66.
Pope, Gen. 132, 136.
Pontoon Bridges, 130.
Prim, General visits the army, 109.
Pleasanton, Gen. pursues Stuart, 169, 268.
Patrick, Provost Marshal, Gen. 213.
Prentiss, Sergt. Edmund F. 236.
Paul Gen. killed, 268,

Q.

Quinn, Rev. Thomas 296, 297.

R.

Rodman, William M. 287. [See sketch 11th Regiment, Appendix.]
Root, Rev. N. W. T. [See sketch 9th regiment, Appendix.]
Rhode Island Troops in Virginia, 3.
Review at Bailey's Cross Roads, 3.
Reconnoissance to Hunter's Mill, 10.
Rebel strength, 25.
"   pursued from Yorktown, 75.
"   mementos, 35.
"   falsehoods, 274.
Regiment, 4th R. I., 38; Sketch of, 303.
Regiment, 2d R. I., 61, 75, 82, 89, 111, 135, 142, 172, 228, 235, 240, 265; Sketch of, 288.
Regiment, Mass. 22d, 67.
"   "   1st and 11th, 69.
"   4th Michigan, 90.
Reynolds, Col. 48.
Raymond, Hon. Henry R. opinion of, 52.
Randolph, Capt. Geo. E. 58, 81, 114, 115, 112, 188, 231.
Randolph, Lieut. Richard K. 79.
Rebel Sharpshooters, 71; losses, 191.
Reno, Gen. 137; killed, 152.
Rodman, Gen. mortally wounded, 150.
Reflections on the War, 165.
Read, Capt. 111; Lieut. Col. 236.

Rice, Lieut. wounded, 111.
Rogers, Col. Horatio, 235, 265, 293.
Reynolds, Gen. taken prisoner, 113;
at Fredericksburg, 188, 210, 228;
mortally wounded, 261.
Rich, Lieut. 276.
Rectorstown, 277.
Russell, Lord John, Speech of, 281.

S.

Stables built, 9.
Sham Fights, 13.
Signal Corps, 22.
Spics, 25
Stoneman's Reconnoissances, 37,
75; Drives in Rebel Pickets, 86;
at Fredericksburg, 186, 210.
Smith's Division, 44, 186.
Sprague, Gov. 48; account of pur-
suit of Rebels, 76; congratulates
Gen. Burnside, 179; [for other
particulars, see Introduction.]
Sears, Lieut. Edward, 50.
Skirmishes, 58, 59.
Scenery on the Peninsula, 67, 87.
Secesh News-boys 108; Souvenir,
158.
Sigel, Gen. 137.
Stevens, Gen. killed, 142.
Scenes at Antietam, 152, 155.
Sharpsburg, 159, 176.
Sumner, Gen. 77, 117; at Freder-
icksburg, 181, 186; death of 205.
Sisson, Col. Henry T. 322, 323.
Stone, Edwin M. 287.
Steere, Col. W. H. P. wounded, 150,
312, 314.
Slocum, Col. John, killed, 288.
Smith, Gov. James Y. [See Intro-
duction.]
Soldier's Home. [See Appendix.]
Sedgwick, Gen. wounded, 154, 228,
237, 268.
Sanitary Commission, 220, 270.
Sears, Capt. Wm. B. 62, 111, 237,
291, 292.
Stanley, Capt. wounded, 111.
Stuart's Raid, 106, 214.
Sackett, Lieut. 167, 231, 240.
Snickersville, 176.
Sayles, Col. Welcome B. killed, 187
Soldiers' Rest, 217.
Sanitary condition of the Army, 219.
St. Patrick's Day, 223.
Sickles, Gen. 228, 224, 268.
Slocum, Gen. 229, 268.
Shurz, Gen. 231, 268.
Shaw, Capt. John P. 236.

Sick and wounded sent to Washing-
ton, 259.
Schell, Dr. 170
Shired, Gen. killed, 268.
Shaw, Col. James, 10th and 11th
R. I. [Appendix.]

T.

Tents, Sibley, 1, 216; shelter, 216.
Thanksgiving, 2.
Tyler, John, 41.
Tompkins, Col. Charles H. 187, 237,
266.
Tyler, Gen. wounded, 191.
Turner, Capt. 236.
Torslow, Lieut. O. L. wounded, 239.
Tew, Lieut. Col. G. W. 315, 322, 325,
326.
Tillinghast, Capt. Charles, killed,
309
Tompkins, Major. [See sketch bat-
tery A, in Apendix.]

V.

Virginia Weather, 8.
    "   Mud, 23.
Vermont Regiment 55.
Viall, Col. Nelson, 185, 293. 11th R.I.
Vinton, Gen. wounded, 191.

W.

Wise and Tyler, views of 19.
Washington's Birthday, 31.
Winthrop, Col. Theodore, death of, 15.
Weeden, Col. Wm. B. 3, 9, 71, 112.
Waterman, Lieut. and Capt. 57, 71,
105, 113, 116, 159, 189, 231, 240.
Wentworth, Capt. Lewis E. 61.
    "   Sharpshooters, 69, 71.
Warwick Court House, 68.
Wells, Lieut. Col. 73.
Wheaton, Col. Frank, 80; General,
185, 186, 235, 292.
White House, 87; evacuated, 124.
Woodbury, Col. 90, 91; killed, 118.
Warren, Col. 91, 92; Gen. wounded,
268.
Wounded left at Savage's Station,
119.
Webster, Col. Fletcher, killed, 142.
Whiting, Lieut. Leonard, wounded,
111.
Warner, Lieut. wounded, 111.
Washington, Birth Day of 31.
Wanderings, 189.
Washington, N. C. relieved, 323.
White, Rev. Henry S. [See sketch
5th regiment. Appendix.]

Warrenton, 177.
Weed, Capt. 232; Gen. killed, 268.
Wadsworth, Gen. 268.
Wayland, Rev. H. L. 300.
Woodbury, Rev. A. 283.

Y.

Yorktown, ball opened at, 45; besieged, 62; evacuated, 73; fortifications of, 74; letter left at, for Gen. McClellan, 75.
Young, Capt. 235.

ERRATA.

Page 27, for ' 12-pounders," read " 10-pounders."

Page 46, first line, for " right," read " left."

Page 46, second line, for " execution on our left," read " still further on the left of Griffin's."

Page 112, sixth line from bottom, for " corps," read " division."

Page 113, eighth line from bottom, for " Bucklin's," read " Buckley's."

Page 115, seventh and eighth lines from bottom, omit " under the temporary command of Col. Nelson Viall." Col. V. took temporary command of the Mass. 10th at a subsequent date.

Page 116, third line from top, for " Lieut. Waterman," read " Capt. Weeden." Lieut. Waterman had command of battery C. Allen's Mass. battery was under the supervision of Capt. Weeden.

Page 116, fifteenth line from top, for "42-pounder," read "32-pounder."

Page 159, eleventh line from top, for "Martindale's brigade," read " Griffin's brigade."

Page 159, third line from bottom, for "12-pounder," read "10-pounder."

Page 166, third line from bottom, for " Martindale's brigade read "Griffin's brigade.

Page 188 eighth line from bottom, for "18-pounders," read "12-pounders."

Page 207, bottom line, bombardment of Fort Pulaski, should read " April 10th and 11th."

Page 295, Major George Metcalf was commissioned in November, 1863.

•

INTRODUCTION.

The strangest occurrence of the Nineteenth Century is the attempt commenced, in 1861, to break up our national Union, and to establish, within its limits, a new nation upon the basis of Slavery. Without stopping to discuss the constitutional rights of that institution, or the right or the wrong of its presence on the North American Continent, it is a marvel scarcely less than that excited by the toleration of its iniquities for eighty-five years, that those who lived in the midst of its immoralities, witnessed daily its inhumanities, and saw, as they must, its antagonism to the purity of social life, and its dangerous nature as an element of State policy, should desire not merely its perpetuation, but its extension over regions still free from its blight. Yet such appears the fact, however unaccountable on purely moral grounds. By the natural growth of public opinion adverse to the chattel idea, and the power imparted to free labor by the agency of education, the friends of slavery saw their cherished system losing its controlling influence; and though, as its candid supporters frankly confessed, there was no just ground for complaint against the Free States on the score of unconstitutional aggression, yet, with suicidal fanaticism, the supporters of slavery resorted to every measure short of personal violence, and in some instances including that, to regain lost prestige and to ensure success to their favorite idea of expansion.

The framers of the Constitution, representing the South, were alive to the evils of slavery, and sincerely wished its abolition. The opinions of Washington, Jefferson, Madison, and other leading statesmen of the Slave States, are too well known to require repetition. They saw the necessity of union on some common ground, and if they adopted the National Compact with the clause touching involuntary servitude less clear, as to its real meaning, than is now seen to have been desirable, they honestly believed that the institution, which was an abiding contradiction of the declaration of human rights which has so long formed the staple of national boasting, was on the high road to its grave. They believed in the Union as an inviolable contract, and never dreamed that it could be cancelled except by the consent of every State party to it. But it now appears that there were those who privately held different views, and though they entered the Union with apparent sincerity, they did so really from considerations of temporary safety, but with the concealed purpose of leaving it, whenever, in their judgment, sectional interests could be subserved thereby. Of this class was Robert H. Lee, of Virginia, grandfather of the present commander-in-chief of the rebel army. In a letter written April 5th, 1800, and recently brought to light, he develops this design. " I confess," he says, " that I feel myself often chagrined by the taunts against the ancient dominion, but disunion, *at this time*, would be the worst of calamities. *The Southern States are too weak at present to stand by themselves,* and a general government will certainly be advantageous to us, as it produces no other effect than protection from hostilities and uniform commercial regulations. *And when we shall attain our natural degree of population, I flatter myself that we shall have the power to do ourselves justice with dissolving the bond which binds us together.* It is better to put up with these little inconveniences than to run the hazard of greater calamities."

This letter shows the early existence of an intention to secede, on the part of the slavery propagandists, when the Union should no longer serve their exclusive purpose, a fact charged upon them by Mr. Benton, in his Thirty Years' Recollections. It is also a key to the mystery of Nullification, in 1832, and of the strange and startling declarations, made in the beginning of 1861, that the President elect would never be permitted to reach Washington alive, or if he did, would not be suffered to be inaugurated. The time had now arrived for decisive measures on the part of the disunion leaders. By the legislation of many years, the Southern harbors had been strongly fortified, custom houses and arsenals built, mints established, and other advantages obtained, necessary to the strength and convenience of a new nation, and it only remained to see that the unreasonable demands of a disloyal minority were yielded to by a loyal majority, or to declare themselves out of the family of States. The latter were true to constitutional obligations, and the former, ill-advisedly for themselves, seized upon the alternative.

When the threats to do this were first made, the Free States were incredulous. The heated declarations, in Congress and out of it, were viewed as ebullitions of passion that would soon exhaust themselves, and all become quiet again. But in this they were mistaken. The mask of a generation was partially removed; and as Mason and Breckenridge boldly talked treason on the floor of the United States Senate, the country, for the first time, became seriously alarmed at the threatened rupture. The Free States had cultivated the arts of peace. The North loved the Union with a devotion deepened by a remembrance of the costly sacrifice at which it had been attained. Detesting the spirit that bold and reckless demagogues had exhibited, deploring the animosity they were exciting among their constituents against a law-abiding people, and shrinking from the calamities of civil war, the friends of the Union in the Free States readily favored the request of the State of Virginia, for a Convention of Commissioners " to confer upon the best mode of adjusting the unhappy differences then disturbing the peace of the country. In the spirit of conciliation, Rhode Island concurred in this request, and on the 30th January, 1861, the General Assembly, by joint resolution, authorized the Governor to appoint Commissioners to represent the State in a Convention at Washington. The appointees were Hon. Samuel Ames, Alexander Duncan, Esq., and Hon. William W. Hoppin, of Providence; George H. Browne, Esq., of Gloucester, and Hon. Samuel G. Arnold, of Middletown.

The Convention met on the 4th of February. Twenty-one States were represented; John Tyler, of Virginia, presided, and the Conference continued until the 27th of February, when, after a free and full discussion, a series of peace propositions were adopted, and referred to Congress for such action, as in the premises and under the circumstances, that body might deem advisable. The plan was, substantially, to guarantee to the Slave States the rights they had always, under the Constitution, enjoyed south of 36° 30′ of north latitude, but prohibiting forever the extension of slavery in territory north of that line where it did not then exist. No slave territory was to be acquired except by discovery, or for naval and commercial stations, depots and transit routes, without the concurrence of a majority of all the Senators from States which allow involuntary servitude, and a majority of all the Senators from States which prohibit the relation. Slavery was to be abolished in the District of Columbia only with the consent of Maryland. Congress was to pass laws preventing the importation of Coolies or persons held to service or labor into the United States and the territories, from places beyond the limits thereof; and in all cases where the United States Marshal was prevented, by violence or intimidation, returning fugitives from labor, the government was to pay their full value to owners from whom they had escaped. The slave trade was to be abolished forever.

These propositions, as a peace measure, failed to obtain the action of the national legislature. They were finally laid on the table, and with the close of the Thirty-sixth Congress, they expired.

The position of the Rhode Island delegation was one of delicacy and difficulty. Opinions at home were somewhat divided as to what should be done, and in the Convention they found extreme views prevailing. The President of the Convention, as afterwards appeared, was secretly committed to secession, and indirectly gave the weight of his influence in that direction, while Mr. Seddon, a representative from Virginia, openly avowed the doctrine. But keeping in view the declared purpose for which they were assembled, and looking at things as they then appeared, rather than as they appeared at a subsequent day, they went into the Convention as pacificators, with minds open to receive whatever light discussion might reflect, and resolved, by fair and honorable means, to do what could be done to restore the harmony of the States, and plant their future upon a basis that faction could never again disturb. But this was not easy. The delegates secretly devoted to a rupture, were constantly insisting upon what could not conscientiously, or upon any ground of justifiable expediency, be granted. The delegates from the border States, who knew more of the impending evil than they chose to reveal, pleaded for something to be done that would save them from a yawning gulf. The position finally taken by the Rhode Island delegates, received the concurrence of Ohio, Pennsylvania, and nearly one-half of New York, together with New Jersey and some others. In their report to the General Assembly, of their perplexing labors, they say : " It will be found, upon an inspection of the Journal of the late Conference of Commissioners, that the undersigned voted against many propositions in themselves just and expressive of *their* sentiments and *yours*, because inopportune and useless ; and against others because introduced for the very purpose of sowing dissention among the Commissioners, and to prevent agreement, by majority, upon anything. In this they must ask your candid construction of their conduct, looking to the crisis, the occasion, the purpose and effect of the matter upon which they were called to act; and their unwillingness to hazard an agreement upon that deemed by them unnecessary, by tacking to it that, which, however true, was at least useless, and might in the result be dangerous."

It is not the intention here to discuss the merits of the plan adopted by the Convention, or to enter upon a critical examination of the general course of debate. This is the more appropriate province of the historian of that body, and who, with full knowledge of the circumstances under which it met, and from a careful analysis of the varied measures urged, will be enabled to treat the subject impartially. The acts of public bodies, like the movements of armies, are to be judged from the stand-point of their own time. The popular voice then was for conciliation, and the report of the Rhode Island delegates shows that, to ensure tranquility to the country, they were willing to make such concessions as could be made without compromising the character of the State. If the Convention failed of its declared object, that very failure was useful in preparing the public mind for measures that followed.

The Peace Congress ended, President Lincoln inaugurated, and his administration organized, the leaders of a thwarted faction applied themselves diligently to their secession schemes. While Mr. Buchanan still occupied the Chair of State, the Country was painfully excited with rumors of a design to seize Washington, and, in view of possibilities, Governor Sprague promptly offered him the services of the Rhode Island militia for its protection. This offer the President saw fit to decline. Assurances of military support were also given to the Secretary of War through Secretary Bartlett, as early as January 12th, 1861. Thoroughly convinced that an eruption was about to take place, and that men for the protection of the Capital would be needed, Governor Sprague verbally instructed Major William Goddard to proceed to Washington, and privately signify to General Scott, the readiness of Rhode Island to furnish troops for that purpose. The facts in the case place the State, through its Executive, in a proud position, and the occasion for secrecy having passed, they are now, for the first time, made public. Major Goddard proceeded with the utmost dispatch to Washington, on, or about January 23d, 1861, and there received the following official communication :

STATE OF RHODE ISLAND AND PROVIDENCE PLANTATIONS.

EXECUTIVE DEPARTMENT,
Providence, January 24th, 1861.

MAJOR :

Under the advice of Senator Anthony, put yourself in communication with Lieutenant General Scott, and say to him that Rhode Island has from 1600 to 2000 uniformed, well disciplined troops, having, as you can inform the General, no superior in those qualifications which make good soldiers. Say that 600 to 700 are Riflemen, the balance Infantry, including 1 Battery Light Artillery, 6 guns,—the latter in excellent state of equipment and efficiency, and of which you can speak more in detail. Say that these troops could be put in almost immediate readiness for service, if intimation was given that all, or any part, would be wanted. Rhode Island would deem it a high honor, to be called upon to furnish her troops to aid in protecting the Constitution and the laws, and the troops would obey, with alacrity, any orders to this end. The troops could also be put in readiness and moved, without the fact transpiring.

Say, in conclusion, that this government would esteem it a great favor, if the General would intimate whether or not the services of the above would be accepted, and this without fear (that if required) it would be known.

I am, &c.,

(Signed)   WM. SPRAGUE.

To Major. Wm. Goddard,
        Willard's Hotel,
            Washington,
                D. C.

In obedience to this order, Major Goddard, accompanied by Senator Anthony, at once waited upon General Scott, and

B*

was received by the veteran commander with that distinguished grace of manner which neither the infirmities of age, nor the anxieties of those days of darkness ever diminished. Upon reading the brief note, in which Governor Sprague commended Major Goddard to the General as an officer of the State of Rhode Island, possessed of his confidence, and sent to Washington upon a special mission, General Scott exclaimed, "I have no doubt that the patriotic Governor of loyal Rhode Island has sent you to me with a tender of troops for the support of the Government." Major Goddard then explained in detail the offer made by Governor Sprague, and commented upon the efficiency of the troops. General Scott said, "I wish I had those fellows; I know the stuff they are made of. In the war of 1812 I commanded all the New England troops, and I must say that for bravery, for resolute endurance of fatigue and privation, for steadiness under trials, for high personal character, in fact, for all the qualities which make a good soldier, the soldiers of the regiment, composed chiefly of Rhode Island men, were the very best troops I commanded." This testimony of the first military commander of the age to the superiority of Rhode Island troops, passed from that moment into the history of the State.

General Scott adverted to the principle of etiquette, which demanded that an offer of this kind should be made to the Secretary of War rather than to him, and while he carefully avoided any expression of distrust in the honor and loyalty of his superiors in office, he made it manifest that he comprehended the reason why *he* was selected. Said he, "I have urged again and again, and in the most earnest manner, both verbally and in writing, upon the President and upon the Secretary of War, that I might be permitted to concentrate here troops for the defence of the Capital, but I grieve to say, in vain. I have even this morning written to the President, that, with 1500 good troops, in addition to those now here, I would undertake to hold the Capital against any force that could probably be brought against it, at this time ; but, alas, I can make no impression upon him. The President, Sir, has a natural dread of blood-shed, and so have I. But, Sir, there are cases in which a little blood-letting is the best, the only remedy, and in my opinion this is one of those cases. I have thought that, taking into account the reluctance of the President to consent to the use of the militia of the States, he might be willing to accept the services of the New York 7th regiment, which, having performed some services of a National character, might in some sense be regarded as a National regiment, which could be used without exciting the prejudices of which both he and the Secretary of War seem in apprehension. But, in spite of all my solicitations, I meet with nothing but refusals. And here I am ! God knows how much I should desire the aid of your gallant troops, but I am powerless ! The inauguration day is fast approaching, and I have but a handful of troops. I am too old to mount my horse again, but I am determined, if God spares my life, to ride in the procession with Commodore Stewart ; and I think, Major, our grey hairs will be worth a thousand men" !

A report of this, and of subsequent interviews with General Scott upon this subject, was carefully prepared and forwarded to Governor Sprague by Major Goddard. It is worthy of note, that, while a traitorous Secretary of War, and a timid, indecisive President, forbade General Scott to adopt a single extraordinary measure for the protection of the Capital, the military family of the General himself was composed in part of traitors and spies. Lieutenant Colonel Lay, an Aide de Camp to the General, constantly strove to prevent Major Goddard from further communication with his Chief, and persistently endeavored to dissuade him from further attempts to carry out his patriotic purpose. And when, a few weeks later, Major Goddard entered Washington with his noble regiment, under the gallant Burnside, and the battery attached to it, both of which he had on this occasion tendered to the Government, it was to find that Colonel Lay, after possessing himself of the plans of his General-in-Chief, had basely deserted to the enemy.

The assault upon Fort Sumter, April 12th, 1861, gave assurance that treason had taken an aggressive form, and the call of President Lincoln on the 15th of April for three months troops, to aid in suppressing it, received from Rhode Island a cordial response. The alacrity with which the First Regiment of Infantry and a battery of Artillery was filled, attested to the soundness of the State. Hon. Samuel G. Arnold, Lieutenant Governor elect, tendered his services to Governor Sprague as Aid de Camp, and as Lieutenant Colonel, took command of the Marine Artillery, Captain Charles H. Tompkins, (by whom it was organized,) which left Providence on the 8th of April, and proceeded to Easton, Pa., where he issued a spirited order, counseling fidelity to the Constitution and the laws, and if need be, "a willing sacrifice upon the altar of our country."

The Artillery remained in camp at Easton, ten days, perfecting its drill. It there exchanged its smooth bore guns for James' rifled cannon. On the 2d of May it reached Washington, the first volunteer battery that entered the field, and the first battery of Rifled cannon ever in the service of the United States. It was mustered out of service August 6th.

At a special session of the General Assembly, held in August, 1861, it was unanimously resolved, "That in the present crisis of our public affairs, there ought to be a full and sincere union of all political parties in support of the constitutionally elected government of the United States; and that this General Assembly pledges to the President of the United States the best exertions of the government and people of Rhode Island, and its entire resources for the preservation of the Union." This resolution was forwarded to the President, and received the following acknowledgment:

DEPARTMENT OF STATE.
Washington, Sept. 5, 1861.

SIR :—The government of the United States is indebted to the State of Rhode Island for a very liberal share of the men and material, as well as of the skill and valor, which have sustained it thus far successfully, against the unnatural and violent assaults of faction, which it has been called to encounter.

The President directs me to express his sincere and profound thanks to the Governor, the Legislature, and the people of that patriotic State, for the support they have thus already afforded to the cause of the Union, and for the assurance of still farther and more effective support which is given by the General Assembly, in the resolutions passed in August last, of which a copy has been transmitted to this Department.

The President feels assured that when, in after times, it shall be asked which of the thirty-four States was most loyal and most effective in saving our country from ruin in its present peril, the State of Rhode Island will have no fear that her traditional fame will suffer in the answer that shall be given.

I have the honor to be your Excellency's obedient servant,

WILLIAM H. SEWARD.

To his Excellency WM. SPRAGUE, Governor of the State of Rhode Island, Providence.

When the call for 75,000 men was made, Ex-Governor Banks, afterwards Major General in the volunteer service, declared that for a speedy and effectual suppression of the rebel uprising, the call should have been for 700,000 ; and the history of events since show the correctness of his opinion. Scarcely had the first regiment reached Washington, when the need of more men was perceived, and a second call was made. It was answered by Rhode Island with the spirit and promptitude of the first. The State was all astir, and every town wore the features of a military camp. In less than two weeks, the 2d regiment was enlisted, organized, and embarked for the Seat of War. Then, as the signs of resistance thickened, the gigantic proportions of the Rebellion gradually developed, and other calls for forces were from time to time made, the State, still faithful in her allegiance, continued her contributions of men. The Third regiment was quickly enlisted, and departed. The Fourth as quickly followed. Then came the Fifth and the Seventh; then the Ninth and Tenth three months' regiment; then the Eleventh and Twelfth for nine months service; and parallel with these came two regiments of cavalry and eight batteries of Light Artillery,; so that at the close of 1863, Rhode Island had sent upwards of 16,000 men into the field. This is exclusive of the 14th regiment, (colored,) and the 3d regiment of cavalry, which would swell the total to upwards of 18,000.

But to fairly represent the State in this contest with treason, there should be added to the number composing the Rhode Island quotas, men equivalent to a maximum regiment of infantry, enlisted in regiments of other States, and not less than one hundred officers serving in the regular army, the navy, and the volunteer regiments of different States, who are natives of Rhode Island. Generals Casey, Arnold, Sherman, Greene, Wheaton, (Burnside a son by adoption,) Captain Samuel T. Cushing, of the Signal Corps, Lieutenant G. S. Green, identified with the glory of the old Monitor, Lieutenant Newcomb, lately deceased, Commander S. F. Hazard, and many more distinguished for bravery, are names that belong to the military history of the State.*

In the Adjutant General and Quartermaster General Departments, the most unremitting activity was visible. To make the necessary arrangements for rapidly organizing and sending forward regiments of infantry and batteries of light artillery, and to clothe and equip them ready for service, involved an immense amount of labor, as well as the most careful pains-taking to ensure completeness; and to the able services of General Mauran, in the former, and of Generals Stead, Frieze and Cooke, successively, in the latter, the State is largely indebted for the reputation it has gained for system and efficiency.

---

*Captain Robert H. I. Goddard, of Providence, was commissioned March 11th, 1863, and is serving on General Burnside's staff.

From the beginning of the rebellion to the close of his administration, Governor Sprague devoted himself, with untiring zeal, to the support of the government and the interests of the Rhode Island troops. Nothing escaped his watchful eye, and nothing was left undone that could contribute to elevate and give power to State example. No Governor was so well known by reputation in the army of the Potomac, and the superior equipment of our men frequently called forth from the western soldiers admiring exclamations.*

When the Southern Atlantic States, following the lead of South Carolina, entered, with others, into a confederacy looking to nationality, it became apparent, that to cripple their energies and prevent a foreign recognition which they were bending all their efforts to secure, a close · blockade would be absolutely necessary. "Stop the rat-holes," was General Scott's comprehensive theory ; but these were numerous on a coast stretching from Cape Charles to the Rio Grande, and required, at least, five times the naval force that could then be commanded. It was vastly easier to bring an army of 600,000 men into the field than to create a navy of two hundred vessels, for a pressing emergency ; and while the Navy Department was exerting itself to the utmost to strengthen the naval arm, by purchasing and chartering steamers and sailing vessels, and by building at the yards, it gladly availed itself of patriotic offers made by wealthy citizens, of such marine aid as would hasten the completion of the blockade.

In this prompt and generous support of the government, Rhode Island was handsomely represented in the person of a citizen of Providence. When the first call for troops was made in April, 1861, Captain Thomas P. Ives, son of the late

---

* To meet the needs of the State Treasury in the emergency, and before definite arrangements were made with the Federal Government, A. & W. Sprague offered the loan of $100,000. The banks also made liberal tenders of money. For these offers, the General Assembly passed votes of thanks.

Moses B. Ives, was confined to his chamber by severe illness; and when the First regiment left for Washington, had not sufficiently recovered to show, by personally volunteering, the loyalty he cherished.   He had long cultivated nautical tastes, had been much at sea, and had attended to practical navigation. In the preceding autumn, he had built for himself a yacht of large size and unusual speed, and before he had sufficiently recovered to leave his room, he sent for the late General James and contracted with him to arm his yacht with the rifle cannon of his invention.   So soon as he was able to be abroad, he offered his vessel and his personal services to the government, in any way in which they could be employed.   His offer was accepted, and he was temporarily commissioned a Lieutenant in the revenue service, and stationed, during the summer of 1861, in the Chesapeake Bay, below Baltimore, where he was engaged in repressing the contraband traffic, then very largely prosecuted in those waters.   He won, during the season, frequent special approval of the successive commandants at Fort McHenry.

As the government drew its military lines more exactly, this kind of revenue service became unnecessary.   Before, however, it was ended, Mr. Ives was invited by General Burnside to accompany him in his expedition to North Carolina. He soon after received the proper commission from the War Department, and was made Captain of the expeditionary steamer Pickett, which bore the General and his staff to Hatteras Inlet.   The Pickett took a prominent part, as a gunboat, in most of the marine operations of General Burnside, especially at Roanoke Island, and in the approaches to Newbern.

Early in the summer of 1862, the duty for which his boat was fitted being all accomplished, Captain Ives resigned his commission, and again offered his services to the government, still as before, upon the water, his favorite element.   In August of that year, he received a commission. from the Navy Department, under the then recent act of Congress for the temporary increase of the Navy, and was soon assigned to the command of the gunboat Yankee, and attached to what is now styled the Potomac Flotilla. The sphere of his service, from that time to the present, has been on the waters of the Potomac, Acquia Creek and the other streams tributary to the Potomac. He has, in all stations, been distinguished for his nautical skill, his firmness in danger, and his fidelity to duty. Although his commission in the Navy is temporary, he has received several proofs of the confidence of the Department, and has been advanced to the post of fleet captain of the Potomac Flotilla, a post which he filled with great credit to himself. In December, 1863, he was detached from this command and assigned to duty in Providence, as Inspector of Ordnance. Captain Ives is thirty years of age. He succeeded his father as a member of the house of Messrs. Brown & Ives, of Providence.

During the process of organizing the army of the Potomac, the commander-in-chief was reported to have said, "This is to be largely an artillery war," and it is understood that he gave more than ordinary attention to increasing this arm of defence. With what rapidity that increase has progressed, few, perhaps, have an adequate idea, and it may awaken surprise, as well as indicate the strength of this department, to know, that since the first battle of Bull Run, the light artillery in the several armies has increased from a few batteries to upwards of two thousand guns. In this mass of power, Rhode Island is nobly represented. On the 1st of August, 1861, Hon. Simon Cameron, the then Secretary of War, authorized Governor Sprague to raise and equip a battalion of artillery, to consist of three batteries, one of which, Captain William H. Reynolds, was then in the field. Of this battalion, Captain Charles H. Tompkins was appointed Major, and proceeded at once to the work of organizing. Battery B, Captain Vaughan, and battery C, Captain Weeden, were soon organized under this order, and left for Washington. Volunteering for the artillery being so brisk, Governor Sprague asked for and obtained, just prior to the organization of battery C, an order to raise and equip two additional batteries, to be added to the battalion. The head-quarters of the battalion were established at Camp Sprague, Washington ; and as rapidly as the organization of the batteries was completed they were sent there. The two batteries—D, Captain Monroe, and E, Captain Randolph—were rapidly organized ; and on the 13th of September, 1861, authority was granted by the War Department to raise three more, the eight to constitute a regiment, and be called the 1st Regiment Rhode Island Light Artillery. Of this regiment, Major Tompkins was appointed Colonel, and Captain Reynolds, Lieutenant Colonel. The former spent most of his time at Camp Sprague, in disciplining and drilling the batteries. Lieutenant Colonel Reynolds most of the time in Rhode Island, superintending the organization of new companies, and forwarding each to Washington as soon as their numbers were full. As rapidly as the batteries arrived at a passable state of drill and discipline, they were assigned by the military authorities to the different divisions of the army of the Potomac. On the 1st of December, the regiment, with the exception of battery H, being all in the field, Colonel Tompkins was assigned to the division of Brigadier General C. P. Stone, then at Poolsville, and with which batteries A, B and G were serving.

Throughout the Peninsula campaign of 1862, Colonel Tompkins commanded the artillery of the second division, second corps, (Sedgwick's,) and was present at the siege of Yorktown, the battles of Fair Oaks, Peach Orchard, Golding's Farm, Savage's Station, Glendale, and the first and second of Malvern Hill. Upon the evacuation of Harrison's Landing, he was sent home to recruit for his regiment, which had become much reduced in numbers. He returned to the army in November, 1862, and since then has participated, as mentioned in other parts of this volume, in the battles of Fredericksburg, December 13th, 1862, and May 3d, 1863, Salem Chapel, Salem

Heights and Gettysburg, besides several smaller encounters. In the "seven days" battles upon the Peninsula, no guns were lost from his command, nor a wounded man left behind. The wounded of each day were added to those of the day previous, and carried from hospital to hospital on the caissons, so that all reached Harrison's Landing. Colonel Tompkins has been favorably mentioned in the reports of his commanding officers, for bravery and efficiency in every action in which he has been engaged. He has been strongly recommended for promotion to Brigadier, and twice recommended for Brevet for gallant conduct in action.

Lieutenant Colonel Reynolds was appointed to an important agency for the government, at Hilton Head, the duties of which he successfully and satisfactorily performed. He resigned his military commission, June 26th, 1862, and the service lost a brave and accomplished officer.

In December, 1862, Dr. Lloyd Morton, of Pawtucket, and Mrs. Charlotte Dailey, of Providence, were appointed a commission to proceed to Washington, on a tour of hospital inspections, having in view the welfare of sick and wounded Rhode Island soldiers. Dr. Morton visited the 2d, 4th, 7th, 11th and 12th regiments of infantry, the 1st regiment of cavalry, a portion of the regiment of light artillery, and twenty-one hospitals, besides the convalescent camps and the camps of distribution at Alexandria. Mrs. Dailey visited sixty-one hospitals. The examinations and inquiries were thorough, and the reports made by the commission to the General Assembly presented many interesting and important facts.

But the humanity of the State did not expend itself solely through official agents. Individual sympathy found free flow through Ladies' Relief Associations, organized in every town, or through personal communication with hospitals and camps. These spontaneous offerings of willing hearts and ready hands have already swelled to an aggregate intrinsic value of more than $200,000, but estimated by their influence upon the recipients, having a value beyond computation.*

Early in the rebellion, Executive attention was turned to the enlistment of colored troops. Out of New England, the employment of colored men as soldiers was an idea in advance of popular opinion. Prejudice frowned upon it, and pride denounced it. In Rhode Island a more enlarged view obtained. In the war for Independence, the State had sent into the field a regiment d'Afrique, which proved to be among the most efficient soldiers of the revolutionary army ; and if it was right to employ blacks in achieving a national existence, no sound logical reason could be assigned why their posterity should be debarred the privilege of defending the government under which they were enjoying freedom. Whatever hostility might have been felt to such a measure, and from whatever cause, the free discussion of the subject by the press throughout the country gradually strengthened popular opinion in its favor. The War Department having signified a readiness to accept a colored regiment from Rhode Island, Governor Sprague, on the 4th of August, 1862, directed an order to be issued for the enlisting of a sixth regiment, to " consist entirely of colored persons." " Our colored fellow citizens," the order continued, " are reminded that the regiment from this State, in the Revolution, consisting entirely of colored persons, was pronounced by Washington equal, if not superior, to any in the service. They constitute a part of the quota from this State, and it is expected that they will respond with zeal and spirit to this call. The commander-in-chief will lead them into the field, and will share with them in common with the patriotic soldiers of the

---

* From official reports, returns from towns and associations, and extended inquiry, it appears that the amount expended for the war, by the State, towns, relief associations and individuals, from April, 1861, to December 31, 1863, exceeds $4,000,000. If the free expenditure of money, to sustain the Union cause, is an evidence of the loyalty of a people, Rhode Island can ask no better record than these figures show.

army of the republic, their trials and dangers, and will participate in the glories of their success."

This call excited a lively interest among the colored population of the State. Public meetings were held in Providence, the subject freely discussed, and a general readiness expressed to form a colored regiment in Rhode Island. A rendezvous was opened, and about one hundred men enrolled; but owing to uncertainty whether they were to be employed as soldiers, on equal terms with other volunteers, or to be assigned to labor with pick and spade, together with other causes, the enterprise for the moment failed.

Governor Sprague having been elected Senator to the United States Congress, resigned the State Executive Chair, March 3d, 1863, and Hon. William C. Cozzens, of Newport, was elected by the General Assembly, then in session, to fill his place for the remainder of the year. Resolutions were passed by the Senate, thanking the retiring Governor " for the efficient and vigorous management of his duties," during the term of his administration, which was appropriately acknowledged in a farewell speech. At the succeeding annual election, Hon. James Y. Smith was elected Governor, and at the May Session of the General Assembly, took the inaugural oath. Governor Smith brought to the service of his new and responsible position, the energy and practical talent that had distinguished and given success to his business pursuits. He had, from the discharge of the first rebel gun at Sumter, given his active support, as a citizen, to the government, and the spirit with which he entered upon the duties of chief magistrate of the State, is perhaps best shown in a brief address, extracts from which are here quoted:

" This period in our history is full of interest. The eyes of nations are fixed upon us. Our national government has been attacked. The responsibility is great upon our people. Let us be firm although danger surrounds. Let us stand united before the world. The obligation of the solemn oath I have taken, demands of me to be watchful, and convey unimpaired to posterity all the blessings we are enjoying. We are admonished by the events surrounding us, that united action should govern. Let every loyal man step forward to the rescue, lay aside all partizan feelings, and join in one grand cry, ' Our country, the Union—it must be preserved.' Our country is the great object to which our efforts should be directed. Let us unite our strength, relying upon the Supreme Ruler to direct our steps, and we shall prevail. We have but one alternative—war—as has been said by an able jurist—'war without remission waged in all lawful modes, and by all classes of citizens, without prejudice to caste or color. A frightful prospect indeed! But let him who shudders at it remember that the God of love is also the God of battles, and that blood is the price of progress.' My experience in public life confirms the opinion, long since advanced, that the destruction of our national government would fasten upon us everlasting revolution. Impressed with these opinions, I shall ever be ready to advance such measures as will secure to us our fixed position under the national Union, jealously watching every event, as without union our liberty can never be preserved. Our brave soldiers must share largely in our sympathy. They are battling for our existence, and nothing should be left undone that will add to their comfort."

The purpose of raising a colored regiment, though temporarily suspended, was not abandoned. Since the first proposition, at which the War Department, from prudential considerations, hesitated, public opinion had been rapidly outgrowing its prejudice. Circumstances had changed. Things appeared in a new aspect, and the clearly revealed popular feeling authorized the government to take a more decided step. One of the early acts of Governor Smith was to communicate with the authorities at Washington on the subject, and obtain permission to enlist a colored company of heavy artillery. This was granted. June 17th. On the 4th of August. the permit was extended to a battalion ; and September 3d, again extended to a regiment. In accomplishing this work, many and peculiar difficulties occurred, but all were successfully overcome. To Colonel Nelson Viall, an officer of large experience, was assigned the work of organizing and disciplining a body of men hitherto not made available for bearing arms. The change in public opinion, alluded to, wrought by the events of less than three years, is among the remarkable facts of the time, and the effect of the early efforts of Massachusetts and Rhode Island to put colored troops in the field; and the success crowning those efforts, must be to strengthen a policy that, consistently persisted in, can give to the government a fresh force of two or three hundred thousand men, better fitted by nature for southern service than whites, and render further draft upon the mechanical and agricultural departments of the country, unnecessary. The successful part taken by Rhode Island in this movement will be a conspicuous fact in her military history.

The exposed condition of the Rhode Island coast, and especially of Narragansett Bay, in the event of war, had been, for many years, the subject of comment, and the importance of putting the approaches to Newport and Providence under sufficient protection, often urged. General Totten, in 1851, made a report bearing favorably upon the matter. In a communication to the Providence Journal, dated January 6th, 1862, Hon. William H. Cranston, Mayor of Newport, pointed out very clearly this need, and urged such defences as would secure the east and west passages from being successfully penetrated by an enemy. On the 14th of the same month, Governor Sprague referred to the subject in his address to the General Assembly; but nothing was done that secured the object. After the confederate government succeeded in getting two or three vessels upon the ocean, it was at once perceived how much mischief could be done by coast piratical operations ; and the bold dash into Portland harbor, in June, 1863, together with the hostile attitude of England, awakened much

alarm along the entire New England coast. An early purpose
of Governor Smith was to secure this protection, and earnestly
pursuing this design, he addressed the following telegram to
the President :

June 27th, 1863.

To His Excellency ABRAHAM LINCOLN,
    President of the United States, Washington, D. C. :
    Great anxiety is felt here on account of the unprotected condition
of Narragansett Bay. There is nothing to prevent a rebel incursion
through the "West Passage," exposing to destruction this city, Fall
River and other towns on the Bay. I respectfully request immediate
authority to construct, arm and man suitable earthworks, at the expense of the Federal Government, and that the plans understood to
be in the War Department for such works, be furnished without delay. Also, authority to cause all vessels to be brought to and inspected before entering the Bay.
                (Signed,)   JAMES Y. SMITH,
                                    Governor of Rhode Island.

To this application, the following reply was immediately
returned :

WASHINGTON, June 27th, 1863.

Governor SMITH :
    I am instructed by the President, to inform you that the authority
asked for in your telegram of this date is granted to you. The Chief
of the Engineer Bureau is instructed to furnish you the plans, and
also an engineer officer to assist in laying out the work.
                (Signed,)   E. M. STANTON,
                                    Secretary of War.

Acting under this authority, Governor Smith at once proceeded with the work. For temporary defence, a light battery, under Colonel Edwin C. Gallup, and a company detailed
from the 1st regiment of Rhode Island militia, composed of
students in Brown University, under Captain John Tetlow,
were stationed at the "Bonnet," near the South Ferry, on the
Narragansett shore, to command the approach to the West
Passage. Here a breastwork was thrown up, and the encamp-

ment named " Camp James Y. Smith," in honor of the chief magistrate of the State. Major E. B. Hunt, of the Engineer department, was sent on by the Engineer Bureau, to lay out and superintend the erection of the fortifications. An eight-gun battery was immediately laid out on Dutch Island, a little south of " Camp Bailey," and as successive companies of the colored regiment were sent there to complete its organization and for instruction, daily details were made to labor on the fort until completed and the guns mounted, saving to the government a heavy expense, and giving to the men a valuable experience. The government has a ten-gun battery in progress in the rear of the light-house, and contemplates another of fifteen guns on the north-west side of the island. It was a part of Major Hunt's plan, to erect a battery for heavy ordnance on the summit of the island.* These works, when completed and mounted, will command all the approaches, and serve alike for offence or defence.†

It will be seen, by reference to page 278, that the narrative of the operations of the Army of the Potomac closes with the battle of Gettysburg, the political effects of which were soon perceptible in England, in the changed tone of the government press, and a semi-official avowal of a strictly neutral position. Similar effects were also made visible in France.

---

* Major Hunt was unfortunately killed at New York, in the autumn of 1863, while testing a shell of his invention. He was an accomplished engineer, and, at the time of his death, was doing government service in several places.

† The government is the entire owner of Dutch Island, having, in 1863, purchased that portion not previously in its possession, of Powell H. Carpenter, Esq., for $21,000. The island contains eighty acres, of which the government, before this purchase, held six acres for light-house purposes. It was originally owned by the Indian sachems, Wequagannett, Kaskasabo and Quissurkqnantt, who deeded it to Randal Holden and " Mr. Brenton," March 28th, 1659. It has one of the best harbors on the coast, is easy of access, and is often sought in stress of thick or tempestuous weather.

Since the victory of July 4th, ushering in the National Anniversary with jubilant shouts from twenty millions of freemen, military operations have taken place that may properly be noticed in this place.

The boldness of the rebel commander-in-chief of the Army of Virginia, is shown in his invasion of Maryland in 1862, and of Pennsylvania in 1863. Though disappointed at Gettysburg, and compelled to beat a hasty retreat behind the Rappahannock, it was not to be expected that he would long be quiet. The barb of that Pennsylvania arrow made a ragged and painful wound, that nothing but the lenitive of a positive success could soothe or heal. For two months or more after his escape, his prolific mind was busy in contriving strategetic plans for recovering lost prestige, and wounding the Union forces in some vital part. To withdraw attention from the disposition he designed to make of his forces, and the uses to which they were to be put, guerrilla raids were multiplied, skirmishes engaged in, and other methods of annoyance practiced. In September there were indications of mischief on his part, and a subsequent change in the position of our army, contracted a line too long for easy defence, and placed it on a better field for observation.

On the 9th of October, General Lee's army was in motion for a new enterprise. The object, as stated in his subsequent report, was to bring on an engagement with the Federal army, which was encamped around Culpepper Court House, and extending thence to the Rapidan. To avoid observation, and ensure success in the choice of position, as well as to come suddenly and unexpectedly upon the Union forces, his march was by circuitous and concealed roads. His movements, however, were observed; and the falling back of our army upon Centreville and Chantilly, where Sedgwick's (6th) Corps occupied the extreme right of the line, with Kilpatrick's Cavalry protecting its flank, completely check-mated his purpose. Another object, not avowed by Lee in his report, as that would

have compelled the admission of a failure, but which the Richmond Examiner revealed, was "to interpose a corps of his
army between a large portion of Meade's force in Culpepper
and Washington;" in other words, to turn our right flank, and
make a push for the Union Capital. Independent of forcing
a withdrawal of the menace of Richmond, the operation, had
it succeeded, would have been good for almost any purpose.
The possession of Washington, in these days of darkness, to the
rebels, when England, alarmed by her own short-sighted
statesmanship—if that which Talleyrand pronounced worse
than a crime, a mistake, can be called statesmanship—was
beginning to look coldly on secession, would have been a glorious stroke of good fortune, and the disappointed rebels could
have afforded to forgive Lee the false report he made, claiming an overwhelming victory at Gettysburg! If, on the other
hand, he had succeeded in simply pushing our army back to
the line of its old encampments, running north from Fort Lyon,
along Munson's and Miner's Hills to Lewinsville and Langley's, and thus gained time for such complete destruction of
the Orange and Alexandria railroad, as would have required
two or three months to renew, he might have felt secure in
largely depleting his army for the benefit of the hard-pressed
confederates in the southwest. But he did neither. At Bristow's Station he lost five pieces of artillery, and a considerable
number of prisoners. He utterly failed in his flank movement;
and though he made very thorough work in destroying the
railroad as far as time permitted—thereby setting the Federals
a suggestive example in their future raids—he was able to
remove and destroy no more than two weeks could restore—a
time totally insufficient to render any extensive relief to his
discomfited brethren, without incurring an unwarrantable risk
of his own safety; and if the events of the month changed
somewhat the relations of the two opposing armies, the disadvantage evidently enured to Lee and not to Meade. The
schemes of Lee were well devised, but though his line of march

was the shortest, Meade had the swiftest feet, and these gained the position that frustrated the plans of the former, and compelled him to fall back.

As Lee retreated, the Army of the Potomac gradually returned to its old position, the Sixth corps finding itself once more in the vicinity of Warrenton, holding Water Mountain for a signal station. It now became General Meade's turn to assume the positive, and on the 7th November, the army made a forward movement. General Sedgwick's corps advanced to Rappahannock Station, where it had a fierce encounter with the rebels, resulting in their rout. The captures were two redoubts, four pieces of artillery, eight battle flags, 2000 stand of arms, one bridge train, and 1600 prisoners. The Federal loss was about 300 killed and wounded. The charge was made by General Wright's division, and the redoubts carried by the 6th Maine and 5th Wisconsin. The 121st New York, 5th Maine, 49th and 119th Pennsylvania, took the line of rifle pits. The third division, with which the 2d Rhode Island was connected, was held in reserve.

General French (third corps) engaged the enemy at Kelly's Ford, driving them across the river, seizing their entrenchments, and capturing over 400 prisoners. His loss was about 70 killed and wounded. The Rhode Island batteries engaged displayed great spirit and bravery. Among the advantages secured by this success was the preservation of twenty-four miles of railroad and an equal length of telegraph between the Rappahannock and the Rapidan. The captured battle flags were formally presented to General Meade, at head-quarters, November 11th, by Colonel Upton, commanding Russell's brigade, by whom they were taken. They bore the inscriptions—" Winchester," " Manassas," " Cedar Run," " Second Harper's Ferry," " Sharpsburg," " Chancellorsville," " Fredericksburg," " Gettysburg," " Gaines's Farm," " Malvern Hill," " Elthain's Landing." indicative of the battles in which the troops from which they were captured had been engaged. In

receiving the trophies, General Meade expressed his gratification at the good conduct and gallantry displayed on the 7th
and his purpose, in a general order, to do justice to all the troop-
who had distinguished themselves. The scene was impressive
and inspiriting.

On the 26th of November, the Army of the Potomac again
advanced, and crossing the Rapidan, encountered the enemy
Sharp fighting followed, resulting on both sides in about an
equal loss of killed and wounded. A large number of prisoners were taken by the Federals. After an absence of eight
days, the army returned to its old encampments. In this ad
vance, the Rhode Island batteries and the 2d Rhode Island
regiment participated. Batteries A, C and E, were hotly en
gaged, and gave their fire with disastrous effect to the rebels
A had one man wounded and another slightly injured; C, one
wounded, and E, two. This demonstration in force apparently
embraced two objects,—first, to prevent Lee sending rein
forcements to Longstreet or Bragg, where they were greatly
needed; and, secondly, if circumstances warranted, to fight a
general battle. The first object appears to have been successfully gained; the second, the position of the rebel army and
the unfavorable nature of the ground for the use of artillery
did not, to the commanding General, seem to authorize. I
regrets found expression on the Federal side, that a decisive
battle was not fought, they were in full measure shared by the
confederates, who confidently anticipated " a Southern victory,"
and evidently felt that Lee had been put at disadvantage by
the falling back of Meade. The Richmond Examiner, of De
cember 4th, said : " Whether to be pleased or sorry at the
retreat of Meade, without battle, is a doubtful question."
" Had a pitched battle taken place," it added, resulting in removing the menace of Richmond, it would have been worth
all the sacrifice of life it must have cost, and " would have
cheered and inspired the heart of the country." But the chee.

D

lid not come, and the third year of the war closed with the menace in full force.

In another part of this volume, reference has been made to the need of a more complete ambulance system. The subject was brought to public attention, by the author, through the Providence Journal, immediately after the battle of Gaines' Farm on the Peninsula, and the correctness of views then expressed subsequent observation has confirmed. After the "seven days" battles, so sanguinary in their results, an improvement was made in the ambulance arrangements, but in no considerable battle fought since has the system been found adequate in its operations to immediate necessities. Even at Gettysburg, where all was apparently done that could be, wounded men lay on the field, as they fell, two or three days before they could be gathered up. A reorganization and expansion of the present system could be made, without arresting for a day its active service. The importance of such a change has become apparent, and is engaging the earnest interest of influential gentlemen of every profession; and it is gratifying to notice, as these pages are passing through the press, that petitions are in circulation, asking of Congress the passage of a law authorizing the adoption of a system such as the humanity due to the volunteer defenders of the Union demands.

In introducing the following correspondence, it may be proper, in explanation, to say, that battery C took its departure for the seat of war August 31st, 1861, and wintered at Minor's Hill, Va.

RHODE ISLAND IN THE REBELLION.

LETTER I.

Sibley Tents — Thanksgiving — Providence Journal — Rhode Island Troops in Virginia — Grand Review at Bailey's Cross Roads — Falls Church — Rumors.

CAMP OWEN, MINER'S HILL, VA.,
December 1, 1861.

Camp life, ordinarily, affords but few incidents for a letter, though the facts of its daily routine may serve as contributions to one's philosophy of human relations. The "tented field," the morning call, the parade, the drill, and other reminders of war, aid in keeping up a healthful activity and open to the mind a broad field for speculation. The most important break in our local affairs is the reception of ten new Sibley tents, which were cordially welcomed. They take the place of the old wedge or A tent, give great satisfaction, and add much to the comfort of the men. A tent of still better construction, I am informed, has been for some time on exhibition at the War Department, and finds favor with experienced officers. It combines roominess with a more approved method of ventilation, two points of importance to the convenience and health of their occupants. The wedge or A tent, so generally in use, is deficient in both these particulars; and when it is considered that the accommodations of an army necessarily affect its

1

physique and *morale*, the motto of the dictionary publishers furnishes an excellent and economical rule for the government to act upon—"get the best." Our own mess arrangement works to a charm. With some of us, Yankee ingenuity has worked out additional conveniences. In our own tent we boast a very respectable fire-place, and though less elegant in appearance than is found in first class dwellings, it has the prime merit of "carrying smoke" well. A fire, and bunks of primitive construction, add much to our comfort. A fire at this season is no slight inducement for one to anticipate reveille and hold communication with distant friends. To this, and the thoughtful service of the corporal of the guard, I am indebted for an early opportunity to fill a sheet that might otherwise, for the present, have remained blank.

Last Thursday, the Puritan institution of New England was duly inaugurated on the "sacred soil" of Virginia. Here, for a short season, *turkey* was the ruling power, and Thanksgiving the expression of many hearts. To-day, in our mess, plum-pudding is in the ascendant, and in trencher service the honor of Rhode Island will be becomingly sustained.

For the last two weeks, the Providence Journal has failed to reach me. This is a real privation. I can do without a day's rations, if need be, and preserve my equanimity, but I cannot so philosophically endure a break in the communication of current events at home. I suspect light fingers have something to do with the matter. "Who steals *my* purse, steals trash," but he who plunders the mail of my newspaper, robs more than one of both patience and enjoyment. We are not Berkleyites out here. To us, the Journal is a luxury, of which we do not like to be deprived. A woe rests upon the offender, if caught, who shall again intercept it in its legitimate destination.

Our battery, as already mentioned, is attached to Gen. Fitz John Porter's division, and there is reason for the belief that he regards it with a partial eye. The other batteries of the

division, Griffin's and Follet's, are distinguished for qualities
that give efficiency to artillery, and whenever called into action, will doubtless make a satisfactory report of their doings.
Gen. Porter is a graduate of West Point, an accomplished and
experienced officer, and in every respect calculated to inspire
with enthusiasm the men under his command. At the close of
a late division review, Gen. McClellan pronounced it a model
for the army.

Rhode Island is now represented on the Virginia side of the
Potomac by a regiment of infantry and four batteries of artillery. The latter are stationed as follows: Capt. Randolph's
at Artillery Camp, near Fort Lyon, below Alexandria; Capt.
Belger's at Camp California, about four miles west of that
place, under the guns of Fort Worth; Capt. Munroe's at Camp
Dupont, near Munson's Hill; and Capt. Weeden's, at this place.
It is but little more than three months since the oldest of these
batteries completed its organization and left Providence for
the field of action, and scarcely two since the last of the number referred to temporarily occupied Camp Sprague; yet, to-
day, as the result of industry and laborious training, they
occupy no second rank in the volunteer arm of the service;
and with the spirit that pervades them all, each month will
witness a closer approximation in details to the proficiency of
regulars. Comparisons are neither necessary nor always in
good taste. To boast of superiority would be folly, as to de-
preciate the truth would be a violation of self-respect. We
hear of many pleasant things said of us by partial friends,
which are received as incentives to merit their favorable
opinions.

The series of division reviews, by Gen. McClellan, closed on
the 20th ult., with a grand display at Bailey's Cross Roads,
when more than seventy (some estimate eighty) thousand infantry, cavalry and artillery covered, in battle array, the plain
spreading south from the foot of Munson's Hill. It was an
imposing spectacle, and worth a long journey to witness.

From an account by another hand, the following details are supplied :

" Bailey's Cross Roads are situated eight miles from Washington, in the direction of Fairfax Court House, at the junction of the Columbia turnpike and the Alexandria and Leesburg turnpike. Between the Cross Roads and Munson's Hill, a mile and a half distant towards Fall's Church, is a plain two miles in length, which was prepared, by clearing off the fences, filling up the ditches, &c., for this grand display.

" During the last two or three days, a rumor circulated among the troops that the publication of the purpose to hold a grand review was intended to cover the preparations for an advance, and when, last evening, the order promulgated for all the infantry regiments to provide themselves with forty rounds of ball cartridges, and, later, for at least one ambulance, with all the surgical appliances, to accompany each regiment, the excitement rose to fever heat. It turned out, however, that these were but prudent precautionary measures against the possible movement of the enemy during the day.

" At half-past nine o'clock, General McClellan, attended by all his staff officers, left his head-quarters in Washington, escorted by a column of eighteen hundred regular cavalry. The array was most imposing as this splendid cortege moved through the streets, the cavalry marching by platoons until it reached Long Bridge, where it was compelled to march by column of fours, and afterwards defiled along the road leading by Arlington Heights to the review ground. Gen. McClellan was plainly attired. As he rode in advance of his numerous staff, he was loudly cheered.

" All of the seven divisions on the Virginia side of the Potomac were represented in the review, but enough were left in each to supply double the usual picket force to guard the camps, and a reserve in addition strong enough to repel any attack in force the enemy could make.

" As early as nine o'clock, the head of the column of Gen.

Blenker's division, the head-quarters of which are nearest to Bailey's, began to arrive at the grounds from the Washington road. Soon after, Gen. McDowell's advance guard appeared. Next came Gen. Franklin's column, and soon after, the division of Gen. Smith. Gen. Fitz John Porter was next on the ground. The troops now poured in from all directions, those under Gen. Heintzelman following Gen. Franklin's division, and the column of Gen. McCall succeeding that of Gen. Smith, and continued without cessation until half-past eleven o'clock.

"The scene was most exhilarating; more than twenty Generals, with their staffs, numbering above 150 horsemen, were dashing hither and thither, arranging their divisions, which presented a total of above 70,000 men, including seven regiments of cavalry, numbering nearly 8,000 men.

"At a quarter past eleven o'clock, the President of the United States entered the grounds, in his carriage, followed by the Secretary of State, also in his carriage, and by the Secretary of War and Postmaster-General, accompanied by Mrs. General McDowell, and by two daughters of General Taylor, on horseback. The party were escorted to a slight elevation near the centre of the area, marked by a white flag, where they were soon joined by Gen. McClellan and his staff. Everything being now in readiness, a salvo to the President and General-in-Chief was fired by four batteries of artillery designated for that purpose. In the meantime, the President and Secretary of State, Secretary of War and Assistant Secretary of War, alighted from their carriages, mounted horses and prepared to accompany Gen. McClellan in his review of the lines. The divisions then passed in the following order:

" First—Gen. McCall's division, composed of the brigades of Generals Meade, Reynolds and Ord.

" Second—Gen. Heintzelman's division, composed of the brigades of Generals Sedgwick, Jamison and Richardson.

" Third—Gen. Smith's division, composed of the brigades of Generals Hancock, Brooks and Benham.

1*

" Fourth—Gen. Franklin's division, composed of the brigades of Generals Slocum, Newton and Kearney.

" Fifth—The division of Gen. Blenker, composed of the brigade of Gen. Stahl, and two brigades commanded by senior Colonels.

" Sixth—The division of Gen. Fitz John Porter, composed of the brigades of Generals Morell, Martindale and Butterfield.

" Seventh—The division of Gen. McDowell, composed of the brigades of Generals King and Wadsworth, and a brigade commanded by Col. Frisbie ; making a total of seventy-six regiments of infantry, seventeen batteries, and seven regiments of cavalry. The time occupied in passing was three hours. The enthusiasm of the troops was remarkable. When the General passed them in review, their huzzas filled the field.

" Upon the right of the General commanding, during the review, were the President, the Secretary of State, the Secretary and Assistant Secretary of War, Quartermaster-General Meigs, and the Prince de Joinville. Upon the ground were also all the rest of the Cabinet officers, and a number of Foreign Ministers and their families, grouped in carriages and on horseback around the carriage of the President, which, containing Mrs. Lincoln and some friends, was immediately opposite the position of the commanding General.

" One of the most interesting features of the day, to many, was the martial music, played by more than fifty bands, most of which were of the first order. In two or three instances the bands of the whole brigades were consolidated. The consolidated band in Gen. Butterfield's brigade numbered 120 pieces, and played, with excellent effect, while the brigade was passing in review, a quickstep, entitled ' The Standard Bearer Quickstep,' composed for and dedicated to Gen. Butterfield. It was a day of compliments, and none were complimented more than Gen. Barry, for the appearance of the artillery, of which he is chief.

" The whole review was most admirably conducted. Infinite

credit is due to Gen. McDowell, who was the commander of
the review, for the promptness with which his vast column was
moved."

The grand review was witnessed by, it is supposed, from
twenty to thirty thousand spectators. As no passes were required, it was free to every one who could procure a conveyance, or who chose to walk. The roads were guarded the
entire distance, so that civilians without written permission
could not diverge from the prescribed limits of travel. Three
Rhode Island batteries on this side of the Potomac, (C, D and
E,) participated in the event, and, in the judgment of many,
were not behind those longer in service in the details of their
movements. We left our camp at an early hour in the morning, and returned about dark, very much fatigued, but well
satisfied with the work of the day.

Situated, as we are, in a wooded country, and sparsely populated, the eye rests upon few objects to excite the imagination.
Outside of our surrounding encampments we see only Falls
Church and Lewinsville, with here and there an intervening
chimney smoke to remind us of the proximity of civilization.
Both these places obtained some military notoriety in the earlier
period of the rebellion. The former is a small village, comprising two houses of worship, a blacksmith shop, and, I believe, a tavern. The principal object of interest to the anti-
quarian, is the Episcopal church, built, so tradition says, by
Washington, of bricks imported from Europe. It is a small,
plain structure, and belongs to a class to be met with between
this post and Mount Vernon, said to have had a similar origin.
Several ancient gravestones are standing in the adjacent burial
ground, which may, ere long, need the attention of some pious
Old Mortality. The other house of worship, occupied by a
Baptist society, is a wooden building with a New England
steeple, and in its interior was badly mutilated by the secesh
while the place was in their possession. Lewinsville is a
smaller collection of houses than Falls Church, and, for some

time past, has been under the supervision of pickets, though
this arm of the service has been extended several miles beyond.

Of late, movements have been made in several divisions of
the army, and particularly in McCall's, Smith's, (both above
us,) and Porter's, that indicate a purpose to extend our lines on
the right and left. Flank movements, should they be made,
may inconveniently disturb the rebels. Many rumors circulate
in camp. One is that we shall soon move towards Fairfax.
Whatever, however, may take place, two facts are clear, the
men are in excellent heart, and will be prompt to meet the
demands of duty.

LETTER II.

Virginia weather—Stables—Reconnoisance—News from England—
Battle at Drainsville—Bucktail Sharpshooters—Lieut. Col. Kane
wounded—Gen. McCall's command—Sham Fights—Christmas—
Pierpont's "E Pluribus Unum"—Foraging Expedition—Review.

CAMP OWEN, MINER'S HILL, VA.,
December 15, 1861.

Virginia is as extreme in her weather as she has shown herself in politics. During the summer and early autumn there
was an almost daily contest between sunshine and rain, and
when the Shower king put Sol suddenly under a cloud, an out-
pouring that would have been creditable to antediluvian times
was quite sure to follow. Then succeeded warm mid-days and
chilly evenings, the mercury often taking a downward slide of
fifteen or twenty degrees, fevering the blood, and touching the
marrow as with an icicle, and preparing many an incautious
one for a typhoid delirium, or for the society of shakers. Subsequently, in fitful moods, came a drizzle, reminding one of a

blue day at Newport or Nahant; then the "latter rain," preparing for hill-side encampments a soap-like surface, and making the thoroughfares to the national capital like so many Sloughs of Despond; then sweeping along from the distant Blue Ridge came the piercing blast, challenging the forecasting soldier to a rough and tumble struggle for his outer gear, as if he had yet to learn that in the uncertainties of a camp "undressing is a woe." And, now, to point a contrast, we have a soft and genial atmosphere, with moonlights as brilliant as ever illumined Prospect Hill, or scattered gems on the ruffled bosom of Narragansett Bay. What will come next, the "clerk of the weather" alone can tell; but with the inspiring news from Port Royal, and the successful cruise of the San Jacinto, we can very calmly endure the severest frown that winter may put on.

"The merciful man is merciful to his beast," and in the spirit of this saying, by the direction of Capt. Weeden, we have all been busily engaged, the past week, in erecting a stable for our horses. For some time they have needed a better shelter than a grove affords, and the beneficial effects of good stabling will, no doubt, soon be visible, especially with those that have been the most worn. Battery service tries horse flesh severely. Activity and precision, whatever may be the ground, are essential to perfection, and as field drills are in some sort mimic movements of an engagement, the guns and heavy caissons necessarily tax the strength of the horses to the utmost; and now, when they return from the field, heated by the exertions of the hour, they will be shielded from the cold winds of winter. Our stable is two hundred and twenty feet in length by twenty-four feet in width. The sides are closely lined with cedar boughs, and the roof is thatched with the same material. The architecture is not of the precise style of any found in the books, nor is its finish quite equal to some model structures in Providence; but it has the merit of harmonizing with its surroundings, and altogether is a comfortable and convenient affair.

Besides, it is economical, and will never come under the ban of the Congressional investigating committee. The materials of which it is constructed were had for the cutting, and the labor cost the government next to nothing. This kind of stabling has been provided for many of the cavalry regiments in the different divisions on this side of the Potomac, and, as a temporary expedient, will come into general use. Whether the work I have described indicates a continuance here through the winter, or whether our labors will be entered into by others, time only can determine. Milton makes one of his characters *guess*, and to do so is accorded to Yankees as their exclusive prerogative; but with an eye to economy, which is also a Yankee trait, I shall leave events to settle the point, while I attend to matters with which I am more familiar.

Of military affairs, outside of one's encampment, comparatively little can be known. What comes to us from head-quarters is borne on the wings of rumor, and is to be received with liberal deductions. When you notice how reporters, with the full command of their time and the free range of the army, are often hard pushed to produce a sensation paragraph, it will not be cause of surprise that one whose time and opportunities are more circumscribed should not be in a condition to relate all that would be interesting to hear. And then, all facts and many fictions reach you by the lightning messenger so instantly, that, by the time a letter reaches its destination, its contents become "stale, flat and unprofitable." Since my last, reconnoisances along the entire line of the army have taken place. A large body of troops have extended their observations as far as Vienna and Hunter's Mill, without meeting any obstruction. Reports are that the rebels no longer hold Fairfax Court House with any considerable force, their army at that place having fallen back to some other position. Vienna, it will be remembered, was, a few months ago, a stronghold of the enemy, and Hunter's Mill was in their possession. These places are in a direct line west from the encampment of Gen. Smith's division.

north of us, and the withdrawal of the rebel troops indicates, on
their part, an apprehension of Smith and McCall. Generals
McDowell, Blenker, Heintzelman, and others, below us, have
been feeling their way forward, and, it is believed, have obtained information that will be turned to good account. From
all that has transpired, it is evident that the rebels are making
new dispositions of their forces,—whether for retreat, assault or
winter quarters, a few weeks will show. It would seem that
the series of federal expeditions, inaugurated at Hatteras, and
followed up at Beaufort, disturb their plans ; and when Butler's
and Burnside's movements reach a *striking* point, their leaders
will doubtless more than ever be troubled. So mote it be.
There is a wisdom higher than man's that will bring confusion
to the counsels of the wicked.

The news from England is variously received in camp, but
by none, I think, with serious alarm. Common sense teaches
that our government is in the right, and, with Mr. Bright for
our advocate, why should we fear ? But will not England side
with the confederates and declare war against us ? Some papers, for reasons not distinctly avowed, but which are pretty
well understood, would have us think so. But her statesmen
are not madmen, and they know that a move in that direction
will authorize a counter-movement by powers who owe her no
large amount of good will. Besides, they have not forgotten
that Canada once rebelled, and may again ; that Ireland is not
the safest of her possessions; and that whatever France may
do about sponging out the record of St. Helena, Russia would
not object to an opportunity to pit her bear against the British
lion. The moment she " lets slip the dogs of war," she will
have her hands full. Judging from independent ground, she
will not commit that folly. But this is speculation.

Pleasant reminders from home give assurance that " Christmas is coming." A Christmas in Secessia will, to most of us,
be a new thing under the sun. With our faces turned to the
east, we shall greet the anniversary of His advent whose life

and death comprehended in their results the welfare of the
world ; and as we open mysterious looking boxes and packages, we will bless the loving hearts and ready hands that prepared them.

December 23. Since my last, several regiments of General
McCall's division, sustained by a battery of two 24 and two 12
pounder howitzers, had a battle with the rebels near Drainsville, a post town on the Leesburg turnpike, six or eight miles
northwest of us. It resulted in the repulse of the enemy, with
a loss on their part of 150 killed and wounded. A shell from
a federal battery struck a rebel caisson and exploded with terrific effect. One of the wounded rebels said, as he was dying,
" We whipped you at Manassas, but you have the best of us
to-day." This victory excited great enthusiasm on the field
and in the camp. The victors returned with fifty wagon loads
of forage, making a valuable contribution to the subsistence
department. The fight is represented as very severe, and the
federal troops stood up under the heavy fire with the coolness
of veterans. Among the troops conspicuous in battle were the
Bucktail Sharpshooters, under the command of Lieut. Col.
Kane, who wear in their hats or caps, as a distinctive badge,
the brush of a deer. They are a hardy set of men, from the
mountain regions of Pennsylvania, many of them experienced
marksmen. They are reported to be as ready for a reconnoisance or conflict as they were at home to pursue their game ;
and the manner in which they conducted themselves under fire,
in the recent engagement, is an earnest of their future. Col.
Kane received a shot in the cheek, which brought him down.
He instantly arose, bound up the wound, and continued fighting until the battle terminated.

General McCall commands the Pennsylvania reserve division, and occupies Camp Pierpont, extending beyond Langley's church and tavern, and stretching towards Lewinsville.
It constitutes the right wing of the army of the Potomac, and

covers Chain Bridge, an important approach to Washington, and interposes an effectual obstacle to a flank movement by the rebels from Leesburg.

Last week was diversified by two sham fights, in both of which our battery participated. The first comprised Gen. Morrill's brigade, consisting of the 9th Massachusetts, 4th Michigan, 14th New York and 62d Pennsylvania, all of them, to use an emphatic phrase, common here, " bully " regiments. A large field in this vicinity was occupied by the troops, who went through the various manœuvres of a battle, with much satisfaction, I believe, to a large body of spectators, and certainly with a corresponding amount of fatigue to themselves. The second took place on Saturday, in which the whole of Gen. Porter's division engaged. It was a splendid and exciting scene, and gave the " boys " an inkling of the mysteries of warfare. If they do as well when in the presence of a veritable enemy, their friends will have no cause for mortification, nor the rebels for boasting. The part enacted by our battery was such as became its position, and if explosive sounds are evidence of merit, we had reason to be satisfied with both guns and gunnery. Having met the imaginary foe and made him ours, we returned to camp without the loss of a man ! The interest of this occasion was enhanced to the 62d and 63d Pennsylvania regiments by the reception of regimental flags, presented to them by Hon. Edward Cowan, in the name of the State. The speeches of presentation and acceptance were patriotic and appropriate.

A recent visit of Gen. McClellan to Porter's headquarters gave rise to various conjectures. As it was previous to the Drainsville affair, it may have been in reference to concerted action with other divisions in advancing our lines towards Fairfax Court House, or, what is quite as probable, to see the men in their encampments when off duty. At all events, nothing perceptible has followed, and the object, if a special one was entertained, is still veiled.

2

December 29. From my earliest recollection, Christmas has been to me a day of joy. I remember with what childish faith, on the eve of the Nativity, I hung my stocking in the chimney corner, and how, as I extracted its varied contents the next morning. I speculated upon the marvellous ubiquity of Santa Claus. Even now, I feel the impressions then received; and while I recognize the higher significance of the day, in its relations to Him who manifested the humanity of heaven to a needy world, I confess it not easy to blot out, as a myth, the queer little old man and his huge pack, whom the pictorials represented to my wondering eyes as entering each dwelling by the chimney, to bless with his gifts good boys and girls. In a spirit becoming the occasion, and with the cordial approbation of Capt. Weeden, it was resolved to celebrate Christmas in camp. A committee appointed for the purpose attended to the preparation of a tent of ample dimensions, beneath which the tables were laid.

Our *chef de cuisine* and assistant laid themselves out on the occasion, with a success that would have done honor to Providence Soyers. Here is our bill of fare: Turkeys, rivalling the noblest Narragansett gobblers that ever graced Market Square; apples, such as the veteran purveyor of South Main street would delight to provide for appreciative customers; cranberries, of which Smithfield might be proud; potatoes, that would inspire the enthusiasm of the most stolid son of Erin; turnips, that "beat the Dutch" for obesity; and onions, that would make a son of Weathersfield weep for envy. These, with other "fixings," and a sprinkling of good things provided by loving and loved friends at home, furnished a banquet fit for the President. Such a dinner, seasonably provided, would have spared Esau the sale of his birthright. Apicius himself, after a treat like this, would have voted nightingale's tongues and peacock entrées of little account, and never have committed suicide to escape starvation. In our table spread, it is true, we could not boast the massive plate of Steeple street,

nor the elegant dinner sets furnished by Hutchins or Whita-
ker; but to our utilitarian notion, steel and tin were satisfactory substitutes for silver and stone china, and to good Union
appetites, the viands were none the less savory. At all events,
ample justice was done to the repast. Pindar was right when
he declared that the turnpike to the heart lies through the
mouth. The difference between a hungry and a well-fed man,
is the difference that distinguishes civilized and savage races.
It is surprising how a well-lined epigastrium humanizes one's
nature, and makes a churl " wondrous kind."

> " All human history attests
> That happiness for man—the hungry sinner—
> Since Eve ate apples, must depend on dinner."

Had that irascible old gentleman, Mr. John Bull, been our
guest, he would have smoothed his gouty visage, and buried
the Trent affair beneath the delights of the table; and it may
be correctly imagined that after such a " dining," a genial
spirit and healthful hilarity prevailed. Songs and dancing
followed, and though

> The sparkling eyes, and flashing ornaments--
> The white arms, and the raven hair—the braids
> And bracelets—swan-like bosoms—the thin robes,
> Floating like light clouds 'twixt our gaze and heaven—

so often seen at Howard Hall, did not grace our festive season,
the " boys " made up for the deficiency by the vigor of their
pedal gymnastics. That closed the day, and to the latest
hours of life, we shall retain pleasant memories of our first
Christmas in Secessia. In other encampments, the day was
variously observed. Our neighbors, the 22d Massachusetts,
had a burlesque dress parade, which afforded much amusement.

A friend has sent me a copy of Pierpont's national lyric,
" E Pluribus Unum," for which my thanks are due. Like
everything from his pen, it bears the stamp of genius, and

shows by its brilliant flashes and vigorous expression, that age has not abated the force of a cultivated intellect, nor diminished the intensity of a fervid patriotism. It admirably blends music, science, and the principles upon which our Union is based, giving point to the latter, by the apposite illustrations drawn from the former. I am reminded by this acceptable souvenir, that we have poets in the army. Not long since, one of them, "after taking a drink" at a modern Helicon, produced the following. If in rhythm it is less accurate than more ambitious compositions submitted to the National Hymn committee, its sentiment, all will admit, does not lack *spirit.* I am at loss to determine whether the author had in mind David's sling or a certain beverage once fashionable, and not yet obsolete, and shall leave the question to be settled by critics:

Plea for the Second Regiment of Sharpshooters.

[Respectfully proffered to the Head of the Ordnance Department.]

While our brothers plead with others,
   We, O Major, turn to you ;
You have all the guns and rifles,
   And the bows and arrows too.
Let, Oh, let us not be idle,
   While you have such lots of things,
If you *cannot* give us rifles,
   Pray, O Major, give us *slings*.

Let our post be one of honor,
   We will prove that "might is right ;
When the *first* their forces marshal,
   Let the *second* have a sight.
Let *them* take the patent weapons ;
   We'll take yours so much derided ;
For we know a nation's fortunes
   Once by one was soon decided.

They may pour their leaden shower,
We'll stand by to end the fray,
And when *they* are driven to cover,
We'll go in and claim the day.
Talk of rifles! we've decided
They'll do well enough to play with,
But before *we* start for Richmond,
Give us *slings* to clear the way with.

Last Friday, a foraging expedition of five regiments, comprising Gen. Wadsworth's brigade, proceeded to the vicinity of Fairfax Court House, without meeting obstructions, and brought away eighty loads of forage. Yesterday, seventy loads more were secured. These operations serve the double purpose of familiarizing the men with road movements and supplying army wants at the expense of the rebels. Such successes keep up the spirit of the men.

Yesterday, another review of Gen. McDowell's division, to which Battery D, Capt. Munroe, is attached, took place at Ball's cross roads, terminating in a mimic battle. To-day, Gen. McCall's division has been reviewed at Langley's, several miles north of us, in the presence of Secretary Cameron, Gov. Curtain, of Pennsylvania, and other magnates. Gen. Ord's brigade, I understand, attracted special attention, and were addressed in complimentary terms by Gov. Curtain for their bravery in the late battle. The colors of each regiment, and also of Capt. Easton's battery, are to be inscribed with the word "Drainsville," by the authority of the State, as an honorable recognition of their services. These reviews consume considerable time and ammunition, but it is time and expense well employed.

2*

LETTER III.

Meditations on guns—Former views of Wise and Tyler—Mementoes from home—Rumors—New Year in Secessia—Signal Corps.

CAMP OWEN, MINER'S HILL, VA.,⎱
December 31, 1861.   ⎰

An old English author wrote "Meditations among the Tombs." With concrete materials for thought in abundance around him, he must have experienced little difficulty in composing the pages of his volume. As he read the epitaphs chiseled on ambitious columns by ostentatious wealth or pretentious meanness, he doubtless could have summed them all up as did a Connecticut clergyman when, as I have heard the anecdote, he wrote, "here lie the dead, and here the living lie;" or, with the softened expression of sadness, have quoted the Man of Wisdom,—"Vanity of vanities; all is vanity." But had he selected a quiet, orderly camp, like ours, for intellectual incubation, he would have found himself as much perplexed in meeting the printer's demands for copy, as were the brickmakers of Egypt in making out a "full tale" of their productions when cut off from the customary allowance of straw. The uniformity of its life would have brought him to a stand-still after the third or fourth chapter. So friends who expect a letter at least once a week, freighted with interesting incident, will understand the condition of one whose range of observation is necessarily limited, and whose themes a few brimming sheets exhaust. As the year approaches a close, we instinctively grow thoughtful, and yield to an unseen influence that moves us to draw lessons from the past and to form resolutions for the future. Wise are they who thus compel the hours to serve them. In this frame of mind, while recently looking at our battery, I found myself meditating on guns. The topic was not entirely foreign to the prolific one chosen by the author referred to, though at this moment more abstract. Our park comprises six as fine rifled brass pieces as a trained gunner could wish to look upon; and as they stood in majestic silence, overlooking the approaches from the west and north, they seemed to me the representatives and expounders of six vital principles,—liberty, law, order, equal rights, constitutional nationality, and a perpetuated Union. It is for these they may yet speak with more than Websterian power.

As I passed in review the events of the year, and recalled the instructions of Virginia to her delegates in 1776, and the patriotic eloquence of Patrick Henry, the contrast seemed humiliating to a State boasting herself the mother of Presidents. Yet not more so, perhaps, than the past and present positions of two of her prominent citizens, one a late Governor and the other once acting chief magistrate of the Union. In 1844, according to a paper from which I quote, John Tyler, in a message sent to Congress, uttered these memorable words:

"I regard the preservation of the Union as the first great American interest. I equally disapprove of all threats of its dissolution, whether they proceed from the north or the south. The glory of my country, its safety and its prosperity, alike depend on union, and he who would contemplate its destruction, even for a moment, and form plans to accomplish it, deserves the deepest anathemas of the human race."

In 1858, on a public occasion, Henry A. Wise, with even more earnest emphasis, expressed himself as follows:

"Listen to me now, and to what I am going to say. I wish that there was no noise, and that there were silence in all the earth, and that I had the trumpet of the archangel to sound it everywhere. When your fathers attempted to form this Union, they did not know beforehand what sort of a Union it was to be. They set to work and did the best they could under the circumstances. What they would accomplish, no man could tell. There was not a head upon either that could foretell what was to be; but they went in for the Union for

Union's sake. By all the gods, by all the altars of my country, I go
for Union for Union's sake. They set to work to make the best Union
they could, and they did make the best Union and the best government that ever was made. Washington, Franklin, Jefferson,—all
combined,—in Congress or out of Congress, in convention or out of
convention, never made that constitution. God Almighty sent it
down to your fathers. It was a work, too, of glory, and a work of
inspiration. I believe that as fully as I believe my Bible. No man,
from Hamilton and Jay and Madison,—from Edmund Randolph, who
had the chief hand in making it, and he was a Virginian,—the writers
of it, the authors of it, and you who have lived under it from 1789
down to this year of our Lord 1858,—none of your fathers, and none
of your fathers' sons, have ever measured the height or the depth, or
the length or the breadth, of the wisdom of that constitution.''

And now where are these men? What has moved them to
contemn a constitution so essentially Virginian as one of them
boasts? Why have they so soon falsified their professions of
attachment to the Union? Is it not because ambition prompts
them to rule rather than serve? and to magnify the importance
of the State at the expense of the nation? So it seems to me.
For the desolation that civil war has caused in this State, they,
as perverters of the truth and leaders of the misguided masses,
are largely responsible. Every dilapidated farm, every dese-
crated church, every ruined country seat, and every prostrate
forest, meeting the eye along the Potomac, are swift and terrible
witnesses against them. By their aid, the good name of a State
that stood shoulder to shoulder with the north in the resistance
of oppression has been destroyed, and her material prosperity
put back for a quarter of a century. What a history are these
men making for themselves. One may be known to posterity
as " great on oysters," and the other as once the commander of
a corporal's guard ; but when the story of 1861 is written, the
black lines of *treason* will wreathe their names, and Wise and
Tyler will be synonyms for recreancy to principles for which
Washington hazarded his life, and the plains of Yorktown were
stained with patriot blood. But enough of guns and their sug-

gestions. May the year, soon to open, be happier for Virginia
and the Union than the past, whose last hour is striking.

Among the pleasing incidents of the camp, next to receiving
a long letter full of neighborhood gossip, or furnishing a synopsis of life on Westminster street, is the arrival of boxes or
packages from home; and when the quartermaster returns from
Washington with tokens of maternal thoughtfulness, sisterly
affection and friendly recognition, which he has disinterred at
the express office from beneath piles of army merchandise, you
may be sure he shares the blessings that spring warmly from
feeling hearts. What pent-up power for good was there in a
Christmas box, eagerly looked for and exultingly welcomed
on the eve of Advent-day. Gauntlets, such as mortal eyes
never before saw in Buckskin land; socks and mittens, just
in the nick of time: blankets for our Rosinantes; (who but a
provident mother would have thought of them?) jars of anti-
scorbutic condiments; delicious condensed Mocha, with lacteal
accompaniments; " Käse " that would provoke a German appetite to activity; saponaceous compounds, teaching us how
near akin is cleanliness to godliness; and nameless other matters for present comfort; these all, as remembrances from
home, carried sunshine to a certain tent, and quickened to full
flow the emotional nature of its occupant. Had Gulliver's
philosopher tried this method of filling his bottles with the
beams of Sol, instead of wasting his genius upon cucumbers,
his experiments would have been crowned with success, and a
fortune laid up " where moth and rust doth not corrupt."
Home is never so dear to a man as when separated from its
cosy enjoyments, and they are " blessed in the deed " who thus
keep the line of communication with the camp unbroken.

Since the Drainesville battle, all sorts of rumors have prevailed in regard to the enemy's forces. One is, that they have
13,000 men at that place, whereas, it is a well ascertained fact
that not a rebel is to be found there. Another report was that
Gen. McCall's pickets had been driven in. This, like the

preceding, proves to be a base coin, as no secesh have, of late, been within eight miles of his picket lines. The truth is, that after the recent acquaintance made with his command, they will be slow to thrust themselves upon his military hospitality.

January 1, 1862. Our first New Year's day in Secessia was made genial by a clear, bright sunshine. In most of the regiments in this vicinity, the customary drills were omitted, and the men were permitted a holiday within division lines, according to their fancy. A few voluntary drills conducted by privates, trials of skill in musket and rifle shooting, exchange of visits, music, dancing, illuminations and serenades, filled the hours of day and evening. Battery C spent a portion of the day in gunnery. The firing was from Hall's Hill, and the target a tree twelve hundred yards distant, in the direction of Fall's Church. Capt. Griffin's battery engaged in a similar recreation. With both batteries the results were satisfactory, and showed accurate sighting.

The army Signal Corps, a new and important feature in the army of the Potomac, has been filled up with the prescribed complement of officers and men. One hundred and two officers have been detailed, and are under the command of Major Meyers, late Assistant Surgeon General. Their camp is in the neighborhood of Georgetown, where they will receive a thorough course of signal instruction. When completed, an officer will be attached to the staff of each Brigadier General.*

---

* The code of signals, by flags, has been brought to remarkable perfection, and during the different campaigns of the rebellion, has been of immense service. In many instances, the firing of artillery has been directed by signal officers stationed where they could overlook the fight, and observe, with a field glass, the effects of gunnery. By their aid, the commanding general is made seasonably acquainted with the movements of the enemy in time of battle, spread over a field of several miles. The signal service is dangerous, and men of bravery and coolness only are suited to it.

LETTER IV.

Virginia mud—Foraging expeditions—Spies—Health of the army—
New guns—Burnside's Expedition—Capture of Forts Henry and
Donelson—Faulkner's opinion—Washington's Birth-day.

CAMP OWEN, MINER'S HILL, VA.,
February 3, 1862.

There has been no perceptible change along our lines, since
the year came in, except the departure of the Fourth Rhode
Island Regiment and Battery F from Camp California, near
Alexandria, to join Gen. Burnside's expedition. It would
have gratified many other Rhode Island boys had they been
included in the call to that service ; but they must wait their
turn.

For several weeks past, the clerk of the weather has
been in fitful moods, and, as if to try human patience, has sent
us a liberal supply of rain, sleet and snow. The result is mud
of the most unmitigated kind. Its grammatic scale would read,
muddy, muddier, muddiest ; over shoes, ankle deep, knee deep ;
or in another form of descending comparison, deep, deeper,
deepest. The mud of Virginia is a compound unlike any substance bearing that name seen north of Mason and Dixon's
line. Take, for example, a quantity of clay thrown out from a
New England brickyard, mingle with it two parts ferruginous
earth, a sprinkling of yellow ochre, and soft soap, *ad libitum*,
and you will have a tolerable specimen of the soil of the Old
Dominion in the region about us. At this moment the roads
are in the worst possible condition, and that the heavy army
teams succeed in moving back and forth between the encampments and Washington, is creditable to the perseverance of their
drivers. Mud is a formidable obstacle to army operations. In
the present state of the roads, a movement of this division, reported to be in contemplation, is a physical impossibility. **The**

regrets occasioned by this temporary embargo are softened by the reflection that the secesh troops are in a similar predicament. A few weeks will change the aspect of our surroundings, and then, if rumor is reliable, another expedition will be set on foot. Who are to compose it, and where its destination, time will reveal. Such a movement will be hailed with satisfaction by men to whom the monotony of camp routine, to say nothing of mud and slosh, has become a bore. "On to Richmond," or anywhere else, would be to them an agreeable change, after a four months' study of the geological structure of Miner's and Hall's Hills. The men, as a body, want a short war, and are now becoming anxious to "put it through" at the earliest possible day.

Reconnoissances and foraging expeditions into the rebel lines, the present winter, have been successful, the former gaining information for use at headquarters, and the latter adding to the supplies of the commissary department. A few weeks ago scouting parties in the direction of Fairfax Court House reported that the farmers had not then commenced their annual hog-killing, for the want of salt, a serious evil to them, but to the lovers of spare-ribs and cracklings among the federals, a decided advantage. It would not be surprising to learn that a respectable number of the swinish multitude, as contraband of war, had yielded to the force of circumstances, and been consigned to some regimental or brigade commissariat.

Since all the particulars of the Drainsville battle have been ascertained, Gen. McClellan has officially complimented Gen. Ord and the men of his brigade for the gallantry displayed on that occasion, and the Secretary of War has addressed a letter to Gen. McCall, commending, in warm terms, all the troops of his division engaged, for their bravery. Soldiers are not insensible to deserved praise, and while it gratifies a natural feeling, it stimulates an honorable ambition. Col. Kane, of the Bucktail Rifles, who was wounded in his cheek, and taken to Washington, has recovered and returned to his regiment.

Lieut. George F. Hodges, Adjutant of 18th Massachusetts Volunteers, died of fever, at Hall's Hill, on the 30th ult. He was a zealous, conscientious Unionist, a valuable officer, and highly esteemed for courteous manners and excellent qualities of heart. He was son of Almon D. Hodges, Esq., of Roxbury, Mass., formerly of the firm of Stimpson & Hodges, Providence.

Our line, on this side of the Potomac, has a front of about fifteen miles, reaching from the head of McCall's division to Fort Lyon. The division encampments, counting from right to left, are in the following order: McCall's, Smith's, Porter's, McDowell's, Blenker's, Franklin's and Heintzelman's. The rebel strength threatening Washington, is estimated at 160,000. At Centreville and Manassas they are supposed, from the best sources of information, to have from 75,000 to 80,000 men. At both places they are strongly fortified.

Spies are still about, watching opportunities to penetrate the Federal lines, for information. Occasionally, one is taken and sent to Washington for examination. In that city, it is understood, female spies have been numerous from the beginning of the war, and, in various ingenious ways, have succeeded in conveying much important information to the rebels. Among those who have been placed in confinement for this treasonable practice, are Mrs. Greenhow and daughter, Mrs. Phillips, Mrs. Levy, Mrs. Hassler, Mrs. Jackson, Miss Markle, Mrs. Onderdonk, Mrs. Lowe, Miss Poole and Mrs. Baxley. Some of these ladies have been released, and have left for more congenial homes, while others are still " in durance vile." Mrs. Jackson is the mother of the assassin of Ellsworth. After a confinement of two days and nights, she was permitted to go south. Miss Poole, whose *alias* was Stewart, came from Wheeling to Washington, last August, and was very successful in obtaining and conveying information to the rebel leaders in Kentucky. She escaped from prison by tying the sheets together and letting herself down from the window. It is said that when arrested a second time, within ten miles of the enemy's lines in Kentucky, $7,500 of unexpended money furnished by the rebels was found upon her person. She is now tasting the sweets of confinement at the Sixteenth street jail, flavored with rumina- tions upon the uncertainties of secession scheming. It may be ungallant to resort to treatment that justice would mete out to derelict *sons* of Adam; but when crinoline or "a love of a bon- net" is perverted to the purposes of treason, the distinguished consideration of the Provost Marshal becomes an imperative necessity.

Of the health of the army of the Potomac, the hospitals are perhaps the best exponents. There are seven hospitals in Washington* and Georgetown and one at Alexandria, besides regimental or division hospitals in the various encampments. In the latter are found, for the most part, men slightly indis- posed, or whose illness is not of a type to require removal to the former. At the last report, 24th ult., the hospitals at Washington and Georgetown contained 575 patients; that at Alexandria 537, making a total of 1,112. Considering the numerical force around Washington, these reports indicate a favorable sanitary condition. Of all in the hospitals, only fif- teen are Rhode Island soldiers. Ten of these are at Alexan- dria—eight from the 4th battery, and two from the 6th. Of the number in the regimental or division hospitals, I have no exact knowledge, but presume they do not exceed what are usually found in a large army. Deaths occasionally occur, and the solemn procession, with arms reversed, the plaintive strains of the band, the brief funeral service, and the volley over the grave, remind us that the end of man is dust, and that the dark- ness of the tomb can be enlivened only by the hope of immor- tality. The exemption of Rhode Island volunteers from fatal sickness is quite remarkable, and may be attributed, in part, to the judicious selection of encampments, and in no small degree to unremitting attentions from home. No State has surpassed, and few States have equalled, Rhode Island in her care for her troops. The government, as well as the soldiers, owe much

---

* They have since been increased to eighteen.

to individuals and associations, from whom have come timely supplies of blankets, socks, mittens, &c., comforting the body and making glad the heart. Patriotic relief associations, loyal workers, and nameless loving friends, will ever be held in grateful remembrance.

February 17. If the condition of the roads is not soon materially improved, our speedy departure from this encampment is problematical. The weather has been as unsettled as the fortunes of this secession-ridden State. Occasionally, we greet the face of a pleasant day, but take them as a whole, the past two months are to be ranked among the disagreeables of tent life. Last Saturday, about four inches of snow fell; yesterday, the heavens were propitious, and all overhead was fine; but, to-day, " the clouds consign their treasures to the fields " again, while men of rueful visage speculate as to what will turn up next.

The principal incident of local interest is the exchange of our old guns (James's) for a new battery. On Friday last, the men went to the Washington Arsenal to obtain new field pieces, with which they returned after a day of fatigue, in braving the mud and facing the rain. It was an occasion of agreeable excitement, and all slept the better for the exercise. The guns are light 12-pounders, gotten up under the sanction of the United States Ordnance Board, and made of wrought iron. The cartridge is attached to the shell, thus facilitating loading. They are an improvement, I believe, by Shenkle, and are said to be superior to anything in the line of field pieces yet invented. A trial of their merits will determine their value.

The news of the success of the Burnside expedition and of the capture of Forts Henry and Donelson, with 15,000 men and large quantities of war stores, was received in camp with strong demonstrations of joy. This afternoon, about two o'clock, the bugle sounded the assembly, and after the men had fallen into line, a dispatch from Gen. Porter, announcing these

splendid victories, was read to them by Capt. Weeden.   The
intelligence was responded to with three cheers and a "tiger"
that would have put the best specimens of Narragansett demonstrations at home quite in the shade.   A salute of thirty
guns was also fired, and as the loud cannon pealed its hoarsest
strains, hill tops and vallies caught the sounds, and sent them
echoing the glad tale to the foot of the distant Blue Ridge,
inspiring the patriotic with noble resolves, and filling the
"weary and care-haunted bosom" of secession with dismay.
At Hall's Hill, Gen. Martindale read the official dispatches to
his brigade, who listened in breathless silence.   When he
closed, four thousand caps were instantly swinging in the air,
and as many thousand stentorian lungs gave vocal expression
to the enthusiasm awakened.   Similar demonstrations were
witnessed in the various encampments, furnishing the boys with
a topic for conversation infinitely more agreeable than Virginia
mud or the weather.

But while joy has found this hearty expression, regret is felt
at the escape of Floyd and Pillow.   The latter, it is true, has
never contributed much to the ease and comfort of the rebels,
and, as superintendent of their military ditches, may still render
service to the Federal cause.   Let him go.   But a general, who,
yielding to constitutional propensities, steals time and two
thousand men, as though they were well-filled treasury bags,
and runs away with them in the dead of night, shows capabilities that deserve suitable recognition.   For such preëminent
merit nothing less exalted than the *Cannabis* order of Knight-
hood should be thought of; and this, if his retreating steps stop
short of Europe, a host of appreciative Kentuckians will, at
brief notice, cheerfully confer.

The fall of Forts Henry and Donelson are, it is hoped, but
precursors of a series of important achievements.   A succession
of such triumphs as have recently been witnessed will not only
stimulate our troops, now quietly encamped, to deeds of daring
when called to action, but must prove heavy blows to an

ephemeral rebellion. A few months ought, and doubtless will,
make still more encouraging changes in the aspects of this great
national struggle. Secretary Stanton evidently aims, by a
wise and prudent exercise of his power, to do whatever lies
within the line of his duties, to bring the war to an early termination. In this he has the sympathy of the great body of
the army. From the beginning they have looked for a short
war, and composed largely of thinking men, they do not see a
necessity for its long protraction.

It is evident that the successes of the federal arms have exercised the rebel leaders with deep concern. It is reported
that Faulkner, the late Minister to France, declared, at a dinner given him at Martinsburg, a few days ago, that it is useless
for the south to contend any longer—that the Southern Confederacy could not stand, and the sooner the war was ended
the better it would be for the people of the south. One swal-
low does not make a summer, nor does a solitary declaration
like this give full assurance of a speedy return of our southern
brethren to their senses. But "straws show which way the
wind blows," and taken in connection with the tone of several
of the leading southern papers, the statement is of deeper significance than would appear, upon a hasty reading. No doubt
it expresses the real feelings of large numbers at the south ;
but the leaders are desperate, and such men as Mr. Davis will
yield only to arguments of iron and lead. That rebellion will
be crushed out is a fixed fact, but we may not hope to witness
such a result without the further intervention of villainous salt-
petre. Of this the Federals have enough and to spare.

With regard to the future movements of the army on this
side of the Potomac, little reliable is known. Many rumors
are afloat. But "rumor's a pipe blown by surmises," and surmises often end where they begin. Camp gossip needs careful
winnowing to obtain the few grains of truth mingled with a
liberal allowance of chaff. We know that it is said this division has been under marching orders for some time, and that

3*

is about all we do know, or at least all that a soldier would feel himself at liberty, without authority, to repeat.

A forward movement may or may not be made at the earliest favorable condition of the roads, as circumstances shall authorize. It is possible, also, that no advance will occur until Burnside, Butler, and Commodore Porter have made a few more strikes. If this be so, then, when Gen. McClellan moves forward, it will be what certain sharp men call the "clearing up deal" with secession. This, of course, is mere speculation, and may prove erroneous; but it does not look reasonable that an army so large as is concentrated along the Potomac should be quietly resting on their arms for nothing. Indeed, for the matter of that, we know they are not. They have already done more than the service of a battle by compelling Beauregard to keep the strength of his army at Manassas, until embargoed by mud for the winter. This silent way of doing things has not the charm that fascinates the popular mind and wins the popular applause; but when the history of the campaign shall be written, this page in the story may be read with quite as much satisfaction as though recorded in gore. Strategy has bloodless victories, not less to be admired than those won by storm and carnage. The story of Capt. Scott and the coon illustrates an important phase in the present conflict. If the rebel army is not treed at Manassas, it has been effectually cooped for the last four months, and is apparently thrown upon the alternatives of assaulting the Federal forces on their own ground, retreating, or surrendering. The former it will be slow to do, and the latter nothing but dire necessity will induce. Retreat is possible. Rumor says troops are already beginning to depart. If true, so much the better. When the last regiment departs, Eastern Virginia will undergo a pancake operation.* If they do not

---

* This prediction is left as originally written. Appearances then, favored its early fulfilment. The causes of disappointment, it is needless to discuss.

retreat, surrender in the end must come. A certain chaplain
may yet have an opportunity to preach from his favorite text.*
For results, we can afford to wait till the ways are settled.

February 26. It is an omen for good that the birth-day of
Washington has been so universally celebrated throughout the
free States. His farewell address is truly a national sermon,
and, at this time, most fitting to be repeated. Its warnings and
counsels, as well as the sound principles of government it un-
folds, need to be uttered in the national ear with all the emphasis that the experience of sixty-six years authorize. The
President showed wisdom and patriotism in recommending this
becoming tribute to the memory of " the founder of our federate
republic," and nothing could have been more impressive than
the scene at the Capitol on the 22d instant. There was something more than local significance in the reäffirmation of fealty,
by the chief magistrate of the nation and the legislative bodies,
to a government based upon human equality and personal
rights. Such an occurrence, in the presence of the representatives of foreign nations spoke more loudly of the spirit and
purpose of those who direct the destinies of this republic than
any set asseverations could possibly have done, and must largely
tend to revive and deepen the love of country in the hearts of
the rising generation. The occasion was celebrated throughout
this division by national salutes from the different batteries,
regimental parades, and national airs played by the several
bands. The day was cold and wet, and perhaps less was made
of it in the way of show than would have been had the surroundings been more agreeable. It was a brazen-faced imper-
tinence on the part of Mr. Davis to avail himself of the day to
inaugurate his rebel administration. Could the marble statue,
beneath whose shadow the outrage was committed, have spoken, it would have said, " shame."

The weather has been at its old tricks again. While the

*" Manasseh is mine."

clerk was supposed to be at Washington, last Monday, looking after demolished church steeples, unroofed houses, dilapidated chimneys, and divers other confusions, occasioned by the boisterous eccentricities of Boreas, that blustering railer rushed with startling violence to our camps, and, on Tuesday, indulged in most unbecoming shindies, such as flooring a number of our tents, blowing the shanty of the sutler of the 4th Michigan regiment, near us, pretty much to pieces, razing the observatory at general head-quarters, and maintaining an uproariousness in minor ways, to the great annoyance of a quiet and order-loving soldiery. Last night, a heavy rain fell. To-day, it is clear, cold and windy. Having no Old Farmer's Almanac at hand, it is impossible to predict what the next change will be.

Our new guns, already mentioned, have been tried, and are regarded as a complete success. The test firing gave Gen. Porter great satisfaction. The men are in excellent heart, and would be glad to introduce the entire battery of ordnance to the secesh at an early day.

LETTER V.

The army moves on Manassas—McClellan's plans revealed to the rebels—Manassas evacuated—Works at Centreville—Fairfax Court House—Address to the army—Stoneman's reconnoisance.

FAIRFAX COURT HOUSE, VA.,
March 12, 1862.

Last Monday was a day of excitement on this side the Potomac. Two weeks ago we had an inkling of coming events. After tattoo, on the 25th ult., an order was issued to pack up and cook rations in readiness for marching the next day. To

what point advance was to be made could only be surmised,
but the order was obeyed with alacrity, for however strong
their admiration of Miner's Hill and its surroundings, the men
were anxious for something more lively than camp life afforded.
They had become infected with the active spirit of the war
department, and welcomed a change that gave promise of a
hand in putting secession *hors du combat* before hot weather.
But eager anticipations were not to be immediately gratified,
and it was not until day before yesterday that the tents of
Battery C were struck and a formal farewell bidden to its old
encampment. At 7 o'clock the battery was in motion. The
day was stormy, and the roads muddy as only Virginia clay,
with due mixture of water, can become; but by dint of perseverance we reached Fairfax Court House, our immediate destination, at half-past twelve o'clock, having made about eight
miles in five and a half hours. It was a fatiguing march to men
and horses, and that night, "tired nature's sweet restorer" was
courted with the assiduity of a rural swain. For the present, Gen.
McClellan's headquarters are fixed here, and an enthusiastic
army are looking forward to a speedy conflict with the army
of treason. They had hoped to catch the birds just flown
from Centreville and Manassas, but must for a time be content
with hunting them elsewhere. The precipitate retreat of the
rebels excited general surprise; but they doubtless were governed by prudential reasons, and these must have been urgent
to induce them to abandon a position of so much importance
without firing a gun.*

---

* This supposition subsequent revelations substantiated. It was stated
by a rebel officer, taken prisoner, that ten days before the army of the
Potomac moved, Gen. McClellan's plans were revealed to the rebel chiefs,
through spies or sympathisers at Washington, and ample time was gained
to shun a battle. At Centreville, the defences, eight in number, and extending five miles, were left without essential injury—"quaker guns"
being placed in the embrasures to give, at the last moment, appearance
of strength. At Manassas Junction, ruin and ravage prevailed. The
torch had been applied to the machine shop, depot, other buildings

Yesterday, General McClellan and McDowell made a cavalry reconnoisance, with a view, probably, of determining the completeness of the evacuation by the rebels of their late strong holds. It is now clear that they have made a successful retreat, carrying off with them most of their ordnance, all their provisions and munitions, and a large portion of the population, slave and free, leaving the country in a measure desolate.

The evacuation of Manassas is the third alternative predicted in my last letter, that the rebel forces would take, though it was not anticipated at so early a day. It was evident they were not disposed to become the attacking party. It was equally clear that they would not surrender, if they could possibly avoid it; and in view of what they saw foreshadowed by the events of the past two months, retreat, as a measure of safety, became a necessity. If the comparatively quiet possession of this stronghold of the rebels has not the prestige of a hard fought battle, it secures advantages that may be accepted as an equivalent for bloodshed. An important post has been gained without loss of life, and the federals hold all the country

---

and camps thereabout, and all were leveled to one smoking, flickering mass. Two camps, however, had been evacuated so hastily that arms, hospital stores, tents and baggage were left behind unharmed, but strewn in infinite confusion.

In a recent volume, entitled "War Pictures from the South," written by an officer in the Confederate army, the author says: "It was no longer a secret to the Confederate Chief that it was General McClellan's intention to transfer his operations to the Peninsula. Large forces were accordingly ordered to proceed there forthwith, and instructions sent at the same time to General Magruder to place Yorktown and Williamsburg in such a state of defence that, if threatened, both should be able to stand a siege. General Magruder, who had for a long time held a command on the Peninsula, lost no time, accordingly, in carrying out these instructions, and he soon fortified Yorktown so strongly that it was in a condition to stand the siege of a large army. . . . . No sooner was his (McClellan's) intended scheme of operations known at Washington, than it was communicated by means of active espionage to the Government at Richmond, where the necessary steps were forthwith taken to counteract it."—p. 269.

east of a line drawn from Manassas to Leesburg. This will soon give us the rebel batteries on the lower Potomac, while our advanced troops are fresh for an onward movement to Richmond or elsewhere.

Fairfax Court House is twenty-one miles west of Washington, and until the rebellion broke out was a quiet little community of some 200 or 300 souls. At present the exact population is unknown. It is a dirty looking village, and bears all the marks of having been under the curse of secession. In a military point of view, its importance, at this time, arises from the fact that it commands the Warrington turnpike, leading to Centreville, seven miles beyond, and thence across Bull Run at Stone Bridge, the Little River turnpike, and the road leading to Vienna, on the Loudon and Hampshire railroad. But a glance at the map will give a better idea of these relations than any description. This place was a scene of a Federal cavalry dash, previous to the battle of Bull Run; here, also, a brave Providence boy* of the Second Rhode Island, captured the secession flag that floated in insulting defiance from the top of the Court House, while halting on the march to that sanguinary conflict. He bears on his person the evidence of his exposure on that memorable day, and deserves well of the country he so faithfully served.

A few rebel mementoes have been picked up in the village. The first is a legal paper of a half century gone by, setting forth why a suit should be brought against Ralph Lane, who " hath hitherto refused and still refuses," to pay Charles J. Love " fifty-four pounds which to him he owes, and from him unjustly detains." The second is a receipted bill of modern date, showing that the " Clerk of the Circuit Court" was successful in obtaining fees due for services rendered; and the third, a grocery order, furnishes evidence that as late as 1854, " good molasses " and " 6¼ cents sugar" were among the articles

* Sergeant James Taggart.

of household comfort used by the "F. F. V's." Did time
permit, an instructive moral discourse might be made from
these three heads, but that is left to those whose province it is
to instruct.

The good news that comes booming to us from the west, is
tinged with sadness by the accompanying tidings of Gen. Lander's sudden death. That sad event has cast a shadow upon
many hearts. His experience on the plains of California, prepared a nature attuned to adventure, for the position to which
he was called at the opening of our national troubles; and his
gallant conduct at Rich Mountain, Edwards Ferry, and in his
last engagement, fully justified the expectations formed of him
by a numerous circle of friends and admirers. Brave and reliable as Junot, and dashing as Murat, he seemed admirably
adapted to play the part assigned him. Gen. McClellan, in
his general order to the army, justly said, " As a man, his devotion to his country, his loyalty to affection and friendship,
his sympathy with suffering, and his indignation at cruelty
and wrong, constituted him a true representative of chivalry."
His loss will be severely felt, and few will be competent to fill
his place.

March 14. To-day, Gen. McClellan has issued an address
to the army in which he says the period for inaction is past.
He commends it for its " magnificent material," and admirable
discipline and instruction. He is soon to bring it face to face
with the enemy on the decisive battle field. " It is my business," he adds, " to bring you there. . . . I shall demand
of you great, heroic exertions, rapid and long marches, desperate combats, privations, perhaps. We will share all these
together; and when this sad war is over, we will return to our
homes, and feel that we can ask no higher honor than the
proud consciousness that we belonged to the army of the Potomac." There is " vim" in this address which tells with
power upon the men. The army, with the exception of Gen.

Heintzleman's division, now rests around Fairfax Court House, ready for the next movement. Quite a mania has prevailed for visiting Bull Run and Manassas, and many officers and men have improved the opportunity afforded them to examine the field of last year's disaster.

March 15. Yesterday, Gen. Stoneman made a reconnoisance in force about fourteen miles beyond Manassas toward Warrenton, to which place the rebels had fallen back. He found the railroad bridge at Bristow's station, on the Orange and Alexandria Railroad, and also Kipp's bridge had been destroyed by fire. The roads were strown with military equipments and baggage wagons, showing that the retreat had partaken of panic. The rebels were several times encountered, and shots exchanged. One man and one horse on our side, were wounded. On the rebel side, one saddle was emptied. After obtaining desired information, Gen. Stoneman returned to Manassas in a drenching rain. Report is, that Gen. Banks has taken possession of Winchester, much to the joy of its inhabitants. The night before, Jackson's troops carried off more than two hundred of its loyal citizens.

March 17. Our mission to Fairfax terminated at the expiration of five days, when orders came for another march. At three o'clock last Saturday morning, reveille was sounded, one day's rations delivered to each man, breakfast served, and everything packed ready for a start. At half-past six o'clock the battery was in motion, and taking the Little River Turnpike, which passes through Anandale, at one time a rebel post, and leads to Alexandria, our faces were set towards the rising sun. As usual, when we move, the superintendent of the weather stepped out, leaving the stop-cocks of the over-head reservoirs open, and we arrived at Camp California thoroughly

4

drenched. A fire was quickly started and the surplus moisture soon evaporated. We occupy the tents vacated by a New York battery, now at Manassas or in that vicinity, and are very comfortable. Our camp was the temporary home of the Fourth R. I. regiment, and of battery F, R. I. Artillery, previously to their joining Burnside's expedition, and a little exercise of the imagination almost enabled one to catch the inspiring tones of "glorious Joe Greene's bugle," as they floated upon the evening air down the valley towards the Potomac. Just above us, Fort Worth lifts its stern head; in our front, towards Alexandria, bristles Fort Ellsworth; and from an eminence on the south-east, stands Fort Lyon, frowning defiance upon the enemies of the Republic. These fortifications effectually guard the approaches to Alexandria. The latter commands the river, and could put a permanent embargo on all rebel vessels attempting to reach Washington from below. Washington is now protected by between thirty and forty defences, and, in the judgment of intelligent officers, 30,000 troops can hold it against any force the rebels can at present hurl upon it.

March 20. A brief visit to Alexandria, a few days since, was an agreeable break in the routine of the camp; and a sight of the Canonicus, as she lay quietly on the bosom of the Potomac, brought up pleasant visions of Rocky Point, Portsmouth Grove and Newport, only, however, to give place to the stern realities of war. Steamboats are not permitted at present to run to Mount Vernon, and the hope of an excursion to the home of the Father of his Country must be for a time deferred, falling back for consolation upon the philosophy that "the best enjoyment is half disappointment." Whether this be so or not, it is a facile method of disposing of "fortune's cheating lottery."

Alexandria looks dilapidated. The objects of interest are few. The Marshall House, where Ellsworth was murdered, has nothing inviting in its external appearance, while its internal parts are disappearing by piece-meal, through the industry of relic gatherers. Many private dwellings belonging to absentee secessionists, are closed or occupied as officers' quarters. The old church, built at an early day of imported brick, and in which Washington worshipped, occupies a somewhat retired spot and is surrounded by a high fence. It is said that his pew, prayer book, cushions, &c. remain as they were when he last attended service there. Last autumn, a large hotel was converted into a General Hospital for sick and wounded soldiers. The last official report shows 519 inmates. Of these, 162 belong to New York regiments, 89 to Pennsylvania, 40 to Maine, and 24 to New Jersey. Only four Rhode Island men are on the list, and one Connecticut. In a former letter it was predicted that the free passage of the Potomac would follow the occupation of Manassas. The prediction has become a verity.

Our army is gathering in this vicinity, with a view of carrying out Gen. McClellan's original plan of reaching Richmond by the way of York and James rivers. The plan, modified by a contingent clause, has received the unanimous approval of the Generals commanding corps, present at a Council of War on Thursday last.* The Potomac, in front of Alexandria, is full of transports, yet not in sufficient numbers to embark the entire force. This will occasion some delay, and subject the troops, deprived of camping accommodations, to temporary inconvenience. It may also give the rebels time

---

*This plan of operations was submitted to the President on the same day, who approved it, but gave directions that such a force should be left at Manassas Junction as would make it certain that the enemy could not repossess himself of that position and line of communication, and also that Washington should be left secure. It is understood, however, that the President preferred a movement on Richmond by way of Manassas.

to prepare for a strong defence, before we can march up the peninsula in sufficient numbers to sweep the way clear to our destination.*

·

LETTER VI.

Embarkation for the Peninsula — Passage to Fortress Munroe — Mount Vernon — The Monitor — Hampton — John Tyler — Gen. Smith's division.

CAMP NEAR NEW MARKET BRIDGE, VA.,
March 30, 1862.

My last was dated at Camp California. The two weeks succeeding were busily occupied in embarking the Army of the Potomac for its important campaign on the Peninsula. Officers and men were full of agreeable excitement in prospect of the active work before them, and the streets and wharves of Alexandria probably never before presented so lively an appearance.

On the morning of the 21st, bowing respectfully to Fort Lyon, and touching my cap to Fort Ellsworth, we bade farewell to the comfortable quarters we had temporarily occupied, and were soon in motion for Alexandria, where we embarked on board the propeller A. H. Bowman and two transport schooners. The embarkation of the artillery of Porter's division was followed by the infantry regiments, and occupied nearly the entire day. Twenty-five steamers and several steam tugs lay

---

*The Prince de Joinville, a member of Gen. McClellan's staff, speaking on this subject, says, " He had been promised transports which could convey 50,000 men at a time. He found vessels hardly equal to the conveyance of half that number. Instead of moving at once, as McClellan intended, a whole army with its equipage, a number of trips had to be made."—*The Army of the Potomac*, p. 20.

in the stream, besides numerous sailing vessels, which were crowded to their utmost capacity. The following steamers were made headquarters of Generals of Porter's division : Daniel Webster, Porter; State of Maine, Morell; Elm City, Martindale; Knickerbocker, Butterfield. Gen. McClellan and staff had their headquarters on board the Commodore, and were conveyed by her to Old Point. The chiefs of artillery, cavalry, engineers, transportation, and the assistant Adjutant General's office were also on board, and until the steamer left, business in their several departments was there transacted.

On the 22d, at 12 o'clock we weighed anchor, and with the transports in tow steamed down the Potomac. We turned our backs upon a city whose flour has a better reputation than its loyalty, without regret, and set our faces with unrestrained eagerness towards our future field of service. As we passed Mount Vernon, the wise counsels of Washington in his farewell address were brought impressively to mind, and it required but a moderate indulgence of the imagination to seem to see his venerable shade stretching forth its arms as if bestowing a benediction upon our enterprise. Sadly has Virginia fallen from her first estate, and bitterly will she yet mourn the folly into which she has been betrayed by unscrupulous and ambitious leaders.

It would have been a pleasant episode in our experiences could we have landed at Mount Vernon for an hour and visited the tomb of one "first in war, first in peace, and first in the hearts of his countrymen;" but the demands of duty forbade delay, and the privilege must be held in reserve for a more propitious season. The mansion, I learn, has been put in good repair, preserving the original style of architecture, and is occupied by two of the regents of the Mount Vernon Association, who have charge of the premises. Mr. John A. Washington, the late owner of the estate, has gone to his account, with secession heading the catalogue of sins to be answered for. Henceforth his name will stand inscribed on the scroll of

4*

infamy, the companion of other names as infamous as his own. Should the "great gulf" that separates him from the Father of his Country ever be spanned, and he be permitted to pass over, his first interview with the founder of a nation he sought to destroy, must present a singular spectacle to the Christian patriots of Bunker Hill, Yorktown and Eutaw Springs. Could it be permitted a mortal to be present on such an occasion, it would be interesting to mark the flashing eye and hear the indignant comment of Patrick Henry, or the emphatic Saxon of "Mad Anthony" of Stony Point memory. All this, however, is on the supposition that the parties are yet in a "sphere" where a little human nature cleaves to the spirit.

The passage down the Potomac was not distinguished by any extraordinary occurrence. The rebel batteries at Shipping Point, Cockpit Point, Acquia Creek and other points, had become silent, and we passed them without any sign of recognition. They have been abandoned, and the navigation of the river is once more free, one of the fruits of our holding Manassas. This places the rebels at Fredericksburg in unpleasant relations with the Federals, and they will probably soon follow the example of their retreating brethren at Manassas and Centreville, and seek some post of greater security.

We arrived off Fortress Monroe about 4 o'clock, on the morning of the 24th. About 8 o'clock, we reached the wharf, and immediately commenced landing our artillery. Owing to the delay in getting up one of the schooners having a portion of our horses on board, the work was not completed until nearly night. Fortress Monroe is a formidable structure, and mounts, including casemates, water batteries and barbette guns, something over four hundred pieces of ordnance. The great Lincoln gun, descriptions of which the illustrated papers have given, is a Behemoth in this great family of defence, and throws a projectile of more than 400 pounds weight. Should it be mounted on the side of approach from Norfolk, and the Merrimac come within range, it might send an unacceptable mis-

sive to that disagreeable neighbor. A large number of United
States craft lay in the bay, among them the Minnesota, which
paid its addresses to the Merrimac a few days ago, and which,
from all accounts, is ready for another trial of strength. The
Monitor also lies at anchor in the bay. In appearance, she has
been likened to a Yankee cheese-box mounted on a scow. But
to my mind, she suggested an image less gustatory. As I
looked upon her, with her two big eyes, the pupils of which
were just discernible, I was reminded of a faithful Newfoundland dog I have often seen on Prospect Hill, guarding his master's premises against unwarrantable intrusion. With his nose
resting lazily between his outstretched feet, and his eyes opening from time to time, to see that all was right, he impressed
the beholder with the fact that beneath an apparent calmness
was hidden a power not safe to encounter. Her conflict with
the Merrimac, when viewed in the light of its consequences, is
the most remarkable on record. It opens a new era in naval
warfare, and the time may not be distant, when, for harbor defence, more reliance will be placed upon an iron-clad floating
battery, like the Monitor, than upon the strongest fortress of
granite. Capt. Errieson may justly be proud of an achievement that has proved a national benefaction, and that crowns
his genius with imperishable renown. Lieutenant Worden and
his gallant crew deserve, as they will receive, an honorable
testimony on the page of history.

Looking upon this immense fortification as a base of operations, the force maintained here for a year past, and the naval
support that could, at any moment, have been concentrated,
surprise is awakened that the Merrimac should have been left
undisturbed in dock until transformed into a formidable iron-
clad, or that a rebel battery should have been suffered to bris-
tle on Sewall's Point. To a practical mind, that Point should
have been early occupied by a Federal force, with defences
seaward and landward, and an attempt, at least, been made to
destroy the Merrimac. These two things done, the freedom of

the James River, which this floating fortress controls, would now be ours. Just at this time, no one, except rebels, Dr. Russel, or his lordship of that name, would object to a small stone fleet finding the bottom of the channel at the entrance of Norfolk harbor.

Immediately on the debarkation of our battery, we took up the line of march, and passing through Hampton, encamped two miles beyond. This town, until the breaking out of the rebellion, a fashionable summer resort, is now a heap of ruins, and the numerous stacks of chimneys stand as so many monuments of secesh vandalism, by whose hand the place was fired. Here John Tyler, " the Accident Presidential," had a residence, to which he gave the romantic name of " Margaritta Cottage." But the place had less attractions to an eye for the picturesque than, from the name, would be inferred, and a magazine writer, with as much truth as sarcasm, has said, " a summer in this site would make any man a bore."

Last Thursday, Gen. Smith's division advanced as far as Great Bethel, but finding no rebels, several of the regiments returned at night. Our battery was hitched up and ready to move at a moment's notice, but its services were not then needed. As our Sibleys were left at Camp Owen, we have extemporized substitutes by setting crotches in the ground to sustain poles, over which are stretched rubber blankets, or tarpaulins. These will serve us a temporary purpose as the season advances, and the weather becomes milder.

LETTER VII.

The advance—Great Bethel—Col. Winthrop—The Ball opened before Yorktown—The first gun fired by Battery C.

CAMP NEAR YORKTOWN, VA.,
April 8, 1862.

Last Friday, 4th inst., Gen. McClellan and staff arrived at Fortress Monroe, and the army commenced its advance. The divisions of Generals Porter and Hamilton took the direct route to Yorktown. The corps of Gen. Keyes proceeded up on the left, by way of Union Mills, and the next day arrived at Warwick Court House. At 6 o'clock A. M., on the same day, our battery broke camp near New Market Bridge, and marched with Gen. Martindale's brigade, to Harwood's Mills, where we encamped for the night. We passed through Great Bethel, made memorable by the fatal conflict with the rebels, last June. There, the accomplished Col. Theodore Winthrop fell, a premature sacrifice to patriotic ardor; and the sound of the "long pealing dirges and muffled drums," that honored his memory, seemed still to float mournfully on the air. Next morning, we resumed our march, and at 10 o'clock came in view of rebel forts and entrenchments. The rebels observed us, and sent their compliments in the form of a shell, which burst in the air some distance in advance of us, doing no harm. Immediately the order "trot march" was given, and being in the lead of the column, we pushed forward. Approaching Fort Magruder, mounting a dozen or fifteen guns, we went into battery in a cornfield, on the right of the road leading to Yorktown, at 1500 or 1800 yards distance, and replied to our quondam friends with a twelve-pound Hotchkiss projectile. For an hour and a half, we had lively work. It was new to us all, but the men took to it with a ready spirit. Presently,

Griffin's battery came up on our right, and peppered away in fine style. Martin's did similar execution on our left. In advance, and about 750 yards from the nearest rebel entrenchment, Berdan's sharpshooters were posted, who, with their telescopic rifles, picked off the rebel cannoneers as often as they exposed their persons above the ramparts. At 3 o'clock P. M., Randolph's battery was ordered to relieve Griffin's, and took position opposite the works at Winn's Mill, on the left of the line occupied by Heintzleman's corps. He was engaged two hours. The 3d and 5th Massachusetts batteries took an efficient part in the fight. Butterfield's and Martindale's brigades reclined on their arms within range of the enemy's guns during the day. The roar of cannon shook the earth like a subterranean convulsion, and the sharp crack of Berdan's rifles told how busily they were employed. We lost one man, John J. Reynolds. At the second fire from the rebels, he was struck by a shell, which terribly shattered his leg. It was immediately amputated, but he lived only about fifteen minutes after the operation. He appeared not to suffer at all. The surgeons said the shock was sufficient to cause his death. He was buried at night. Two men belonging to Martin's battery were killed, and five reported wounded. Thus, Rhode Island and Massachusetts share the honor of shedding the first blood in this preliminary engagement. One of our horses had two of his front teeth knocked out. It is remarkable, that with shot and shell coming thick and fast from three forts, one in the centre, one on the right, and one on the left, (though that on the right fired, I believe, but a single shot,) we did not have more casualties. Griffin's battery did not lose a man or horse. Randolph's lost eight horses, and had a spoke knocked from the wheel of a carriage. Martin's had three horses killed and five wounded. One of Berdan's sharpshooters was killed, and three were wounded. We remained in our position till night, the fighting during the day being mostly carried on by artillery and sharpshooters. Our battery had been in position but a

short time, when, hissing with secession spite, came a shell from
a rebel breastwork, which passed directly over the heads of
Gen. Porter, Gen. Morell, and several other officers, and struck
the ground beyond them, without injury to any one. Other
shells threatened much by their erratic movements, but proved
harmless. In the rear of our caissons, on the brow of a hill,
were the 62d Pennsylvania volunteers, who had just come from
our extreme left, and had halted in the form of a square. The
sharp-eyed rebels, discovering them, let fly a thirty-two-pound
shell, which went buzzing like a hornet's nest over our heads,
and struck a rail fence with a furious crash, wounding three of
their men, one of them so severely that he has since died.
Fortunately the shell did not explode, or it would have swept
away an entire company.

In review of this first experience under fire, truth demands
no record which a Rhode Island man would be unwilling to
read. With the conduct of his men, Capt. Weeden was much
gratified, and Gen. Porter, whose head-quarters are close by,
spoke of them in high praise—a praise deserved by all the batteries.

While encamped at Newmarket Bridge, I visited the 2d
Rhode Island regiment, which had encamped about a mile from
us, and enjoyed the pleasure of greeting a few old friends whom
I had not seen since they left Providence. The half-hour
allotted me passed like a dozen seconds, and left many friends
to be seen at a more convenient season. The regiment has
advanced, and is somewhere in our vicinity. They are in excellent spirits, and eager to pay off an old score. " Slocum "
and " Ballou " will be terrible battle-cries when the contest
rages, or the order to charge is given.

Gen. McClellan was here yesterday, and, I learn, has examined the rebel lines. They have a long line of defences
stretching between York and James rivers, and their breastworks mount many heavy guns. Yorktown is the key to Richmond on the route from Fortress Monroe. If this stronghold

falls, Richmond and Norfolk will follow, Virginia will be swept of secession, and Gov. Wise, if he continues successful in keeping out of harm's way, may have an opportunity to revive his famous and once popular sentiment, "The Union for the sake of the Union."

April 14.   Last Wednesday, Gov. Sprague and Col. Reynolds visited the 2d Rhode Island, and were greeted with a hearty welcome. To-day, the Governor was expected to pay us a visit, but did not arrive. The flying visit to our encampment last December, as well as the substantial tokens of his interest in the comfort of the Rhode Island troops, are pleasantly remembered. His presence again will be the signal for three cheers and a Narragansett.

.
————

LETTER VIII.

Picket duty—A brush with the rebels—Gen. Porter's balloon adventure—Rebel works—Siege preparations.

CAMP NEAR YORKTOWN, VA.,
April 16, 1862.

Since our engagement with the rebel entrenchments, our battery has been chiefly engaged by sections in picket duty, at times tedious for want of adventure, but sometimes lively and exciting, and always profitable as a practical exercise.

Last Thursday afternoon, the centre section, under Lieut. Clark, while on picket, had a smart brush with the rebels. From their works they poured shot and shell, with a profusion worthy a better cause. The fire was returned with great spirit, and with fatal effect. Forty rounds were bestowed upon them, killing and wounding, as is understood, at least twenty of the

rebels. At one time, the position of the battery was somewhat
critical. A regiment of the rebel infantry deployed, for the
purpose of closing round and cutting it off, but a few well-
directed discharges frustrated their design, and drove them
back. A body of our infantry who advanced to support the
battery, encountered the foe, and performed important service.
Capt. Randolph was also out, and put two of his guns in battery to cover an exposed point, but necessity for testing their
power did not occur. During the contest, heavy shells were
thrown from mortars by the rebels, while Minie bullets from
their sharpshooters flew like hail. No injury was sustained by
our men or horses. Two fixed canister lying beside one of the
guns, had their cartridges ignited and exploded by the bursting
of one of the enemy's shells, but without harm. A sponge
bucket was also knocked to pieces. No other casualties occurred. An unexploded shell was brought back to camp. It
was a percussion 32-pounder, and of good finish, showing that
the rebels have formidable appurtenances of warfare as well as
ourselves. Four batteries besides our own—Captains Tompkins', Randolph's, Bartlett's and Owen's—are here, and ready
to do any work in their line. Last Saturday, Gen. Barry and
Major Webb visited our camp. Both are accomplished artillery officers. Friday, Lieut. Buckley's section was on picket.
Sunday, the right section, Lieut. Waterman, was out. We had
a quiet time and saw nothing alarming. No occasion offered
for firing a gun. We witnessed the ascent of a secesh balloon,
which came down almost immediately after it went up. Monday night, about 12 o'clock, our battery, in conjunction with
Griffin's, went out again, and addressed our compliments to the
rebel works, with which we just made acquaintance on the 5th
instant. Both batteries fired about fifty shells, and retired before the occupants of the forts were fairly awake, or had opportunity to ascertain who had so early disturbed their repose.
The flashing of the guns in the darkness of the morning was an
interesting sight, and whatever may have been the effect of our

5

missiles, the unseasonable reveille was doubtless as surprising
as unwelcome.

Last Friday, an incident occurred, which, for a moment, excited amusement, but soon assumed too serious an aspect to be
classed with jokes. Gen. Porter, who has a habit of knowing
everything from personal observation, proposed to make a balloon reconnoissance in the usual way. He accordingly stepped
into the car alone, and was soon mounting into the upper air.
At an elevation of several hundred feet, and just as he was
preparing to get a good observation of the rebel entrenchments,
the guys, by which the balloon was held, parted, and the gaseous
vehicle sailed away before a wind that drove its passenger towards the enemy's lines. The first impulse was to laugh, as is
ordinarily the case when an unfortunate slips upon an icy side-
walk and falls, but the next was to shout, "open the valve."
But the General had too little respect for the secesh to drop
himself in the midst of their encampments, which he would
have done had he acted upon such advice, and too much regard
for the feelings of his division to make a visit to Richmond
alone ; and so, with the calmness of Capt. Allen or Prof. Lowe,
let things remain in *statu quo* till he reached an upper current
that swept him back over the point from which he started, when
he let off the gas, and came down in the neighborhood of Gen.
McClellan's head-quarters, with a velocity that nothing but the
exigencies of the case would have justified. Fortunately he
was not injured, and still more fortunate was it that the upper
current did not hurry him off to the capital of Virginia rebel-
dom, or force him across the James river to Norfolk. That
he obtained valuable information during his aerial voyage is
probable, but none will wish him to increase his knowledge of
the rebel defences at the price of a similar risk.

A section of Battery G, under Lieut. Edward Sears, has
been out on picket the past forty-eight hours. In some artillery
practice upon the rebels, two of the gun carriages were disabled by recoil. The enemy have three lines of defences in

rear of each other, on the other side of the Warwick river. '
Opposite, the Federals have three earthworks, behind which
artillery is posted, having range on their guns. Between the
first and second earthworks, counting from the left, are two
chimneys, the remains of a dwelling burned by the rebels.
Here, two sharpshooters, with telescopic rifles, are stationed, to
pick off every gunner who may have the temerity to show
himself.

The rebels are busy in building fortifications on the Gloucester side of the York river, which are protected by guns of
long range. To-day, the Federal gunboat Tobago, mounting
an hundred-pounder rifled Parrott gun, took position and sent
a number of shells into their works with fatal effect, causing the men, for a time, to suspend their labor. They were
seen carrying off their dead and wounded.

Great strictness is now exercised among the soldiers. No
one is allowed outside of his camp without a pass signed by a
general officer. Those who stray beyond their bounds are soon
escorted back by the provost guard. Sutlers are quite scarce,
and when one arrives, his stock is soon disposed of at an ex-
orbitant advance. Butter, (a luxury with which a soldier is
not frequently acquainted,) has been sold as high as sixty cents
per pound, and other articles in proportion.

Gen. McClellan has appropriately named his head-quarters,
Camp Winfield Scott. He frequently reconnoitres in person,
and is said to know, from observation, all the rebel positions.
Some of these positions are strong, and from the wet character
of the ground around them, are not easy of approach ; others
are comparatively weak, and, it is believed, can be taken without much difficulty. The preparations for the reduction of this
rebel stronghold are progressing steadily, and on a formidable
scale. Rifle pits have been dug, roads and bridges built, earth
works thrown up, heavy siege guns mounted, and other preparatory labor done, that would surprise the uninitiated. A
work on our right mounts 100 and 200-pounder rifled ordnance,

to take care of a strong point in the rebel defence. It is obscured by a forest, that, at the appointed moment, will be instantly prostrated, and leave no obstruction to the transmission of deadly missives.* Prisoners report that about two thousand negroes have been at work, for two months, on the rebel fortifications. A supply of shelter tents to the 4th Michigan regiment, has put the men in excellent spirits. They have occupied the advance, in Gen. Howard's brigade, and been much

---

* By the following statements, it appears that besieging Yorktown was not a positive part of the original plan:

"In order to gain time, and avoid the tedium of a siege, General McClellan had thought out the means of turning the position. The enemy held the James, with the Merrimac and his gunboats; the York was closed by the Yorktown and Gloucester Point batteries. Nevertheless, by a disembarkation on the Severn, beyond Gloucester, we might carry the latter position and open the way of the Federal gunboats into the river York. A subsequent movement up the left bank, in the direction of West Point, would put us so far in the rear of the army charged with the defence of the lines of Yorktown that it would have been in a most perilous position. This accomplished, the confederates must have abandoned Gloucester, and fallen back hastily upon Richmond. The execution of this *coup de main* had been left to a corps of the army commanded by Gen. McDowell. This corps was to be the last to embark at Washington, and it was calculated that it ought to reach Yorktown, in a body, on its transports, at the moment when the rest of the army, moving by land, should appear before that port from Fortress Munroe. Instead of finding it, we received the inexplicable intelligence that this corps of 35,000 strong, had been sent to another destination."—*De Joinville's Army of the Potomac, p.* 41.

"His original plan, as I have already stated, was to send a *corps d'armee* to the rear of Gloucester,—to reach West Point, twenty-five miles above Yorktown, and then, by combined attack in rear, in front and on the flank from our gunboats, to compel a surrender. This plan he was under the necessity of changing when Gen. McDowell's corps was withdrawn and sent to the Rappahannock; because he was then left without a force sufficient to warrant the detachment of so large a body as this operation would have required. His only resource, therefore, was to make the attack in regular form and by a regular siege operation,—running no risks of defeat by undue haste or inadequate preparation, and making it absolutely *certain* that he could hold every step he might take in advance."—*Letter of Hon. Henry J. Raymond, in N. Y. Times.*

exposed to inclement weather. When all things are ready, and the order to open fire passes along the line, there will be a thundering of artillery such as America never before dreamed of. That Yorktown must fall, is the common sentiment of the army. That conviction inspires every heart and nerves every arm. In the way of prophecy, an old authority may be cited : " The thing that hath been, it is that which shall be ; and that which is done is that which shall be done." Nearly eighty-one years ago, Rhode Island men led the attack upon the British entrenchments Yorktown, which resulted in the surrender of Cornwallis, and ensured to our country an independent nationality. Rhode Island men are again before this same Yorktown. Let the record of the next few weeks complete the story of the coincidence in its bearing upon secession.

[It was the opinion of General Heintzleman, as expressed before the Committee on the Conduct of the War, that when our army first reached Yorktown, it could have forced the rebel lines " at or about Wynn's Mills, isolated Yorktown, so as to prevent the enemy from re-enforcing it, when it would have fallen in the course of a little while." General Keyes, also, gave it a. '' impression that " if the whole army had been pressed forward, we should have found a point to break through." He did not think, however, that Yorktown could have been taken by assault, except at great expense of life.

General Hooker, in his testimony, said, " From my examination of the works at Yorktown, and reaching away beyond the position that I occupied, I felt that their [rebel] lines could be pierced without any considerable loss, by the corps with which I was on duty—Heintzleman's corps. We could have gone right through, and gone to the rear of the enemy. . . . . I would have marched right through the redoubts which were a part of the cordon they had, and got on the road between Yorktown and Richmond, and thus compelled the enemy to fight me on my ground, and not have fought them on theirs."

5*

The President was desirous that this breach should be made, and telegraphed to the Commander in Chief, April 6th, "I think you had better break the enemy's line from Yorktown to Warwick river, at once;" to which Gen. McClellan replied, on the 7th, "The whole line of the Warwick, which really heads within a mile of Yorktown, is strongly defended by detached redoubts and other fortifications, armed with heavy and light guns. The approaches, except at Yorktown, are covered by the Warwick, over which there is but one, or at most two, passages, both of which are covered by strong batteries. It will be necessary to resort to the use of strong siege guns, and some siege operations, before we can assault. Our prisoners state that General J. E. Wharton arrived in Yorktown yesterday, with strong reinforcements. It seems clear that I shall have the whole force of the enemy on my hands, probably not less than one hundred thousand men, and possibly more." Before the Committee on the Conduct of the War, Gen. McClellan gave it as his opinion that Yorktown could not have been captured by a rapid movement immediately upon landing upon the peninsula. "We found," he says, "the enemy intrenched and in strong force wherever we approached. The nature and extent of his position along the Warwick river was not known to us when we left Fort Monroe. . . . . Movements of troops had been going on across the James river to the peninsula for some days before my arrival. Immediately upon my arrival at Fort Monroe, I was told that quite a large number of troops had been crossed over to Yorktown, from the south bank of the James. I therefore hurried my own movements, and started from Fort Monroe sooner than I would have done. From the best information I have been able to get, I think that the large masses of the reinforcements arrived at Yorktown from one to two days before I reached its vicinity. Johnston himself arrived there the day before I did. . . . I resorted to the operations of a siege, after a more careful personal examination than a commanding general usually gives to such things; and I was fully satisfied that the course I adopted was the best under the circumstances." These different opinions are here cited, to give more completeness to the narrative, without design to decide between them.]

LETTER IX.

Assault by a Vermont regiment—Battery skirmishes—Picket firing discountenanced — Incidents — Berdan's, Wentworth's, and Sanders's sharpshooters—Battery C on the right of the line—Morale of the army.

CAMP NEAR YORKTOWN,
April 18, 1862.

Besides the ordinary picket duties, in which both artillery and infantry have been engaged the past week, pretty active attention has been addressed to the rebels employed in throwing up outer works in their line of fortifications, very much to their disgust. By day, and sometimes under cover of night, they have been visited by batteries and other respectable bodies of Federals, and though proffered the most substantial articles of our military commissariat, they have, for the most part, tartly declined them, and precipitately retired. In several instances their work has been effectually stopped. Generally, these neighborly movements have been satisfactory to our men, giving them exciting exercise, as well as familiarizing them with the practical movements of the field. In some instances, however, they have led to sharp encounters, in which the prowess of our troops has been placed beyond question. A case of this kind occurred day before yesterday, at a point between Lee's and Winn's Mills, on a tributary of Warwick river. Here the rebels had been at work for several days, in making secure an important pass, which being discovered, two Vermont regiments and four batteries of artillery were sent out to dislodge them. A severe engagement followed.

In this assault, the Vermonters displayed the energy of their mountain sires. The free air of their native State had quickened the blood-flow of their hearts, and imparted force to a determined will. Before them, to impede their advance, was a stream that had been dammed; and on the opposite bank an entrenchment, protected by cannon and a thousand rifles. But to water and fire they were alike indifferent. Into the first, several companies rushed with alacrity, and were soon wading waist deep, and some even to the arm-pits. The second, they faced with the coolness of veterans, and under a perfect storm of lead and iron, and amid deafening explosions, that seemed as though Jupiter was "cleaving the clouds with flashing lightning," and driving his "thundering horses and swift chariot through the sky," they pushed steadily on, as if moved by the spirit of Ethan Allen. Bennington and Plattsburg were never represented by truer men. Sustained by several batteries, they stormed the enemy's works, which they held for a short time, but upon the approach of heavy rebel reinforcements, it was deemed prudent to recross the stream, which they did without confusion. Loss reported is, 32 killed and 132 wounded. The color-bearer was shot, but by the bravery of Sergeant Holton the colors were secured and brought off. Mott's battery, which was prominent in the fight, suffered a loss of 17 men killed and wounded, and seven horses. The other batteries, Capts. Ayers, Kennedy and Wheeler, conducted themselves with great bravery, and fortunately escaped with few casualties.

The skirmishes of the day brought out the Rhode Island batteries B, E and G—Capts. Bartlett, Randolph and Owen—who spoke to the rebels in very decided tones. Of the latter, two or three men are reported wounded by the explosion of a rebel shell. Beam's New Jersey battery was also in position, and took part in the work.

During the day more than 1700 projectiles were fired. The Vermont troops engaged have been complimented in a general order for " the invincibility of spirit " shown by them while exposed to a terrific fire, and Gen. McClellan spoke in warm praise of the manner in which the artillery performed their part. It appears that our recent night reconnoissance produced great consternation in the rebel camp. I hear that they formed in battle array and remained so for several hours. Had we been on the ground an hour and a half earlier, the annoyance could have been made still more disagreeable, as their camp fires were then brightly burning, which would have proved of service in more accurately sighting the guns. But perhaps the scare we gave them was enough for a first experience.

Wednesday, Lieut. Buckley's section went out on picket. There was some firing from the gunboats, and in Gen. Sedgwick's division. On our left, the cannonading was incessant all day, and, towards night, rapid discharges of musketry were heard. Several casualties occurred, and among the killed were an orderly sergeant and a lieutenant of infantry. The former was shot through the body by a cannon ball. The batteries reported engaged were Randolph's, Mott's, Carlyle's and Gibbon's. They battered away at a secesh fort, and, it is said, with famous execution. About four o'clock, a light battery was seen to leave a fort and move off to the left, probably to assist or relieve the one assailed, and our right section, Lieut. Waterman, was ordered out to take care of it. At five o'clock, the two sections united. We took post just under the brow of a hill, and waited the appearance of the foe ; but the rebels smelt a rat, and the first thing we knew, three regiments of infantry and a light battery were coming down on our right, to flank us. We were not to be caught, however, in that manner, and quietly limbering up, moved to the rear, where we halted for a short time, and, as the enemy did not choose to favor us with another manœuvre, we returned to camp about half-past seven, without damage.

Yesterday, Capt. Owen's battery threw some two hundred rounds at the rebel works. While firing, Gov. Sprague rode up. He dismounted and sighted one or two guns, making very good shots. He remarked, with a smile, that he had " wasted ammunition enough," and then mounting, rode off.

To-day, we have had no call from camp. Griffin's battery has been out, and expended a little ammunition. The gunboats in the river have thrown several shells at the rebel fortifications, to which they responded from their heavy guns, but without effect. There was cannonading at intervals, all last night, and towards morning musketry was heard on our left. We had orders to hitch up, which were soon countermanded. To-day, the firing has been irregular. What will be on the morrow, the morrow alone can declare. It may be, we shall again hear

> "The rattling musketry, the clashing blades,
>   And ever and anon, in tones of thunder,
>   The diapason of the cannonade ;"

or, before many weeks, we may be called

> "To sit and muse, like other conquerors,
>   Upon the fearful ruin "

secession hath wrought, in this once powerful Old Dominion. I will here correct an error into which I notice several reporters of our fight, of the 5th instant, have inadvertently fallen. In that attack upon the rebel fort, the first gun was fired by Battery C, Rhode Island artillery. So please stick a pin there, that in after years history may give credit to whom credit shall be due.

Gen. McClellan is discountenancing the firing of pickets upon each other, when posted on extreme lines, and engaged in ordinary duties, as barbarous. The rebels show less inclination

to adopt a pacific practice than our own men, though they are
gradually coming to a comprehension of its correctness. Occasionally, the pickets on both sides hold conversations in which
the jokes are more frank than elegantly expressed. A short
time since, the following colloquy across Warwick river occurred :

"What regiment do you belong to?" shouts Union.
"Seventh Georgia," responds secesh. "What regiment do
you belong to?" "The 102d Rhode Island, and we are going
to whip you like ——" was the reply. The conversation
dropped. Another specimen runs thus : "What regiment do
you belong to?" is the rebel question. "Massachusetts," is the
reply.

"How about *sugar ;* have you got any?"—this intended as
a thrust.

"Yes, plenty," answered Massachusetts.

"That's an infernal yankee lie," responded the nettled ques-
tioner. "We know better. Raise the blockade, and we'll let
you have sugar."

"How about *salt?*" retorted Massachusetts.

"Go to ——," was the blunt response, and expressive silence
reigned.

A vein of humor sometimes shows itself even in the midst
of deadly strife. The other day, so the story goes, during a
skirmish, a Maine and a Georgia soldier posted themselves
each behind a tree, and indulged in sundry shots, without effect
on either side, at the same time keeping up a lively chat.
Finally, that becoming a little tedious, Georgia calls out to
Maine, " Give me a show," meaning step out and give an opportunity to hit. Maine, in response, pokes out his head a few
inches, and Georgia cracks away and misses. "Too high,"
says Maine. " Now give me a show." Georgia puts out his
head, and Maine blazes away. " Too low," says Georgia. In
this way the two alternated several times without hitting.
Finally, Maine sends a ball so as to graze the tree within an

inch or two of Georgia's ear. " Cease firing," shouts Georgia.
" Cease it is," responds Maine. " Look here," says one, " we
have carried on this business long enough for one day. 'Spose
we adjourn for rations ?" " Agreed," says the other. And so
the two marched away in different directions, one whistling
Yankee Doodle, and the other, Dixie.

April 21. Since I last wrote, the weather has alternated
with sunshine and storm. Saturday night, considerable rain
fell. Wrapped in a poncho, I slept very comfortable, however, though my cover was not entirely impervious to water.
Yesterday forenoon was cold and stormy. To-day, at intervals,
it has rained again, with the prospect of another wet night.

In military matters, things, for the last three days, have not
materially changed. More or less, every day, the rebels try
the range of their guns, and get, in return, specimens of our
shot and shell. A few shells from one of their large guns have
exploded in the vicinity of a steam saw mill, which they forgot
to destroy, and which the Federals have converted to constitutional uses. Their range being short, no damage was done.
The mill is a very handy contraband. Firing by night and
by day is quite frequent ; and while I am writing, a large secesh
gun has belched forth at some of our boats in the river.' But
all this is the pastime of war, though it may be regarded as a
motion towards something more serious.

Berdan's Sharpshooters are still troublesome to the rebels,
picking them off whenever they come in range. One of them
told me a few days ago, that while on duty that morning, he
brought down his man. The telescopic rifle brings the object
so near as to render the aim, within a given distance, almost
certain. So shy have the rebels become, that in repelling assaults upon their earthworks, they often employ negroes to load
their cannon. The Massachusetts 22d has a company attached,
under the command of Capt. Wentworth, highly skilled in the
use of the rifle, and who are constantly engaged in hard duty

on the outposts.* The first company of Andrew Sharpshooters, Capt. John Saunders, attached to the 15th Massachusetts, are also a terror to rebel gunners, and highly effective in their line of service. The 2d Rhode Island regiment has men who draw a bead with great accuracy. One of them, I am informed, rivals the California prodigy of Berdan's corps, and woe betide the secesh who shows his head within three hundred yards. The regiment, after moving from Newmarket Bridge, was posted, for a short time, near Warwick Court House, where a post hospital has been established; but since I last wrote, it has advanced several miles to a position nearer the rebel lines, and is ready for the work to which it may soon be called. Judging from the spirit of the men, they will be found busy in the thickest of the fight. They have several times been under arms for a brush, but as yet, have not had an opportunity to meet the enemy.

The rebels have lately taken quite a dislike to a large Parrott gun mounted in our lines, and with whose conversation they have been considerably annoyed. Last week, under cover of night, they resolved to obtain possession of it, and put a stop to its insolence. They "plotted brave schemes," but were doomed to disappointment. War sharpens wits, and anticipat-

---

* Captain Lewis E. Wentworth is a native of New Hampshire, and at the breaking out of the rebellion, was doing business in Salem, Mass. He marched to Washington for the protection of the Capital, as lieutenant of infantry, and participated in the battle of Bull Run, July 21, 1861, where he exhibited great bravery, and rendered important service. On his return home, he was authorized to raise a company (the Second) of Sharpshooters, which he did in brief time. The company broke camp at Lynnfield, October 8, 1861, and reached Hall's Hill, Va., on the 13th, where it remained till the following March. Its position before Yorktown was one of great danger and of severe labor. It was at Gaines's Farm, Malvern Hill, the second Bull Run, Antietam, and Fredericksburg, and has obtained an honorable reputation for efficiency. Capt. Wentworth is a skilful officer, a thorough disciplinarian, courteous in manners, and is held in universal esteem. He has suffered much from sickness induced by exposure.

6

ing some such movement, an entire brigade of ours was ordered to receive them. Lying flat upon the ground in the form of a harrow, (thus >,) with the coveted gun in the centre, they waited the arrival of their expected visitors. On approaching within speaking distance of the Federal guns, they rose and gave them a leaden welcome, for which they were not grateful, and from which they retired with " curses not loud, but deep." The loss on the rebel side is reported considerable. Of ours, if any, I have not yet ascertained.

The rebel entrenchments extend across the peninsula, from York to James river. Some of them are heavily mounted, and strongly manned with infantry. Many others are not completed, and are defended only by infantry and sharpshooters, who cover the workmen while throwing up embankments. What is doing in the rear of these visible defiances we shall soon learn. At present, all knowledge of rebel doings in that direction is confined to those who best know what use to make of it. Day before yesterday, Capt. Sears, Co. F. 2d Rhode Island, with two hundred men, went out to assist in strengthening our earthworks. Platforms are now laying for fifteen 100-pounder guns. The infantry deserve great praise, not only for the spirit with which they engage in picket and skirmishing duties, but for the hearty will with which they handle the pick and spade.

Our battery is on the right of the line, and it is expected will hold that position during the campaign. Gen. McClellan has been pleased to speak of it in very complimentary terms. I believe he appreciates the reliability of the other batteries Rhode Island has given him. Here, or elsewhere, they have been under fire, and shown a steadiness reputable to the State they represent.

The *morale* of the army before Yorktown is good. The men composing it who are here from a conscientious sense of duty, may be reckoned by thousands. They are thinking men, and understand the interests at stake. They are men who have much to live for, to whom life is sweet, and yet who know that some must fall. But they are ready to sacrifice everything earthly for the sake of this glorious Union. Such men will stand firm in the hour of conflict. As well might it be hoped to "entice the sun from his ecliptic line" as to turn them back from the work to which they have put their hand.

Yesterday, Isaac B. Cowdrey, a member of Wentworth's Sharpshooters, died after a few days' confinement in the hospital. He was a favorite with the company. He was buried near night, and his mortal remains rest, as will thousands, in a strange soil, far from the home of kindred and friends.

LETTER X.

Rebels attack the 7th Maine—Rebel deserters—California Joe—News from home—Col. Bissell—Topography of the country—Rebel deserters—Contrabands.

CAMP WINFIELD SCOTT, NEAR YORKTOWN, VA., \
April 24, 1862.

The rain, for a week past, has, at times, been copious, and rendered active operations less agreeable, though the military work has gone steadily on. Reconnoissances, picket service, and an exchange of shots, along the line, have been continued, as mentioned in former letters. Occasionally, a shot comes from the rebel fort on the right, termed, by us, the hospital fort, but as yet its missiles have proved harmless. Monday night, the Federal gunboats tried their range upon the rebel fortifications, with what effect, I have not learned. Tuesday afternoon, the rebels expended a quantity of powder and shells upon a party of our troops at work in front of the entrenchments on their left. Their shells fell short, and the attempt resulted simply in noise and smoke. In the evening, there was an interchange of shots between our gunboats and the rebel works on our right. The enemy's shot failed of effect, while a number of the Federal shells fell within their forts, and exploded, it is reported, disastrously. Yesterday, a brisk encounter took place above Lee's Mills. An attack was made, by two hundred rebels, on the pickets of the 7th Maine regiment. The assailants were driven back at the point of the bayonet, having had several fatally wounded. One prisoner was taken, and sent, for examination, to Gen. Sumner. To-day, the weather is charming, and our battery have drilled at the manual. The gunboats have fired several shots, to which the rebel forts have a few times responded. As I am writing, a shell has just burst over in the woods, doing no damage.

Deserters are frequently coming into our lines, who bring reports of disaffection among the Irish in the rebel army. It is said they have refused to fight. How much truth there is in the statement, we shall shortly learn. From all accounts, Gen. Magruder has his hands full. Six weeks ago, he issued a vaporing address to his soldiers, to encourage those to reënlist whose term of service was about to expire, and to soothe the disappointment of the men from whom furloughs to visit their homes had been withdrawn. He admits that " disasters and reverses have recently befallen " the rebel arms, and boasts loudly of what he is going to do. He uses as grandiloquent invectives as he perhaps ever indulged in when in peaceful command at Fort Adams; but when the hour for closer intimacy arrives, he will probably find the sons of Bellona before his entrenchments less agreeable than the company of the Naiads of Newport Beach, or the daughters of Terpsichore at the Ocean House.

After the disasters that have followed the rebel arms elsewhere, it is evident the leaders look with great anxiety to the approaching struggle before Yorktown. One of their papers, in speaking of the troops under Gen. McClellan, says, " If we decline to fight them, we must yield Richmond, and that is giving up Virginia. If we fight them, and are signally defeated, Richmond and Virginia are lost. Let us be assured," the writer continues, " that McClellan does not take the field and risk his fame, without the means to back up his ambition. This is the army we have got to whip, or Virginia is lost." The sequence of the failure we readily accept.

Last Monday, a Federal sharpshooter shot a rebel picket, while the latter was attempting to surprise him. He was brought into the hospital, and died in the night.

In previous letters, I have spoken of Berdan's Sharpshooters, as an important feature of our advance. They comprise two regiments, and are held to be among the best, if not the very best, marksmen in the world. Some of them are armed with Colt's revolving seven-shooter rifle, and others with rifles of heavier calibre. Every day they send unwelcome messages into the rebel lines, and cause a vacancy in some mess. Among them is one, to whom I referred in my last, bearing the sobriquet of California Joe, who is something of a character, and bids fair to become " famous throughout the world for warlike praise." In manners, Joe is not a Chesterfield. Grace is not in his steps, and no rebel, confronting him, would discover heaven in his eye ; but beneath a rough exterior beats a warm, patriotic heart ; and, after disabling a foe, he would readily share with him the contents of his canteen and haversack. Joe carries a rifle weighing thirty-two pounds, and may be regarded as a movable fortification. He takes pride in the reputation of a crack shot, and holds himself good for anything covered by his telescopic sight at a thousand yards. Every success he marks upon his ramrod, and it is said the tally is nearly full. Joe greatly restricts the freedom with which the enemy would be pleased to use the guns mounted upon some of their works, and with the sharp vision of the backwoodsman, should he escape the casualties of his hazardous vocation, will doubtless prove to many of them a deadly northern hornet. If he falls, it will be

> "With his face to the foe,
> Cheering his comrades on."

Tuesday was a red letter day in camp. Providence smiled as Providence alone can smile. The welcome post courier brought up a generous number of letters and papers that had accumulated at Washington, waiting the convenience of arrangements for conveyance to their destination. How eagerly seals were broken, and contents devoured, can easily be imagined by one who has long been separated from loved ones at home. And then, what glorious stories the Journal told us about Island No. 10, Pea Ridge and Newbern, old at this time to those who have the news fresh from the bulletin three times a day, but, in their details, new to us who enjoy no such advantages. The tale of Island No. 10 is a marvel of the age, and will suggest new modes of operation elsewhere. That aquatic saw was worth half a dozen gunboats, even though clad in armor, and Col. Bissell will rank in history with the genius that conceived and perfected the Monitor. The doings at Newbern, following closely upon the capture of Roanoke, are what might have been expected of one who conquered the storm, in spite of rotten hulks, at Hatteras. Men taking their inspiration from the face of such a leader, are bound to conquer. So much for letters and papers—the former warm with heart sympathies at home, and the latter talking to us of local occurrences, as we intensely listen, and passing, as a panorama, the bustle of Market square, and the show windows of Westminster street, fresh before us. The Egyptian who originated the power to do this deserved a temple to his honor. He little thought that at the end of four thousand years, more or less, his invention would be sunlight to the thousands before Yorktown to-day.

The next visitors that would, at this moment, meet the warmest welcome, are the paymasters. With empty purses and four months' arrearages due, the men naturally look with special interest for the advent of these important personages. It is understood they are on their way, and may have already reached some portions of the army. The more promptly the men are paid, the better will it be for those who have families at home. And that consideration leads to another topic, which it is hoped the press will agitate until the object is gained, viz., pensions for soldiers' widows. In the army, this is a subject of universal interest. I do not know of a married soldier who did not understand, when he enlisted, that if he fell, his wife would receive a pension ; but it is now understood that no such provision exists, and the fact has awakened feelings of disappointment. Every man here, having a dependent family, would fight better and lay down his life more cheerfully, could he but be assured that his wife and children would not be left wholly destitute when deprived of their natural guardian. A matter involving so many interests should not be hidden from view, nor passed lightly by. It certainly deserves a place in the sympathies of Congress alongside of the contraband confiscation question.*

This morning, six companies of the 22d Massachusetts and a small detachment of sharpshooters, were sent on a reconnoissance. Having accomplished their object, they returned about noon.

April 28. The peninsula between Fortress Monroe and Yorktown is diversified in its topographical features, as well as in its soil and culture. The soil is generally light and easy to work, and well adapted to the production of turnips, beets,

---

* Soon after this letter was written, the attention of the government, as well as of influential members of Congress, was drawn to the neglect here spoken of. It has since been remedied, and the widows of Rhode Island soldiers, by a noble provision of the public authorities, can have all the necessary papers for obtaining a pension, and the pension itself secured, free of cost.

carrots, and other vegetables; but the prospects for farming in this region, the present year, are not encouraging. The secession owners of farms, together with their slaves, have, in many instances departed, leaving the estates to take care of themselves, or what amounts to about the same thing, consigning them to the care of a few worn out inefficient negroes. This is the case with a large landholder by the name of Young, the owner of mills bearing his name, who has abandoned a beautiful home to unite his fortunes with rebellion. There are many fine localities along the route of our march, which eastern enterprise and taste would soon convert into Edens; but the general appearance of the country betrays the sad effects of civil war. Hampton, which was burned last year by the rebels, to prevent it falling into Federal hands, presents only a collection of chimney stacks, to mark the spot where it once was. The Bethels, big and little, look forsaken of the Lord. Warwick Court House is a small dilapidated place, appearing as though it fell into syncope about the time Rip Van Winkle took his long repose in Sleepy Hollow, and the worn out lands of the county bear evidence of the exhaustive tendencies of the "peculiar institution."

The swamps and low grounds of this vicinity are thickly inhabited by the posterity of the ancient Rana family, and though less obtrusive than their Egyptian kindred, have quite as strong musical propensities. As their concert season has arrived, we may count on nightly treats, vieing in sounds with

"The brazen trump, the spirit stirring drum,
That bid the foe defiance e're they come."

The rebels on our left have lately been disposed to be troublesome, but have been admonished of their folly by the 2d Rhode Island and some other troops. Deserters are continually coming within the Federal lines, and prisoners are frequently taken. One fellow had his fears of abuse allayed by a cup of coffee, which he said was the first he had tasted in four months. He had been informed by his officers that the "Yankees" tortured their prisoners, and said that were it known by the rebel soldiers that it was not so, many would desert. Day before yesterday, companies I, II and A, of the 1st Massachusetts, under Lieut. George D. Wells; two companies of the 11th Massachusetts, under Major Porter D. Tripp, and two pieces of artillery, under Lieut. Butler; all led by Gen. Grover, made an early morning advance upon a rebel lunette, which had been a cover to their sharpshooters. The contest was brief and sharp, and the work taken at the point of bayonet. The Federal loss was three killed and fifteen wounded, one mortally. Thirteen rebels gave themselves up — coming in under a white flag. The main body fled. After getting possession, the work was partially levelled by pick and spade, under a constant fire from the enemy. Berdan's sharpshooters continue their daily avocation of picking off the enemy who may have the temerity to expose their persons to view. Sunday, four were victims to a single rifle.

It is now understood that to Gen. Porter is assigned the work of beseiging Yorktown proper. In this work, battery C will have a share. How soon the attack will be made, no one can tell. But begin when it may, one of two things is certain: the rebel army will be captured, or they will evacuate.

Contrabands began to come into our lines soon after our army reached the peninsula, but not in great numbers into camp. The rebels took the precaution to carry them off, and use them in erecting their defences. Of the colored population, who have not seen the advantage of hunting up their fleeing masters, and who exhibit the characteristics of their race, a writer relates the following:

"One, any day, may gather up a great deal of wit, folly, wisdom and such like intellectual coruscations that furnish food for the metaphysically inclined, by going among them and talking with them. I met one, the other day, of Jim Crow expression of face and hair, who says he was in Yorktown at the time of the Revolutionary seige. I left him, profoundly impressed with his Gulliverian aptitude at story telling, and I doubt not the reader will be so impressed on reading the following portion of my confab with him :—

"Did you see the shooting," I inquired.

"Yes, indeedee, Massa ; I seed it all."

"How did you like it ? "

"The musketry wasn't nuffin, but seein' the big cannon balls skeered me some."

"How did you escape getting killed ? "

"I stayed hid in a deep, big cellar all de 'hole time, massa," responded the catechised Ethiopian representative, with a breadth of grin and compass of guffaw that showed very clearly that, in his own estimation, he had done one smart thing in his life, if he had never done another.

A second colored brother I have met in my wanderings, whose notions of personal smartness do not reach the altitude of the one mentioned. His modesty, what is more, takes a direction many white folks would do well to imitate. He said he had been a slave all his life, and his last owner was Mr. Clark, who owns a large amount of property, and who, by the way, is a corporal in the Peninsula Guard, a rebel regiment.

"Do you think slavery right or wrong ? " I asked him.

"Wrong, of course, Massa."

"How so ?"

"I know it be wrong, massa, but I can't arger."

Here is a portion of a conversation with a third negro, and with it, I will wind up the negro question. He had insisted that the negroes were as well off slaves as they were free.

"They orter 'have themselves," remarked the argumentative individual referred to, putting himself in an oratorical attitude, "and get good massas, like me, and they will be well taken care of."

"And you have always been well taken care of ? " I remarked, in a congratulatory tone ; "you are one of the lucky ones."

"It is not ebery one hab the same luck as me."

"In what regard ? "

"Why, my massa was my own fadder."

Mrs. Stowe has not written any thing that has opened more clearly to view the domestic life of the South, than this last sentence—" my massa was my own fadder."

May 2. For a week past we have kept up a daily familiarity with the booming of cannon, the whiz of solid shot, and the bursting of shells. Our great battery, No. 1, near the river, has made a number of splendid shots, and given the enemy trouble. At times they have responded with spirit. To-day they have tried some of their heavier guns in the direction of General McClellan's head quarters, several of their shells passing directly over. Last night, the right section of our battery, under Lieut. Waterman, was ordered out, and took position under the edge of an embankment, to look after the enemy, who it was supposed designed to stampede us. The left and centre sections were hitched up and held in readiness to go out at a moment's warning, should they be needed. The rebels, however, did not appear, and about seven o'clock, we returned to camp, without having had occasion to unlimber the pieces. Griffin's battery was likewise out all night. Day before yesterday, the rebel gun boats Teazer, (rightly named,) and Yorktown, appeared up James River, off our left, and sent in a number of shells, which did no damage. The former carried the black flag at her mast head.

This morning, Capt. Wentworth's sharp-shooters marched up to General Porter's head quarters, where they were provided with shovels, and then proceeded to the bank of the river, to open a new intrenchment. The task allotted to each man for the day, was to dig a space six feet square by four deep. The rebels discovered them from the opposite side, and opened a fire, which was continued at intervals, until the work was completed. One hundred and seventy shells were thrown, some of which burst near the working party; but the attempt to drive them from their labor failed.

The rebels have for sometime employed a negro rifleman, and skillful marksman, to ascend a tree within range of our rifle pits, and pick off our sharp shooters, as opportunity offered. In this work he had considerable success, and it was determined to terminate his operations. Last Tuesday he smuggled himself into position, as he thought, unseen. But sharp eyes were upon him, and the following brief conversation opened:

"I say," called out one of our men, "you had better come down from there."

"What for?" responded the colored confederate.

"I want you as prisoner."

"Not as this chile knows of," replied the concealed Ethiop.

"Just as you say," replied our sharpshooter.

In about an hour he peered his head out. Our man was on the look out for him; he had his rifle on the bead line ready —pulled the trigger—whiz went the bullet, and down came the negro. He was shot through the head.

While rejoicing over the inspiring news from New Orleans, the papers brought intelligence of the death of Capt. Frank Ferris, of the 12th Illinois, who fell mortally wounded in.the terrible carnage at Pittsburg Landing. So, clouds obscure the sunlight of earthly friendships, and " that same day that highest glory brings," comes full freighted with sorrow. Capt. Ferris was a native of Providence, and several years since emigrated to Princeton, Illinois. He was a man of generous nature, and among his numerous circle of acquaintances in the West, bore an honored name. "They never fail who die in a great cause," and a life like his has not been laid down in vain. Lieut. Richard K. Randolph was taken prisoner while ministering to Capt. Ferris, on the battle field, a noble sacrifice of personal safety at the shrine of humanity.

LETTER XI.

Yorktown evacuated—Union flag planted on the rebel defences—
Strength of the place—Secesh letter—Concealed torpedoes—Pursuit of the enemy—Governor Sprague's account—Battle of Williamsburg — Federal Success — Second Rhode Island regiment—
Randolph's battery—Rebels retreat.

CAMP WINFIELD SCOTT, NEAR YORKTOWN, VA., }
May 6, 1863. }

To the surprise of the entire army, Gen. Magruder has
withdrawn his forces from Yorktown and from his long line of
defences in our front, and fallen back to Williamsburg. Saturday and Sunday he kept up a brisk fire on our intrenchments from his heavy guns, and to the last hour maintained
an appearance of a determined resistance. But it was under
the cover of this, that he beat a retreat. It seems that the
withdrawal of his army commenced on Wednesday, and when
the last brigade was ready to depart, the torch was applied to
the barracks and a store house, which accounts for the brilliant
illumination seen Sunday night. On our side, preparations
for a general assault had been completed, and yesterday a fire
was to have been opened from all our batteries. But it proved
too late, and our monster Parrotts stand silent as moody
mastiffs. The elaborate work of nearly a month, as the eye
now rests upon it, tells of what would have been had the
enemy risked a decisive engagement.

The first intelligence of the evacuation was brought into the
camp of Col. Black, of the 62d Pennsylvania, by deserters,
and immediately communicated to General Jameson, who telegraphed the same to Gen. Porter, director of the siege. To
determine the accuracy of the report, he ordered the advance
of a small force. This comprised detachments of the 22d
Massachusetts, Col. Gove, and 62d Pennsylvania, Col. Black,
supported by two companies of the 1st Massachusetts, under
Lieut. Col. Wells. These advanced without opposition to the

7

rebel entrenchments, and finding the way clear, entered the works with great enthusiasm. General Jameson and Col. Black first mounted the parapets. Col. Gove, Capt. Hassler and Lieut. Crawford followed. The 22d Massachusetts were first to enter the deserted defences and plant the national standard, which they did amidst deep and heartfelt cheers.* The town was also visited by Capt. Weeden and lieutenants Buckley and Clark.

The fortifications, for strength, are all that engineering skill and the labor of a large working force for nearly a year could make them. The ditches are unusually broad and deep, the embankments ten to twelve feet thick, and the embrasures thoroughly constructed of sand bags, sods or gabions. With 75,000 men behind his line of works, wonder is increased that the rebel commander should have abandoned them without a hard struggle. It is an inconsistent commentary upon his emphatic declaration that every man should die in the entrenchments before the army should fall back. But the army did not die in the entrenchments, and did fall back, to be fought, if it makes a stand, elsewhere.† In the haste of the

---

* Col. W. R. Brewster, of the 73d N. Y. Vol., Hooker's division, claims for his regiment, " the honor of first planting the stars and stripes upon the rebel fortifications in the town of Yorktown." His dispatch, making this claim, is dated " Yorktown, Sunday, May 4—5 A. M." There is no necessary conflict with the statement above made. He may have entered Yorktown at a different point,—unaware, at the hour designated, that the Union flag had been planted elsewhere.

† It now appears that the abandonment of Yorktown was not voluntary on the part of Gen. Magruder. The author of " War Pictures from the South," says, he " had assembled a force at Yorktown strong enough to enable him, if necessary, to take the open field and give battle to the enemy. While thus actively at work and animated by a feeling of confidence, Magruder received an order from the Secretary of War to evacuate Yorktown as quietly as possible—leaving all his guns in position — and fall back upon the second line of defence at Williamsburg. This unexpected order gave, as may be supposed, the greatest annoyance to Magruder, who, most reluctantly, issued directions for the retirement of his troops. To conceal his movement from the enemy, he ordered all the guns to open a heavy fire upon the besiegers, and at the same time sent two or three regiments to make a demonstration by way of feint.—p. 276.

rebels to quit, they left tents standing, with their interior fix-
tures untouched, and in private houses occupied by officers,
books, papers, correspondence, and other personal effects.
Upon a table in one house, several letters were found. One of
them, addressed to Gen. McClellan, makes a lame attempt at
wit. It reads thus:

GENERAL McCLELLAN—You will be surprised to hear of our departure at this stage of the game, leaving you in possession of this
worthless town; but the fact is, McClellan, we have other engagements to attend to, and we can't wait any longer. Our boys are getting sick of this damned place, and the hospital likewise; so, good-
bye for a little while. Adjutant TERRY, C. S. A. M.

The possession of Yorktown has added fifty-one guns and a
mortar, left in position, to our ordnance, besides placing in our
hands a large quantity of military appliances. One of the
guns is a 10-inch columbiad, and upwards of twenty are thirty-
two and forty-two pounders. The largest gun in the fortification was burst, in firing, last Friday.

In abandoning their works, the rebels left behind them
abundant evidence of a barbarous spirit. They buried in the
ground, hid in barrels and boxes, and laid around elsewhere,
large numbers of infernal machines in the shape of torpedoes
and bombs. These were connected with coffee pots, pincush-
ions, officers' chests, and such other articles as it was supposed
our men would seize as trophies, when an explosion, blowing
them "sky high," would follow. All this preparation for
wholesale destruction was in keeping with shooting pickets,
poisoning water and food, bayoneting the helpless wounded,
violating graves, and other infamies practiced elsewhere. Men
were detailed to search for these concealed missiles, to mark
their localities or remove them; but with all the care taken,
explosions occurred, and several men were killed and wounded.

As soon as it was known that the rebels had fled, Gen.
Stoneman, with two regiments of cavalry, the 2d Rhode Island,
8th Illinois, 6th Regulars, 98th Pennsylvania, and a battery

of Regular artillery, was sent in pursuit. The enemy had the advantage in the start. At 9 o'clock, as discovered by a balloon ascension, his rear had placed four miles between it and the deserted works. The pursuit was hot. To the infantry and artillery, the rain and mud rendered marching very fatiguing. In the mean time, the divisions of Generals Kear‑ ney and Hooker, and the balance of Gen. Keyes corps, were put in motion. The two former moved by the direct road to Williamsburg, while the latter took the road from Warwick Court House. Sedgwick's, Porter's, and Richardson's divisions were held back, to support our advance, or to move up to West Point by water, as exigencies should require.

[In March, after the army had entered upon the Peninsula campaign, Governor Sprague joined the head-quarters of General McClellan on the staff of General Barry, Chief of Artillery. He came to look after the Rhode Island troops, and by the invitation and request of the Secretary of War, connected himself with the movements of the army until the latter part of May. He was present at the preparations for besieging Yorktown, and joined General Stoneman in his pursuit of Magruder. The following account of it was given by him before the Committee on the Conduct of the War:

"About 11 o'clock or thereabouts, the cavalry started in pursuit, the enemy having been gone some six or seven hours. We moved through Yorktown on the heels of the retreating enemy. The arrangement was that this cavalry force, with some light batteries, should move rapidly forward, being supported by General Hooker's division. There was some difficulty after we got through Yorktown, because the enemy had placed explosive shells in the roads where our troops had to move, which exploded when trod upon. We lost several men and horses in that way. That delayed the progress of the column through the intrenchments and along the roads. Otherwise, however, the roads were very good. At, perhaps, one o'clock, General Stoneman received a communication from General McClellan to push on with all speed, and to follow closely upon the enemy, and that he would be supported by General Hooker's division ; that had been ordered to move on immediately. General Stoneman had, up to that time, been pushing forward, halting occasionally to remove the torpedoes from the road. The column moved with such rapidity that General Stoneman, after stopping to write a despatch to be sent back, would be obliged to trot briskly to resume his place in the column. When we had come to within about four or five miles of Williamsburg, we came up with the Hamilton Legion, of the enemy's forces. We had at first only cavalry there, the artillery not having come up. We were received by an artillery fire from the enemy. As soon as our light artillery came up, we pressed the enemy closely. They would retreat for a time, then come to a stand as we pressed upon them ; then, after a short resistance, retreat again, and so on. In that way we kept up a running fire, I should think, for about three miles. When the rear of the enemy made its first stand, General Stoneman sent me back to hurry up the infantry. About six miles from Yorktown are two roads—one the regular road, that General Stoneman took ; the other a road diverging towards the position General Sumner afterwards occupied. General Hooker's division, which had left Yorktown about one o'clock, and which was the one assigned to our support, when it got up to those two roads, found General Sumner's troops occupying the road before him, and was delayed for some time. I found General Negley's brigade in the advance of General Sumner's column, and had about got him moving up to support us, when General Sumner countermanded it, saying that he had had no directions to move on. I requested General Negley to report to General Sumner the fact that General Stoneman was on the heels of the enemy without an infantry support and that it was important that the enemy should find some infantry there with us. There was a delay of nearly two hours,

7*

until finally, after solicitation, General Sumner concluded to move up his troops. I returned and reported to General Stoneman, and remained with him until we had been driven back from immediately under the fortifications of Williamsburg, the rear guard of the enemy occupying the works. It was then late in the afternoon, perhaps five or six o'clock. It had commenced raining. The troops came all mixed up together—those of General Sumner, General Heintzelman, and General Keyes, all together, without any order or preparation. In falling back, having no infantry support, in going through the woods, some of our guns got stuck in the mud, and the enemy captured some three of them. We fell back to a clearing, a mile and a half or two miles from the works occupied by the enemy. The road divided some distance back from Williamsburg. General Stoneman divided his cavalry force, and sent a portion of it on the road leading off to the left of the fortifications at Williamsburgh, and the other portion he sent off to the right. When General Hooker came up with his division, he was sent to the left to support the cavalry there, and it was there that the main contest took place the next day. The cavalry to the right was supported by General Sumner's troops. As the infantry came up they were moved forward; but night came on while they were in the woods, and, with the rain and mud, it was impossible to extricate them that night. The whole army lay there that night upon their arms, within a mile of the enemy's works. The pickets were within half a pistol shot of each other. Many of our men straggled off in the woods, not being able to extricate themselves in the darkness, and were captured by the enemy. As soon as General Sumner arrived on the ground, he took command. The cavalry, of course, had done all that could be expected of it. During the night, General Sumner himself became lost in the woods, and there was no one there exercising supreme command. I speak minutely of these things, because it was a very anxious period for us. I had been with the advance, and was in a situation to know the position of the enemy, and could give information to the general in command, which would enable him to determine the best course to be pursued in attacking the enemy's works. But this information, which had been gathered by General Stoneman's advance, and which I was anxious to communicate to General Sumner, could not be communicated all that night, because there was no one exercising command there. General Sumner and his staff, in going too far down, had got into the woods, and almost surrounded by the enemy, and the only way they could get off safely was by remaining still, all the night, in the woods. We slept there in the mud and rain, that night, without cover. We had started off from Yorktown so hurriedly that no preparations for rations had been made, and many of the regiments had nothing to eat."

To the foregoing, a few particulars are added. The following morning, May 5th, the battle before Williamsburg commenced in earnest. It was begun by Gen. Hooker, with two regiments of skirmishers — 1st Massachusetts and 2d New Hampshire, who drove the enemy in the rifle pits into Fort Magruder. The batteries of Webber, Osborne and Bramhall, were then brought into position, and opened upon the fort. Their fire was very accurate, and with the sharpshooters silenced that of the enemy until afternoon. A pouring rain, and the tramp of infantry, cavalry and artillery, put the roads in a terrible condition, which greatly impeded the operations. For this cause, and from the nature of the ground, it was difficult for artillery to act. The rebels were strong in earthworks —thirteen in number—rifle pits and men. They fought as though intending to redeem themselves from the shame of their recent evacuation; but they were met with an invincible determination. Sumner, who commanded the centre and right, Hooker, Heintzelman, Kearny, Keyes, Hancock and other generals, were seen in every part of the field, directing the conflict. Jameson, Berry, Birney and Peck handled their men with vigor. Casey did not reach the front until the battle was nearly over, but was in season to render important service to Hancock, who took two redoubts, repulsed Early's brigade by a bayonet charge, and captured 150 prisoners.

At one time, Heintzelman was sorely galled, by an immensely superior force, when, opportunely, Berry's brigade rushed through the mud to his support. It was welcomed by shouts of gladness, the bands playing Yankee Doodle and the Star Spangled Banner. Towards the middle of the day, things looked uncertain, and at 12 o'clock, Governor Sprague rode to Yorktown, and communicated the condition of affairs to Gen. McClellan. Late in the afternoon, he arrived, and took command of all the troops. At dark, the fighting ceased—the enemy beaten in the field, but still in possession of Fort Magruder.

Gen. Heintzelman estimated the men on the Federal side, actually engaged, at less than 17,000. The rebel forces were rated at 30,000 to 40,000. In the heaviest of the fight by Hooker, he was hard pressed by a force three or four times his numbers, led by Johnston, Longstreet, Pryor, Gholson and Pickett. Between four and five o'clock P. M., Kearney, with great effort, came to his assistance, and relieving his worn men, held the positions in front until the battle ended. About five o'clock, Randolph's battery arrived on the ground, but was not ordered into action. The fighting, at some points, was terrific. Men, on both sides, went down in heaps. The rebel loss was reported at upwards of 3,000. On the Federal side, it was about 2,000, in killed, wounded and missing. Of this number, Hooker's division lost 1,700.

In this hard-fought battle, the 2d Rhode Island bore a part. They were ordered to relieve a regiment engaged in front. They moved promptly forward, and remained under fire several hours. Gen. Devens, commanding the brigade, complimented the men for their coolness and fidelity. Col. Wheaton had a narrow escape from a shell, which cut away a portion of a tree near him. Col. Tristam Burges, son of the distinguished Rhode

Island lawyer and orator, was wounded in the leg. He was acting, at the time, as volunteer aid to Gen. Stoneman. As the night shut down, the Federal army bivouacked. It was a sad night for the wounded and the dying. Let the curtain drop before the scene.

During the night, the rebels commenced a retreat, leaving their works and the ancient seat of learning they were designed to protect, in Federal hands.* A section of Randolph's battery, and one of Thompson's (G, 2d United States,) under him, were the first to enter the town the next day. The generals all rode in together. The rebels, in their escape, as one writes who was an eye witness, "left one large gun in their works, abandoned a splendid brass piece on the road, with two caissons; strewed every rod of their path with muskets, bayonets, knapsacks, blankets and overcoats; littered the way with all the wreck and ruin of a beaten and demoralized army in full flight from imaginary as well as real terrors. There was a harvest for the blacks who had not been driven in cofiles, by their owners, to Richmond. From all parts they alighted upon this abandoned property, much of it new and valuable, fresh from the commissary's stores, and left upon the roadside in wagons, only because it impeded flight." A force of cavalry and infantry pursued the rebels a few miles, but owing to the

---

* This retreat was also involuntary, and much against the will of Gen. Magruder, who had great confidence in the strength of the fortifications, erected under his own inspection. The rebel author of the War Pictures, already cited, says:—" General Johnston having now arrived, he was intrusted by the Confederate government with the chief command of the army. He at once ordered the retreat to commence, although Magruder insisted that he could still hold Williamsburg against the enemy. But the Federal General Keyes had already taken up a position between Williamsburg and Richmond, a manœuvre which allowed us no time to hesitate, as he not only menaced the retreating troops from Williamsburg, but threatened the safety of Richmond itself. General Magruder consequently made the necessary dispositions to rejoin the main body of the army at Richmond."—p. 280.

state of the roads and other causes, were not followed up. Taken in battle and captured as stragglers, the prisoners amounted to 2,000. The hospitals were crowded with their wounded.

On the 10th May, Gen. Keyes marched his corps to Burnt Ordinary, and thence to Bottom's Bridge. The roads were heavy, and the marching necessarily slow. Stoneman's cavalry, the 2d Rhode Island and a Pennsylvania regiment were then in advance, harassing the rebel rear. On the 23d, the divisions of Casey and Couch crossed the Chickahominy. On the 25th, Heintzelman, with Hooker's and Kearney's divisions, crossed at the same place, in preparation for coming events.]

LETTER XII.

Battery C embarks for West Point—March to Cumberland Landing—General Franklin's division goes up to West Point—Battle at West Point—Narrow escape of General McClellan.

CAMP AT CUMBERLAND LANDING, VA., }
May 14, 1862. }

From Sunday morning, the 4th inst, when the flag of our Union was unfurled upon the ramparts of Yorktown, and the shout of exultation ran along our line from river to river, " mightier than the voice of many waters," until Friday, the 9th, we remained in our encampment with little to disturb its quietness. On that day the order was given to embark for West Point. To get our battery and its appurtenances aboard the transports was the work of an entire day. We lay off in the stream all night, and Saturday morning bade farewell to a spot which the capture of 1781 consecrated to civil liberty, and the occupation by the Federal army in 1862, has forever linked with the triumph of constitutional law, in which this war is to issue. As we lost view of the frowning fortifications, and thought of the traps left by the rebels for the destruction of life, and the hidden missiles of death scattered along the road to Williamsburg, Byron's words came fresh to mind,

> "All the devil would do, if run stark mad,
> Was here let loose."

We reached West Point at night. Sunday we debarked and went into camp, where we remained till yesterday morning, when we moved forward to this place, a distance of about thirteen miles. The day was warm, the roads dusty, and rest refreshing. We are about thirty miles from Richmond.

About the middle of last month, General Franklin, with his division, arrived below Yorktown in transports, and anchored in the Poquosin river. On the morning of the evacuation, he was ordered round to Yorktown, to proceed up to West Point, but owing to bad weather did not start until the morning after the battle of Williamsburg. The object of this movement was to cut off the retreat of Johnston and Magruder, who were making their way back to Richmond; but in this he was disappointed. The rebels were too fleet, and found safety beyond the Chickahominy. To gain time for the escape of their main body, the rebel generals commenced an attack on General Franklin the morning after he landed. The fight was severe and continued most of the day, when the enemy were driven back with heavy loss. The Federal loss in killed, wounded and missing, was about 300. In this affair, the 1st New Jersey, 31st and 32d New York, 95th Pennsylvania and 5th Maine regiments were engaged. The 1st New Jersey artillery did great execution. The 95th Pennsylvania suffered severely in officers and men. Capt. Richard Arnold, Gen. Franklin's chief of artillery, is spoken of as having contributed essentially to the success of the day.

Cumberland is a little hamlet on the bank of the Pamunky

river, which at West Point unites with the Matapony, and
forms the York. It now, for the first time, becomes a historic
spot, as a depot of supplies for the army of the Potomac.
Gen. McClellan has temporarily established his headquarters
here. Yesterday, an unsuccessful attempt was made by the
enemy to capture a wagon train on the road between this place
and Buck House Point, and it is reported that the General in
Chief, while making a reconnoisance with his staff, had a narrow escape from the rebel cavalry. Troops are rapidly concentrating here, and the advance upon Richmond may now be
considered as fairly in progress.

LETTER XIII.

Battery C moves to White House—Norfolk surrendered and the
Merrimac destroyed—Stoneman drives in the rebel pickets—White
House estate—Encampment.

CAMP NEAR WHITE HOUSE, VA.,
May 20, 1862.

My last letter was dated at Cumberland Landing. On the
morning of the 15th, the men turned out at four o'clock, and
packed up for a march. At ten o'clock we moved forward.
The night previous had been stormy, and the rain continuing,
rendered the roads almost impassable ; but perseverance surmounted the obstacles that strewed the way, and with much
weariness of the flesh, drenched with rain, and covered with
mud, the battery encamped seven miles nearer Richmond.
The team containing our tents not arriving in season, we extemporized temporary habitations with the tarpaulins, and laid
ourselves down to rest. I never slept better. Army life has
its amusing side, as well as its serious aspects. In camp and

on the march, one having a keen sense of the ludicrous, can always find something to excite his mirthfulness. Laughter is healthful, and amazingly promotes digestion. The buoyant Winthrop once wrote of his army life, " I have fun—I get experience—I see much—it pays ;" and the soldier has yet much to learn who does not understand how to turn the experiences of the day and the annoyances of the night, including spiders, wood-ticks and gnats, to profitable account.

The news of the evacuation of Norfolk and the blowing up of the Merrimac, was received with lively demonstrations of joy, and operated like electricity upon the *physique* of the men.* For more than two months the Merrimac has been the terror of the whole country. Imagination, taking counsel of fear, conjured up a multitude of disasters she was destined to inflict. Excited vision saw the commerce of New York and our entire navy, sinking beneath the heavy blows of her iron beak. But these apprehensions were, in a measure, dispelled by the providential advent of the spunky little Monitor ; and now that this ogre has received death at the hands of its friends, the timid will once more breathe freely. This information, following close upon the rebel discomfitures at Williamsburg and West Point, it is said, caused great consternation at Richmond.

[The author of " War Pictures " says : " The dread that then prevailed at Richmond, must be ascribed chiefly to the conduct of President Davis and his wife, who, as soon as in-

---

* These events occurred on the 10th and 11th of May. On the 10th, General Wool landed 5,000 men at Willoughby Point, Va., and marched upon Norfolk. Slight skirmishing ensued, without hindering the movements. At five o'clock P. M., a deputation of citizens of Norfolk met the United States troops, and the town was formally surrendered and occupied, General Viele being appointed Military Governor. The same night, the rebels set fire to the buildings of the navy yard at Gosport, and attempted to blow up the dry dock, in which they partially succeeded. The next morning the Merrimac, or Virginia, as she had been newly christened, was blown up by her officers, and destroyed.

telligence of the advance of the enemy reached them, not only took every precaution to place their family in safety, but despatched to North Carolina all the valuable property at Richmond which had been placed at the President's disposal, such as plate, pictures, works of art, jewels, &c. . . . . This was not considered a becoming example of the firmness and magnanimity expected from the elected head of the Confederacy for the purpose of encouraging the citizens. The effect was, as may be supposed, to bring about a general removal from the town. Great confusion also prevailed at the various public offices. The government property was removed to North Carolina, and all the bank-note presses to Columbus. The Secretaries of War and Navy, Randolph and Mallory, proceeded to Norfolk and Portsmouth ; not, as might have been supposed, to take measures for saving what could be preserved at those important naval stations, but to destroy everything. A humiliating day for the cause of the Confederacy was now at hand. Gen. Huger was entrusted with the disgraceful task of destroying the valuable docks and government stores at Portsmouth. Although there were no less than 30,000 excellent troops in and around Norfolk, the order he received was fully carried out, and thus the docks and building yards became a prey to the flames. . . . . Property to the value of millions, much of which might have been saved, was destroyed in the most reckless manner."]

Yesterday, General Stoneman marched to Coal Harbor, on the road leading to Richmond, and drove the rebel pickets in to within two miles of their main force. The enemy have destroyed the bridges over the Chickahominy, and in strong numbers are encamped on the other side. Our army is spread along their front, with suitable supports, and every day making changes that are bringing on the crisis of deadly conflict.

The general deportment of our army towards the people of the country through which it has passed, and the tender care bestowed upon the rebel sick and wounded, who have been taken prisoners, is in striking contrast with the atrocities committed upon the wounded and dead Union soldiers that have fallen into rebel hands, the account of which the papers have not exaggerated. But a day of retribution draws nigh, and those monsters in human form will yet learn that

> "Cruelty's a prodigal, that heaps
> A suicidal burthen on itself."

From Old Point Comfort to Richmond the country is full of interest, and at this season of the year, in a time of quiet, would afford delightful rambles to an excursionist. A trip up the York river to West Point, and thence up the Pamunkey to some twenty miles above White House farm, where the navigation has been impeded by the rebels, would be scarcely less attractive than an excursion from Providence round Point Judith to New Haven, or up the Hudson from New York to Albany. The shores on either side of the York and Pamunkey are quite as picturesque as those of the Narragansett, and it will not be strange, when rebellion is crushed out and Virginia restored to her right mind, to find some enterprising Perham introducing northern lovers of " spontaneous joys where nature has its play," to scenes of quiet beauty but little known.

A horseback ride up the peninsula would prove equally pleasant. Yorktown, Warwick Court House, Williamsburg, New Kent Court House, and White House farm, on the Pamunkey river, nearly midway between West Point and Richmond, all have attractions for the student of American history. The latter place is one of the largest plantations in this part of the country, and is in a fine state of cultivation. On the arrival of our troops here, a large quantity of wheat and corn was found on the premises, which was very properly appropriated to army use. At this place, it is said, Washington first saw, wooed and won the Martha whose name crowns the list of patriotic women of the revolution. The present owner, Gen. Lee

of the rebel army, became possessor of the estate through his
wife, to whom it was bequeathed by the late George Washington Parke Custis, the adopted son of the Father of his Country.
If Shakespeare tells the truth of Hamlet's father, surely the
recusancy of one whose ancestral name stands among the honored of Virginia patriots, is enough to disturb the grave-sleep
of the venerable patroon of Arlington House to the end of time.

The colored population along the route of our army is less
numerous than it was a few months ago, large numbers of
slaves having been sent towards Richmond, or in other directions, as the Federal forces advanced. Some extensive plantations are left in charge of a few venerable sons of Ham, while
on others considerable gangs remain under the charge of over-
seers. It is understood that the house servants belonging to
the White House estate, (which, by the way, takes its name
from the color of the mansion,) were recently removed to
Richmond. The field hands continue on the place, and show
a readiness to supply the Yankees with such camp dainties as
are at their control.

Though good authority tells us that " our stomachs will make
what's homely, savoury," yet we do not object occasionally to
sandwich our goverment rations with such delicacies as the
sutler's wagon can furnish ; but just now this class of purveyors
are scarce, and the nearer we approach Richmond, the more
costly this sort of cheer becomes. With his list of prices star-
ing me in the face, I was prepared to give a hearty welcome
to an iron bound box which arrived this morning, and whose
judiciously assorted contents, reminding the receiver of warm
hearts at home, were all right.

We are now encamped on one of the most beautiful spots I
have seen in Virginia. Berdan's Sharpshooters are encamped
on the right of us, and on the extreme right, on the summit of
a high hill, Gen. McClellan has his head-quarters. The numerous camps around us, dotted with tents, wagons, and parks
of artillery, interspersed with patches of green, impart a beau-

tiful effect to the scene, while the national airs played by the bands, fall upon the ear with inspiring power. We, of course, shall remain here but a short time, and then "on to Richmond." That the rebels intend to stand there "the hazard of a die," is probable, unless the last ditch, so long sought, lies somewhere beyond.

LETTER XIV.

Battery C advances to Kidd's mills — A bath — Fight near New Bridge, by the 4th Michigan — Old Church — New arrangements — Reconnoissance to Hanover town — Battle of Hanover Court House — Battles of Fair Oaks and Seven Pines — Old California — Slave population.

CAMP AT GAINES'S MILLS,)
Eight miles from Richmond, June 2, 1862.)

For the last two weeks, our army, with its six miles of front, has been making steady progress towards Richmond. Almost every mile of the march has been resisted by rebel pickets and skirmishers, or by larger bodies of their troops, but Gen. Stoneman's advance corps, including the 2d Rhode Island regiment, has been uniformly successful in opening the way, and as the main body has come up it has been enabled to hold every point gained in its forward movements. Since the battle of West Point, our right has gradually stretched itself north, beyond Hanover Court House, which looks like a flank movement. What it really means, a few days will show.

My last letter left our battery near White House. Since then, little opportunity has occurred for deliberate writing, and as a substitute for a letter, I send a few rough field notes, hastily jotted down. On Monday, 19th May, we marched to Tunstall's station, on the railroad line from White House

8*

to Richmond. Wednesday morning, 21st, at 3 o'clock, the reveille was sounded, and at about six we left camp. The day opened warm and muggy, and topped off hot. We marched four or five miles, and at half-past ten o'clock went into camp. We should have gone further, but the roads were so blocked up with teams and baggage wagons as to render it impossible to move fast enough to make it an object to keep up the march. We passed through a fine country, and the fields in which no encampments had been made looked promising. The wheat fields in which batteries of artillery had been parked, were, of course, destroyed. The people along the route complained of the scarcity of provisions, and doubtless with good reasons. This is an effect of rebellion they did not anticipate, but which, like other foul birds, has "come home to roost." Thursday morning, 22d, we advanced to Kidd's Mills, a place boasting a saw and gristmill. Our camp ground was in a pleasant locality, with a pond in the rear, which was soon filled with bathers. More than one Providence boy was reminded of the aquatic pleasures of "Sandy Bottom," now no more. The discomforts of a severe thunder shower in the afternoon were more than offset by the report that Halleck had defeated Beauregard at Corinth. On the supposition of proximity to the enemy, bugles were not allowed to be sounded, drums to beat, or bands to play.

May 25. Yesterday the rain fell copiously, from 7 o'clock A. M., till afternoon. The battery was hitched up, and at a quarter before twelve we moved from camp, leaving behind blankets and equipage of every sort, as though we were going out merely on picket, or to have a skirmish. We proceeded about two miles, and halted near Gen. Porter's headquarters, where we learned that the 4th Michigan regiment, under Col. Woodbury, had successfully measured strength with a rebel brigade in the neighborhood of New Bridge. It was a sharp contest of two hours, terminating in a bayonet charge. The enemy fled, leaving upwards of one hundred killed and wounded on the field. Thirty-seven prisoners were taken, twenty-two of them belonging to the Louisiana Tigers, whom I saw as they came in. The Federal loss was three killed and seven wounded.

[General McClellan, having received intelligence of this affair, rode towards the river and met the regiment on its return. He grasped Col. Woodbury warmly by the hand and said, " Colonel, I am happy to congratulate you again on your success. I have had occasion to do so before, and I do so again with pleasure." He also shook hands with Captain Rose, of the first company, which was deployed as skirmishers, and discharged the first volley on our side, and said, " I thank you, Captain ; your men have done well." To some of the men he said, " How do you feel, boys?" They exclaimed, " General, we feel bully."]

Turning from the General's quarters, we proceeded to a post town consisting of several private dwellings and a tavern, and known as Old Church, so a member of the " peculiar institution " informed me. We are here to protect this point to prevent the enemy from turning our flank. The 5th regiment New York volunteers, (Zouaves) are encamped just in front of us. Their colonel, Warren, is acting Brigadier. The 1st Connecticut, heavy artillery, and the 13th New York, are in our rear. The Connecticut regiment is the same that manned and were to work the siege guns at Yorktown. They are now acting as infantry, their siege train being left behind. A regiment of cavalry, the 6th Pennsylvania Lancers, are also here. Mrs. Col. Lee and daughters are under Federal guardianship about a mile above us, very much to their chagrin ; but such is the fortune of war, and secesh officers who permit their families to wander about like so many " unprotected females," may be thankful when they fall into Union hands. Some have surmised that this capture was sought by the parties interested to insure to them a safety they could not hope for in the rebel capital.

This morning, Col. Warren rode up to Capt. Weeden's quarters and requested him to hitch up as quickly as possible, information having been received that the enemy were advancing. This was done, but the enemy did not appear, and the battery moved to the rear of the camp and went into park, to be called out at any moment. A portion of our blankets were brought up last night, and the residue to-day. To add to our comfort, the negroes come into camp with hoe cake and milk to sell,—an agreeable episode in gustatory experiences.

May 27. New arrangements have been made in the commands of General Porter's division. Gen. P. is now commander of the 5th provisional corps. Gen. Morell commands his old division, and Colonel McQuade, of the the New York 14th, is acting Brigadier of Morell's brigade. Yesterday, three guns of the battery, under the command of Lieut. Buckley, went out to Hanover town, on a reconnoissance, accompanied by the 1st Connecticut and 5th New York infantry, and a company of cavalry. One gun went with the cavalry, in advance. The rebel pickets were driven in, one prisoner taken, and a bridge crossing the Pamunkey destroyed. About 6 o'clock they returned to camp.

Last night about 10 o'clock rain commenced, and continued falling without intermission till to-day noon. If, after the copious outpourings of " watery treasures " for the last two weeks, any " thirsty ridges " are still to be found, they will have ample opportunity to " drink their fill." Judging from past experiences and present appearances, the weather, so far as human agency is concerned, has been left to indulge its humor without stint, and generally it has given its services to the rebels between the Chickahominy and Richmond. A Virginia rain of ten hours is about equal to a picket force of

twenty-five thousand men in retarding the rapid advance of
the grand army ; and if there is any virtue in the supervision
of " wandering cisterns in the sky " by a loyalist,` a spare as-
sistant from College Hill would prove a valuable accession to
our numbers about these days.

This morning, at 4 o'clock, reveille sounded, and at 6, much
to general satisfaction, we were on the march for Hanover
Court House where the rebels were understood to be in force,
ready to accept battle should it be offered.   The gaining of so
important a position, and the destruction of certain bridges that
connect rebel approaches to Richmond, were sufficient stimulants to the men, and they pushed forward to the encounter
with a will.   Gen. Morell's division, consisting of three
brigades, commanded by Generals Martindale, Butterfield, and
Col. McQuade, and Berdan's regiment of sharpshooters, moved
briskly from their camps for the field of action, fifteen miles distant.   Gen. Porter was with the advance of the column.   Gen.
Martindale had only the 22d Massachusetts, 25th New York
and the 2d Maine with him, the 18th Massachusetts and 13th
New York being detached on duty elsewhere.   The artillery
led the van.   Then came Berdan's telescopic men.   Martindale's diminished brigade marched next.   Butterfield, who left
a sick bed to be in the fight, followed, while McQuade brought
up the rear.   The 25th New York was sent forward to act as
skirmishers, and received the first fire of the enemy.   Berdan's
men early found employment.

Our battery, the 5th New York regiment (Zouaves), the 1st
Connecticut, 13th New York and 6th Pennsylvania cavalry,
were to take the road on the right, while other regiments and
batteries were to come up more on the left.   We were on the
extreme right, and the rebel Gen. Branch, who by some means
had, as early as 10 o'clock, learned we were approaching, prepared to give us a warm reception.   Battery C appears to have
been an object of special interest to him, and he made liberal

arrangements to escort it within his lines. At a narrow part
of the road, which he supposed we should pass, he stationed
for this purpose a brigade of cavalry and artillery; but he was
doomed to disappointment by our taking another road, which
brought us on to the field about 3 o'clock. The rebels had promised us "fits," but as they were not so great in that line of the
the profession as they pretended, the effort proved a failure.
They received what they proposed to give, for while bestowing their courtesies upon us, and before they knew it, other
troops were upon them with a peppering of Minie balls and
artillery "fixings," for which they had little relish. A body
of the Federal advance encountered a rebel regiment, about
two miles from the Court House, which they drove back, and
when we arrived on the ground we could see them about a
mile distant, drawn up in line of battle. We cut round to the
right to follow them up, but after going about two miles we
received intelligence that they were coming down upon our
rear, when our pieces were immediately reversed and we returned to our position.

The principal artillery work on our side was done by Griffin's and Martin's batteries. The former fought his Parrotts
with galling and fatal effect. Capt. Martin was in the thickest
of the danger, and at one time during the day came near losing
two of his pieces, but by the timely support of infantry, they
were saved. Although, to the regret of officers and men, it was
not permitted us to take further active part in the contest, we
were witnesses of all that could be seen on so large a field, and
of the bravery of those engaged. The roar of artillery and the
rattling of musketry was terrific; yet, as we listened to their
thunder and marked the flashes of fire, the effect was like the
sound of the trumpet to the war horse. Every man's blood
was stirred for the fray. Such is human nature.

The fight of to-day was in the highest degree sanguinary,
and will be conspicuous among the battles of the peninsula.
On both sides the utmost determination was displayed. "'Twas

blow for blow, disputing inch by inch." In numbers, the rebel force greatly exceeded the Federals, but they could not stand before bayonets pressed forward by principle. At every point they yielded and fell back, leaving between 600 and 800 prisoners in our hands. Their killed and wounded swell their loss to 1,500. Several cannon and 500 or 600 rifles and muskets were also captured. The Federal loss, in killed, wounded and prisoners, amounts to between 300 and 400 men. Among the regiments engaged that suffered most, were the Maine 2d and the 25th New York, the latter under the command of Col. Johnston. The 44th New York regiment, Col. Stryker, lost 27 killed and 50 wounded. They behaved with great gallantry. Berdan's Sharpshooters had several wounded. The Massachusetts 9th and the New York 14th were also engaged; the loss of the former, one killed, nine wounded, and one missing. The rebel troops are largely North Carolinians. They are a hardy looking set of men, but miserably clad and poorly armed. As one result of this battle, the Virginia Central Railroad has been cut, by the removal of several hundred feet of rails, and the large bridge on the Fredericksburg Railroad completely destroyed. A large quantity of army stores has also been destroyed.

The appearance of the field after the battle, as described by those who passed over it, was sickening. Youth and mature age, dead and wounded, lay thickly mingled, and many a poor fellow breathed out the little remnant of life there, before the hand of humanity could be stretched out to seal his glazed eyes, or the voice of sympathy inquire his last wishes.

May 28. After the fatigues of yesterday, the battery has remained in park all day. Hanover Court House, the scene of our recent action, is a small post town of Hanover county, and is distinguished as the birth-place of Henry Clay. It was in the slashes of the Chickahominy, that the mill boy received the inspirations of freedom, and became imbued with a love of country that so conspicuously displayed itself in after years.

In the defeat of yesterday, the rebel General Branch must have felt the presence of the spirit of the great statesman, rebuking the treasonable resistance of a government, to the support of which, during a long life, he had devoted his transcendent talents. A great many prisoners have passed to-day. The cavalry brought in one company of upwards of ninety men, including the captain. I went down to the woods this morning, and counted twenty-five North Carolinians, who lay

> "In the deep stillness of that dreamless state
> Of sleep, that knows no waking joys again."

They were all shot either in the head or breast, none lower, showing with what accuracy our men sighted their guns. It was a horrible sight, and the deluded victims of secession were buried by our troops. To-day, General McClellan has visited the division, and expressed his warm commendation of the good conduct of the men yesterday.

May 30. Yesterday, we started on a reconnoitering expedition, but went only two or three miles, when several of our pieces were put in battery. We remained till afternoon, and returned without having discovered any rebels. In some of the houses on the road, wounded secesh were found by the Federals, whose wounds had not been dressed. They were sent to our hospitals to be cared for. At seven o'clock, we left for Old Church, and arrived at our camp about ten o'clock. To-day, we left camp at half past two, and proceeded to near Gen. Porter's head-quarters. A severe shower set in while on the march. "The clouds their thunder anthems sang," the rain descended in torrents, and soon we were in the condition of the man whom a joker boasted he could throw across the North River, but who, in the experiment, was dropped in the stream. The lightning was very sharp, and struck the camp of the 44th New York volunteers, killing one man and wounding four or five.

June 1. The rebel commanders, alarmed at the steady advance of our army upon Richmond, appear to have resolved to concentrate their strength upon our left wing, and, if possible, break our line and gain our flank. Yesterday, they made a spirited assault upon Gen. Casey's division, which, after a short struggle, was forced back. Some of the regiments, it is said, fought well; but a considerable portion of the men had never been under fire, and broke, causing great confusion.

[This is known as the battle of Fair Oaks, taking its name from a grove of oak trees near the field of action. It is sometimes called the battle of Seven Pines, from seven pine trees, near which General Casey established his lines, on crossing the Chickahominy. In describing his position before the Committee on the Conduct of the War, he says, " My division, composed of raw troops, with no support on their right or left, were pushed like a wedge up into the presence of a strong force of the enemy, my troops having suffered severely in coming up the peninsula. However, that was the order, and I obeyed and went to work with all my energy, to dig rifle pits, make abatis, &c. For two nights, the enemy attacked my pickets in force, but were repulsed with loss. I kept my line in position. My pickets frequently killed the enemy 700 or 800 yards from my line. That was our situation.

" About 11 o'clock, the pickets reported, by a mounted vidette, that the enemy were approaching, evidently in force. I immediately called in all the men I had working in the rifle pits, &c., called out the division, and got them into line. I fought the battle in two lines, by which means I think I saved an hour; that is, I kept the enemy back an hour by fighting them in two lines. I put a force in the rifle pits, and then went out and established a line about one-third of a mile in advance, five or six regiments and four pieces of artillery. . . . . . The enemy crowded upon me, and attacked me in front and on both wings, in force, I suppose of about 35,000."

9

Gen. Casey's division consisted of only 4,380 men. The enemy pressed upon him so hard, that, to save his artillery, he ordered a charge of four regiments of infantry, which was handsomely executed, and the enemy driven back; but to hold his ground against such an immensely superior force was impossible. He, in turn, was driven back, and night saw the enemy in possession of his camp, and several pieces of artillery. The loss in his division was 1,433, killed, wounded and missing. General Casey had a horse shot under him, and was wounded in the leg.

When the battle commenced, General Sumner, with his command, was on the east bank of the Chickahominy. He immediately crossed over and advanced rapidly to Fair Oaks, with Sedgwick's division. In his testimony, he says : " On reaching Fair Oaks, I was met by General Couch, who told me that he had been separated by the enemy from the rest of the army, and was expecting an attack every moment. I formed this division of Sedgwick's together with Couch's troops—assuming the command of the whole—as quickly as possible, with a battery of artillery between the two divisions. Before the formation was completed, the enemy made a ferocious attack upon my centre, evidently with the expectation of getting possession of my battery. I had six regiments in hand on the left of the battery. After sustaining a severe fire for some time, these six regiments charged directly into the woods, crossing a broken fence in so doing ; the enemy then fled, and the action was over for that day.* During that night, I succeeded in getting

---

* " Pickett's brigade now turned and hastily retired. This necessarily led to the retreat of the divisions of Anderson and Hill. Johnston vainly put himself at the head of his best troops in order to reopen the action. All his efforts were useless. The victorious enemy pressed on with loud cheers. The generals halted to make a last effort; but it was of no avail. Sumner rushed on our troops who had lost all self-possession, and drove them back to Fair Oaks, until night put an end to the struggle."—*War Pictures*, p. 287.

up Richardson's division, and formed it parallel with the railroad. About $7\frac{1}{2}$ o'clock on Sunday morning, the troops became engaged on the railroad. A very severe fight continued there for the space of three or four hours, in which I lost many valuable men and officers. The enemy were then entirely routed and fled."

In this engagement, Generals Kearny, Sedgwick, Franklin, Sickles, Keyes, Heintzelman, Couch, Hooker, French, Howard, and others, acted a conspicuous part. Randolph's battery was stationed in two small redans, on either side of a line of rifle pits held by Kearny's division as a second line ready for action, but did not engage. Of Heintzelman, at a critical period of the battle, a rebel officer bears the following testimony: "At this moment, Heintzelman rapidly brought up his division to stem the pursuit of the Confederate troops, and planted himself like a rock between the pursued and their pursuers. His men, Irish and Germans, fought and died like heroes in this work of salvation. All Hill's and Anderson's attempts to repulse them were futile; the Germans and Irish kept their ground, and succeeded in covering the flight of their vanquished comrades. They steadily opposed every fierce onset of our elated troops, and stood like a wall between them and their own defeated forces, in order that some of the fugitives might be enabled to reform their ranks, and thus, in their turn, try to assist those who had come to their rescue."

Two days after the battle, General McClellan issued a spirited commendatory order, which was read at the head of every regiment. General Kearny, proud of the bravery of his division, did the same to the men under his command. The rebel force engaged was estimated at 75,000. The Federal loss, in killed, wounded and missing, formed a grand total of 5,739, including many valuable officers. The rebel loss must have greatly exceeded this, though their generals reported it less. General Johnston was wounded, and General Lee took the command. About 1,000 rebel prisoners were taken, among whom were General Pettigrew, Colonel Loring and Lieutenant Washington, an aid to General Johnston. Rhode Island battery G, Capt. Owen, arrived at the scene of action on Sunday morning, but owing to the nature of the ground and the position of our troops formed in front, did not take an active part in the battle.

At the moment, under misapprehension of facts, the conduct of General Casey's division on this occasion, met with severe reproach; but subsequent developments showed that it did as well, under the circumstances, as was possible. The General, in his official report, gives instances of great bravery, and says : " From what I witnessed on the 31st, I am convinced that the stubborn and desperate resistance of my division saved the army on the right bank of the Chickahominy from a severe repulse, which might have resulted in a disastrous defeat. The blood of the gallant dead would cry to me from the ground on which they fell fighting for their country, had I not said what I have to vindicate them from the unmerited aspersions which have been cast upon them."

The scene on the field, after the battle, gave appalling evidence of its desperate character. Within the square of a mile, lay more than seven thousand dead and wounded of both sides, the first to be buried as quickly as possible, and the latter to be gathered up and sent to the Savage Station Hospital—the work of more than a day. The sight was too ghastly to dwell upon.]

From the commencement to the termination of the firing, yesterday, the booming of cannon and the rattling of musketry, told us of what was going on, and towards night we could see the flashing of shells as they burst in the air.

Reveille sounded, this morning, at half-past two o'clock, and having no part in the contest going on within our hearing, we left camp about 5 o'clock, in a misty, muggy atmosphere, for picket duty, all day, on the banks of the Chickahominy, together

with seven or eight other batteries stationed at different points.
Our business was to protect a pontoon corps, who were throwing a bridge across the river. The rebels let a dam loose
above, flooding the land on either side so as to render the
swampy passage impassable to artillery. We could distinguish
the rebel pickets on the other side of the river, and also a battery on the top of a hill, manœuvering. They fired no shots
at us, and their attention was not courted. Some of the other
batteries, however, fired at intervals during the day, but with
what effect is unknown. To-day, I saw our quondam Yorktown friend, Old California, of Berdan's Sharpshooters. He
looks much as usual, and in personal appearance is a fair representation of some of our scouts of the revolution. He made
a pile in California, and is reputed to be worth $100,000. He
heartily hates secession, and engaged in the war from purely
patriotic motives.

June 2. The day is warm and pleasant, and I have indulged
in the luxury of a bath. As we approach Richmond, the slave
population appears in greater numbers. They visit the camps
with freedom, but do not find the Yankees to be the barbarians
they have been represented. All with whom I have conversed
repeat substantially the same story: "Massa told 'em dat der
Yankees would cut off their ears, and sell dem into Cuba."
From personal experience, they have learned the falsity of such
statements, and compliment us for our politeness. compared with
the white secesh. Some of them are intelligent and shrewd,
and seem well to understand the difference between "de norf"
and "de souf" side of Mason and Dixon's line.

At White House are a couple of negroes, Robert Meekum,
and Diana his wife, the chattels of Colonel Lee. Diana was
born on the plantation eighty-three years ago, and had never
been beyond its boundaries. Both were leading characters
among the colored population, and both devout. Though not
well informed in regard to political and social changes outside

9*

their limited world, they appeared to have a dim perception of
the "good time coming," when every yoke should be broken.
In relating her experience to one conversing with her, Diana
said, " We hab seen a heap ob ups and downs, crosses and come-
backs, but my desire is unto de end." When told that the
Yankees would be very likely to kill Massa Lee, she replied,
very complacently, " De Lord's will must be done unto him."
She knew that a man had been hung for fighting for the slaves,
and that his name was John Brown. To the enquiry, if the
colored folks ever entertained a hope of being freed, she answered, " Well, I hab hear some say so ; but others said it
would neber be. A good many years ago, de vessels used to
come up dis yere ribber and get a great deal ob timber, and
de cap'n ob one ob dem vessels tole me when I was mournin'
'cause my daughter was sold away, dat I should lib to see de
day when all would be free, but it nebber come."

A few days ago, Colonel Ingalls, who has charge of the
quartermaster's department at this point, went to Diana's cabin
and directed that her husband should assemble all the able-
bodied negroes on the place, and he would set them to work for
the United States. The old woman was much excited, and
exclaimed, repeatedly, after the Colonel was gone, " Dear
Lamb ob God ! I know'd it would come. Now I know I
hab got a Lord and Saviour, and I tank him."

Many of the slaves, alarmed by the frightful stories told
them of Yankee ferocity, will probably remain docile in their
master's families ; but that some of them estimate the worth
of freedom, and will improve the providential opportunity for
self-emancipation now offered, the following extract from a
letter of a wife to her husband, a rebel officer, captured by our
cavalry and found on his person, is one of a multitude of testimonies that might be given. After relating, in no amiable
mood, her experience with the " vile Yankees," and uttering
the wish that a clover field in which she saw two cavalry squads
of " these horrid devils," had been " the crater of the infernal

regions and every man and horse swallowed up in it," she adds: " Most of our servants have proved themselves our most devoted friends, standing by me in all my trials and dangers, and protecting, as far as lay in their power, our interests. But I regret to say that Sally Cary, Edmond and Sam have gone to the Yankees. Sam went the first day they came to this part of the country, four weeks ago. S. C. went this day week. She and Phillis, after having matured all their plans, started off last Sunday, but were captured and brought to us by one of the pickets in two hours after they left. They fastened Phillis up in one of the closets in her room, and I put my prisoner, with some exultation, in the smoke-house. Next morning, when I went to bring my captive forth, to my surprise, I found she had been gone since the night before. Her bed had not been touched. How the girl opened the door, I have never been able to ascertain."

June 6. Yesterday, Davidson's and Hancock's brigades crossed over to the other side of the Chickahominy. As they were crossing the bridge, they were fired upon by some of the rebel batteries on the other side. To these attentions the Federal batteries on this side soon returned their compliments, and for a short time there was quite a lively artillery fight. Tuesday we were out on picket, but since then have been occupied only with camp duties. The weather is fluctuating. A great deal of rain has fallen, rendering movements very disagreeable. A recent storm probably postponed a battle, which must be near at hand. Hereafter, the bayonet will be largely used. The rebels have never stood a bayonet charge, and that made by our troops on Sunday was terrifically destructive. In the use of this weapon our infantry maintain superiority.

The health of the .rmy is occupying the attention of the commander-in-chief. As a preventive of fever and ague, which the miasma of this region produces, half-rations of whisky, medicated with quinine, have been ordered to be dealt out morning and evening.* In matters of the *cuisine*, sweet potatoes have recently given variety to ordinary camp fare. These, and other vegetables, when they can be obtained in sufficient quantities, will prove a valuable counteractant of scurvy, induced by salt diet.

CHAPTER XV.

The weather—Bridge-making and picket duties—Secessionists—Rebel raid—Army supplies and foraging—Hospital stores—Newsboys—Misstatements of Davis.

CAMP AT GAINES'S MILLS, VA., }
June 18th, 1862. }

The past two weeks, in their general features, have not been unlike their predecessors since we moved forward from West Point, or rather from Cumberland Landing. The weather has continued fitful, bestowing upon us a mingling of sunshine and cloud, hot days and cool nights, (the right hand powers of typhoids and ".chills"), rain and mud, with a superabundance of the latter, much to the inconvenience of artillery movements, the annoyance of army teamsters, and the discomfort of infantry. There has been more activity, however, than may have appeared to those at a distance. Bridge-making, picket duties, reconnoissances, skirmishing, with an occasional brush of a more serious character, have filled up the time, and though our entire line occupies mainly the ground it held at the battle of Fair Oaks, in preparation and renewed energy it possesses advantages that promise well for the future. On our left, picket duty has been engaged in on a somewhat extensive scale. I understand that Sedgwick's entire division, including batteries, has been thrown forward, probably to see that all is

---

* This order was soon after rescinded, and hot coffee substituted.

clear in front, or to remove whatever impediments may be found. To this kind of service Battery C has devoted a due share of time. It has been out frequently by sections, under Lieuts. Waterman, Buckley and Clark, and though the duty is monotonous and dull, except when enlivened by an opportunity to send a few shell compliments to our secesh neighbors, the work has not been without important uses. Our pickets and those of the rebels are in some places stationed not more than ten rods apart. They often exchange papers and enter into friendly conversation. Generally, the persons of pickets are held sacred, though occasionally an ugly secesh disregards the rules of honorable warfare. Officers and sharpshooters, however, are held as exceptions to the law of custom, and those who wish to escape the risk or consequences of a shot do well to shun exposure.

The number all through the peninsula, who are decided in their hostility to the Union, though they are careful not to exhibit it offensively, is very considerable. The minister of the Episcopal church at Old Church, mentioned in a previous letter, believes in rebellion, and lends his influence to the cause. Dr. Gaines, who lives near by our camp, and over some part of whose farm I daily go, is a rank secessionist, and so are scores of others between White House and this place, who are ready to avail themselves of Federal guards to protect their property, and quite as ready to give intelligence of our movements to the rebels. Such persons ought to be consigned to the care of Gen. Stoneman, who understands how to deal with them. The bitterest spirit is often manifested by women. I was informed, a few days ago, that the grand-daughters of a late ex-public functionary, on hearing that our wounded had, in some instances, been tied up by their heels, and had their throats cut by the rebel soldiery, clapped their hands and exclaimed, " good, good." These young ladies, it will be remembered, are not of the vulgar herd, but *educated*, and what is termed *refined!* At the north, in the same position in society, where would the parallel of this spirit be found? Yet we can hardly be surprised when it is recollected that these cultivated feminines are the descendants of a man, who, while acting on a commission for the preservation of the Union, was secretly in league, and afterwards openly acted, with those who were plotting its destruction! But this betrayer of his country has gone to his account, and "his name remains to the ensuing age, abhorred."

Last Friday, 13th, a body of rebel cavalry, infantry and a section of artillery, made a sudden dash into Old Church, causing the Federal cavalry there to retire. They then pushed on to Garlick's Landing, on the Pamunkey river, a few miles above White House, where they burnt two schooners and several wagons, and drove off a number of mules. From thence, they proceeded to Tunstall's Station, where they fired into a train, as it came in from Fair Oaks, with several hundred sick and wounded men, destined to the hospitals at White House. One man was killed and several wounded. The engineer, seeing his danger, put on a full head of steam, and escaped. After cutting the telegraphic wires and tearing up the railroad, they pursued their way to New Baltimore, and crossed the Chickahominy in the neighborhood of Bottom's Bridge. The raid was led by General Stuart. It was a daring affair, and created a good deal of excitement. Stuart's movements were so rapid, that before troops could be put in motion to pursue him, he was beyond harm.

It is said to have been the practice of the First Napoleon, to quarter his army upon the inhabitants of cities and parts of the country through which he passed, and to that end, sent officers in advance to notify them to have the necessary provisions in readiness. This reduced the supply train, relieved quartermasters of much vexation and labor in getting up forage and rations, and ensured the prompt feeding of both men and horses. The levy may have been onerous to those upon whom it was made, and often inconvenient; but it facilitated the movements of the army, and that, with the great captain, was a prime consideration. The example of the French Emperor is not, in this respect, followed in providing for the army of the Peninsula. To supply its daily needs, a fleet of vessels larger than the entire navy of some European powers, and thousands of teams, are kept constantly employed; and at this time, in bustle and activity, White House landing resembles a quay in London, and the Pamunkey, another Thames.

We marvel at the capability of "mine host," who can daily dine his three or four hundred guests upon the abundance of the land, or of the purveyor, who, under a mammoth tent, provides satisfactorily for twelve or fifteen hundred hungry mortals. What, then, must be the brain-work and administrative power of the man who, for an entire campaign, calculates, to a ration, and provides, seasonably, for an army of one hundred thousand men? To the unseen power, giving motion to the complicated machinery producing this wonderful result, no small praise is due. But with all the liberality of provision indicated by the immense operations here mentioned, there are times when it is needful to increase supplies by availing of local resources, and foraging becomes an important feature of a day. Our government, however, respects private rights, and generously compensates loyal citizens from whom articles for the use of the army are of necessity taken. Such seldom have cause for serious complaint. Occasionally, a professedly Union man, but secretly a rebel sympathizer, reveals his interior nature, and has to abide the pecuniary consequences. The following incident, related of Colonel E. G. Marshall, of the 13th New York volunteers, illustrates the statement. The Colonel, on one occasion, not long since, had been reconnoitering, and encamped in a clover field. As was natural under the circumstances, the horses, being in clover, lost no time in taking advantage of it. The proprietor of the field, having made remonstrance without effect, demanded payment for his loss, when the following brief conversation ensued:

Proprietor.—Col. Marshall, I believe?

Col. M.—You believe right, sir.

P.—Well, Colonel, you have trampled down my clover field, and completely destroyed it. Do you intend paying for it?

Col.—Well, sir, are you loyal?

P.—Yes, sir!

Col.—Are you willing to take the oath of allegiance to the United States?

P.—No, sir.

Col.—Then get Jeff Davis to pay you, and get out of my tent, you infamous traitor.

And so the parties separated.

A few days since, acceptable hospital stores, for the battery, were received from Rhode Island friends, through the Sanitary Commission. A good deal of sickness has prevailed in the army for some weeks past, though, perhaps, not more than is to be expected among so large a body of men subjected to the hard labor and exposures they have seen. One of the best auxiliaries to health in the army that could be supplied, is good cooks—men who have been educated to the profession. The advantage of such an arrangement was seen at Camp Sprague, near Washington, last year, while occupied by the first regiment of Rhode Island volunteers. The subject involves interests that render it worthy the attention of the Sanitary Commission.

Day before yesterday, a novelty was seen in the Federal lines, in the form of a secesh newsboy, fresh from Richmond, with a supply of papers. He was taken to Gen. Franklin's head-quarters, where he will probably be detained until his real character is made clear. He stated, among other things, that there had been a fight between a North Carolina regiment and other rebel regiments, on account of the former having refused to serve longer. Whether this statement is true or not, a similar report has been current in camp for some time. Upwards of thirty contrabands, escaped from Richmond, were taken to head-quarters on the same day, who reported that an alarmed state of feeling existed in the city, and that the soldiers received only half rations of pork and bread.

Among noticeable events of less importance than fighting, yet pleasantly exciting, that have recently occurred, was a review of Porter's corps, on the 10th inst., apparently for the gratification of the Spanish General Prim, who is now on a visit to the army of the Potomac. The day, fortunately, was propitious, and the display brilliant and satisfactory. The distinguished stranger expressed himself highly gratified with the appearance of our troops. He is apparently about forty years of age, and has an eminent military reputation. After the review, he visited our outposts, and took a distant view of the rebels.

Mr. Jefferson Davis, it appears, has found it necessary to show himself at Richmond. His recent address to the rebel army, as published in the papers of that city, is characteristic, and may properly be assigned a place in the next edition of the "curiosities of literature." He claims for the south a marvellous victory at Fair Oaks, precisely as a victory at Pittsburg Landing was claimed, and without half the grounds of plausibility. As to victory, another such an one, following immediately upon the fight at Fair Oaks, would have proved the, utter ruin of the rebels. The most that in truth can be said, is that they gained an advantage on our left on the first day, which they not only lost on the second, but were compelled to fly precipitately from the camp they occupied, leaving things essentially as found, to safe distance towards Richmond. I give them credit for fighting desperately in a bad cause; but when Mr. Davis claims a victory, he must count largely upon the credulity of men who "will believe, because they love the lie." But what can exceed the effrontery that charges the Union troops with a disregard of "many of the usages of civilized war," and claims for the confederates a "humanity to the wounded prisoners" who fell into their hands, that "becomes a fit and crowning glory" to their valor! With ill grace is this accusation made by one whose army has been noted for the deeds it charges upon the Federals, and who, within a few weeks, have illustrated their ideas of the "usages of civilized war" by shooting down men decoyed into their power by a flag of truce and a request of humanity! But "treason and murder ever keep together as two yoke devils sworn to either's purpose," and the "fit and crowning glory" of such conduct is what God awarded to the first secessionist and the perverted spirits he drew after him.*

The recent visit of Gen. Burnside to Gen. McClellan's headquarters, has naturally awakened speculation as to its cause, without leading to any definite conclusion.

LETTER XVI.

Battle of Five Oaks—Battles at Mechanicsville and Gaines's Mill— Battle of Malvern Hill—Batteries A, C and E—Casualties—Sick and wounded left at White House and Savage's sta'ion—Federal losses in various battles—General order on 4th July.

HARRISON'S BAR, VA.,
July 2, 1862.

The details of the movements of the army of the Potomac for the last ten days would fill a volume more stirring than the most exciting romance. Seven of the ten have been days of battle excitement, such as was never before witnessed in our land,

-----

* In manly contrast with the unfounded charges of Mr. Davis, is the following testimony of a rebel officer who fought at Fair Oaks: "The humanity displayed by the general commanding the enemy's forces, created a feeling of warm admiration among our troops, great numbers of whom had near relations among the wounded we had been compelled to leave behind in the dense woods and sickly swamps, and who were out of the reach of any succor from us."—*War Pictures, p.* 283.

and finding few parallels in modern story. On the morning of the 25th June, the curtain rose and disclosed preparations for a mighty struggle. At an early hour, Generals Hooker and Kearny commenced advancing their divisions with a view of occupying a new position, which brought on a severe engagement in front of Seven Pines, lasting until a late hour in the afternoon. It was the precursor of more bloody battles yet to come. In this conflict, the 2d Rhode Island, which had returned to its old position in Couch's division, participated, and stood a galling fire of shot and shell. It lost five men killed, and twenty wounded; among the latter, Captain Stanley, who was slightly injured by a fragment of a shell. Capt. Sears was struck by a splinter, but not hurt. The companies of Captains Read and Dyer, while acting as pickets, were much exposed. The latter had two men killed and two badly wounded. Lieutenant Whiting, an aid of General Palmer who commands the brigade, had an arm taken off by a shot.* The 2d New Hampshire regiment suffered heavily, as did Sickles' brigade. The 1st Massachusetts, Colonel Cowdin, lost 6 men killed and 55 wounded. Lieutenant Charles B. Warner, of the 19th Massachusets, was killed, and Lieut. James H. Rice, of the same regiment, wounded. Lieutenant Warner belonged to South Danvers, Mass. The enemy were repulsed, the position sought gained, and "The Battle of the Five Oaks," as it is called, closed. The Federal loss in killed, wounded and missing, is set down at 600.

The next day, June 26th, the grand ball opened near Mechanicsville, and McCall's division, which had recently arrived to strengthen our right wing. led the "dance of death." He occupied a defensive position along the line of Beaver Dam Creek. Griffin's and Martindale's brigades were in position

---

* Lieutenant Leonard Whiting is the son of Colonel Whiting, of the 5th New York Cavalry, and a grandson of the late Nathan Waterman, of Providence.

for supports on his right and left. On the afternoon of that day, our battery hitched up and proceeded to near Mechanicsville, and in proximity to the enemy, where it stood under fire, but did not engage. When we approached the fighting ground, the roar of musketry and the thunder of artillery on both sides, told of the sharp practice going on. A rebel battery to our left and front, and not more than 700 or 800 yards distant, was blazing away constantly, and occasionally a secesh shell or solid shot would come screeching over us, and tearing through the trees, burst in the distance without serious damage. As we stood in the road, I saw several poor wounded fellows pass by to the rear, and also five prisoners, one of them a young lieutenant of the 3d Louisiana regiment. The action continued until night, and the enemy were repulsed with severe loss. About 9 o'clock P. M., we went into a field on our right and bivouacked.

The following day, June 27th, the fighting was renewed at Gaines's mill. Porter's corps took position behind a deep ravine. On the right was Griffin's brigade, on the left Butterfield's, while Martindale's held the centre. Gen. Reynold's brigade, of McCall's division, was called from the reserve, and was engaged for the greater part of the afternoon. Most of the artillery was formed in line about one-fourth of a mile in rear of the infantry, in the second line of defence. Porter's line extended about two miles, the left resting on the Chickahominy and the right on Coal harbor. The face of the country was broken by hill, vale and meadow.

At daybreak, battery C advanced to its position. Captain Weeden having been appointed Chief of Artillery for the corps, the immediate command devolved on Lieutenant Waterman. At 2 o'clock, Lieut. Buckley was ordered to take his section to the front line, and support or assist General Martindale's brigade. He took position on a slight elevation on the bank of the ravine, and in the centre of the brigade. At this time, the fighting was principally on our right. About 3 o'clock,

the enemy charged on us, and were handsomely repelled. Two
of Lieut. Bucklin's guns were sighted at the rebel colors, and
at the second shot they fell. The rebels fought with a determination to conquer, and were met in a corresponding spirit.
The thunder of artillery and the roar of musketry was perfectly deafening. " Death spoke from every booming shot that
knelled upon the ear." Our artillery mowed them down like
grass, "and slaughter heaped on high its weltering ranks."
Three times they charged with the fury of a tornado, but were
as often driven back. But worn out human nature could not
longer resist such fearful odds. Our corps, rated at 30,000,
probably counted not more than 25,000 fighting men. Against
this number, the rebels massed and hurled 60,000 to 70,000,
supported by eighty pieces of artillery. At their fourth onset,
our lines were broken, and the infantry fell back. In our battery, officers and men were cool and determined. The gunners, streaming with perspiration and begrimmed with powder
and smoke, worked their pieces with vigor and effect, though
Minies fell like hail stones around them. The sections of
Lieutenants Waterman and Clark belched forth vollies of
death. But fourteen men had fallen, killed and wounded;
sixty horses had been shot; Lieut. Buckley had not enough
left to take off his guns: and the order to retreat became a
necessity. It was obeyed only when a squadron of rebel cavalry had charged within a few rods, and then their contents
were bestowed upon them as a parting gift. Three guns and
three caissons were lost—two guns left on the field for the reason above stated, and one mired. Lieut. Bucklin's horse was
shot. General Reynolds was taken prisoner. Among the officers killed, were Col. Gove, of the 22d Massachusetts, and Col.
Black, of the 62d Pennsylvania. He was a noble officer, and
fell at the head of his regiment while leading a charge. The
loss on both sides, in killed and wounded, was large. The
rebels, from their superior numbers, and reckless rushing up
to the cannon's mouth, suffered most.

10*

When the order to retire was received, we moved to the Chickahominy, crossed that stream at Woodbury's Bridge, and encamped for the night. Saturday morning, I went round and took a look at the hospital and wounded. Many poor fellows were writhing in agony; some with shattered arms; some pierced through the lower limbs, and others through the body, with Minies. It required strong nerves to witness the scene unmoved, and no small amount of self-control to restrain a vocal call of curses upon the heads of men "composed and framed of treachery," who, reckless of consequences, and consulting only their mad ambition, had involved their country in all the horrors of civil war.

The hospital was located near Gen. McCall's head-quarters. There I saw George W. Ham, Jr., of Providence, who was mortally wounded. He was shot during the retreat. A round bullet entered his back to the right of the spine, which followed round the ribs and came out in front, just below the short ribs. He was in Lieut. Buckley's section, and did his duty manfully, till ordered to retire.

Sunday morning, at 8 o'clock, we left our encampment, at White Oak Bottom, and continuing our march, arrived at Turkey Bend on Monday, and took position on Malvern Hill. The battles at Peach Orchard, Savage's Station,* Golding's Farm, White Oak Swamp, Charles City Cross Roads and Glendale, which would make graphic pictures of valor, were but a continuation of the line of fire running from Mechanicsville to the James river.† At the latter place, Capt. Randolph had the four rifled pieces of his battery on the right front, with the division of General Slocum. His two howitzers were a mile

---

* Dr. Newell, of Providence, was taken prisoner at Savage's Station, with twelve other surgeons, and a large number of wounded men. He was sent to Richmond with the wounded men under his care, but in the course of a few days, was released.

† At Glendale, June 30, battery A had four men wounded, and battery B, three.

to the left, with Kearny's division, and, for a short time, in the thickest of the fight. One howitzer was taken by the enemy.

Yesterday, the battle of Malvern Hill took place,—a fight as exciting and sanguinary as those of Thursday and Friday, at Mechanicsville and Gaines's Mill. In the order of battle, General Franklin held the right, resting on James river; General Porter, the extreme left ; Generals Keyes and Heintzelman occupied the centre, and General Sumner's corps was held in reserve. The right was supported by the gunboats Galena and Jacob Bell, whose 100-pounders were useful in searching the woods, and interfering with the advance of rebel reinforcements, as they came down in heavy numbers within range. The day was clear ; and the rolling country covered with with moving thousands, the glittering of bayonets and burnished artillery, the verdant forest skirting the field, and the sparkling waters of the James, seen in the distance, all combined to open the day with a picture of surpassing beauty. It soon vanished, and the eye rested on a scene of blood and slaughter.

The battle began at 3 o'clock P. M., by a heavy musketry fire from the rebels upon our centre, and soon a general engagement ensued. Our line was in the form of a semi-circle. For several hours, the conflict raged with unmitigated fury. Here, as at Gaines's Mill, Porter's corps did some splendid fighting. The troops, under Heintzelman, Sumner, Sedgwick, Kearny, Keyes, Couch, Morell and other generals, fought with the steadiness of veterans. The 2d Rhode Island held an important position, and deserves honorable mention. The 10th Massachusetts, under the temporary command of Colonel Nelson Viall, of the 2d Rhode Island, in connection with the 36th New York, assailed and nearly annihilated a rebel brigade. Randolph's battery occupied a position on the right, within one thousand yards of the rebel batteries stationed in a wheat-field. He had a severe artillery fight, losing one man killed and four wounded, while the regiments in support in front and rear lost fifty men.

At half-past 8 o'clock in the morning, the three remaining guns of battery C, with a section of Allen's Massachusetts battery, all under the command of Lieut. Waterman, (Capt. Weeden being Chief of Artillery,) moved to the hills, and proceeded off to the left of the line to protect the left flank. The battery with Allen's section was stationed on the brow of a hill, and commanded a plain below. A sharp look-out was kept along the edge of the woods beyond the plain, to see that no rebels came out, and if they did, to give them a becoming reception. Shot and shells from the rebel batteries on our right were constantly flying over our heads, but we had, for the moment, less to fear from them than from some of our own guns on the extreme left of the line, which were obscured from our view by woods, and were shooting over our heads. Some of their shells were fired at too short range, and a 42-pounder shell burst close by one of our pieces, instantly disabling six of its men, and fatally wounding Lieut. Waterman's horse and that of Sergeant Hunt. It was little less than miraculous that their riders escaped. Two of the men were instantly killed and four wounded, one severely. The explosion was stunning. Shells were coming from right, rear and left, and our position being too hot, we were ordered to retire ; and moving further to the right, very soon relieved Griffin's battery, which had expended all its ammunition. After getting in battery, firing was commenced, dropping shells in various directions in the woods in front of us. A rebel battery somewhere in front of us responded to our civilities, and sent us specimens of their ordnance stores, but as most of them overreached, no injury was done.

In a short time, a rebel regiment was seen coming down a road to our left and front, and deploying into the field as skirmishers. Attention was also arrested by a rebel battery just in the edge of the woods in the rear of the regiment, whose position could be discerned only by the smoke of its discharges. A few well directed missiles put a stop to impertinences, and firing from that quarter soon ceased. Most of its shots over-

reached, and did comparatively little damage. One was made,
however, which told on our ranks. A shrapnell burst splen-
didly, (for so are death missives often viewed on the battle-
field,) and one of the fragments struck Corporal William B.
Thompson in the thigh, making a mortal wound. Another
man, working the gun, was struck in the arm by a piece of the
same shell, and died in twenty minutes. The rebel infantry
came within 300 yards of our battery, but we could not poke
cannister at them from fear of wounding our own men in front ;
so we gave them shrapnel, (shells filled with sixty bullets and
nearly as destructive,) which were fired over the heads of the
infantry. The batteries, in their several positions, mowed
down the rebels with terrible certainty, as did our infantry
along the entire line ; but life seemed of no consequence to
their officers, and relying on their superior numbers, they filled
every breach made in their ranks with fresh men, maddened
and made reckless with whiskey and gunpowder. Though they
numbered three to our one, it was in vain that they rushed upon
our men. It was only to meet certain death and final repulse.
Our men stood up bravely to the work, as they did six days
before, and when they saw the rebel infantry deploying, cheered
and waved their hats, crying, " give it to them, give it to them,"
—and it was done. In this battle, four men of the battery
were killed, eleven wounded, and several missing. We lost
ten horses and one caisson. About half past seven o'clock, we
were relieved, and returned to the camp we left in the morning. Late in the night, the battery proceeded on its way to
Harrison's Landing, where it arrived at four o'clock A. M., very
much exhausted. At midnight, terminated a week of battles,
the enemy driven back, and the Federal army holding the
field. The Federals captured twenty-nine cannon and lost
twenty-eight. The slaughter on both sides was immense—the
rebels·suffering largely in excess. To describe the appearance
of the ground the next morning, covered with wounded, dead
and dying men, carcases of horses, and strewed with fragments

of gun carriages, muskets, and other military accoutrements,
would only be to describe the horrors of previous battles, mag-
nified. Imagination can scarcely exceed the reality.

The question is sometimes asked, How does a man feel in
battle? The testimony of the bravest generals in this country
and in Europe is, that at the commencement of a fight, they
experienced a certain trepidation that soon wore off. To stand
unconcernedly before an opposing force, especially of superior
numbers; to abide the calm that precedes the first flash of artillery or volley of musketry, thinking of home and the possibilities of the hour, requires some nerve; and the man who
trembles when he first hears "the death-shot hissing from afar,"
is not to be branded as a coward. He may be brave as Cæsar,
but his blood will quicken, his heart beat with increased force,
and through his whole frame "some sense of shuddering" be
perceptible. But the first discharge of artillery or infantry
from his own side breaks the charm, and in a few minutes the
strange sensation, not easy to describe, that had run over him,
passes away, and in the din and wild excitement of the battle's progress he becomes oblivious of danger, and even finds
in the last exploded shell, or shower of Minies, subjects for a
jest.

Roll-call, after a battle, tinges success with sadness. Many
of our regiments have been decimated. The gallant 4th
Michigan, which left Miner's Hill with full ranks, now numbers less than 300 men. The brave Colonel Woodbury was
killed yesterday, while leading it on. Col. Cass, of the Massachusetts 9th, was severely wounded. Both belonged to Morell's old command, now under Gen. Griffin. Not more than
1500 men are left in the whole brigade, and but two or three
field officers. Col. McQuade, of the 14th New York, is the
only colonel that escaped injury. All the New York, Pennsylvania, New Jersey, Vermont, New Hampshire, Massachusetts, Connecticut and Maine regiments engaged, suffered
severely. On the fatal fields of the Chickahominy and of

Malvern Hills, many noble fellows lie low, "no more to hear the victor's shout or clashing steel;" and when the historian shall record the daring deeds of the Army of the Peninsula, he will not fail justly to eulogize the patriotism and fidelity of the men who supported law and sustained the integrity of the government by the sacrifice of their lives.

[Perhaps the most trying experience in war is the necessity, that sometimes occurs on a retreat, for leaving sick and wounded men behind, and this was sadly realized in the late retreat of our right wing and centre. By sickness and the casualties of battle the hospitals at White House and Savage's station had become crowded, and when the evacuation of the former had been determined on, the means for removing the helpless ones were found to be totally inadequate. It only remained for those superintending the operation, to take away as many as the hurry of the time, and the limited number of vehicles would enable them to do, and leave the residue to be made prisoners by the rebels, sent to Richmond to struggle with death, and if successful, to find themselves transferred from the discomforts of poorly provided hospitals to the even greater discomforts and worse provided Libby Prison, or another equally miserable place of confinement. In such a prospect, there was nothing to inspire, but everything to extinguish, hope, and the feelings of the unfortunate victims can easily be conceived. Dr. Thomas T. Ellis, an acting medical director at the White House, speaking on this subject, says:

" At daylight on Saturday it was known that the army was to evacuate its line of entrenchments. To do this with sufficient celerity, it was necessary to move only the most essential baggage, and leave behind everything ponderous and bulky. An order was issued to officers to discriminate between necessaries and luxuries. Even the sick had to be told that to but few of them could ambulances be allowed. The wounded were told nothing, but the ominous silence must have convinced

them that they were to be left on contested ground, at the
mercy of the enemy, while the army would, column after column, recede to the distant James river by a doubtful and dangerous route. None who witnessed it, will ever forget the
scene on Saturday morning. All knew that the White House
had been abandoned, thus cutting off the depot of supplies—a
part of the line of earthworks deserted, and the tentless army
lay on the open field, many sleeping after the labors of the
battle, but by far a greater number were grouped in anxious
conversation. Hundreds also were limping along, or with an
arm in a sling, inquiring eagerly for their own regiments.
Many, very many, started on the painful and hopeless pilgrim-
age to the now coveted James river, where they hoped to find
the Union gunboats, feeling that under their port-holes alone,
could they find rest or safety. The long and straggling lines
of these left many a drop of blood on the sandy track as they
filed through brook and wood, and over hill and dale, traced
by the certainty of deliverance which each step secured to
them. Some of them hobbled ten miles the first day, upon
crutches; and one poor fellow, who had received a ball
through the hip and had the ankle of the other leg broken,
kept up with an ambulance for eleven hours. The ambulances
were crowded so full that the springs, often breaking, were all
bent flat on the axle. Many poor wounded fellows sat on the
tail of the ambulances, their blood-dripping feet dangling behind. . . . Over a thousand wounded were left in the
hospital at Savage's station. This was unavoidable under the
circumstances, and every arrangement that could be made was
attended to, to insure their comfort and secure them good
treatment from the enemy whose bloody greeting they were
a second time destined to hear. But not a few of these poor
fellows were unwilling to remain, and made desperate efforts
to get away. Scarcely able to drag themselves along, they
clung to the skirts of their stronger comrades, or hobbled on
crutches, apparently dreading, more than death itself, falling

into the hands of the rebels. Many became so exhausted that they fell by the wayside and could only be roused and helped forward by the greatest exertion.

The Federal losses in the various battles preceding and during the retreat, according to General McClellan's official report, were as follows:

		Killed.	Wounded.	Missing.	Total.
Gen. Sumner's,	Second Corps,	176	1,088	848	2,086
Gen. Heintzelman's,	Third Corps,	189	1,051	883	2,073
Gen. Keyes',	Fourth Corps,	69	507	201	777
Gen. Porter's,	Fifth Corps,	873	3,700	2,779	7,352
Gen. Franklin's,	Sixth Corps,	245	1,313	1,179	2,737
Gen. Stoneman's,	Cavalry,	19	60	97	176
The Engineers,			2	21	23
Total		1,555	7,711	5,958	
Grand Total..15,224					

Of any single division, that of General McCall suffered the greatest loss. Killed, 251; wounded, 1,223; missing, 1,607; total, 3,081. Of the rebel casualties, no authentic statement has been seen. A Richmond paper admits the loss to have been not far from 18,000; but there is good reason for the belief that 20,000 to 25,000 would be nearer the fact.

The army of the Potomac, after the battle of Malvern Hill, established its lines at Harrison's Landing, in the form of a crescent, the right and left wings resting on the James river, supported by gunboats. Fortifications were soon thrown up, which rendered its position secure. On the fourth of July, General McClellan reviewed the troops, at which time the following general order was read:

HEAD-QUARTERS, ARMY OF THE POTOMAC, }
July 4, 1862. }

SOLDIERS OF THE ARMY OF THE POTOMAC:

Your achievements of the last ten days have illustrated the valor and endurance of the American soldier. Attacked by superior forces, and without hope of reinforcements, you have succeeded in changing your base of operations by a flank movement, always regarded as the most hazardous of military expedients. You have saved all your material, all your trains, and all your guns, except a few lost in battle, taking in return guns and colors from the enemy.

Upon your march, you have been assailed day after day, with desperate fury, by men of the same race and nation, skilfully massed and led.

Under every disadvantage of numbers, and necessarily of position, also, you have, in every conflict, beaten back your foes with enormous slaughter.

Your conduct ranks you among the celebrated armies of history.

No one will now question that each of you may always, with pride, say—"I belong to the Army of the Potomac."

You have reached this new base, complete in organization and unimpaired in spirit.

The enemy may, at any time, attack you. We are prepared to meet them. I have personally established your lines. Let them come, and we will convert their repulse into a final defeat.

Your Government is strengthening you with the resources of a great people.

On this our nation's birthday, we declare to our foes, who are rebels against the best interests of mankind, that this army shall enter the capital of the so-called Confederacy ; that our national Constitution shall prevail, and that the Union, which can alone insure internal peace and external security to each State, must and shall be preserved, cost what it may in time, treasure or blood.

GEORGE B. McCLELLAN,

Major General Commanding.

LETTER XVII.

Rebels fought under disadvantage—Cause of the evacuation of White
House.

HARRISON'S BAR, VA., }
July 8, 1862. }

Ever since the army left Yorktown, we have fought the
rebels under great disadvantage. They were on their own
ground. They were familiar with the country. They knew
every nook and corner, every swamp and hiding place, and the
direction of every road and cross-road. They had plenty of
spies in the people among whom we encamped, to give them
warning of all our movements. They were thus able to choose
their positions, and take advantage of every circumstance that
could be turned against us. We, on the contrary, had everything to learn, with few reliable sources of information, and
constantly liable to be misled. Nearly all the knowledge that
could be depended upon, had to be obtained by reconnoissance.*

---

* General McClellan, in his testimony before the Committee on the Conduct of the War, said : " Our maps proved entirely inaccurate, and did us
more harm than good, for we were constantly misled by them." General
Barnard, chief of engineers, before the same committee, said : " We found
ourselves in a *terra incognita*. We knew nothing of the roads; nothing
of the country. I had supposed that all these matters had been investi-
gated; that in choosing such a route, there was, at least, such a knowledge of it as would have justified the choosing of it. The country between Fort Monroe and Yorktown was almost a perfect wilderness. It
had been stated so often, that I felt that it was an assured fact, that the
roads were hard and sandy; whereas, they were everywhere of the most
terrible character—what there were of them; and with the roads we had
there, we never had heard, up to the day we arrived before Yorktown, of
the fact that there were any other defences except the mere defences of
Yorktown. But when we got there, we found a line of defences stretching across the isthmus."

Yet, with all these unfavorable conditions, the Federals have ever been more than a match for the rebels. They beat them at Williamsburg, at West Point, at Hanover Court House, and in every considerable fight along a line of some twenty-two miles extent. Gaines's Mill may be regarded as the solitary exception. By the time our army had fought its way to the Chickahominy, disease had begun to make serious inroads upon its ranks, and on the day that arrangements had been completed (including the building of bridges and corduroy roads) for advancing it across that stream, 30,000 or 40,000 men were needed to make it as strong as when it commenced pursuit of the retreating foe. In the meantime, rebel tactics had been changed. Raids were organized and put in active operation, to gain time for the accumulation of an overwhelming force at Richmond. When Gen. Porter's division was thrown forward to Hanover Court House and the Junction, it was mainly to cut off northern communication with that city.

It had been hoped that Stonewall Jackson would have been kept in the valley of the Shenandoah, in which event the right wing of our army would have been safe. But he escaped. And when it was found, on the 24th June, that he had broken through his barriers, and was sweeping down upon our right with 30,000 men, it became evident, that with such a force in conjunction with that in front, nothing could prevent his seizing White House and the military supplies there deposited, and attacking our army on the flank and in the rear, with the almost dead certainty of its annihilation. All this foreseen, the immense stores were speedily transferred to the shipping in the Pamunkey, and the chagrined rebel leader disappointed in his hopes of booty. The double movement of throwing the left wing forward to the James river, where the gunboats rendered it secure, and swinging round the right, required great skill, and the success with which it was accomplished in the face of formidable obstacles, places it among the most remarkable of military achievements.

[To go back a little and make the record more complete and intelligible, it should be remarked that, upon the request and earnest representation of General McClellan, the President, on the 17th May, acceded to his request to have General Mc-Dowell, then before Fredericksburg, form a junction with his right wing, to coöperate in his advance on Richmond. This would have added thirty-five or forty thousand men to his army, and rendered an entrance into the rebel capital, early in June, before the enemy had time to increase their strength, comparatively easy. This junction, it is now understood, was to have taken place about the time, or soon after the battle of Hanover Court House, which, as already described, occurred on the 27th May. But, in the meantime, the rebel movements elsewhere had become alarming. The critical condition of General Banks's position, the push upon Harper's Ferry, the threatening of Leesburg, Geary, and, to a certain extent, Washington itself, induced the President, from prudential considerations, to countermand the order to General McDowell, which he did on the 24th May, and on the same day notified General McClellan that he had been compelled to suspend the movement of General McDowell to join him. In the place of Mc-Dowell, General McCall's division of ten thousand men was sent forward to strengthen his right. They began to arrive at White House on the 11th June, and before the 26th, were ready for the battle they so bravely fought on that day. Meanwhile, the rebel force had concentrated on the Federal right, in superior numbers, and the ten thousand auxiliaries were insufficient for the exigency. To fight, and hold the ground; to fight again, and fall back, was all that could be done. Ten thousand additional troops might have changed the day on the 27th. But they were not to be had, and retreat and evacuation, as before stated, of necessity followed.]

11*

LETTER XVIII.

Reconnoissances—President's visit—Exchange of prisoners—Sickness—Harrison's Mansion—Ancient will—Flies.

HARRISON'S LANDING, VA., }
August 12, 1862. }

Since the battle of Malvern Hill, the army has been chiefly occupied in reconnoissances, reviews, and such attention to its *personnel* and material, as would prepare it for the offensive service to which it may soon be called. Skirmishes have been of frequent occurrence, keeping up the *esprit de corps* of the troops. Last Tuesday, (5th,) Hooker and Sedgwick had a sharp contest with the rebels at Malvern Hill, and drove them off at the point of the bayonet. The Federal loss was about forty in killed and wounded. A considerable number of the enemy were taken prisoners. Twenty-eight of their captured cavalry men passed our camp at night. The affair, it is said, created a strong sensation at Richmond, and forty thousand men were sent down in the direction of the Hill, to look after matters. If the design was to divert the rebels from Pope and Burnside, the movement may be reckoned successful.

On the 8th of last month, the President made a brief visit of inspection to the army, by whom it was reviewed. He was welcomed with the customary official salute, and as he rode along the lines of each division, by the stentorian cheers of the men. General Halleck and other high military dignitaries have also been here, for consultation, as is supposed.

Vessels are constantly descending the river with flags of truce, bringing large numbers of our sick, wounded, and able-bodied men, taken prisoners in the late battles. Equivalents in kind are almost daily returned. The river, at the landing, displays all the activity of a commercial city. At times, more than one hundred sailing vessels and steamers may be seen laying in the stream, waiting to discharge or receive cargoes. Among the latter are the Canonicus, Commodore, State of Maine, Nantasket and South America. The ironclads Dacotah, Monitor and Galena, move back and forth, watchful of their defenceless proteges, and looking well to rebel demonstrations on either bank. The shore on the western side is lined with officers' quarters, hospitals, ambulances, commissary stores, wagons, mules, disabled horses, post office, express office, and photographic establishment. These, with a host of contraband men, women and children, of all shades, from neutral tint to jet, present a picturesque scene, while their shouts, laughter and loud lingo, remind one of the confusion of tongues.

Compared with the swamps of Chickahominy, the location occupied by the army is healthy ; but tested by sanitary laws the entire country, at this season of the year, must be pronounced sickly. Much of the sickness now prevailing, (though the health of the army is understood to be better than when our right wing rested on Gaines's farm,) was engendered by fatigues and exposures previous to the battle of Malvern Hill. Besides diarrhœa and fevers, scurvy has, to some extent, prevailed, the latter aggravated, if not induced, by an inability to obtain a sufficiency of vegetables. The man who said he was tempted to cry " liberty and onions, now and forever, one and inseparable," understood the needs of men whose staple of food has, of necessity, been salt junk and hard tack. The government has not been unmindful of these wants, and the beneficial effects of the recent provision made for a mixed diet will undoubtedly soon be visible.

Harrison's Landing receives its name from Benjamin Harrison, the friend of Washington, and a signer of the Declaration of Independence. It possesses additional interest from being the birth-place of the late President William Henry Harrison. He doubtless little thought, when " Tippecanoe and Tyler too" was the popular refrain of 1840, that in twenty years Virginia would became a hot-bed of rebellion, and a leader of it his associate in the Presidential canvass. But times change, and men of feeble principle, or victims of ambition, change with them, only to build for themselves a monument for true men's scorn. The old family mansion is still standing near the river, and is used for hospital purposes. On the roof of the house the signal corps has a look-out, which commands the surrounding country. The granary of the old mansion is occupied by Dr. Holmes, of Brooklyn, N. Y., as an embalming house. A relic of interest, in this connection, is the following copy of the will of Benjamin Harrison, picked up among scattered papers at Warwick Court House, where the registry was made. It is witnessed by Thomas Read and Samuel Harrison, and the record attested by Miles Carey, clerk of the county court. What relation the testator held to Governor Benjamin Harrison, if any, is by me unknown.

In the name of god, Amen. I, Benjamin Harrison, being sicke & weake in body, but in perfect sence and memorie, blessed bee God for it, finding my selfe to bee of noe longe continvance doe make this my last will & Testament as followeth—first, I give my Soule to god my maker, hopeing through the merritts of Jesus Christ my Saviour, to attaine to Everlasting life and my body to my mother, the Earth, to bee buried after a Cristian maner, and all the rest of my worldly Estate, as followeth :

1. I give and bequeathe unto my son, Benjamin Harrison, my negro boy Called Billic, to bee delivered to him by my Executors when he is Twentie one years of age, and when he, my sd son, hath the sd negro Delivered to him that then, he shall pay unto his Sisters, as many of them as shall bee then alive, to Each of them twenty Shills : and I give alsoe unto my sd son, my Gun and sword. And alsoe my Desire is, that my sd son shall bee bound to a Trad as he most desires, at the age of thirteen or fourteen years, att the Discrettion of my Executors : but if the above named negro boy should Die before (2) that my son is of age, then my will is that my sd son shall have a proporsonable share with my wife and the rest of my Children of all the rest of my Estate, but at the receitt of the above sd negro, my sd son shall give a discharge for his full share of my Estate.

3. I doe lend unto my loveing wife, Ann Harrison, all the rest of my Estate, dureing her widdow-hood, without Inventory or Apraisement: and if my sd wife should marry, that then it shall bee Equally Devided betwen my sd wife and the rest of my Children: and I doe alsoe make my loveing wife and my Son-in-law, John Langhorn, my whole and Sole Executors of this my last will and Testament, revoakeing all other wills by me made, as wittness my hand and Scalle this — day of Apprill, 1715.

BENJAMIN B. H. HARRISON.

[At this season of the year, the surrounding country here affords an inviting field for exploration to the enthusiastic amateur or professional entomologist. Between the " sweet musician" who seldom forgets to thrust his bill for payment in the face of one whose unwilling ear is compelled to listen to a nightly serenade to that member of the *Pediculus* family, celebrated by Pindar, is to be found " every creeping thing" that Noah permitted a place in the ark, and perhaps some that he did not. Some of the specimens are as ill-favored, and by no means desirable companions. But whatever pleasure may be derived from pursuing sientific investigations through this wide field, it is not far separated from discomforts, among the chief of which, in the present lull of war, may be reckoned flies. Talk of " Rats in Brazil," or " Cockroaches in Japan; " they are not a circumstance to the *Diptera* tribes, at Harrison's Landing. Pharaoh was never more effectually plagued, and it is not a wonder that he regarded the toleration of Hebrew worship in his dominions, a cheap payment for their expulsion. Here, the most hardened and impracticable rebel would give up, and take the oath of allegiance, rather that endure their torment a week. Remember, the mercury is at 100° or 110° in the shade. You write, and flies cover your paper. You read, and flies usurp the page. You attempt a siesta, but it proves an abortion. You " saw the air," with a quick irregular motion of the hand, but your tormentors only double their torments for this attempt at self-defense. Buzz, buzz, buzz; flies on the nose; flies in the ears; flies on the table; flies in

the food ; flies in the tent ; flies outside ; black, biting, merci-
less flies, everywhere. Look at those poor horses at the picket
rope, and under yonder shade. Flesh has gone and flies have
got it. You count their ribs, and you mark their almost expression of despair. How they stamp, and shake their heads,
and whisk their brushes, and pull at the halter for release.
But all in vain. Flies have them. Flies are consuming them.
Of many of them, flies will be the death. No marvel that
they are often frenzied beyond recovery. Next to a miracle
will it be if any escape. In a fair fight, the rebels can be
vanquished, though three to our one ; but flies, in fly time,
never. Like hungry contractors, they stick till gorged, and
then retire, only to return and gorge again.

LETTER XIX.

Withdrawal of the Army of the Potomac from the Peninsula.

NEWPORT NEWS, }
August 17, 1863. }

The shadow of coming events at Harrison's Landing was
resolved, early last week, into tangible substance. Rumors that
had freely circulated in camp, then issued in facts, and preparations by the army to retire from the Peninsula, were everywhere seen. On the 10th, the baggage of Battery C was
placed on transports. Thursday, the 14th, we were prepared
to vacate our camp. On the night of that day the order " forward " was given, and turning our backs alike, upon the enemy
we had beaten at Malvern Hill, and the entomological tribes
that shared our tents and disturbed our repose, we took up our
line of March. Our course lay through Charles City Court
House. We crossed the Chickahominy at its mouth, over a
pontoon bridge 1,400 feet in length, built under the direction

of Captains Spaulding and Duane, of the 50th New York
regiment. The bridge was a fine specimen of engineering,
and greatly facilitated the withdrawal both of the army and
the immense baggage trains of the commissary, quartermaster's
and ordnance departments. Our march was through Williamsburg, Yorktown and Great Bethel, and this morning we arrived
at Newport News, dusty and weary. A salt water bath at the
beach, was among the earliest refreshing experiences. The
march was pleasant, and an abundant supply of poultry and
fruit, obtained by the way, were very satisfactory contributions
to the gastronomic department.

[After a change of base became necessary, and the army
had taken up its new position on the James river, the question
of evacuating the Peninsula was privately discussed. This
discussion was connected with the visit of General Burnside,
referred to on a preceding page. The President and General
Halleck visited General McClellan at his head quarters, for
consultation, to ascertain from observation and inquiry, the
morale of the army, and perhaps, to obtain with greater defi-
niteness, the views of the General. The review of the troops,
mentioned in a preceding letter, was embraced within this design. On the occasion of General Halleck's visit, an informal
consultation of the corps commanders was held, at which General Burnside was present, and the subject of the removal of the
army fully discussed. A difference of opinion existed. Some
were decidedly in favor of withdrawal; others were disposed
to make another trial for the capture of Richmond. This was
the earnest wish of General McClellan. For this purpose, he
asked a reinforcement of fifty thousand men, but as that number were not immediately available, expressed a willingness to
make the attempt with twenty thousand, which General Halleck
informed him he could have. But the rebels had been diligent
in making Fort Darling, near the river, impregnable to our gun
boats, and in otherwise strengthening their position around Rich-

mond.   Piles had been driven in the river, and obstructions
sunk in the channel, which rendered abortive any attempt to approach within range of the city by water.   Recruits for wasted
regiments came in slowly, and although considerable activity on
our side prevailed, little was accomplished that gave promise of
immediate success.   At this time, the rebel army in front of
Richmond, for its protection, was estimated at 200,000 men.
According to a statement based on official reports, made by
General McClellan to the President, July 15th, the number of
men under his command, then present for duty, was 88,665.
Upwards of 38,000 were absent, with and without authority,
while the sick present, amounted to more than 16,000.   On
the return of General Halleck to Washington, he was accompanied by General Burnside, to receive his instructions about
taking up reinforcements to General McClellan.   The next
morning, he was informed that a message from the General
made it necessary to change the plan which had been decided
upon, and that he must wait for further instructions.   A few
days subsequent he was ordered to move his whole command to
Acquia Creek, and from thence to Fredericksburg, to relieve
General King, who rejoined General McDowall's corps, then
on the upper Rappahannock with General Pope.   In the then
existing state of affairs, it was deemed by General Halleck
a military necessity to concentrate the forces of the Peninsula
with those of General Pope, on some point where they could,
at the same time cover Washington, and operate against Richmond, and accordingly the order to withdraw was given.

To remove without loss, in the face of a powerful foe, the
army and its entire material, was an undertaking requiring
forecast and skill.   It was done.   It was intended to conceal
the movement from the enemy.   How successful the attempt
proved could only be conjectured.   If, with numerous spies,
prowling cavalry, and the almost free control of the opposite
side of the river, they discovered nothing in appearances to
awaken suspicion, they must have been more dull of appre-

hension than would be reasonable to suppose of a vigilant adversary. To common discernment, the massing of vessels and transports near the various landings, the activity of numerous tugs, and the nightly departure of full freighted steamers, would naturally suggest something unusual as going on, and stimulate curiosity to ascertain what it all meant. But, however that may have been, no proper caution, on the Federal side, was omitted.

To cover appearances, the gunboats were kept up towards City Point, watching the enemy, and appearing as if waiting for the coming of the formidable ram from Richmond. The balloon regularly visited the upper regions, to view—ether, and the surrounding country enveloped in smoke. The tooting of bugles and beating of drums in the camp were, if possible, more stentorian and defiant than ever, as much as to say,— "Here we are, come if you dare." The siege guns continued to show their black mouths to the enemy's pickets, from the intrenchments at the front. The usual parades, reviews and guard mountings went on, just as if nothing unusual was about to happen. Steamers coming up the river brought large companies of returning convalescents and stragglers, which aided to keep up appearances. Meantime, all the sick were sent away. The surgeons in charge of this department literally had their hands full. Dr. Bradley shipped 1,908 patients on board of the State of Maine, Louisiana, Knickerbocker and John Brooks—mostly light cases of fever and diarrhœa, the men walking on board. They had been reduced and broken down by climatic and other influences.

Dr. Dunster, the director of the transports, arrived on the Webster, Friday evening, August 15th, and immediately took up the business of getting off the sick. He sent on board of eight steamers, 3,149 persons. As fast as one steamer was loaded she was sent away. The estimated number of sick and wounded dispatched north, by different transports, was 11,000, 3,000 of whom were prisoners from City Point. These included those sent from White House before the change of base. Surplus tents were struck; regimental baggage, by the hundred tons, was shipped, and eight days' rations ordered for each of the commands—five days to go on the transports, land and water, and three to be carried by the men.

The gunboats engaged in shelling the woods along the banks of the James river opposite this place, elicited no response from the enemy. It was doubtful if there was any near enough, in force, to be hit. A balloon reconnoissance revealed no important change of the enemy's position. It was too smoky to see much. A cavalry reconnoissance as far as Sandy Point found no enemy.

The landing of express baggage was stopped, transportation being now the other way. The mail steamer, John A. Warner, hauled out into the stream to evade the rush of passengers on board before the time of departure. Mountains of knapsacks, belonging to the various departing regiments, lay piled upon the bank opposite the landings. At the upper wharf, men were busy all through Monday night, in pulling field and siege caissons and ammunition wagons on board the transports. Such, in brief, was the work of a week. The general plan of evacuation was, to send away the larger portion of the troops, with the necessary artillery and transportation wagons, by land, moving them in two or three columns towards Williamsburg, and then embark the remainder of the troops and material upon transports, under cover of the gunboats if we should be attacked. For the purposes of embarkation, no better position could be found on the James river. With the low and swampy region of Herring Creek protecting the rear and right of our encampment, no force could annoy us with impunity from the land side, for the gunboats could effectually keep such a force at bay there, and at the same time render it impossible for it to approach from the direction of our intrenchments at the front and right, after those works were abandoned.

On Thursday night, August 14th, the forces departing by

land were in motion. General Syke's division led the advance, followed by the divisions of Generals Morell and McCall. The other troops pursued the way assigned them. General Heintzelman's corps crossed at Jones's Bridge, covering, by its march, the movement of the main column. Unmolested, and with only the loss of a single baggage wagon of the immense train, which broke down and had to be left behind, the army was soon beyond danger of attack, on the northern side of the Chickahominy. The 2d Rhode Island made its encampment on York river, two miles below Yorktown, where it remained a week, occupied in destroying earthworks thrown up during the siege. On the 29th August, it embarked on board the steamer S. R. Spaulding, for Alexandria, accompanied by General Devens and staff and a part of the 36th New York regiment. They reached their destination on the 31st. General Keyes, with Peck's division and all the reserve artillery of his corps, established his head-quarters at Yorktown.

Thus closed the Peninsula campaign. It failed of the final success it deserved. Disappointment was felt alike by the country and the army. But upon that army no stain of dishonor rested. For five months it had been familiar with disease in malarious swamps, and fought superior forces with honorable bravery. It had approached within sight of the rebel capital, inspired by the expectation of celebrating our national anniversary there, and of seeing the monster, grown into huge proportions in Virgina, destroyed. It was hard to turn back from a work auspiciously begun, and to yield a prize that seemed almost within its grasp. But the sacrifice was made, and a record, of which the army had no cause to be ashamed, committed to the keeping of history.]

LETTER XX.

Embarkation — Pope's situation—Battles of Bull Run and Chantilly—Death of Generals Stevens and Kearny.

CAMP NEAR FORT CORCORAN, VA.,
September 14, 1862.

To keep my narrative unbroken, I must go back to the 17th ultimo, which day found us at Newport News. As early as the 20th, the army of the Peninsula was occupying camps in the vicinity of Fortress Monroe and Yorktown, as convenient places for embarkation to another field of service. Immediately on his arrival at Newport News, General McClellan established his head-quarters in a grove in the neighborhood of Camp Hamilton, to give direction to the further movements of his troops. On the 18th August, our battery marched to Hampton and embarked. In the Roads were several hundred vessels of all descriptions, some full-freighted and others waiting to receive their cargoes of human kind. Our destination was to reinforce General Pope, who, at that time, was pressed hard by Stonewall Jackson.

[Of his situation, he makes the following report: " From the 12th to the 18th of August, reports were constantly reaching me of large forces of the enemy reinforcing Jackson from the direction of Richmond, and by the morning of the 18th, I became satisfied that nearly the whole force of the enemy from Richmond was assembling in my front, along the south side of the Rapidan. and extending from Raccoon Ford to Liberty Mills. The cavalry expedition sent out on the 16th, in the direction of Louisa Court House, captured the Adjutant General of General Stuart, and was very near capturing that officer himself. Among the papers taken was an autograph letter of General Robert Lee to General Stuart, dated at Gordonsville, August 15th, which made manifest to me the disposition and force of the enemy and their determination to overwhelm the army under my command before it could be reinforced by any portion of the army of the Potomac. I held on to my position thus far to the front, for the purpose of affording all time possible for the arrival of the army of the Potomac at Acquia and Alexandria, and to embarrass and delay the movements of the enemy as far as practicable.

"On the 18th August, it became apparent to me that this advanced position, with the small force under my command, was no longer tenable in the face of the overwhelming forces of the enemy. I determined, accordingly, to withdraw behind the Rappahannock with all speed, and, as I had been instructed to defend, as far as practicable, the line of that river, I accordingly directed Major General Reno to send back his trains on the morning of the 18th, by way of Stevensburgh, to Kelly's or Barnett's Ford; and, as soon as the trains had gotten several hours in advance, to follow them with his whole corps, and take post behind the Rappahannock, leaving all his cavalry in the neighborhood of Raccoon Ford, to cover this movement. General Bank's corps, which had been ordered on the 12th to take position at Culpepper Court House, I directed, with its trains preceding it, to cross the Rappahannock at the point where the Orange and Alexandria Railroad crosses that river. General McDowell's train was ordered to pursue the same route; while the train of General Sigel was directed through Jefferson to cross the Rappahannock at Warrenton, Sulphur Springs. So soon as these trains had been sufficiently advanced, McDowell's corps was directed to take the route from Culpepper to Rappahannock Ford, while General Sigel, who was on the right and front, was directed to follow the movement of his trains to Sulphur Springs. These movements were executed during the day and night of the 18th, and the

12*

day of the 19th, by which time the whole army, with its trains, had safely recrossed the Rappahannock, and was posted behind that stream, with its left at Kelly's Ford, and its right about three miles above Rappahannock Station, General Sigel having been directed, immediately upon crossing at Sulphur Springs, to march down the left bank of the Rappahannock until he connected closely with General McDowell's right.

" Early on the morning of the 20th, the enemy drove in our pickets in front of Kelly's Ford and at Rappahannock Station ; but finding we had covered these fords, and that it would be impracticable to force the passage of the river without heavy loss, his advance halted, and the main body of his army was brought forward from the Rapidan. By the night of the 20th, the bulk of his forces confronted us from Kelly's Ford to a point above our extreme right. During the whole of the days of the 21st and 22d, efforts were made by the enemy, at various points, to cross the river, but they were repulsed in all cases. The artillery fire was rapid and continuous during the whole of those days, and extended along the line of the river for seven or eight miles. Finding that it was not practicable to force the passage of the river in my front, the enemy began slowly to move up the river for the purpose of turning our right. My orders required me to keep myself closely in communication with Fredericksburg, to which point the army of the Potomac was being brought from the Peninsula, with the purpose of reinforcing me from that place by the line of the Rappahannock. My force was too small to enable me to extend my right further, without so weakening it as to render it easy for the enemy to break through it at any point. I telegraphed again and again to Washington, representing this movement of the enemy toward my right, and the impossibility of my being able to extend my lines so as to resist it without abandoning my connection with Fredericksburg. I was assured, on the 21st, that if I would hold the line of the river two days longer, I should be so strongly reinforced as not only to be secure, but to be able to resume offensive operations; but on the 25th of August, the only forces that had joined me or were in the neighborhood, were two thousand five hundred men of the Pennsylvania reserves, under Brigadier General Reynolds, who had arrived at Kelly's Ford, and the division of General Kearny, four thousand five hundred strong, which had reached Warrenton Junction."]

To embark the troops gathered in the neighborhood of Fortress Munroe and Yorktown, together with their baggage trains, ordnance stores and other material, was a labor of even greater magnitude than their removal from Harrison's Landing the previous week, and taking the two events together, they are without parallel in the military history of our country. This more particularly deserves attention, because work of this sort, in connection with the active operations of an army, is seldom appreciated. Yet, upon the promptness and care with which it is executed, may depend, in no small degree, the suc- of an enterprise involving momentous consequences. The delay of a day, or misjudgment in the arrangements, may be fatal to the best laid plans. In the present instance, the embarkation was seasonably commenced and industriously pursued, until every transport had received its full complement of men, horses, and munitions of war; and great credit is due to those under whose immediate supervision the whole was effected.

On the 19th of August, battery C left Hampton Roads, and steamed away for Acquia Creek Landing, which we reached on the 20th, and debarked. From thence we marched to Barnett's Ford on the Rappahannock; thence to Kelly's Ford; and on the 27th arrived at Warrenton Junction. The next day we proceeded to Gainsville. The march was one of the most trying to men and horses that had yet been made. Owing to some delay in the supply train, rations and forage were deficient. The weather was hot, the travel hard, and the necessity for a rapid advance, urgent. But neither equine nor human nature were proof against the influence of a stinted commissariat; and when they reached the scene of action, had the rebel army, under some magicians touch, been transformed into droves of beef and sacks of grain, both men and horses would have foraged with a voracity surpassing the lean bovines of Egypt.

[For the previous nine days, General Pope's army had been kept in motion, marching and fighting, with various results. On both sides it was an adroit game. In the mean time, Hooker, Heintzelman, Kearny and Franklin had placed themselves in active relations with him. On the 22d August, Stuart made a raid upon Catlett's Station, capturing two hundred horses, and the camp equipage of General Pope and staff, including instructions, maps, and topographical charts. On the 27th, Hooker made battle with the rebels near Bristow station, and after a smart skirmish, caused them to retreat with considerable loss. Randolph's battery, and a section of a New York battery were engaged, and drove the batteries of the enemy from a superior position. The former lost two men killed and two wounded. On the 28th, General Pope reached Manassas Junction with Kearny's division and Reno's corps, shortly after Stonewall Jackson had departed. Hooker, Reno and Kearny were immediately pushed forward upon Centreville. Late in the afternoon, the latter drove the enemy's rear guard out of the town, and occupied it with his advance beyond.

On the morning of the 29th of August, General Sigel opened the first day of the second Bull Run battle, by an attack on the enemy a mile or two east of Groveton. Kearny, Hooker, Heintzelman, Reynold's, McDowell, and other generals, fought their commands. Our battery took position on the left of the line, but was not called into action. The battle was bloody, the Federal losses amounting to not less than six or eight thousand killed and wounded. The rebel loss was vastly more.

The results of this battle were not satisfactory.* On the following day came the renewal of the fight. Of this, General Pope, in his report, says: "During the whole night of the 29th and the morning of the 30th, the advance of the main army, under Lee, was arriving on the field, to reinforce Jackson, so that by twelve or one o'clock in the day, we were confronted by forces greatly superior to our own; and these forces were being every moment largely increased by fresh arrivals of the enemy from the direction of Thoroughfare Gap. Every moment of delay increased the odds against us, and I therefore advanced to the attack as rapidly as I was able to bring my forces into action.

Shortly after General Porter moved forward to the attack by the Warrenton turnpike, and the assault on the enemy was begun by Heintzelman and Reno on the right, it became apparent that the enemy was massing his troops, as fast as they arrived on the field, on his right, and was moving forward from that direction to turn our left, at which point it was plain he intended to make his main attack. I accordingly directed McDowell to recall Rickett's division immediately from our right, and post it on the left of our line. The attack of Porter was neither vigorous nor persistent, and his troops soon retired in considerable confusion. As soon as they commenced to fall back, the enemy advanced to the assault, and our whole line, from right to left, was soon furiously engaged."

On the morning of the battle, our battery marched to the field, and at 10 o'clock went into position, and opened on the enemy. At 12 M., the position was changed, and again at 3 and 4 o'clock P. M. Two men were wounded and two horses disabled. Randolph's battery was posted on the left of the

---

* The failure to obtain a decisive victory, General Pope, in his report, ascribed to the inaction of General Porter, who suffered his troops "to lie idle on their arms, within sight and sound of the battle, during the whole day." General Porter was subsequently court-martialed on specific charges, and dismissed from the service of the United States.

Leesburg road, and delivered an effective fire. He lost two
men killed and three taken prisoners. For hours the battle
raged with fury. As on the previous day, the losses on both
sides were heavy—on the Federal side, estimated at 500 killed
and 5,000 wounded. The enemy greatly outnumbered the
Union forces, but the latter held their ground till dark. General Pope claimed a victory, but dear bought. Ten field officers were killed, among them Colonel Fletcher Webster, of
the 12th Massachusetts. Of the wounded, were Generals
Duryea, Towers and Hatch. At night, the Federals fell back
on Centreville. In the battles of the 29th and 30th, Munroe's
Rhode Island battery, (D,) was warmly engaged, and suffered
severely in men and horses.

The day after the battle of Bull Run, (September 1,) a severe fight took place at Chantilly, in which the rebels were
routed by a general bayonet charge. The 2d Rhode Island
formed a part of Hooker's force in this battle, but were not
called actively into engagement. Randolph's battery was in
the action, and by its destructive fire did much to decide the
day. His only loss was one horse. The Union loss, in killed
and wounded, was estimated at one thousand, and the rebel loss
not less. Among the killed on our side, were Generals Isaac
L. Stevens and Kearny. The latter was shot by a rifle bullet,
while riding out to examine the position of the enemy, and died
almost instantly. He had, but a few moments before, been
cautioned against going farther, but thought there was no danger, and continued his way. He was an officer of large experience and chivalrous spirit, and, by deeds of valor, had won a
name that will be perpetuated on the roll of patriot heroes.
General Stevens was an excellent officer, of noble character, and gave promise of becoming a successful leader in our
army. His untimely death caused general sorrow throughout
the country.

The defeat at Bull Run, for such practically it was, and the
proximity to Washington of so large a rebel force, excited much

alarm for the safety of the capital, and, on the 2d of September,
General McClellan was put in command of its fortification and
all of the troops for its defence.* But the rebel leaders had
other objects in view, and did not press the assault. General
Lee pushed a heavy column into Maryland, threatening Baltimore, and also Pennsylvania. This movement was to be looked
after and the rebels to be driven out or captured. For this
purpose, General McClellan was invested with the command of
General Pope's troops, including his own army of the Potomac,
which he speedily reorganized and set in motion.]

On the 31st of August, our battery marched to Fairfax
Court House, and thence to Alexandria, where we arrived
September 3d. We encamped opposite Fort Lyon, whose
frowning brow had not softened its stern expression since we
last gazed upon it, some five months ago. The next day we
marched to Miner's Hill, where we took possession of our old
camp ground. Six months had made but few changes in the
features of the spot, or of its surroundings. The old fields, the
scenes of many thorough drills, the adjacent hills from whose
summit skillful gunnery was occasionally displayed, the prostrate forest on the west, opening uninterrupted prospects of
Falls Church, (recently used for hospital purposes,) and Lewinsville, and the distant Blue Ridge, lifting its head to the skies
" in the wild pomp of mountain majesty," remained essentially
as they appeared when we first pitched our tents in Secessia ;
and though memory recalled amusing episodes in the camp life
spent there, roll call cast a shadow upon mirthful thought, by
reminding us that some who marched with us from Camp Owen
last spring, were folded in the leaden arms of death, far from

---

* It was bold and characteristic of Jackson to make this dash for
Washington, but he was not quite quick enough to accomplish his purpose. Had the first battle been fought a day or two earlier, there is no
telling what mischief might have speedily followed. As it was, he was
checked in his career, and the capital freed from his grasp.

the homes they loved, noble sacrifices to their country's cause. The lesson will not be void.

Two days sufficed for indulging in local reminiscences. The battery was held in readiness for any service. On the 6th, at 10½ o'clock P. M., we once more bade farewell to our old military homestead, and marched back to Alexandria, where we arrived at daylight. A Sabbath sun broke upon the various encampments as brightly as though the blast of war had not been heard, or the black cloud of rebellion had not obscured a southern sky. But the calmness of the day was followed by the excitement of night. Report came that the rebels were moving in force to make a raid on Alexandria, and a little past midnight, the battery was hitched up and on the advance to meet the foe. No enemy was discovered, and at early dawn we returned to camp with excellent appetites for " peas on a trencher." Subsequently, we moved half a mile to the front, near Gen. Morell's head-quarters, and encamped within the line of breastworks, about forty rods from Fairfax Seminary, an Episcopal theological institution, occupied as a hospital for the sick and wounded of our army. From the cupola of this handsome building, a splendid prospect of the surrounding country is obtained. On the 10th, we broke camp at 7 o'clock, proceeded to Fort Corcoran, opposite Georgetown, and encamped on the ground we occupied when we crossed into Virginia last October.

The daily mails are looked for with eager interest. Nothing contributes so much to keep up the spirits of the men as the privilege of frequent correspondence with cherished friends at home. Letters from distant ones, filled with local gossip and words of cheer, as loving mothers and sisters only know how to fill them, are " like glow-worms amid buds of flowers," casting a pleasant light upon the beautiful treasures of memory, and inspiring courage that nerves the arm for deadly strife.

LETTER XXI.

March to Antietam — The Battle.

CAMP BEYOND SHARPSBURG, MD,
September 20, 1862.

My last, dated at Fort Corcoran, left us at the close of a mounted inspection, in momentary expectation of a forward movement. The experienced eye of Col. Webb relieved the battery of two pieces and caissons worn out in the severe service of the peninsula, and some twenty horses unfit for present use. On the morning of the 12th inst., the line of march was formed, and bidding adieu to Camp Randolph of last October, and with a farewell recognition of Fort Corcoran, the battery crossed the Potomac. Passing through Georgetown and Washington, we were soon on the road leading to Leesboro, at which place we arrived about 6 o'clock P. M., and encamped for the night. The next morning we proceeded through Rockville to Clarksburg, where we made our second encampment. Leaving Clarksburg at 5 o'clock A. M., on the 14th, our march was continued through Harrisville and Urbana, and the battery went into camp just in the outskirts of Frederick city. Heavy firing was heard all day, particularly in the afternoon, in the direction of Harper's Ferry, stirring the boys' blood for the strife, as the trumpet blast causes the war-horse to "arch his high neck and paw the ground with restless feet." The night was, however, passed quietly, and the next day, (Monday,) provided with three days' rations of hard bread and bacon, the march was resumed in the direction of Middletown, in the neighborhood of which we arrived at dusk. Before reaching our camp, we were passed by a squad of 180 rebel prisoners. Departing from this place, we continued our course through Boonesboro, with Martindale's brigade in our advance and

13

Berdan's Sharpshooters in our rear, halted for a short time, in Keedysville, and, late in the afternoon, reached the summit of a range of hills where our infantry and artillery were drawn up in battle array, and from which we could distinctly see the rebel lines. Between Bolivar and Boonesboro, I counted by the roadside, ten bodies of rebels, killed in last Sunday's fight, and in the woods just beyond Bolivar, were several hundred dead rebels, unburied, (killed on the same day,) in an advanced stage of decomposition, so as to render the atmosphere exceedingly offensive. They may yet receive the rites of sepulture, though the chances are that some of them will supply feasts for the fowls of the air. Such is one of the possibilities of war. Well would it be could the plotters and supporters of this infamous rebellion be made the grave diggers of every battle field. With thousands of eyes unsealed in death, glaring upon them, and the dread thought of an untried eternity quickening the moral sense, they could see nothing but frightful shadows, clouds and darkness gathering as a winding sheet round the criminal disloyalty, a presage of their own deserts.

On our march to this place, we passed through a number of pleasant villages, indicating, in their appearance, a higher refinement than we have been accustomed to witness in Virginia. The country is diversified with hills and valleys, fertile fields and dense woods, imparting to the scenery a highly picturesque character. The people along the route appeared loyal, and hailed the presence of the Federal army with marked evidences of satisfaction. The ovations to Generals McClellan and Burnside, on entering Frederick city, were inspired with intense enthusiasm, such as might be expected from a rescued people towards their deliverers. If any of the throng sympathized with Jackson in his invasion of Maryland, they were prudent enough to conceal their predilections.

On the 17th, the battle of Antietam took place, when the hosts of McClellan and Lee measured strength. The fights of previous days were only preliminaries to the great struggle between constitutional law and the inviolability of the National Compact on the one side, and of treason on the other.

[To form an adequate idea of this great battle, it is needful to have some knowledge of the topography of the country, and of the relative positions of each army. In the absence of a map of the field, showing the line of battle, the following diagram, with accompanying explanation, prepared by Mr. Coffin, the accomplished army correspondent of the Boston Journal, is given. Mr. Coffin, widely known as " Carlton," was on the ground, and witnessed much of what he describes.

" The enemy selected the ground, choosing a line where the two armies would be face to face, with but little opportunity for flank movements ; a line about four miles long—a gateway four miles wide, where he put up his batteries. Harper's Ferry was in his possession, also Shepardstown ; Williamsport in ours, so that the enemy could not flank us in that direction, neither escape them if defeated. McClellan could not flank Lee, or get in his rear. Neither could Lee outflank McClellan. Neither was there an opportunity for the cutting round policy pursued against Pope. It must be, then, a square fight. Let it be kept in mind that the nature of the ground was such that there were necessarily wide gaps between some of the corps. Gen. Hooker was assigned the extreme right near Poffenburgh's house. Next Gen. Mansfield, commanding Bank's army corps, next Sumner, next Franklin, next Richardson. All of these were west of the river, extending from the Sharpsburg and Booresboro turnpike bridge to the Potomac. East of the Antietam was Porter and Burnside, the latter at the lower stone bridge. Franklin did not arrive on the ground till Wednesday forenoon. He came up Pleasant valley, crossed the upper bridge, turned in column to the left, moved over the fields and took his position partly between Richardson and Sumner, his right overlapping Sumner's left. Let me endeavor to make the plan by a few lines and figures.

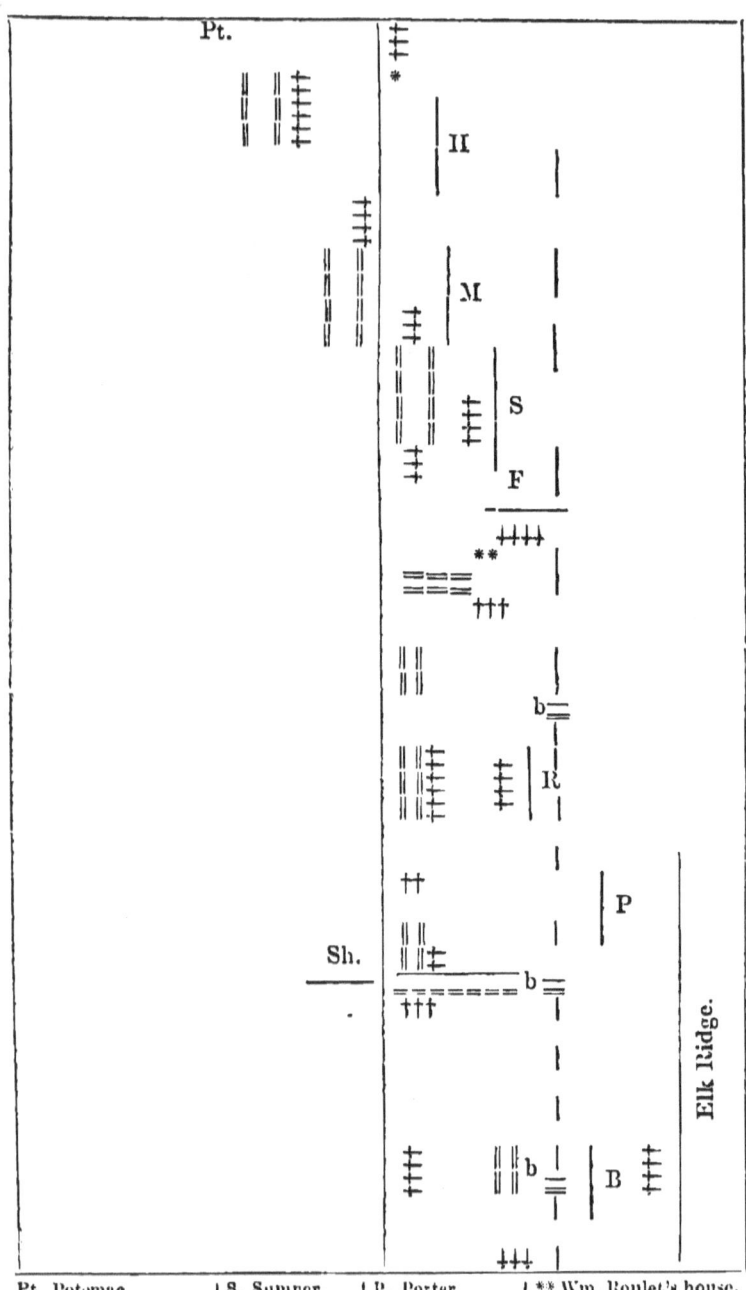

Pt. Potomac.
*   Poffenburg house.
H. Hooker.
M. Mansfield.

S. Sumner.
F. Franklin.
=   Rebels.
R. Richardson.

P. Porter
B. Burnside.
b. Bridges
Sh. Sharpsburg.

** Wm. Roulet's house.
— Union.

"The straight line in the centre of the diagram is the Sharpsburg and Hagerstown pike; the dotted line, the Antietam river.

"Of course, this is but approximately accurate,—as nearly accurate as can be made by straight lines, which must be used in print. I have shown Franklin at right angles with Sumner, and the rebels also at right angles, but an angle of forty-five degrees would more nearly represent it. You are to imagine an elevation in front of Sumner's left, crowned by the grove before mentioned. It was high land, owned by William Roulet. It was a pivot on which the varying fortunes of the day turned and trembled like the mariner's compass in a tornado. The right and the left wavered, swung backward and forward, but the centre was stationary. Mr. Roulet's house is in a ravine, three-fourths of a mile northeast of Sharpsburg. A road runs up the ravine toward the turnpike, northwest; beyond it, is a large cornfield. Between Franklin and Richardson, and between the rebels in front of Richardson, three-fourths of a mile, is an unobstructed sweep of ground. The distance between Sumner and the rebels in front of him is not more than a third of a mile. Sumner is in a western border of a grove, the rebels in an eastern—the rebels on ground fifty to seventy-five feet highest. In front of Mansfield is a grove. In front of Hooker, the mown land, the cornfield, and the wood-crowned ridge beyond, already mentioned, occupied by the rebels. The batteries in front of Richardson are fifty feet above him, on the highest land in the vicinity, and were turned, at times, upon Sumner, Franklin, Richardson, Porter, and Burnside. The rebel batteries at Sharpsburg played upon Richardson, Porter and Burnside. Burnside also had a heavy rebel battery in front and on his flank.

"It will be seen that the lines were near together in the centre, opposite Sumner, but more widely separated on the flanks. The centre was the rebel stronghold. Hooker took the extreme right, having Doubleday's Rickett's and Meade's

13*

divisions. He did not know that the enemy were in full force. Jackson, when last heard from, was at Harper's Ferry, with only Longstreet's, A. P. Hill's and Ewell's corps, in the vicinity of Sharpsburg. I do not think our generals comprehended that Lee had chosen the locality for a great battle till the batteries began to play on Tuesday afternoon."]

To describe, in detail, all the movements of the day, would weary rather than edify. In the centre, on the right wing and on the left, the contest fiercely raged. Sumner, Hooker, Mansfield, Doubleday, Sedgwick, Meade, Richardson, Howard, French, Pleasanton, Rickett, Slocum, and other generals, spared no energy and shunned no exposure. The hundreds of subordinate officers, and the thousands of privates comprising the army, whose services will be honored when their names cease to be mentioned, were inspired by the occasion to deeds of martial daring. The Rhode Island batteries, A, D and G, were in the thickest of the fight. The 4th Rhode Island regiment stood up bravely in the face of a murderous fire, and recorded ninety-three of its number killed and wounded, among the latter, Colonel William H. P. Steere. General Isaac P. Rodman, an honored son of the State, was smitten down by a shot that proved fatal, as was his Aide, Lieutenant Ives.* To

---

* Of General Rodman, a more particular notice is given in the appendix. Lieut. Robert Hale Ives died at Hagerstown, Md., September 27th, of the wound received at Antietam. His age was 25 years, 5 months and 24 days. He was the only son of Robert Hale and Harriet Bowen (Amory) Ives, of Providence. After graduating at Brown University and spending some time in Europe, he entered into commercial pursuits in his native city. In August, 1862, he was commissioned as Lieutenant by the Governor of Rhode Island, and attached to the staff of Brigadier General Rodman, as a Volunteer Aide, he modestly preferring to serve at his own charge. He soon afterwards joined his General, who had then just been assigned to the command of a division in the corps of General Burnside in the army of the Potomac. The army was already moving into Maryland, to repel the invasion of the rebels, and Lieutenant Ives found himself at once engaged in the most arduous service. He speedily displayed

the commander-in-chief, who visited every part of the field in person, it was an anxious day; but not more so than to the gallant commander on the left wing, to whom was assigned the hard duty of forcing the bridge across the Antietam, and in the face of a deadly artillery fire, with insufficient numbers, to take and hold a position on the heights beyond. The quick eye of the rebel chief saw the importance of regaining that position, and massed a heavy force to fall upon his exhausted divisions, and sweep them into the stream they had passed. What consequences then hung upon the hour! What interests imperilled! Of what value a fresh brigade, at that critical moment, to renew the strength then waning. But it did not come.

When Marshal Ney, at the battle of Waterloo, his command exhausted, and weakened by loss, sent to Napoleon for a reinforcement of infantry, the Emperor, who had none to spare, exclaimed, " Infantry! where does he expect me to take them? Does he expect me to make them?"—and the Marshal maintained his fight without them. The parallel of this military incident was found at Antietam. Burnside had fought his command with the vigor of a Ney. His men had faced the foe with veteran coolness. Each volley of the rebels thinned his ranks while their own were augmented by fresh supports.

---

the qualities requisite for an efficient staff officer. He was alive to responsibility, exact and persistent in the discharge of duty, cool in danger and courteous in manner, and he speedily won the confidence and esteem of those with whom he served. On the fatal 17th, Lieutenant Ives was, throughout the day, near the person of his General, save when sent to execute orders at a distance. At about four o'clock in the afternoon, when the battle was nearly ended, General Rodman, at the head of one of his brigades, charged upon a battery of the enemy which had given special annoyance to our troops. The battery was taken, but both the General and his Aide fell, mortally wounded, within a few feet of the guns. He survived the battle ten days, bearing his sufferings with great fortitude, and yielding up his life in the spirit of a Christian believer, in humble submission to his Heavenly Father's will.

Pressed by superior numbers, nerved to the attack by the energy of desperation, and with clouded prospects, he sent to McClellan for aid. " Give me infantry," was his request ; but the answer came back, that not a regiment was available. "Tell General Burnside," was added, "that this is the battle of the war. He must hold his ground till dark, if possible. All I can give him is a battery of artillery. If he cannot hold his ground, then fall back and hold the bridge at all hazards. If the bridge is lost, all is lost." He obeyed. He fell back to his first position after crossing. A night and a day he held it, at a terrible cost. The rebel fire was deadly, and by hundreds his men bit the dust. But there was no wavering. Volley answered volley ; and when the fiery tempest hushed, the enemy had been driven back, the bridge secured, and the left wing of the army saved. History will record the deed as one of the most brilliant achievements of the war.*

It was the fortune of battery C to be in the reserve, on the field, ready for service, but not called into action. Improving an opportunity, I went to the top of a high hill, and witnessed a portion of the engagement. The battle array, with banners flying, bayonets gleaming, and countless hosts moving in every direction, was a magnificent spectacle, such as I never expect to behold again ; while the steady roar of musketry and the loud pealing of four hundred cannon spoke in unmistakable language of the determined spirit in which assaults were made and resisted. It was a battle of Titans—the ablest generals of both sides, leading the flower of the Federal and rebel armies to

---

* On the 14th of September, the battle of South Mountain was fought under the direction of General Burnside, who held the centre, with the troops of Hooker on the right, and of Franklin on the left. The field was strongly contested by the rebels, led by Generals Longstreet, D. H. and A. P. Hill, Garland and Stuart. They were defeated, with a loss in killed, wounded and prisoners, of 4,000 men. General Garland was killed. On the Federal side, the loss was 443 killed, 1,806 wounded, and 76 missing— total, 2,325. Among the killed, was the brave General Jesse L. Reno, an able officer, and greatly endeared to his men.

almost hand to hand encounter. Before the setting of the sun
the fate of the nation was to be decided. And when I thought
of this, you will not wonder that I, at times, held my breath to
catch, if possible, the first shout that should proclaim a victory
for freedom, and announce to the anxious millions of our land
that we had still a constitutional government. The cry came,
an I the country heard it. Henceforth Antietam will be a syn-
onym for indomitable courage and triumph.

But however magnificent a battle appears to a spectator,
posted at a safe distance, when over, an inspection of the field
dissipates the illusion, and the shocking details of carnage speak
m re emphatically, than words can express, of its sanguinary
fruits. Let us make the rounds. Here are the mangled remains of a noble fellow who held a front rank in the charge.
A cannon ball carried away the upper part of his head. He
could never have known what hurt him. There lies one
pierced by a bullet through the heart. He fell forward, holding still his musket in the strong grasp of death. These heaps
of dead bodies tell of the fatal effects of the Federal artillery,
as it poured upon an advancing column of rebels an enfilading
fire. This ditch, used as a rifle pit, strown with men sunk in
sleep that knows no waking, shows with what certain aim the
enemy sent leaden death among them. Yonder windrow of
the dead has been hastily collected to fill the long trench which
will soon be thrown open for their reception. Time presses,
and no formal rites of sepulture will be observed here. An
hour hence, course upon course will rest in silence beneath the
sod, without stone or tablet to tell their names; and long before
the field can be searched by anxious friends or loving kindred
from home, festering mortality will have blended in one indis-
tinguishable mass.

Near that small, solitary house, shaded by a neighboring
wood, stands a caisson, and around it the bodies of six confederate artillerymen, as they fell beneath a deadly Federal fire.
One horse, shot in the traces, mingles his blood with theirs to

enrich the soil. The group is not easily forgotten. Close by yonder fence, a Louisiana regiment was severely pressed. These are of its men, as they fell. That one, with raised arm and head thrown back, must have died hard. But his pains are over. Here lies a manly form. A deadly missile shattered his thigh, and severed the great artery. He must have soon sunk to rest from loss of blood, and his fixed expression indicates the determined heart that so recently beat within his bosom. The poor fellow under this tree, mutilated and weltering in gore, dragged himself out of the line of the enemy's fire, and the equally fatal trample of cavalry, as they charged across the field, hoping, perhaps, to be taken up and carried to the rear. He still breathes, but his eyes are glazed, and his spirit will soon be where the cannon's roar is never heard, " and gory sabres rise and fall" no more. This barn, now a temporary hospital, is crowded with victims of the day. Around, lying upon the ground, waiting to receive the surgeon's attention, are numerous wounded, imperfectly screened from night chills, rain or autumn sun. Their shelter is of the rudest kind. By and by, those who survive will fare better. But let no sensitive, imaginative one, look upon the sight, lest some "horrid apparition, tall and ghostly, that walks at dead of night," should ever after haunt the sleeping hours. Thus the day closes, and night shuts the scene, leaving ten thousand men, helpless and bathed in blood, to watch the return of light, for removal and the dressing of their wounds. Who can imagine the sufferings of that night, and the work for surgeons on the morrow!

[By official reports, the Federal loss in this battle was 2,010 killed, 9,416 wounded, and 1,043 missing—total, 12,469. The rebel loss was upwards of 20,000. 15,000 small arms were collected on the field. On the Federal side, beside General Rodman, already mentioned, General Mansfield was killed, and Generals Hooker, Sedgwick, Dana, Richardson, Hartsuff, Duryea, Weber and Meagher, wounded. Of the rebels, Generals Branch, Starke, Anderson, Whiting and Colquitt, were killed; and Generals Wright, Ripley, Hayes, Lawton, Ransome and Armistead, wounded. From the time the enemy was first encountered in Maryland until driven back into Virginia, the Federals captured 13 guns, 7 caissons, 9 limbers, 2 field forges, 39 colors and one signal flag, with no loss of gun or flag on their side. The expulsion of the rebel army from Maryland was officially recognized by the thanks of the governor, "for the distinguished courage, skill and gallantry with which that achievement was accomplished."

On the morning after the battle, General Lee sent in a flag of truce, asking a suspension of hostilities for the purpose of burying the dead, which was granted until 4 o'clock P. M. On the part of the rebel commander, this was strategy. The living occupied more of his thoughts than the thousands of his killed that lay scattered over the field. He was in close quarters. How to escape, was a prime consideration, and the rites of sepulture, for his slain, suggested the method. Under cover of an armistice, ostensibly for the performance of this sacred duty, arrangements were made for retreat. Late in the day, a heavy rain set in, which favored the design. All night, the rebels were expeditiously moving, and by break of day next morning, the entire army, except the rear guard, were once more in Virginia. As soon as discovery of the retreat was made, troops were put in pursuit, but not in season to seriously molest the retiring foe. How many of his dead Lee caused to be buried, or how many of his wounded he carried off, is unknown; but twenty-five hundred of the former were left on the field, to be interred by Federal details, and of the latter, a large number were abandoned to Federal humanity. These were mostly wounded in the lower limbs.]

LETTER XXII.

Lee's disappointment—Loss of Harper's Ferry—Temporary hospitals
—New guns for Battery C—Bolivar, Loudon and Maryland Heights
and Harper's Ferry retaken—A better organized Ambulance Corps
needed—Statements of Dr. Bowditch.

CAMP BEYOND SHARPSBURG,
September 27, 1862.

The invasion of Maryland was a bold conception, and had it
succeeded, would have put us *hors du combat* for the present,
at least. That General Lee was encouraged to make it, upon
representation that an extensive uprising of the people would
follow his appearing, is not improbable. In Baltimore, Frederick, and in other parts of the State, there were men of high
social and political positions, who sympathized with rebellion,
and who would have rejoiced to witness its complete triumph.
They represented that it was only by the presence of Federal
force that the people were kept down, and that they were panting to be delivered from Federal rule. Under these considerations, the rebel chief, on arriving near Frederick, issued a
proclamation " to the people of Maryland," in which they were
reminded of " the wrongs and outrages " that had been inflicted
upon them, and declared his belief that they possessed " a spirit
too lofty to submit to such a government " as ours. " The
people of the South," he said, " have long wished to aid you in
throwing off this foreign yoke, to enable you again to enjoy
the inalienable rights of freemen, and restore the independence
and the sovereignty of your State. In obedience to this wish,
our army has come among you, and is prepared to assist you
with the power of its arms, in regaining the rights of which
you have been so unjustly despoiled. This, citizens of Maryland, is our mission so far as you are concerned."

If General Lee relied on the disloyalty of the controlling

influence of the State, he must have been sorely disappointed. The masses did not respond to his call. They did not appreciate the benevolence of his mission. The heart of Maryland was loyal, and this experiment of winning it over to Secession proved a costly failure.

A heavy drawback upon the triumph of Antietam, is the surrender of Harper's Ferry, on the 15th instant, by which more than 11,000 Union troops, with scarcely any resistance, were taken from our strength, a gate opened for the escape of the rebel army into Virginia, and a temporary paralysis inflicted upon the coöperative movements of Heintzelman and Sigel from near Washington.* Viewed from any point, it was a disgraceful affair, and involved consequences that should visit the responsible parties, if living, with merited severity. When the tidings first reached the army here, they were received as incredible, so confident were we that the place could be held against any force that could be brought against it, at least till reinforcements could be thrown forward. Never was the spirit of old John Brown so needed there as on that occasion. A tithe of the determination manifested by him when his soul commenced "marching on," would have prevented the shameful catastrophe, Lee and Jackson, with their army, would have been cooped, and rebellion sent to the receptacle for things lost on earth. As it is, we must possess our souls in patience—a mighty hard task—repair damages, and finish up the work at a later day elsewhere.

Going over to Frederick on business for the battery, a few

---

* By this disaster, 73 pieces of artillery, 11,000 stand of arms, 1,800 horses, and a vast amount of military stores, fell into the hands of the rebels, and more than 30,000 of their men left free to coöperate with Lee's army, from which they had been detached. The night before the surrender, the Federal cavalry departed, and reached McClellan's lines in safety, capturing a rebel ammunition train on the way. Soon after the terms of surrender had been agreed upon, Colonel Miles was killed by the explosion of a shell.

14

days since, I found that place one vast hospital. Churches, hotels, seminaries of learning, private dwellings, and a large barrack, used by Gen. Banks, last winter, twenty buildings in all, were occupied by upwards of 4,000 sick and wounded. On my return, the road was filled with ambulances, employed to transport the wounded from various places to that city. Yet, with the means at command, their removal has not been sufficiently rapid to secure to all the early attention they needed; and such will necessarily be the case after any great battle hereafter, until more ample arrangements in the ambulance department shall be made. Many of our wounded are in temporary hospitals at Middletown, Keedysville, Boonsboro', and in this vicinity. Not far from us are a considerable number of wounded rebels, left behind in charge of their own attendants and surgeons. Some of the men have lost an arm; others, a leg; and others have been variously wounded by Minie balls. One man, I saw, who had lost both legs. This assemblage of mutilated human beings was a sorry sight, yet the men appeared cheerful, and certainly devoted to rebellion. I conversed with several of them from Georgia, North Carolina, Virginia and Louisiana, and they all expressed their belief that the south would never be subdued, and rather boastfully added, that, with a navy like ours, they would have whipped us long ago. They bore their reverses with apparent philosophic indifference, yet were not insensible to common civilities. When I offered one of them a drink of water, he said our men had more sympathy for them than their own ; and then laughed and joked as though nothing was the matter. But all this may have been a counterfeited glee, covering a sad and disappointed spirit. From a prisoner belonging to a Louisiana regiment, I received, as a souvenir, a secesh button. The emblem, (the pelican and her brood,) aptly illustrates the condition into which rebellion has brought the seceded States—feeding on their own vitality. In return for his civility, I presented him a Rhode Island Union button, as a reminder of the folly into which he had fallen, and as suggestive of the line of duty when he should be exchanged.

General Porter's corps, which, in the battle of the 17th, formed the reserve, has been assigned to the front, and holds position about two miles from the river. Last week, Lieut. Buckley came up from Washington, with the new pieces, caissons, and several horses, to supply the places of those condemned by Col. Webb when we moved to join the army at Antietam, putting the battery in good working order. Last Saturday, (20th,) it was brought into position on the banks of the Potomac, and Gen. Martindale's brigade crossed the river to feel the position of the enemy. He was suddenly pounced upon by a heavy column of rebel infantry, and forced to retire. Eight or ten batteries opened upon the advancing foe, to protect the brigade as it fell back. But, with more spirit than prudence, they came rushing on, and were cut down fearfully by our artillery. In this affair, battery C expended about five hundred rounds of case shot and shell. Capt. Waterman, while on the top of a hill near by, received a shot through a leg of his pantaloons, but, providentially, was not injured. Early the same forenoon, Griffin's brigade captured three pieces of artillery, one a Parrott gun, said to be the same lost by him at the battle of Bull Run last year. On the 21st, our battery fired at intervals all day, with what effect is unknown, the rebels keeping wide as possible of our range. An occasional occupation of our own and the rebel sharpshooters has been to pop at each other across the river, an amusement that tyros in war would scarcely crave, but which those inured to peril are ready to seek.

Sharpsburg, in advance of which we now are, was, not long since, a neat village of 1,500 inhabitants, but, at present, wears a dirty, dilapidated aspect. Scarcely a house or barn has escaped the effects of shells and musketry. Here a dwelling has been pierced by a 12-pounder Parrott; there a chimney-top unceremoniously knocked into the street; and yonder a stable, consumed with its equine victims—a destruction anticipating the waste of all-devouring years. Such is war. Loudon Heights, Bolivar Heights, Maryland Heights and Harper's Ferry are again in our possession.* The bridge destroyed is fast rebuilding. A pontoon bridge across the Potomac is in rapid process of construction, and divers other things are in contemplation. We hear of masked batteries on the other side of the river, of rebels concentrating at Winchester and Martinsburg, and hanging round favorable points below us, watching opportunities to dash into Maryland again, and, by some brilliant operations, recover the reputation lost upon her soil. All this may or may not be true. In due time we shall know. Both in Pope's campaign and in the present, the battery horses have suffered severely from overwork and the want of sufficient food. After the battle of Manassas, three dropped dead from exhaustion, having been without grain for five days. From the 30th August to 15th September, fifteen died, or were abandoned dying on the road, from the causes here stated.

In a preceding letter, the importance of an ample ambulance corps, trained to the service of removing the wounded from the field during a battle, was incidentally mentioned. Observation since has confirmed the view then briefly stated. In all the principal battles fought since the rebellion begun, the wounded have been largely disproportionate to the killed. Thus far in the war, it has appeared to be the policy of the rebels in battle to wound quite as much as to kill. Beauregard, at the first, and other rebel generals after him, instructed their men to fire low, as every severely wounded man would require the services of two other men to remove him from the front, thus weakening, in that proportion, the fighting power of the opposing forces. A body of men, employed exclusively for this purpose, would

---

* The rebels evacuated Harper's Ferry, September 20th. While in their hands, they destroyed the railroad and pontoon bridges across the Potomac, together with much other property. Soon after, General Sumner occupied Bolivar Heights, General Williams, the Maryland Heights, and General Geary, Loudon Heights.

prevent any such result, besides obviating the confusion incident
to considerable numbers breaking ranks. A properly organized ambulance body attached to each regiment, brigade or
division, would insure the security of the wounded from what
is so much dreaded, and frequently happens in the haste and
confusion of falling back,—being left on the field of battle, to
fall into the hands of the rebels. Men shrink from this, who
would bravely meet death at the cannon's mouth.

Not only should the supply of ambulances be sufficient for
every conceivable exigency, but they should be constructed
with special reference to the comfort of the wounded—with
springs so arranged as to prevent, as far as possible, all painful
jar. And above all, the drivers should be men of humanity.
For the want of a system, on a scale such as here suggested,
an untold amount of needless suffering has been caused.

[The character of that suffering, the following statements of
Dr. Henry I. Bowditch, an eye witness, made before the Boston Society for Medical Improvement, will perhaps best illus-
trate.

" As an illustration of, and in addition to what has been already published by others, as well as by myself, I beg leave
to state that Lieut. Bowditch, having been mortally wounded,
in the first charge made after leaving Kelly's Ford, lay helpless
on the ground, for some time, by the side of his dead horse.
Two surgeons saw him, but they evidently had no means for
carrying off the wounded officer, and it is believed *no one connected with an Ambulance Corps ever approached him there.**

" A stranger horseman,—probably from the Rhode Island
forces,—finally assisted him to get into a saddle; and he rode

---

* " Three days after the fight, I heard several staff officers,—one of
whom, certainly, was a surgeon,—talk, not as if they approved of the fact,
but as if it were a matter of course,—saying that they ' thought' a flag of
truce ought to be sent over the river, to see to our wounded, many of
whom were then, as they believed, still lying on the field! "

14*

off, leaning over the neck of the animal,—a terrible mode of proceeding, considering his severe wound in the abdomen. All this happened *when he was in the rear of our victorious army,* or, in other words, at just the place and time at which a thorough Ambulance Corps should have been busily at work, *seeking out,* and relieving, with every means *a great government should have had at its disposal,* the wretched and, perhaps, dying sufferers.

"After Lieut. Bowditch arrived at the ambulance carriage, there was no water to be found in the casks, connected with it, although, by law, there should have been. The driver was wholly ignorant of the names of those whom he was carrying. He actually, and in answer to a direct question from Colonel Curtis, denied that Lieut. Bowditch was one of them. He did not get any water for the Lieutenant and his still more suffering comrade, although both *longed and asked for it!* A *wretched and dying Sergeant begged much for it, and in vain!* Had it not been for the kindness of Col. Curtis. who, after *much difficulty,* found out where my son was, no water would probably have been procured for either of the parched sufferers. As it was, it arrived at last, *too late* for the Sergeant, who was so much exhausted as to be unable to avail himself of the cup, finally proffered him by his wounded comrade."[*]

Again :

"On the evening of Friday, September 5th, at the request of the surgeon-general, I joined an ambulance train that was just starting to go to the relief of our starving and wounded men near Centreville. There was a train of fifty carriages. I subsequently learned that three of the drivers, afraid of entering the enemy's lines, escaped with their ambulance wagons before we reached Long Bridge. This was easily accomplished, as there was no escort; and, as it subsequently appeared, no power

---

[*] "A brief plea for an Ambulance System, for the Army of the United States."

to prevent such an event. It is true that an army-surgeon accompanied and gave general directions to the train, but he was in the first wagon, and could not know what was doing towards the end of the long train. I soon perceived that the drivers were men of the lowest character, evidently taken from the vilest purlieus of Washington, merely as common drivers, and for no other qualification. Their oaths were flaunted forth without the least regard to the presence of superiors, and with a profusion that was really remarkable, even in the vicinity of Washington. The driver of my ambulance became sleepy as the night wore on, and as his zigzag course over a Virginia road was rather perilous, and as he informed me that he had been overturned a few weeks previously, I thought it more prudent to drive myself, rather than to allow him to do so. While the moon was up, this was comparatively easy. He accordingly slept inside of the carriage until 3 or 4 A. M.; he then reluctantly again took the reins, because I was unwilling, owing to the darkness, to drive further. His whole deportment, during the night, showed a disregard for everything save his own comfort.

"About mid-day we arrived, and found our men in a most piteous condition, lying everywhere, inside and outside of every building connected with a small farm-house. The negro-quarters was a palace,—the manure-heap was a soft bed. The fairest place was under a wide-spreading tree. I found the drivers did not feel it to be their duty to help the sufferers, but sulked, or swore, or laughed, as it pleased each. On the following morning, it is true, I did persuade my own driver to bring to me water, as I was dressing the wounds of the soldiers; but it was difficult even to get that, and he aided me because I asked him to do so, and not because he had any heart in the work.

"On Saturday, P. M., we started for Washington,—all the sick having been arranged in different ambulances, under charge of various surgeons. That night I shall never forget.

I had taken one of those most severely wounded under my own special charge. The ball had passed into his chest, and caused intense difficulty of breathing. He was a German, and one of the most uncomplaining of sufferers ; and his broken words of gratitude for the slightest token of kindness, were most touching. None but a brute could have failed to be kind tô him. He could lie only on one side, and consequently his head was placed directly behind my driver. During the first part of the way, I did not think that the driver paid the least attention to the road with reference to the comfort of the patient. In early night, his tongue ran glibly on in loud, indifferent talk, or the vilest profanity,—thus preventing all sleep. As the night progressed, I was distressed to find that the whiskey, with which he probably had supplied himself, was having its usual soporific effect, and he fell back upon the panting form of my patient. I lifted him up, and told him I could not allow such treatment of the sick man. The only response I got was a muttered oath of ' men complaining,' &c. But it was all in vain. Again and again did he fall back, until at last I took the reins, and drove most of the night with one hand, while with the other I supported this snoring drunkard!' "

With deep feeling, naturally intensified by what he had seen, and the knowledge of facts gained by inquiry, Dr. Bowditch says : " The people are willing their sons should dedicate their young, heroic lives to this Holy War, this blossoming-out of centuries. We have, even in our bereavement at their death, a certain triumphant joy, if they, as the instruments of High Heaven, be accounted worthy to be martyrs in so sacred a cause. But we have a right to demand that they shall not be *needlessly tortured*, or thrown aside, like their own wounded steeds, to die perhaps by the wayside, for want of proper care."]

It may be that the war has attained proportions unthought of at its commencement, and for which reason the provision in this department has been less ample than it otherwise would have been. At all events, in every great battle thus far, the deficiency has been painfully apparent. But this should no longer be. Except in extraordinary cases, for which it may be impossible to provide, the wounded should all be brought off, and spared the anguish of lying uncared for on the field, one, two, and even three days, before receiving surgical attention. The discussion might be largely amplified, and its importance illustrated by facts of the current year; but it may be enough to say that the humanity for which our government has been distinguished demands that something of this sort should be done. In the varied service of the army, a body of men such as indicated could be advantageously employed, when not on the field, in duties for which men are often detailed from the ranks.*

LETTER XXIII.

Reflections—Artillery practice—President's visit—Harper's Ferry—
Tokens from home—Stuart's raid—Sharpsburg—Army in motion.

CAMP NEAR SHARPSBURG, VA.,}
October 14, 1862. }

A year since, the army of the Potomac, stretching some twenty miles, from Fort Lyon, on the left, to beyond Langley's, on the right, was passing through a series of brigade and divi-

---

* Since the date of this letter, attention has been widely drawn to this subject. In the ambulance department, improvements have taken place, but leaving a wide margin for the perfection shown in the French system, and which the cry of the wounded from every battle-field demands. In the National House of Representatives, last winter, a bill providing for organizing an Ambulance Corps was passed. It reached the Senate, and there rested. The subject is doubtless environed with difficulties, but they are not insurmountable.

sion reviews, which culminated in a grand display of seventy-
five thousand troops at Bailey's Cross Roads. It is safe to say,
that such a body of men, with such *physique* and *morale*, had
never before been seen in warlike array, in this or any other
country. They were the cream of the patriotism of the day,
and affected less by mercenary considerations than is commonly
the lot of human nature. They were there to fight, not for sectional ends, but for the perpetuity of a government and consti
tution under which a feeble people had risen to a foremost rank
among nations. Rebellion was then strong—stronger than even
the most credulous imagined. Its backbone had not, as many
supposed, been broken. It had powerful friends in the capital
of the country, and, by some mysterious process, government
plans were gained possession of and made known to the rebel
leaders almost as early as they were communicated to our own
commanders. The magnitude of the work to be done and the
embarrassments that environed it, were not then comprehended
as they are now, and for this reason, possibly, public expectation became unduly large. But be this as it may, the men of
the army were inspired by a noble spirit, and felt equal to the
service to which they were called. They were animated, too,
by the hope of speedy results. "We want to do this work up
quick and go home," was the frequent remark of our brave
neighbors at Miner's Hill, the Michigan 4th, and this expressed
the common feeling along the entire line—a feeling that has
not yet died out. If the hopes of the army and the people
have not yet been realized, it is owing to occurrences, some of
which, it may be, were not anticipated, and could not seasonably be provided for. The army has certainly fought hard
enough, and endured enough, to deserve not only the successes
it has achieved, but the crowning triumphs which are to make
its glorious future.

Since covering the retreat of Gen. Martindale's brigade
across the Potomac, mentioned in my letter of the 27th ultimo,
nothing material has occurred until last Tuesday, when a body

of about two hundred rebel cavalry approached the river on the other side, a mile below Shepherdstown, to relieve guard. So tempting an opportunity for artillery practice could not be allowed to pass unimproved. Accordingly, Lieut. Sackett opened his section upon them, and a few well-directed shots caused a speedy retreat to the village above. Shepherdstown is about three-quarters of a mile from where we are on picket, and has been filled with the rebel wounded. It is a place of fifteen or sixteen hundred inhabitants, and before the rebellion broke out, carried on considerable trade. The bridge connecting it with the Maryland shore has been destroyed, nothing remaining but the abutments and two or three piers.

For two weeks, firing has been daily heard in various directions, some of it quite heavy, indicating skirmishes with the rebels, but more of it merely artillery and infantry practice.

The late visit of President Lincoln to the head-quarters of Gen. McClellan proved a gala occasion to the army, which was reviewed by him. Its general appearance is understood to have been satisfactory. What movements are to follow this visit will be made known in due time. In the meanwhile, the army will exercise the virtue which it is said the President recently recommended to a gentleman seeking a solution of our *quiet* problem—patience.

At Harper's Ferry, a good deal of activity is manifested in the way of strengthening its defences. Report says it is to be made the Gibraltar of the Potomac, and not to be used again by the rebels as a free passage to and from Maryland. Within the camp lines of the army, the regulation in regard to straggling is, at present, more stringently applied. No one is allowed to leave camp without a pass from head-quarters, and any one taken who cannot produce that necessary document is immediately sent to Harper's Ferry to work on the fortifications there. Under this rule, several officers have had an opportunity to practice the pick and spade manual.

The Quartermaster Sergeant, on his return from Washington a few days ago, brought to camp numerous boxes, among them one provided by thoughtful hearts, and packed by skillful hands, that has been seventy-two days on its winding way. Of course, the perishable articles had become foregone conclusions, and though summer gear, looked for and needed last July, with the thermometer at 100° in the shade, was a little out of season, other matters saved under seal were adapted to quicken the appetite of even dispeptics who quarrel with minced pies, and disparage their best and dearest friend, plum-porridge, to say nothing of fat pig and goose. After this, who will despair of the Express that puts things through in four days, or a week at most, or the safety of government storehouses, where, Mr. Olmstead of the Sanitary Commission assures us, many hundred tons of presents prepared by loving sisters and fond mothers, for brothers and sons in the army, are now piled uselessly away. It is good to have faith in men and institutions, for " faith evermore looks upwards and descries objects remote," as far off, at least, as Washington or Fortress Monroe.

Could the commission aid in forwarding those many hundred tons to the army, they would add another to the many valuable services they have already rendered, and ensure the perpetual gratitude of their recipients. Many of the boxes and packages contain wearing apparel sent by friends, to supply loss incurred in battle, and which is quite as much needed now as then. There need be no apprehension that the men will just now be burdened with an excessive amount of clothing, as an inspection of some of the regiments will clearly prove. Soldiers who have not had a change of under garments since they left the Peninsula, in August last, and who are obliged to appear on parade in nether integuments minus one leg, and even worse, run little risk of being broken down by the weight of knapsacks, on the first long continued hard march. At all events, while the army is in camp, and all is quiet along the Potomac, let the many hundred tons now piled uselessly in storehouses and yards, and upon old camp grounds, be sent along, and the boys will take the responsibility of consequences. The beneficial effects of these tokens of the affectionate interest of their friends, will a hundred fold compensate the cost and trouble of transportation.

The late battle at Antietam is still a topic of conversation in camp, and speculations are free as to what could or could not have been done. Among other statements made concerning the rebels, it is said they were short of ammunition, and that they could not have held out with artillery more than an hour longer. Their ammunition train did not arrive till 4 o'clock or later, and then could hardly reach them, the roads were so blocked with ambulances and wagons. Stuart's raid into Pennsylvania, on the 10th inst., and escape back into Virginia, after making the circuit of our army, capturing 1;000 or 1,200 horses and a large amount of other property, has occasioned many witticisms, and not a few expressions unauthorized by the decalogue. As an equestrian feat, it surpasses in boldness and success any event of its character on record. The rapidity with which he was followed by Gen. Pleasanton, who made a march of seventy-eight miles in twenty-four hours, without change of horses or rest, is proof that, with a body of cavalry such as might be selected from the force in the field, the rebels could easily be matched in this kind of warfare. On the morning of the 12th, Pleasanton's advanced guard met Stuart's, disguised in Union uniform, who, before their character was discovered, opened an artillery fire. The latter had only two pieces with him, with which to reply, the rest of the battery being unable to keep up on account of the exhausted condition of the horses. Subsequently, they arrived, and the rebels retreated. They crossed the river into Virginia at White's Ford. Pleasanton sent a regiment of cavalry and some infantry down the tow path to intercept their crossing, and used every exertion to get his guard of artillery to follow them; but the horses could not pull up the hill, and he was obliged to employ men, which caused delay. He held the rebels in check for two

15

hours, but the delay gave them time for a successful "skedaddle." In this raid, Stuart had the advantage of Pleasanton in two particulars, viz., the start, and in the relays of fresh horses seized on his course. To this last fact, he mainly owes his escape. Under the circumstances, Pleasanton made the best time.

Sharpsburg, in front of which is the head-quarters of our battery, is about sixteen miles south from Hagerstown, ten or twelve west of Middletown, from which it is separated by South Mountain, eleven north of Harper's Ferry, and about three from the ferry on the Potomac at Shepherdstown. The location is generally healthy, the only diseases to excite fear being bilious fever and fever and ague. Very few are on the sick list, and Dr. Schell, the battery surgeon, reports that the general health of the men is better here than it had ever been before.

[From the battle of Antietam until the latter part of October, the army lay stretched some thirty miles along the Potomac, guarding the numerous fords. But this time was not spent wholly in inaction. A number of reconnoissances were made to the enemy's lines, to gain knowledge of his movements and position. Several conflicts also occurred in the neighborhood of Martinsburg, Charlestown, John's Run, Snickersville, Hedgesville and other places, resulting in rebel defeats, and the capture of prisoners and army supplies. As September drew to a close, General McClellan considered his army "not in a condition to undertake another campaign, nor to bring on another battle unless great advantages were offered by some mistake of the enemy, or pressing military exigencies rendered it necessary;" and this owing to the absence of officers, the reduced condition of many of the old regiments, and the instruction needed by the new. Several weeks later, he represented that the army was not in situation to move, on account of deficiency of clothing and shoes. It was shown at the

Quartermaster General's department that a sufficient supply had been issued; but, as up to the 18th October, it had not been received at the army depots, it must have been delayed somewhere on the way. But the country and the government were impatient of further delay, and on the 6th October, the President directed General McClellan to "cross the Potomac and give battle to the enemy, or drive him south."

By correspondence published in the report of the Committee on the Conduct of the War, it appears to have been the purpose of the commanding general, "after a full consultation with the corps commanders" in his vicinity, "to adopt the line of the Shenandoah for immediate operations against the enemy now [then] at Winchester," though he did "not regard the line of the Shenandoah valley important for ulterior objects." "The objects I propose to myself," he says, "are to fight the enemy if they remain near Winchester, or, failing in that, to force them to abandon the valley of the Shenandoah, there to adopt a new and decisive line of operations which shall strike at the heart of the rebellion." It was the desire of the President, however, though he did not so order, that the army should "cross the Potomac below instead of above the Shenandoah and Blue Ridge." "Recurring to the idea of going to Richmond on the inside track, the facility of supplying from the side way from the enemy," he considered remarkable. "I should think it preferable," he added, "to take the route nearest the enemy, disabling him to make an important move without your knowledge, and compelling him to keep his forces together for dread of you. The gaps would enable you to attack if you should wish. For a great part of the way, you would be practically between the enemy and both Washington and Richmond, enabling us to spare you the greatest number of troops from here." On the 22d October, General McClellan informed General Halleck, that, after full consultation, he had "decided to move upon the line indicated by the President," and had accordingly "taken steps to execute the movement."

On the 26th October, the crossing of the army into Virginia was commenced. The dispositions made for defending the extended line in the rear, were as follows: ten thousand men to be left at Harper's Ferry; a brigade of infantry in front of Sharpsburg; a brigade at Williamsport; another at Cumberland and between that point and Hancock. Four small cavalry regiments were also left to patrol and watch the river and the Baltimore and Ohio Railroad from Cumberland down to Harper's Ferry.]

LETTER XXIV.

Group of incidents—March of Battery C—John Brown—Colonel Miles—Snickersville—General McClellan relieved of his command —Farewell order—General Burnside succeeds him—His order on taking command—Letter of Governor Sprague.

CAMP NEAR WARRENTON, VA., }
November 10, 1862. }

Since my letter of the 14th ultimo, the telegrams have kept you hourly advised of what has been going on along the Potomac. They have told you how the rebels again crossed the river at Hancock, disturbing the Sabbath quiet of the good people of Hagerstown, by apprehension of a second raid; how two brigades of Gen. Couch's division, including the 2d Rhode Island regiment, moved from near Williamsport, up the river to Clear Spring, a position held by Gen. Howe's brigade since Stuart's celebrated equestrian feat; how several brigades of Gen. Smith's division had taken their departure from the neighborhood of Hagerstown, which, with other movements, indicated something in the wind; and besides nameless similar incidents, how the President, on his late visit to the army,

drank Union cider with an old farmer, at the Mountain House.
Do not smile at this potation, and call it folly. Remember, it
was not John Barleycorn's decoction that inspires scorn of
dangers, nor brandy, "spring of tumult, source of strife," but
juice of the apple, sweet from the press, awakening recollections of boyish delights with straw and noggin, and bringing
up visions of mince pies and thanksgiving. If hard cider accomplished a mighty revolution in 1840, what may not be
hoped from the sweets extracted from the "apple of discord"
in 1862? A governor of Rhode Island understood human
nature, when he solicited a quid of tobacco from a constituent.
The President was no less discerning. There was wisdom in
that "stirrup cup," and henceforth the old farmer and his posterity may be counted in with those who go for the union of
the States, "one and indivisible, now and forever!"

The weather, during the month of October, was generally
pleasant, and, for military operations, more favorable than
September. While detachments, regiments and batteries were
occupied on picket, or making reconnoissances, with now and
then an interchange of leaden civilities with the secesh, our
army was slowly moving its huge proportions towards the sacred soil from which it had so recently retired. At Sharpsburg, the monotony of camp life was diversified by picket service, team and mounted inspections, and such other duties as
pertained to a battery. In the meantime, the military authorities seized a Rev. Mr. Douglass, residing near the river, who
proved to be a traitor, and sent him to Harper's Ferry, to answer for having communicated with the rebels, at Shepherdstown.

For ten or twelve days previous to the close of the month,
orders were several times issued to Porter's corps, and as often
countermanded, to prepare to move. On the night of the 27th,
two days' rations were cooked for the battery, expecting to be
off the next morning. Morning came, but we did not move.
The 28th and 29th found us still lingering; but on the 30th, the

15*

order "forward," so welcome to all, was heard, and eagerly obeyed. At 6 o'clock P. M., we broke camp, and turned from the fields that had but lately been scenes of bloody strife. There was something touching in the memories of the hour, and as we moved along, the winds, in sympathy, sweeping through the trees, sighed out the requiem of the sleeping heroes of Antietam, and the falling leaves, like tears of nature, dropped upon their honored graves. We marched all night, over the roughest road I have yet seen in our campaigning, now climbing sharp ascents, and anon diving down steep declivities. At 3 o'clock the next morning, we halted and made camp about two and a half miles from Harper's Ferry. At 10 o'clock, we broke camp again, and crossed the Potomac at the Ferry, halting only long enough to partake of slight refreshments. Pursuing our way, we crossed the Shenandoah on pontoon bridges, and about three miles beyond, encamped once more in Virginia. Harper's Ferry is too well known to require description. Nestled at the base of a high hill, and surrounded by scenery of the most picturesque character, it was, three years ago, a place of unusual charms. But now the village everywhere gives evidence of the desolating effects of war. The seizure of the arsenal by John Brown and his eighteen " merrie men," in 1859, and subsequent occurrences resulting from their doings, has given to the place a permanent historic character ; and though the body of the bold leader " lies mouldering in the ground," the historian, in coming ages, will trace the progress of his spirit, as it kept step with the march of years along the highway of human freedom.

Although Brown organized a provisional government, with its legislative, executive, judicial and military departments, and took possession of the United States Armory, to aid in carrying out his purposes, it is a singular fact, that Mason and Jefferson Davis, of the investigating committee, were careful to denominate this invasion of Virginia and attempt at insurrection as simply the act of lawless ruffians, and, if my memory serves me

correctly, declined suggesting any legislation that might prevent like occurrences in future. Did they not then contemplate that future as near, when they were to throw themselves
into the lead of a rebellion on a national scale, and for that reason, refrained from giving a character to Brown's conduct that
would condemn their own? The coolness, not to say indifference, with which they treated the subject, inclines one to the
belief that they were influenced by this consideration.

From the commencement of the rebellion, Harper's Ferry
has been an important military position. It was unfortunate
for our campaign in Maryland, that this post was left in charge
of Col. Miles. His surrender lost us the best fruits of the battle of Antietam. Whatever plausibility or truth there may
be—and I do not pretend to judge—in the criticisms upon
events subsequent to that battle, had Col. Miles maintained his
ground, the strength of the rebel army would have been ours,
and rebellion have received its death-blow. And all this is the
more aggravating from the fact that Gen. Wool says that had
Col. Miles obeyed his orders, he could have held the place
against any force the rebels would have had it in their power,
at that time, to bring against him. What motives influenced
Col. M. to adopt the course he pursued, it is impossible now to
say. He was reputed an able officer, and his friends claim for
him devotion to the Union. Whether the infirmity imputed to
him at Bull Run incapacitated him here, or whether he was
affected by other causes, the committee of investigation may be
able to decide.

The day we passed through Harper's Ferry was hot, and a
day of rest at our camp, on the east side of the Shenandoah,
was agreeable alike to men and horses. On the 2d instant,
the battery was in motion at $7\frac{1}{2}$ o'clock A. M., and continuing
our march up the river, we arrived at Snickersville at 5 o'clock
P. M., and went into camp. On our way, heavy firing was
heard in front. It proved to be by Gen. Sumner's corps, which
arrived at Snickersville just in season to drive back the rebels,

who were then coming through Snicker's Gap. The village, a smart little place, is situated directly opposite the Gap. It communicates by turnpike with Winchester, some twenty-three miles northwest, where the rebels are reported to be in considerable force, and Leesburg, eleven or twelve miles east. Thirteen miles southeast is Aldie, on the direct route to Alexandria, through Pleasant Valley and Fairfax Court House. Thirty miles southwest is Front Royal, commanding the railroad through Manassas Gap. All these places have obtained considerable notoriety since the rebellion begun, and several of them possess military importance. Winchester, like Martinsburg, is a convenient position for the rebels, either as a base for raids, or for the concentration of forces for heavier work. They can approach Harper's Ferry by way of the Winchester and Potomac Railroad, or dashing through the Gap by way of Berryville, range between the Blue Ridge and the Shenandoah, with fair prospect of escape if pursued by our troops. The present disposition of forces left behind will probably keep them from doing any essential mischief.

From whom or what Snickersville derived its not very euphonious name. I am not apprised. It may have been from an old inhabitant, addicted to laughing in his sleeve at human credulity, or a company of settlers habituated to cachinate "with small audible catches of voice," at the discomforting experience of every new comer. Be that as it may, the modern Snickervillians do not differ essentially from the dwellers in other villages through which we passed. Had inquisition been made, we should probably have found, as at Sharpsburg, a fair per cent. of Union feeling, with a smart sprinkling of secesh proclivities. Immediately on our arrival, our battery was put in position, together with all others in this division, to command the Gap, and had the rebels shown themselves, the " snicker " would have been on our side and not theirs. After their experience with Gen. Sumner, they prudently declined making our acquaintance, and having held our position till Wednesday last, (5th.) we again took up our line of march. Continuing our course through Middleburg, we arrived, without noticeable incidents, near Warrenton, on the morning of the 8th, and went into camp. Yesterday, we moved forward two and a half miles, where we now are. The weather, on the march, has been variable, but mostly cold. Last Friday, snow fell all day. Yesterday threatened rain. To-day is pleasant.

Warrenton is about fifty miles from Gordonsville, where it is supposed the rebels have a large force, and design to make a stand should they be attacked. It is also some thirty-eight miles from Fredericksburg, which may soon become a base of supplies for our army. It is situated in the midst of a fine agricultural country, and, before our present troubles, did a flourishing business. But a small number of the sick and wounded in the rebel hospital have recovered. Our front extends some distance beyond Warrenton, and Burnside's forces rest on Waterloo. The concentration of troops, at this place, indicates some active operation at an early day. How long we shall remain here is uncertain, but probably not many days.

The most exciting event of the week has been the retirement of Gen. McClellan from the command of the army of the Potomac. The rank and file, who have shared with him the toils and dangers of the Peninsula, and were enthusiastic in their devotion, were taken by surprise, and were deeply moved when the tidings spread from camp to camp. Yet, to their honor, and to the praise of their patriotism and discipline, they quietly acquiesced in this military necessity.

The following Farewell Order of the General, brief and affectionate, was read to the army of the Potomac at dress parade :

HEAD-QUARTERS, ARMY OF THE POTOMAC, }
Camp near Rectortown, Va., November 7, 1862. }

OFFICERS AND SOLDIERS OF THE ARMY OF THE POTOMAC :

An order of the President devolves upon Major General Burnside the command of this army. In parting from you, I cannot express the love and gratitude I bear to you. As an army, you have grown up under my care. In you I have never found doubt nor coldness. The battles you have fought under my command will probably live in our nation's history. The glory youh ave achieved; our marches, perils and fatigues; the graves of our comrades fallen in battle and by disease; the broken forms of those whom wounds and sickness have disabled; the strongest associations which exist among men, unite us still by an indissoluble tie. We shall ever be comrades in supporting the Constitution of our country, and the nationality of its people.

GEORGE B. McCLELLAN,
Major General United States Army.

This forenoon, the General took personal leave of the army. As he rode through the double lines of his veterans, music swelled upon the air, colors were dipped, cannon boomed their deep-toned farewell, and cheers, like the voice of many waters, burst from every lip, as spontaneous heart expressions. Gen. Burnside, who arrived here with Gen. McClellan, day before yesterday, bore himself grandly on this trying occasion, and paid every attention to his old friend and companion in arms, that could tend to make pleasant the memories of the hour. Last night, at tattoo roll-call, the following order issued by General Burnside, on taking command of the army, was read to the line. In expression and spirit it is excellent, and was cordially received :

In accordance with General Orders No. 182, issued by the President of the United States, I hereby assume the command of the Army of the Potomac. Patriotism and the exercise of my every energy in the direction of this army, aided by the full and hearty co-operation of its officers and men, will, I hope, under the blessing of God, ensure its success.

Having been a sharer of the privations, and a witness of the bravery of the old army of the Potomac, in the Maryland campaign, and fully identified with them in their feeling of respect and esteem for General McClellan, entertained through a long and most friendly association with him, I feel that it is not as a stranger I assume command.

To the Ninth Army Corps, so long and intimately associated with me, I need say nothing. Our histories are identical.

With diffidence for myself, but with a proud confidence in the unswerving loyalty and determination of the gallant army now entrusted to my care, I accept its control with the steadfast assurance that the just cause must prevail.

(Signed,) A. E. BURNSIDE,
        Major General Commanding.

As I saw General Burnside yesterday, he had the same noble mien and sunshine of expression that long ago won the respect and affection of Rhode Island men. No other officer could, at this time, succeed General McClellan with so general approbation of the men,—no other could at once so universally win their hearty good will. He is looked upon as prudent, yet prompt and vigorous in action. They expect under him, what they crave, lively times. His antecedents give them confidence in his ability, and they hope to make short work in doing up rebellion. The battle which shall give assurance of this, will be marked by a repetition of the best fighting of the Peninsula.

[Immediately on the announcement of the accession of General Burnside to the chief command, the following letter of congratulation was despatched to him by telegraph, from Governor Sprague, of Rhode Island :

STATE OF RHODE ISLAND, EXECUTIVE DEPARTMENT, ⎰
    Providence, November 10, 1862.   ⎱

GENERAL :

Allow me to tender you my sincere congratulations on your appointment to the command of the army of the Potomac. Your well known energy, skill and patriotism, will, I feel sure, restore confidence to a disheartened people, and lead them to expect active operations and the speedy success of our brave army, in the suppression of treason and rebellion.

Rhode Island regards your appointment with unfeigned pride and pleasure.

(Signed,) WILLIAM SPRAGUE.
To GENERAL BURNSIDE,
 Commander-in-Chief, Army of the Potomac.

To which, through the same medium, the following reply was returned:

HEAD-QUARTERS, ARMY, }
November 10, 1862. }

To GOVERNOR WILLIAM SPRAGUE:

Your despatch of this date is received, and I thank you for it. It is a great support to me, in the assumption of so great a responsibility, to know that I have your confidence, and that of the State of Rhode Island.

(Signed,)   A. E. BURNSIDE,
Major General, Commanding Army of the Potomac.]

LETTER XXV.

Wanderings—Life in camp and on the march—Hoof-rot in horses—General Porter relieved of his command.

CAMP SIX MILES FROM ACQUIA CREEK, VA., }
November 26, 1862. }

We arrived here yesterday, from Warrenton, by the way of Elkton and Spotted Tavern. Our march brought us over a portion of the road we travelled last summer, when we went up from Acquia Creek to Warrenton, and thence, via Bull Run, reached our old quarters at Miner's Hill. If our wanderings, since the 10th of last March, have not equalled those of the Israelites, our exposures, privations, sacrifices of life, and patient endurance, deserve the reward finally bestowed upon that very respectable army of contrabands. The land of promise has been seen, and it may be our privilege, before many months, to possess it. In the advance of our army towards Fredericksburg, the rebel scouts hung closely upon its rear, watching its movements, and keeping the rebel commander apprised of every appearance worthy special attention. These impertinences frequently issued in skirmishes, with little disaster on our side, and pretty uniform skedaddling on the part of the secesh. Our temporary camp in the neighborhood of Falmouth was not far from the head-quarters of Gen. Burnside, and though burdened with the responsibilities of an immense army, a weight sufficient to crush an ordinary mind, his expression was as cheerful as though a stranger to "carking care." All the way between Warrenton and Falmouth, the people were strongly secesh, and some of them more than intimated that we should be driven back. As we held a different opinion, and for satisfactory reasons, we felt that we could afford to indulge these sons of Belial in their harmless taunts.

Life in camp and life on the march have some features in common, yet, in prominent characteristics, differ. In the former, monotony soon rules, and weariness of spirit, when off duty, enters largely into the daily experience. In the latter, there is a constant shifting of scene to refresh the eye, a prospect of adventure that feeds the imagination, and an amount of fatigue that gives sweetness to the slumbers of the bivouac. And then, when, as sometimes happens, rations are scant, foraging by the way becomes an agreeably exciting episode, in matters gustatory. Thus, on the route from Harper's Ferry to Warrenton, salt junk and hard tack were often diversified with poultry, fresh meat and vegetables, purchased, of course, sometimes with government postal and sometimes with secesh money, that the confederate treasury would hardly receive in payment of taxes, or accept as a voluntary contribution to the war fund, if such exists. A very proper order against pillaging existed, which I fear that now and then a man of unbounded stomach, stimulated by the incentive of savory meat, may have less scrupulously observed, than comported with due reverence for law. If any such exceptional cases did occur, and in some unexplained way a barnyard representative found its way into camp, charity remembered how hard it must have been for men, under the potent sway of appetite and the tempting pres-

16

ence of dainties, to "defy that which they love most tenderly," and spread her mantle over the deed.

For a few weeks past, the army supplies have scarcely exceeded daily consumption, rendering any movement dependent on a surplus, unsafe. But the railroad bridge on the road from Acquia Creek Landing to Fredericksburg, destroyed by the rebels, has been reconstructed, so that hereafter the needs of the army, for any emergency, will be speedily supplied.

The " hoof-rot," or, more properly, " grease," a disease that has prevailed to a considerable extent among the horses of the army, and that, at one time, assumed an alarming aspect, appears to be subsiding. It was first noticed in our battery at Warrenton, and occasioned the loss of a number of horses. Since leaving that place, but few severe cases have occurred. The disease is of singular character. It commences with inflammation of the heel, which soon suppurates, spreads, and in time the entire hoof comes off. Its origin in the army, has not, to my knowledge, been explained. It may have been caused by hard service and exposure on the peninsula, connected with wet or muddy picketings, so often unavoidable.

General Fitz John Porter has been relieved from the command of the Fifth *corps d'armée*. On the afternoon of the 12th, he took formal leave of the men he had led in the hard-fought battles of the peninsula. All the troops were formed in line, and as he rode past with his staff, accompanied by Gen. Hooker, Martin's battery fired a salute of honor of thirteen guns. The General seemed deeply affected, and it was not without evident sorrow that the men parted with one under whom they commenced military life. But, as on the occasion of a former military necessity, no breach of soldierly propriety has, on that account, occurred. Gen. Hooker, or Fighting Joe as he is familiarly called, comes to the chief command, with the well-earned fame of peninsula exploits, and the prestige of Antietam.

LETTER XXVI.

Battle of Fredericksburg—Rhode Island regiments and batteries engaged—Recrossing the river—Disappointed feeling—The President's address to the army—The weather.

CAMP NEAR POTOMAC CREEK, VA.,
December 24th, 1862.

The ominous preparations of a month found an explanation on the 13th inst. On that day, a great and bloody battle was fought at Fredericksburg; and now, at the end of two weeks, after opportunity to gather up particulars, I propose to give, not a complete detail of all that occurred, but such points (glancing at the parts in which Rhode Island was represented,) as will convey a pretty clear idea of the fearful contest.

Immediately on assuming the command of the army, General Burnside prepared to act with promptness and vigor. His plan was to concentrate his forces in the neighborhood of Warrenton; to make a small movement across the Rappahannock, as a feint, with a view to divert the attention of the enemy, and lead them to believe he was going to move in the direction of Gordonville, and then to make a rapid movement of the whole army to Fredericksburg. In doing this, he would still be near Washington, having an unobstructed rear for the reception of supplies, and nearer to Richmond than he would be were he to take Gordonsville. This he considered preferable to taking the Gordonsville line, as, in that event, the enemy had it in their power to defend the place until they had given the Federal forces a check; and then, with so many lines of railroad open to them, they could move upon Richmond or upon Lynchburg, making it difficult, in either case, to follow them, and, at the same time, keep open the line of communication with the base of supplies.

This plan was arranged on the 9th November, and, in ac-

cordance with it, pontoons for crossing the Rappahannock at
and below Fredericksburg, were to be sent at once from Washington. In pursuing its course to Warrenton, the army
marched in three columns, within striking distance of each
other, the Second and Ninth army corps being on the right,
the Third and Fifth in the centre, and the First and Sixth on
the left. The pontoons were expected to be ready for use, at
Fredericksburg, on the arrival of the army. On the 17th,
General Sumner, with his command, arrived before that place,
but the pontoons had not yet come. Had all things been in
readiness, he could at once have crossed over, and taken possession of the heights commanding the town, as the force of
the enemy was then comparatively small—report says not over
five hundred—and the position had not been fortified. This
would have enabled General Burnside to keep possession of
the line of the railroad to Richmond, pressing the enemy off,
and if not able to precede them into their capital, yet to keep
so close to them as to afford no time for building fortifications.

[Directly upon the appearing of General Sumner's troops
on the ridge back of Falmouth, a battery of rebel artillery
opened upon them, and the General was strongly tempted to
go over, seize the guns and occupy the city ; but his orders
being to hold Falmouth but not to cross, he suppressed the
impulse. In his testimony before the committee on the Conduct of the War, he says : " That same night, I sent a note to
General Burnside, who was some eight or ten miles distant,
asking him if I should take Fredericksburg in the morning,
should I be able to find a practicable ford, which, by the way,
I knew when I wrote the note, that I could find. The General
replied, through his chief of staff, that he did not think it advisable to occupy Fredericksburg until his communications
were established ; and, on reflection, I myself thought he was
right ; that it was prudent and proper to have the bridges ready
before we occupied Fredericksburg."]

On the 21st, General Sumner formally demanded the surrender of the city, allowing sixteen hours for the removal of women and children, the sick and wounded, the aged, &c., at the expiration of which time, if not given up, he proposed to shell the town. Subsequently, eleven additional hours were granted. The pontoons did not arrive until the 22d or 23d November. In the meantime, the alarm had been given in Richmond, and with the facilities of the railroad, the rebels continued day and night to roll in their forces, until by the time the necessary arrangements for attack had been made, an army of more than one hundred thousand men had come to the rescue of the city, while the heights were fortified with strong redoubts, bristling with heavy cannon.

On the 11th, the pontoons in front of Fredericksburg and two miles below had been laid, under a galling fire from the rebel sharpshooters, and our army began to cross. It was a time of impressive excitement, awakening at once serious and animating emotions. The chances of battle passed swiftly before the mind, and men of thoughtful mood disposed themselves to meet, with heroic firmness and in a trusting spirit, the dread issues of the hour. Then came the inspiration springing from the consciousness that a blow, hoped to be decisive, was to be struck in vindication of law, order, and that fundamental principle of our Federal government—the will of the majority of a free people, fairly expressed through the ballot-box. Men of high resolve held their muskets with firmer grasp, and moved at the word of command with quick and determined tread.

In the general disposition of the forces, General Sumner held the right, General Franklin, the left, and General Hooker, the centre. Of General Franklin's command, the 2d Rhode Island, under Colonel Frank Wheaton, were the first to cross the river. On ascending the bank, they instantly deployed as skirmishers, driving the rebel pickets back, who took refuge in the woods. It was a perilous moment. Between the river and the neighboring heights, occupied by a heavy body of the

16*

enemy's infantry and artillery, lay a plain three-quarters of a mile in width, across which they had to pass, exposed to the deadly aim of an almost unseen foe. But they executed the movement with the coolness and precision of a regimental drill. Those who witnessed it pronounced it one of the most finished evolutions of the day, and it drew from the entire corps of beholders loud cheers of commendation. The next day, Colonel Wheaton took command of the brigade that had been under General Howe, and the command of the regiment devolved on Colonel Nelson Viall. It was brought into the brigade line, occupying front lines in support of batteries—a position of great exposure. When the grand division of Franklin recrossed the river, two companies of the regiment were assigned to guard the bridges. They held their post until the pickets were withdrawn, and were themselves the last to follow.

At 6 o'clock in the morning of the 11th, General Burnside ordered the artillery to open upon the city, and soon the sky was wreathed in the smoke of conflagration. All day long the immense line of batteries in front filled the air with deafening sounds. The town was carried, and the troops inspirited with confidence of success. Next day came the heavy conflict, when General Meade, of Franklin's corps, made the first attack on the left of our lines, and drove the enemy from his advanced works; but not receiving seasonable support, was unable to hold his ground. Out of 4,500 men, he lost 1,740. General Birney, of the same corps, punished the rebels severely as they advanced, and caused them, for a time, to reel and fall back. Generals Gibbon, Smith, Stoneman, Doubleday, Vinton, Bayard and others, were hotly engaged. The entire command of General Reynolds suffered much, his aggregate loss being 3,144.

General Sumner fought his men with great energy. He pushed forward Generals French and Howard, to assault the enemy's works, which rose in triple strength on the heights. Intermediate, and the most powerful obstacle to their advance

was a stone wall of four hundred or five hundred yards in
length, which had been raised and strengthened, and enfiladed
by artillery at both ends. When the Federals approached
within a distance ensuring deadly aim, a tremendous fire was
poured upon them from behind the wall, together with a storm
of shell from the enfilading artillery, which sent scores of brave
men to the ground. It was in vain that repeated assaults were
made. It can only be said they did their best, and failed to
carry the position.

General Hooker's command were not behind the right and
left, in spirit and activity. A portion of his troops were sent as
supports to Franklin, and a division sent to relieve General
Howard, in the upper part of the city. General Humphries,
with 4,000 men and Sykes' division for a support, made a
spirited assault upon the enemy's works, but was unable to
accomplish his object. He was compelled to retire, leaving
1,760 men behind—the work of one-fourth of an hour. The
total killed, wounded and missing in Hooker's grand division is
reported to be 3,548, and in Griffin's, to which our battery is
attached, 1,190. His troops, to a man, fought like veterans.

In this battle, Rhode Island was more largely represented
than on any previous field. The 2d, 4th, 7th and 12th regiments volunteers, and batteries A, B, C, D, E and G were
there. The 2d Rhode Island, first in the fight, added to its
reputation for bravery and efficiency. It reckons eight wounded. The 4th discharged its duty manfully, and mourns the
death of its accomplished Lieut. Colonel Curtis, then in command. The 7th was finely handled by Colonel Bliss, and won
honor on this first experience under fire. It counts 12 killed
and 140 wounded. Of the former is Lieut. Colonel Welcome
B. Sayles, and, of the latter, Major Jacob Babbitt. The 12th,
like the 7th, were, for the first time, under fire ; and under the
eye of Colonel Browne, delivered their own in return, with
coolness and spirit, losing six killed and ninety-four wounded.

On Colonel Charles H. Tompkins, of the Rhode Island artillery, a heavy responsibility devolved, which was discharged with the efficiency of an accomplished soldier. Eighty-eight guns were under his direction, and the work of bombarding the town, on the 11th, fell mostly upon his command. Battery A, Captain Arnold, who came to the command just in season for the battle, won deserved commendation. Battery B, Captain John G. Hazard, fought bravely under a hot fire, losing sixteen men killed and wounded, and twelve battery horses killed. The horses of himself and of Lieutenants Bloodgood and Milne were also shot. Battery G, Captain Charles D. Owen, behaved gallantly. Before crossing the river, it was posted on the extreme right of the artillery line. On going over, it took position in the rear of Gordon's house. Coveting its possession, the rebels approached within one hundred and fifty yards, but were driven back with cannister and the support of the 5th Michigan infantry. Battery D, Captain Buckley, who had been in command but a single day, contributed of its projectiles to the discomfort of the enemy.

Battery E, Captain Randolph, was attached to General Birney's division, which reported to General Franklin, and was placed in support of Meade's Pennsylvania reserves, about a mile down the river from Mansfield Estate, General Franklin's head-quarters. When Meade attacked, Captain R. relieved his batteries, he (R.) commanding the batteries of the line. When Meade was repulsed, the enemy, covered from his fire by the ground and the retreating troops, pushed within thirty yards of his line. Not daring to leave their cover and face his light 18-pounders, loaded with cannister, they laid down and commenced picking off the cannoneers. After waiting a short time, in the hope that they might be tempted a little further to their destruction, General Birney advanced his infantry and drove them in confusion into the woods. In this battle, Captain R.'s three batteries were well posted, covered by a ridge running the entire length of his line. He had two men killed and three wounded, and lost six horses.

Of battery C, Captain Waterman, the following is the sum of its ten days experience. On the morning of the 10th, it moved from camp and took position on the bank of the Rappahannock, opposite the lower part of Fredericksburg. During a first attempt to throw a pontoon bridge across the river, the time was occupied in firing at the houses sheltering the enemy's sharpshooters, sometimes rapidly, and occasionally at intervals. On the 12th, the fire was turned upon the town until late in the afternoon, when a successful attempt to complete the bridge being made by the engineer corps, it was concentrated upon the buildings and terraces which protected the enemy's riflemen. The expenditure of ammunition on the 11th and 12th was about 800 rounds. At the commencement of the action on the 13th, the battery coöperated, as far as possible, with our advancing lines, by firing on the enemy's artillery and skirmishers, until our lines approached so nearly those of the enemy that continued fire became dangerous to our infantry, when it was discontinued. Up to this time, about three hundred rounds of ammunition had been expended.

About one o'clock P. M., the battery crossed the river, and was placed in position under General Couch, by Major Doull. At two o'clock, it commenced shelling the enemy's artillery and skirmishers, at a range of about 850 yards. The fire was continued rapidly for about two hours, when, from information that our forces held the ridge on our left, to which the fire had been mainly directed, the battery concentrated its fire upon the batteries directly in front, which for an hour had been firing upon it. This appeared to have the effect to silence the enemy's guns, until after dark, when they fired a few random shots in the direction of our position. The men were held to their posts during the night, and the horses in harness. During Sunday, the 14th, but a few shot were fired from the battery. The men were exposed to a fire of sharpshooters most of the day, but no men or horses were wounded.

At 7 o'clock on Sunday evening, the 14th, the battery recrossed the river and bivouacked for the night. At 9 A. M., of the 15th, it moved to a position in rear of the Lacy House, and bivouacked until the morning of the 16th, when it was placed in position in rear of the plain commanding the lower part of Fredericksburg, in readiness to repel an attack on the engineer force detailed for the removal of the pontoon bridge. It remained in position there until 10 o'clock of the 20th, when it returned to its former camp. One man and three horses were lost, and two gun carriages disabled. The poor fellow who fell a victim to a deadly aim, had both legs broken and his jaw shot away. He lived but a short time. The men behaved finely, though they passed four nights with little or no sleep.

During the action, the head-quarters of Generals Burnside and Hooker were at the Phillips House, and of Sumner, at the Lacy House, as the most favorable positions for observing operations. Professor Lowe employed his balloon for watching the movements of the enemy, but the state of the atmosphere precluded any important discoveries. The battle closed, and a few words will suffice to sum up the beginning, progress and end. The enemy was driven at different points, and in turn they drove our troops. They took seven hundred of our men prisoners, and we took as many of theirs. Our forces held the city twenty-four hours after the termination of the fight, and, in the opinion of General Sumner, could have continued to hold it " with a single division, by posting our batteries right." Our right and centre stood in front of the rebel breastworks, and they behind them. They held no ground they did not hold before the battle begun. Our army rested a day in the city before evacuating, and no successful attempt was made to dislodge it. It recrossed the river on the night of the 14th— Egyptian in darkness—without the loss of a man, horse or gun. The bridges were taken up without the destruction of a single pontoon, and, on the morning of the 15th, the two armies faced each other, with the Rappahannock between, as they did on the morning of the 10th. On the field of strife lay min-

gled their dead and ours. Of the terrible magnificence and
awful carnage of the 13th, no words can convey an adequate
idea. The roar of musketry and thunder of artillery, the
screeching of shells and the whir of Minies was incessant, and
it seemed as though the fabled battle of the gods had been renewed. Generals Jackson and Bayard were killed, and Generals Tyler, Meagher, Vinton, Gibbon, Kimball and Caldwell,
wounded. From description, the appearance of the field, covered with the slain and wounded, and the subsequent hospital
scenes, were sad and sickening.* Having made himself acquainted with the story of the battle—its courageous deeds and
mournful losses—the President, day before yesterday, issued
to the army the following address :

EXECUTIVE MANSION, ⎱
Washington, December 22d, 1862. ⎰

TO THE ARMY OF THE POTOMAC:

I have just read your Commanding General's preliminary report of
the battle of Fredericksburg. Although you were not successful, the
attempt was not an error, nor the failure other than an accident.
The courage with which you, in an open field, maintained the contest
against an intrenched foe, and the consummate skill and success with
which you crossed and recrossed the river in the face of the enemy,
show that you possess all the qualities of a great army, which will
yet give victory to the cause of the country and of popular government. Condoling with the mourners for the dead, and sympathizing
with the severely wounded, I congratulate you that the number of
both is comparatively so small, I tender to you, officers and soldiers, the thanks of the nation.

ABRAHAM LINCOLN.

That the army feels disappointed at the unsuccess, it were
useless to deny. Still, in view of what they suffered, and the
thinned ranks of many regiments, they are in better spirits

---

* The rebel loss was large, though, from their sheltered position, much
less than the Federal. The Richmond Despatch admitted " 2,500 wounded." General Cobb was killed, and General Greeg mortally wounded.

than could have been anticipated. "Cast down, but not destroyed," may be written as their motto. They believe in their General still, while they marvel at his tenderness of everybody but himself. The plan of attack was well laid, but the hindrances to success were unforeseen and unexpected. Had the pontoons been sent forward from Washington with the celerity that the army moved from Warrenton, no failure could have occurred; but that delay proved fatal. It gave the rebels ample time to concentrate their forces and fortify their position, and prevented results that were confidently expected.

The year draws to a close under a cloud, but the hidden sun of success is not blotted out. Its light of promise will yet be seen. More than 1,200 noble fellows sleep the sleep of death on the banks of the Rappahannock, and more than 6,000 of the living bear honorable marks of the patriotism that inspired their bravery on the field. And these, the dead and the living, speak to their countrymen of the spirit that should actuate every breast while rebellion exists.

From all accounts, Fredericksburg has been essentially ruined. An immense destruction of property was caused by the bombardment and pillage. Many years must elapse before its past prosperity can be restored. In the tobacco business, its merchants have found temporary competitors. Two or three weeks ago, large quantities of the article were thrown into the river to prevent it falling into Federal hands. This the soldiers have been fishing up, and selling to ready purchasers. To-day, some of them have disposed of thirty or forty dollars' worth apiece—quite a nice operation for the lucky fishers.

The weather, during the month, has been variable, furnishing about equal proportions of sunshine and rain, snow, mud and frost. In a time when men are liable to be aroused at any hour of the night, they may be pardoned if they turn in with their boots on. Taking advantage of an illustrious precedent, I did so a short time since, and woke in the morning to find them frozen stiff. Luckily the frost did not penetrate the quick, so no harm was done. To-day, the temperature is too low for comfortable epistolary work without a fire; but in a few days we shall rise from the humble conveniences of tarpaulin or poncho shelter to the elegance of a shanty, with the luxury of a fire-place, when old ideas may be thawed out, if new ones are not warmed into life. To-morrow is Christmas. May its coming prove the precursor of brighter skies.

LETTER XXVII.

Christmas—New Year—Rebels tired of the war—Forty millions of dollars due the army—Review—Rosecrans' success—Reflections—Vegetables for the army.

CAMP NEAR POTOMAC CREEK, VA.,
December 26, 1862.

Christmas came and passed as pleasantly as could be expected in the midst of civil war, on rebel soil, in front of a rebel army. Dreams of home, "a dearer, sweeter spot than all the rest," ushered in the morning that commemorates the chief event in the world's history since the creation; and memories were fresh of by-gone days, when a visit from the jovial Saint, with his queer face and huge pack, as delineated in the annual pictorials, was expected, and stockings confidingly hung in the corner were made plethoric by his munificence. But here no such anticipations were realized. No stockings were hung expectant, and therefore no disappointments were experienced. The venerable Patron, yet always youthful in spirit, was too

17

busy with Spanker and Jumper elsewhere to visit a spot so near the recent scene of bloody strife, and, as an equivalent for the fun his presence always imparts, resort was had, in some encampments, to athletic sports, while in others, some spent a portion of the day in writing to friends at home, or in social calls. In culinary matters, there were differences of experience. In some messes, the capture of a grey-back, whose nimble bound was overmatched by the swifter feet of biped pursuers, supplied savory meat for Christmas dinner, while a chicken graced the festivities of others. Those less fortunate had opportunity to test their skill in conglomerating a dish from pork, salt junk and hard tack. A lean larder arouses ingenuity, and men who are equally at home in building railroads, making engines and fighting secesh, could hardly fail in getting up a respectable feed. Report, "that blunt monster with uncounted heads," gives currency to various novelties as distinguishing the day. In one encampment, it is averred that an officer, in a highly imaginative mood, was seen astride a log, spurring it to a charge, while another gravely ordered the arrest of a rail-fence for neglecting to salute the general. It is possible that the reporter himself saw double. At all events, I can affirm that nothing of the sort fell under my observation. Emerged from shelter tent to hutted life, the sense of progressive civilization has become somewhat quickened and the area of ideas enlarged. If our nine-by-nine does not show the highest order of architectural skill and finish, it affords an amount of comfort unknown for many months past.

January 2, 1863. The departure of the old gentleman with the venerable beard and ominous scythe, whose portrait has so often arrested childhood attention, was not attended by any special demonstration of nature, and his successor was ushered in to meet a cool, not to say freezing reception. It was impossible to part with our old friend without throwing the mind into a retrospective mood. It was remembered, that nine

months before he had witnessed our exultant farewell to Miner's Hill, and had smiled approvingly upon our battery as it
opened the ball with artillery music before Yorktown. He
had seen the struggle and carnage at Gaines's Farm, and the
triumph achieved at Malvern Hills. He had noted our voyage
to Acquia Creek, our wearisome march to Warrenton and Bull
Run, our return to our old camp, our march thence to Antietam, and thence to Fredericksburg, culminating in the fierce
and deadly encounter of December 13th. And when we said,
with a slight tone of sadness, " Good bye, old fellow, we shall
never look upon your like again," he responded, cheerily,
" Keep up good heart; all will yet issue well. Never mind
criticisms, nor tirades against the best government beneath the
sun. You saw the spires of Richmond, and if you failed to
possess that stronghold of rebellion, it was for causes that reflect no dishonor upon the army of the Potomac, and that my
successor will more fully explain. History will set all right.
Deeds of valor, never surpassed, will not pass into oblivion.
Stand firmly for the right. Sustain the constitution and laws
from principle. Confide in your noble general, and repose
faith in the just aims of the government. Take courage from
what has been accomplished. Feel yourselves strong in an
army and navy competent to cope with the strongest nation on
earth. Disasters may yet occur. Disappointments may still
be a part of the nation's experience. Much treasure and blood
may yet be required to be poured out, but justice will triumph
over injustice, freedom over oppression, and the fruit of patriotic sacrifice shall be a vindicated Union and a higher plane
of national civilization, that will send down its blessings to re-
motest posterity." Thus speaking, with outstretched hand, as
if to scatter the nation's path with the benedictions prophesied,
the Father of Years passed from view, and the reverie into which
the mind had sunk was broken.

January 5. " All 'quiet along the Rappahannock," might

answer for a daily record during the past ten days. In several divisions, the monotony of camp life has been diversified by reviews, and a general smoothing of the kinks taken up at Fredericksburg. A line of pickets, extending over twenty miles, indicates that our General-in-Chief does not intend affording the rebel raiders opportunities to make unceremonious visits to any portion of the army. It is singular how soon the animosities of contending parties pass away, and the era of good feeling is restored, after a hard-fought battle. Federal and rebel pickets, with only the river between them, frequently engage in friendly conversation, mutually forbearing the use of deadly weapons, and occasionally the latter cross to our side in boats, and spend an hour in discussing public affairs, and exchanging tobacco for a cup of coffee or other article of refreshment, unknown to their *cuisine*. They repeat the old story, that they are tired of fighting, and wish the war was ended. They are short of clothing, and when relieved from guard, transfer their overcoats to their successors. Yet they express themselves strongly for the confederacy, and show no disposition to abandon the bad cause they have espoused. How far this intercourse is advisable may be an open question. As yet no evil is known to have arisen from it, and if our pickets are the prudent, reliable men they are supposed to be, none is likely to occur. Still, one can imagine how it might be availed of by a shrewd secesh for indirectly gaining valuable information. But then the same may be said for the Federals, thus balancing the account.

The rebels have been quite busy since our army returned to its present position, in fortifying along the banks of the river, evidently apprehensive of another visit from us. A small fort has been thrown up opposite where we had a bridge. No guns are yet mounted, and if there were, it would be of little account should we wish again to cross at that point, as a few shells from our siege guns could, in a few minutes, demolish it.

January 9. Since the opening of the new year, the weather has, for the most part, been fine. The first day was signalized by mustering in the men for pay. Six months have passed, with no chink from our excellent Uncle at Washington. His liberal heart has never been doubted, and a large allowance is to be made for the obstacles in the way of supplying paymasters with a sufficient amount of green-backs to promptly meet the treasury obligations. Forty millions of dollars, however, is too large a sum to longer remain unpaid, without causing complaint among the men, and seriously affecting their families, dependent, to a great extent, upon regular remittances; and it is gratifying to see that the Secretary of the Treasury has put himself earnestly to the work of liquidating this immense liability. The military committee in Congress, I observe, are preparing a bill to equalize the condition of the first and second quotas of three years men, in regard to bounties and other matters. It is understood here that this movement originated in Providence. Whoever did the deed will be sure of the thanks of the army. In view of the feeling awakened in consequence of the disparity referred to, no measure could be more timely, or better adapted to harmonize the spirit of the men.

Yesterday, there was a grand review of the first divisions, by Generals Burnside, Hooker and Meade. Gen. Meade, at present, commands the 5th army corps. Daily drills, dress parades, and camp duties, fill the time that would otherwise hang heavily on the army. Our new quarters are quite cosy, and are in agreeable contrast with former accommodations.

The news from Rosecrans is exhilarating, though shaded by the heavy cost at which success was won. His hard-fought battle has deservedly gained for him the praise due to a brave soldier. The fall of Port Hudson and Vicksburg is next to be looked for. Those places in Federal hands, the course of the Mississippi will be free. Time speed the events. Our rebel neighbors are not idle, though it is difficult to tell precisely

17*

what they are about. Report is that they amuse themselves with nocturnal incursions in the neighborhood of King George Court House, seizing the colored population and sending them south. It is also said that a portion of their forces have been withdrawn from their works in the rear of Fredericksburg. But little reliance can be placed upon these stories.

January 15. We are still here, nursing our future as a glorious uncertainty. The camp feeling is kept in gentle undulations by a succession of contradictory rumors. One day, old madam's runners tell us the army will move soon ; the next, declare that winter quarters in front of Fredericksburg is our destiny ; and, on the third, affirm that Gen. Burnside has received marching orders, and to-morrow we shall be in motion, sure. Thus swings the pendulum of time, moving the machinery of speculation to the point, whether our war is an objective certainty or a subjective nonentity. Decisions are reversed at each vibration, now affirmative, now negative ; and then, like the Dutch justice, massing the testimonies, and accepting them all. In regard to this matter, I shall not assume to be wise above the written order. What is to be, we shall in due time know. Every one knows that inactivity is not a proclivity of our General. He has already shown that he arose too early, and marched too rapidly for somebody in Washington. We may reasonably believe that he is as ready to rise early and work late, as ever, and that if he does not " march with vigor on," it will be for the best of military reasons. Now and then an occurrence happens that awakens suspicion of something being in the wind. For example, week before last, a number of siege guns came up. The surgeons are removing patients from the hospitals, and sending them to some other place. This is supposed by some to indicate immediate action ; but, per contra, it is said a government hospital on a larger scale is to be established at Acquia Creek, and that looks like no apprehension of danger or design to leave this quarter ; so

our gleams of light vanish, and darkness wraps its mantle about
us. But whether fighting is speedily renewed or not, a full
preparation should be made, and the amplest provision also,
for the removal of the wounded. Our arrangements, in this
particular, however better than on the peninsula, are suscepti-
ble of further and important improvement. The men need this
stimulus as an energizer, when they meet the enemy on a field
of mud, where to fall wounded and lie a day, before removal,
must inevitably be attended with fatal results.

With an hour of leisure at command, the temptation is strong
to spend it in a general review of the past year, and in the indulgence of "a few brief remarks," as long-winded orators say,
in prefacing interminable speeches, on the prospects before us.
In regard to the first particular, the inclination will be resisted,
except to say that the Federal armies on the Peninsula, at
Antietam, South Mountain, Fort Donelson, Roanoke, Port
Royal, Island No. 10, Forts Philip and Jackson, Murfreesboro,
and elsewhere, have shown themselves capable of great things.
Many of the battles, for gallantry and grandeur, are not surpassed by any on the record of modern warfare; and the advantages gained, though at an immense expense of life, are of
vital importance to the perpetuation of our nationality, and
must tell disastrously, in a corresponding degree, upon the rebel
confederacy. Yet, the rebels possess wonderful recuperative
powers. They have the advantage of position. They fight
with their homes in sight, and, made to believe that this war is
one of extermination, they fight with desperation. We can
fight them and drive them every day, and with the doggedness
of an English mastiff, they will return to the conflict. Their
policy of warfare is shrewd, and calculated to realize the most
from limited resources. It is what may be called the exhaust-
ing system. They mass their men when possible, and when
not, harass by dashes, fight where success is doubtful up to a
given time, and having effected all the slaughter possible, leave
the Federals in possession of the field, often too much wearied

and depleted to follow up instantly the advantage left in their hands. They fight and run, on the maxim, probably, that they may thus " live to fight another day." Now, it seems to me, they should be met in their own way. Our armies should be massed. Overwhelming force should be brought to bear on single points, so that victory may never be equivocal ; and that when the rebels are put to a skedaddle, there may be an abundance of spare power to follow them up, and make a complete finish of the work. The massing of our artillery at Malvern Hill gave us that splendid victory. Nothing else could have done it. A braver army of infantry than ours never engaged in action, but except sustained by the vast artillery force, they would have been overpowered by the immense hordes massed against them. These may, to the more experienced in the art of war, seems but the crude words of a tyro. They express, however, an opinion, the result of some thought, a careful study of the various campaigns since the war begun, and a tolerable knowledge of the animus of the army. With 800,000 men in the field, and one of the largest navies in the world, rebellion ought to be crushed out before next July.

If one in a comfortable shanty, listening to the patter of rain, or the music of the wind, were inclined to be cynical, and to engage in special fault-finding, it would be at the irregularity of the mails. But " hard words butter no parsnips," and it is wiser to regard disappointment as Sam Foote did a hole in his stocking, " an accident of the day," and take refuge in the pleasures of hope. Letters tell us that a vessel is on the way to our base of supplies, full-freighted with vegetables for the Rhode Island troops, and boxes for individuals from thoughtful friends. They will appreciate the tokens of remembrance. For some weeks past, potatoes and onions have been drawn from the commissary, and though not in sufficient quantities to make them a daily ration, they have served a good purpose in making a healthful change of food. Many eyes will be turned towards the Potomac, and the arrival of the Elizabeth and

Helen will be greeted with a heartiness that such a presence is calculated to awaken. Propitious breezes fill her sails and speed her course.*

·

LETTER XXVIII.

Events of three weeks—General Burnside plans an aggressive move-ment—Is delayed—The army moves—Is compelled by a severe storm to turn back—Terrible condition of the roads—General Burnside relieved—Is succeeded by General Hooker.

CAMP NEAR POTOMAC CREEK, VA.,}
January 30, 1863. }

The events of the past three weeks may be grouped thus: A plan, bold and promising success, to drive the rebels from their stronghold in the rear of Fredericksburg, was formed; but something happened to cause delay. The secesh got knowledge that a new scheme was on foot, and improved the opportunity the information afforded, to prepare for a Federal visit. When obstacles were removed, the army was put in motion; but " the rain descended and the floods came," and the mud deepened, and transformed from fitness for brickyard purposes, became a sea of mortar. The men waded, the horses floundered, and the artillery mired. Sixteen horses and a hundred men pulled at a single gun, to hasten it forward, but almost in vain. Pontoons, as on a former occasion, were late, and helped to disappoint a purpose. The elements, with a perfectly resistless power, did what the enemy could not have

---

* The Helen and Elizabeth, after a long and boisterous passage, in which she met with considerable damage, arrived at her destination. The cargo of vegetables was in good order, and made a welcome addition to camp fare.

done—brought the army to a stand-still—and finally forced it back to its old encampments.

[To make this synopsis more intelligible, it should be stated that, though disappointed of success on the 13th December, it formed no part of General Burnside's programme to pass an idle winter in front of the enemy's lines. He at once devised a plan for an aggressive movement, and took prompt measures to carry it into execution. Of this plan he gave, when called before the Committee on the Conduct of the War, the following history:

"On the 26th of December, I ordered the entire command to prepare three days' cooked rations; to fill their wagons with small stores to the amount of ten days' supply; if possible, to have with them, at the same time, from ten to twelve days' supply of beef-cattle, with forage for teams, and cavalry and artillery horses for about the same length of time, and the required amount of ammunition,—in fact, to be in a condition to move at twelve hours notice. I had determined to cross the river some six or seven miles below Fredericksburg, at a point opposite the Sedden House, a short distance below Hayfield. The positions for the artillery to protect the crossing had all been selected, the roads surveyed, and the corduroy necessary to prepare the roads had been cut. It was my intention to make a feint above the town, which could have been turned into a positive assault if I found we were discovered below. But if we were not discovered below, it was my intention to throw the entire command across at the point opposite the Sedden House, and points in the neighborhood where bridges could be built.

"In connection with this movement, I had organized a cavalry expedition, to consist of some two thousand five hundred of the best cavalry in my command; a thousand of them, with four pieces of artillery, to be picked men. And I had detailed a division of infantry from General Hooker's command to accompany this cavalry as far as the upper fords of the Rappahannock, and aid them in crossing. The thousand picked men, with the four pieces of artillery, were to cross the Rappahannock at Kelly's Ford; the Rapidan at Raccoon Ford; the Virginia Central Railroad at Louisa Court House; the James River at either Goochland or Carter's; the Richmond and Lynchburg Railroad at a point south of there; the Richmond, Petersburg and Weldon Railroad at or near the crossing of the Nottoway; and then to move on through General Pryor's command, and join General Peck at Suffolk, where we were to have steamers in waiting to bring them back to Acquia Creek,—at least, the men, with their arms and accoutrements; and, in case their horses had to be left behind, new horses would be supplied to them. The object of this cavalry expedition was to attract the attention of the enemy, blow up the locks on the James River canal, blow up the iron bridge on the Richmond and Lynchburg Railroad at the place of crossing, and destroy the bridge on the Richmond and Weldon Railroad over the Nottoway; and, during this movement, I intended to throw my command across the river at the point I have named. The remainder of the cavalry, other than the thousand picked men, was to break off from the main body in the following order: a portion to go up to Warrenton; another portion to go to the neighborhood of Culpepper; another portion was to accompany the thousand picked men as far as Raccoon Ford, from which point they were to turn back. The object of these dispositions was to deceive the enemy as to which one of the columns was the attacking column.

"This expedition had got under way, and the brigade of infantry had, I think on the 30th of December, crossed at Richard's Ford, and come back over Ellis's Ford, which would have enabled the cavalry to cross at Kelly's Ford. On that day, I received from the President of the United States a telegraphic dispatch in, substantially, these words: 'I have good reason for saying that you must not make a general movement

without letting me know of it.' I could not imagine, at the
time, what reasons the President had for sending this telegram,
but supposed it related, in some way, to some important military movements in other parts of the country, in which it was
necessary to have coöperation. I at once despatched a messenger to overtake the advance of this cavalry expedition, and
order them to halt until further orders ; and I simply suspended
the order for the general movement. My messenger overtook
the cavalry just as they were ready to cross at Kelly's Ford.
In the meantime, I heard of the raid Stuart had made in the
direction of Dumfries, and the rear of Fairfax Court House,
and sent a second order for a portion of this cavalry to endeavor
to cut off Stuart in the neighborhood of Warrenton, in which
they did not succeed. I then determined to come up to Washington to see the President, and, if possible, to ascertain the
exact state of the case.

" I came up to Washington, saw the President, and he frankly
told me that some general officers of my command had called
upon him, and represented that I was on the eve of another
movement ; that the order for the preparation of rations, ammunition, &c., had already been issued, and all the preliminary
arrangements made ; and that they were satisfied that if the
movement was made, it would result in disaster. That was
about the substance of what the President told me, although
he said a great deal more. I was so much surprised at the
time, at what I heard, that it did not make an active impression on my mind as to the exact words. But I am sure that
was the nature of it ; and I think he said that he had understood that no prominent officer of my command had any faith
in my proposed movement.

" I then sat down and gave the President a detailed account
of my plans for this movement, at the same time telling him
that I was satisfied there was some misgiving on the part of
some of my general officers as to making any movement at all
at that time. But I said that I was myself satisfied that that

movement ought to be made, and I had come to that conclusion without any consultation with the other generals.

" The President still expressed misgivings as to the feasibility of making the entire movement, but expressed some regret at the cavalry portion of it being stopped. I told him that that was a portion of the general movement, and that, if these picked men were to go around Richmond without having any general movement in coöperation with them, and were to meet with disaster and be captured, it would be a very serious loss to us ; and even if they were to meet with success, it would not compensate for the risk, unless we were to take advantage of that success by a general movement ; and, besides, if the details of this cavalry movement could be kept quiet—kept secret—it might yet be made, in conjunction with the general movement, as I had proposed.

" The President then said that he did not feel willing to authorize a continuous movement without consultation with some of his advisers. He sent for General Halleck and Mr. Stanton, and the matter was very fully talked over. He told them, what they then for the first time heard of, that these officers had called upon him and made these representations to him, resulting in his telegram to me. I asked him if he would give me the names of those officers. He said he could not. I expressed some opinions in reference to what ought to be done with them, but, at the same time, said that I should not insist upon having the names, as he had a right to withhold them. General Halleck, at the same time, expressed the opinion that officers making representations of that kind should have been dismissed the service at once, or arrested at once, or something of that kind. My view was that they should have been dismissed the service.

" No definite conclusion was come to during that conference in reference to the subject of a movement. I was here at that time for two days.

" When I returned to my camp, I found that many of the

18

details of the general movement were already known, and was told by a general officer that the details of the cavalry movement were known here in the city of Washington to some sympathizers with the rebellion. I was told that by General Pleasanton. This was some two or three days after my first interview with the President. Of course, I then abandoned the movement in that distinct form, intending to make it in some other form within a few days."]

On the 20th instant, General Burnside announced in a general order to the army, that they were to meet the enemy once more ; that the auspicious moment had arrived for striking " a great and mortal blow to the rebellion, and to gain that decisive victory which is due to the country." He had personally reconnoitered the ground above Falmouth, which determined him to make preparations for crossing at both Banks's and the United States Fords, and in their neighborhood ; and also for crossing six or seven miles below. To that end, all the necessary roads were prepared, the pontoon trains placed in position, and the artillery detailed to cover the crossing. In carrying out the plan, General Sumner had the right, Hooker the centre, and Franklin the left. Hooker and Franklin began to move their columns up by different roads, while Sumner was to make a feint with pontoons below. The design was to turn the rebel stronghold in the rear of Fredericksburg, while Sumner was to cross the river at the old place opposite, and attack simultaneously in front.

The plan was well conceived ; but its success depended upon secrecy, celerity and propitious weather. By some means yet unexplained, the rebels became aware of the contemplated movement some days before it occurred. Conflicting intelligence of spies, in regard to the position of the enemy, caused delay, and when, at last, the march commenced, a severe rain of three days duration set in, converting the whole country, under the tread of men and horses, into a vast morass, and ren-

dering further march impossible. The rebel pickets across the
river saw our discomfiture, and gave expression to their delight by exhibiting sarcastic placards. " Stuck in the mud,"
was their legend.

To further contest the supremacy of the elements were folly,
and it only remained to accept the alternative—return. But
this was scarcely less difficult than to advance. Artillery, ambulances and pontoon trains blocked the roads; men, horses
and mules, sunk to their knees in mire, could only with the
utmost exertion move. But by dint of whipping, spurring, and
of shoulders put to wheels that horses could not stir, the army
finally reached the vacated encampments, but in no enviable
plight. Horses, cannon and caissons were cased in clay, and
thousands of men who by a misstep had measured their length
in the plastic bed, resembled, in outward appearance, a body of
ditchers or brickyard workmen. Except for recollection of the
hundreds of poor fellows who gave out and fell by the way, to
be taken up sick or dying, the return would have been irresist-
ably ludicrous; and as it was, mirthfulness predominated.
Jests were freely bandied, though mingled with a liberal
amount of emphatic expletives. In the memorable experiences
of these few days, battery C. in common with the other Rhode
Island artillery, participated, and shared in the universal regrets at a failure for which neither the army nor its leader were
in fault.

Through the entire four weeks covering the planning and
attempted execution of this expedition, and perplexed as he
was in no common degree, the Commander-in-Chief bore himself with characteristic equanimity. Every movement and expression was indicative of the high-minded, conscientious patriot. On going to Washington, for reasons which it is not the
purpose here to discuss, he tendered to the President his resignation. But the President said, " We need you, and cannot
accept your resignation." In its stead, a thirty days' leave of
absence was given, at the close of which he was to be invested

with the command of an important department.* Last Monday, (26th,) General Burnside, by general order, announced the transfer of his command to General Hooker. He complimented the army for its courage, patience and endurance, and urged the men " to be true in their devotion to their country and the principles they had sworn to maintain," and to give their new commander their " full and cordial support and co-operation." His departure awakens wide regret. His genial smile will be missed by the men, and he carries with him their confidence and affection. General Hooker has announced his staff, at the head of which is Major General Butterfield. To a speculative mind, the year entered upon, as the year closed, furnishes materials for the construction of a philosophy of contingencies, or for an elucidation of the science of probabilities. Fortune is certainly an untrustworthy dame ; but if they who " braveliest bear her scorns awhile," are those " on whom at last she most will smile," the army of the Potomac need not abandon hope of brighter skies. All, in national life, is not exclusively in the control of man. God is over him, and in the end will vindicate his cause.

---

* General Burnside was assigned to the Department of the Ohio. General Sumner was at the same time, at his own request, relieved of his command. He died, after a short and severe illness, at Syracuse, N. Y., while on a visit to that place, March 21, 1863, in the 68th year of his age. He was a native of Boston, and making arms his profession, he served his country long and faithfully. A short time before he died, a few drops of wine were given to revive him, when he seized the glass and waving it above his pillow, exclaimed, " God save my country, the United States of America." His decease was appropriately noticed by his successor, General Couch, in a general order to the Second army corps, and also by General Howard, commanding the second division in the same corps.

LETTER XXIX.

Mud, king—Changes in command—Hospital incident—Rebel relics—
Washington's birth-day.

CAMP NEAR POTOMAC CREEK, VA., }
February 6, 1863. }

Mud is king, and top-boots for subjects are in requisition.
Since the army returned to its encampments from the attempt
to cross the Rappahannock, snow, rain, frost and drizzle have
preserved the monarch's domain from all attempts of sunshine
and wind to diminish its extent. Let one undertake a pleasure
jaunt of twenty miles just now, and he will be convinced that
the story of a battery gun being sunk, on the late expedition, until nothing remained visible but the rims of the
carriage wheels, was but a slightly exaggerated form of speech.
In the course of a few weeks the fitful season will be past, and
active movements can then be more satisfactorily made than at
present possible.

Various changes have taken place in commands. General
Smith has been transferred from the Sixth to the Ninth army
corps, which won noble distinction under Gen. Burnside, at
Antietam. Gen. Smith's old command held a front position
before Yorktown, showed great valor at Williamsburg, and
claims to have saved the right wing at Antietam. The record
of his new command, he can look upon with satisfaction. Gen.
Couch, who has succeeded Gen. Sumner, has the reputation of
a brave and skillful officer.

The autumn campaign was very severe on horses. According to official report, nearly 12,000 unserviceable animals were
turned into the depot at Washington, between September 1st
and December 1st. It is said the larger portion of these were
disabled by hard usage and want of proper attention. Both
these causes were often of necessity and not inhumanity.

18*

Yesterday, a cavalry reconnoissance was made to Rappahannock Station, in search of a pontoon bridge which it was reported the rebels were constructing in the vicinity. No discovery was made, and the pontoon is probably a myth.

February 8. Since Gen. Hooker assumed the command of the army of the Potomac, a reorganization has taken place which it is supposed will give it greater efficiency. Army corps take the place of the grand division system. The commanders of these stand in the following order : Major Generals John F. Reynolds, Couch, Sickles, (whose command is reported to be temporary,) Meade, Sedgwick, Sigel, Slocum. The batteries are to be a unit under a chief of artillery, and the cavalry are to be consolidated under Gen. Stoneman, who led the advance on the Peninsula. For several days past, considerable stir had been visible in the Ninth army corps, which proved to have been caused by preparation for leaving the scene of its late encampment. Last Friday, it moved for Fortress Monroe. In this corps are included the 4th, 7th and 12th Rhode Island regiments, and the 8th, 11th, 15th and 16th Connecticut.

The war has given birth to many gems of poetry, patriotic, humorous and pathetic, illustrative of the spirit and varied impressions of the times. A volume compiled from the newspapers of the day would prove a rich contribution to the military literature of the country. Here is a touching morceau, from an unknown pen, suggested by an affecting scene in one of the army hospitals. A brave lad of sixteen years, belonging to a New England regiment, mortally wounded at Fredericksburg, and sent to the Patent Office Hospital, in Washington, was anxiously looking for the coming of his mother. As his last hour approached, and sight grew dim, he mistook a sympathetic lady who was wiping the cold, clammy perspiration from his forehead, for the expected one, and with a smile of joy lighting up his pale face, whispered tenderly, " is that mother?"   "Then," says the writer, "drawing her towards him with all his feeble strength, he nestled his head in her arms like a sleeping infant, and thus died with the sweet word 'Mother' on his quivering lips."

"IS THAT MOTHER?"

"Is that mother, bending o'er me,
  As she sang my cradle hymn—
Kneeling there in tears before me?
  Say?—my sight is growing dim.

"Comes she from the old home lowly,
  Out among the northern hills,
To her pet boy, dying slowly
  Of war's battle wounds and ills?

"Mother! oh we bravely battled—
  Battled till the day was done;
While the leaden hail-storm rattled—
  Man to man and gun to gun.

"But we failed; and I am dying—
  Dying in my boyhood's years,—
There—no weeping, self-denying—
  Noble deaths demand no tears!

"Fold your arms again around me;
  Press again my aching head;
Sing the lullaby you sang me—
  Kiss me, mother, ere I'm dead."

There is pathos in this incident—one only of hundreds similar,—to inspire the artist's pencil.

February 14.   Nothing of exciting interest has occurred the past week, and little of incident of any sort worth noting. The battery stands parked in grim silence, ready to report when called upon, and the encampments of the army generally are in quietude. The rebels, on the contrary, are reported busy on the other side of the Rappahannock, along our entire front.

Earthworks have been thrown up opposite Falmouth, and rifle pits near the margin of the river. Whether these additional preparations for visitors are based upon a supposition that the Federals design to revisit their old battle-field, or upon positive information, is unknown; but our apparent quietness evidently alarms them, and they intend to be in readiness for whatever may turn up. On our side, sharper attention is p..id to picket duties. By a late order, corps commanders are held responsible for the proper position and strength of their picket lines, and their proper connection on the right and left. This is a wise and judicious measure, and will tend to prevent sudden surprises by rebel raids.

A few epistolary relics from the rebel encampment, scattered by the battle of December 13th, have fallen into my hands, together with a few secesh envelopes, which bear strong external evidence of northern manufacture. The letters are from home, to relatives in camp. One from a wife, is full of solicitude for her husband, whom she learns is sick, and begs, if he cannot obtain a furlough to come home until he recovers, to be kept constantly informed of his situation. Another, from a brother, relating to some business transactions with a neighbor, shows that Mr. Jefferson Davis has at least one man in his domain who needs sharp looking after. But the most significant one is from a mother, who exclaims, "Oh, how I long for this terrible war to be over, so that our poor soldiers may return to their homes and friends, and peace be restored to our troubled country." Doubtless this is the daily wish of thousands of mothers in Dixie; and if they will persuade their husbands and sons to abandon a wicked rebellion, that if persisted in, must issue in their utter ruin, they may hope, at an early day, to realize their wish. The process is simple and practical, and the experiment worth trying.

February 23. Yesterday, the birth-day of Washington was ushered in by one of the severest snow storms of the winter;

grand in itself, as a natural phenomenon, but shorn of poetic sublimity, when viewed from the long line of tents scantily provided with fuel, or deficient in extra blankets. A national salute of thirty-four guns was fired at noon, by the artillery of the different divisions, and, had the weather permitted, the army would have been paraded to hear read portions of the Farewell Address. To the loyal States, and to loyal men in the rebel States, the wise counsels of that address were never so full of expression as now. The angry whirl of the snow, and the hoarse voice of the storm, were appropriate demonstrations of the spirit in which, if living, the founder of the Republic would rebuke the men seeking to destroy it. Under canvas, the hours of discomfort were whiled away by ingenious attempts to keep out the sky dust, or in running a parallel between a winter in front of Fredericksburg and a Revolutionary winter at Valley Forge.

Provost Marshal General Patrick is vigorously exercising his functions against sutlers of feeble conscience. At Belle Plain, a few days ago, a cargo of forbidden goods were seized and confiscated—a significant warning to all minor and major offenders. An extensive contraband traffic between the rebels in Maryland and Virginia has also just been broken up. The supply party run their merchandise, and with it important information of Federal positions and designs, across the Potomac near the extremity of the peninsula. The seizures comprised horses, mules, and a large quantity of provisions, destined for Richmond. A number of vessels employed as transports were destroyed, and several citizen smugglers, together with a rebel signal officer, captured. This operation has stopped, for the present, the enforcement of the rebel conscription, in what are called the Neck counties of the peninsula, then about to take place.

March 20. Last Tuesday, (17th,) Gen. Averill had a sharp engagement of four hours duration, with the rebel cavalry un-

der Stuart and Fitz Hugh Lee, beyond Kelly's Ford. Gen.
Averill's command consisted of the 1st Rhode Island cavalry,
Colonel Duffie, 1st and 5th regulars, 4th New York, 6th Ohio,
16th and 34th Pennsylvania, and the 6th New York light
battery. The enemy were routed with the loss of one hundred
men and fifty prisoners. The Federal loss is reported at about
forty. The fight is considered the most brilliant cavalry affair
of the Rappahannock campaign, and reflects high credit on the
spirit and skill of General Averill. The Rhode Island cavalry
were in the hottest of the fight, and displayed great bravery.
They lost Lieut. Nichols and two privates killed, and had
eighteen men wounded. Lieut. Colonel Farrington narrowly
escaped with a wound in the neck, but continued on the field.
Lieutenant Bowditch, an estimable officer of 1st Massachusetts
cavalry, and Assistant Adjutant General of the first brigade,
was mortally wounded. Of his sufferings, mention has already
been made.

General Stuart appears to have an exalted estimate of female influence, and begun to turn it to account in the rebel
cause, by appointing a Miss Antonia J. Ford an honorary
Aide-de-Camp, and, as such, requiring her to be "obeyed, respected and admired, by all the lovers of a noble nature." Miss
Ford has been styled "a modern Delilah." She was recently
arrested at her home, near Fairfax Court House, by the military authorities, which act may save the Federal Samsons of
that outpost from betrayal into the hands of the Philistines.

March 29. Day before yesterday, Gov. Curtain of Pennsylvania, who is visiting the troops from that State, was entertained with an exhibition of skill in various athletic sports,
enlivened by the music of several bands. A stand, some two
hundred feet in length, was extemporized from pontoons and
bridge materials at hand, near the encampment of the Second
army corps, which was occupied by Gov. C. and suite, division
and brigade officers, and a number of ladies, whose temporary

presence has of late graced the camp. The amusements comprised a steeple chase, scrub, foot and sack races, greased pole
climbing, and other like gymnastics. If they were less classic
in order and execution than those of Isthmian fame, they were
quite as amusing and satisfactory to the large assemblage of
spectators. For several weeks past, occasional episodes of this
kind have received the sanction and presence of the Commander-in-Chief, giving healthful excitement to the soldiers, amid
the graver duties of military routine. Human nature is the
same in the army as out of it. The men crave provocations to
mirth, and Mars does wisely by now and then yielding a point
to Momus.

Under the judicious arrangements of General Hooker, the
morale of the army has been constantly improving for the last
two months. Its present condition is in agreeable contrast
with its jaded spirit immediately after what has been facetiously
called the "mudlarking expedition." Rest, brief leaves of
absence, a full supply of vegetables, soft bread, and other special attentions to the comfort of the soldiers, have invigorated
the atmosphere of the camps. Cheerfulness prevails, the jocund
laugh rings out with hearty sound, the fire that burned at Antietam is again kindling, discipline improves, confidence in-
creases, and, to all appearance, by the time a movement shall
be possible, the men will be ready for any good service to which
they may be called.

The experiences of ten days' leave of absence are not without interest, especially to those who have enjoyed the privilege
for the first time in eighteen months. Suppose the somewhat
tedious preliminary of obtaining the necessary papers, duly
signed, to be over, and the lucky recipient safely embarked on
board the government mail steamer, the fasts thrown off, and
the vessel headed for Washington. Fancy now plumes her
wings for a speedy flight to distant waiting joys. But fancy
and fact are in conflict. Imagination succumbs to stern reality.
Expectation drinks from the cup of disappointment. The tide

is low, the channel tortuous, and in a few moments the steamer "misses stays," and is brought up all standing on a sand bar, where, for three hours, she lies puffing and floundering like a stranded cetaceous monster, affording the meditative mind ample opportunity, amid the noise and confusion of a not over pious crowd, to philosophize upon the uncertainties of this nether world, and to test its patience, while reflecting that the delay necessitates the using up of the next twenty-four hours at the wrong end of the route. But the capital is finally reached, and a much needed bath at Willard's makes partial atonement, by its refreshing influence, for the vexations of the day.

But another trial is in store. Night comes, but " sleep is no servant of the will," and is courted in vain. A generous host can only provide a luxurious feather bed. Here come no "rosy dreams and slumbers light." Half smothered in the plumage of Rome's deliverers, rest is as impossible as peace to a troubled conscience, and tossing from side to side, while waiting coming day, the mind reverts to blanket, tent, or bivouac, when sleep was both deep and sweet, and sympathizes with the boy whose painful endurance of a single feather caused him to marvel that human nature could abide the effects of a sack full. The time of departure at last arrives. Turning the back on steamer and city, the cars are taken at 6 o'clock P. M., puff, puff, goes the iron horse, as he rushes over the road with lightning speed, and, at the end of thirty-six hours, the traveller finds himself at his destination, to give unexpectant friends an early morn surprise. Then come the hearty greetings, the multiplied seals of affection, the social *divertisements* that awaken memories of more peaceful days, beguile the hours, and bring so soon the moment of departure, that one is disposed to think old Father Time has been rejuvenated, and, for the purpose of hastening matters, has borrowed the famed seven league boots.

The recent address of Mr. Jefferson Davis to the confederate States indicates apprehensions on the food question. The deficiency in the supply of meat for the rebel army, is acknowledged, and a full avowal of the fact is made, that "the production of corn, oats, beans, peas, potatoes, and other food for man," is of more consequence than the "production of cotton and tobacco." Cotton is no longer king, and the dethroned monarch shrinks away from the cry that is daily coming up with stronger emphasis, "what shall we eat?"

The condition of the rebel confederacy, as here virtually confessed by its chief, is in remarkable contrast with the state of things in the loyal States. While the south is trembling in prospect of "embarrassments in military operations, and sufferings among the people," arising from deficiency in the food supply, the vast grain regions of the west have scarcely been touched by the devastating hand of war ; the immense granaries of Chicago pour out their supplies in unstinted measure, and the mills of St. Louis, Rochester, Patapsco, and elsewhere, run with increasing vigor. While at the south, a depreciated currency, deranged business, and desolated fields, show how terrible is the calamity of war when brought home, the most striking feature at the north is the almost total absence of its signs. With this, I was strongly impressed on my late brief visit there. In Washington and Baltimore, the evidences of existing war were abundant, but in Philadelphia and New York they had nearly disappeared. The noble Soldier's Rest, in the former city, which has refreshed so many thousands of our weary men, indeed reminded us that sympathy for the defenders of the Union was still warm ; but Chestnut street was as gay as in the palmiest days of peace, and the squirrels on Independence Square gamboled undisturbed by national turmoil. In New York, Broadway teemed with busy life. Merchant princes were making more princely fortunes than ever. Fashion had never been more costly in expenditures, promenades never more brilliant, and places of amusements never more crowded. Except the old barracks on the Park, and the few soldiers met, who find a temporary home at the Rest, superintended by Col.

19

Howe, little was to be seen indicative of civil convulsion. The same was true of Providence. Westminster street was as lively as before the first gun was fired on Sumter; familiar faces were met at every corner; the cars were, as usual, bringing and carrying away their living freights; the ships at the wharves were lading and unlading, with unabated activity; the smoke was going up from numerous factories, foundries and machine shops, and scarcely a noticeable depletion in population had been made by the thousands sent from the city to sustain the government in suppressing rebellion. And so it is throughout the north. Except here and there a recruiting station, nothing looks like war. When one witnesses the profusion that prevails, and sees, as he must, that all the north has done to support the Union has been from her abundance ; that sacrifice has not yet touched her fountains of wealth, the contrast between the condition of the north and the south becomes too palpable to escape attention, and too significant not to awaken practical reflection. Still, it may not be safe to count largely on the fatal effects of the present scarcity of food upon the rebel cause. The leaders are in earnest, as men to whom results will be life or death. They have a faculty of inspiring the masses with their own spirit, and whatever change they propose for mending their fortunes, will probably be adopted. If a cultivation of the cereals, to the exclusion of cotton, is urged as a necessity, the grain fields will at once be multiplied, and the crops of a favorable season will contribute largely to relieve them of the embarrassments now felt. It may be true that a diminished crop of cotton will injuriously affect the confederate finances; but credit in Europe will be quite as much strengthened or weakened by the probabilities of final success or disaster, as by any temporary advantages to foreign manufacturing interests accruing from a larger cotton supply. The effectual Federal counteractive of Mr. Davis's new policy, is to be found in good fighting.

Under the President's proclamation, many absentees have

returned to their respective regiments. They were largely men who had enlisted under the high bounty system, and had deserted to enlist again under assumed names, to improve their finances. Many of them enlisted and deserted several times. Probably no system designed to encourage patriotic enlistments was ever so widely abused. Bringing to the army thousands actuated solely by pecuniary considerations, and who never intended to fight, the moral effects were only evil, and a plan intended to strengthen it, proved, for the time, an expensive failure. The interesting and important report of Major Hamlin to Gov. Sprague shows that, in common with other States, Rhode Island has suffered severely from this evil. The return to their regiments, through his efforts, of between eight and nine hundred deserters and stragglers, affords commendable evidence of the persistence, vigor and success with which he has pursued his duties. At Washington, as I have incidentally learned, the United States Provost Marshal's office in Providence is considered the most thoroughly organized and efficient of any in commission.

LETTER XXX.

Health of the army—Hospitals—Sanitary Commission—The work of Mrs. Fales, Mrs. Chittenden and Mrs. Jillson—St. Patrick's day—Death of Young Fales—Distinguished visitors—Reviews—Rebel Pickets—Movement of General Stoneman—General Fogliardi—Pay day—Army in motion.

CAMP NEAR POTOMAC CREEK. VA..)
April 4th, 1863. {

The sanitary condition of the army is favorably reported. The number on the sick list, in the camp hospitals, does not exceed the usual average, and is less than might have been

expected after the fatigues and exposures of the earlier part of
winter.   Our camp hospitals are not intended for patients requiring serious treatment, and are usually occupied by men
whose cases call for only the simplest prescriptions.   As soon
as it is evident that some weeks or months will elapse before
recovery, the patients are removed to Washington, and thence,
if they can bear the fatigue of the journey, many of them are
distributed to hospitals in Baltimore, Philadelphia, or Portsmouth Grove.   The hospital department has been constantly
expanding to meet the exigencies of a constantly expanding
war, and the arrangements are considered as well systematized.
In the beginning, no one foresaw or imagined, that in less than
two years, nearly one hundred and fifty thousand sick and
wounded men would require medical and surgical treatment;
yet this has actually occurred since the 1st of November, 1862.
From the most reliable sources of information, it appears that
upwards of one hundred and thirty thousand men are now in
the various hospitals of the country.   With limited conveniences, and an inadequate number of skillful surgeons, it is not
surprising that, at first, complaints were numerous and emphatic;
but early measures were adopted to remedy evils that a short
experience had developed.   In Washington, temporary hospitals took a permanent form; large and commodious buildings
were erected, and others at hand were taken by the government, and converted to hospital uses.   These are now in good
condition.   Patients sent there find the comforts and attention
that make sickness endurable, and that relieve the ennui of
confinement from wounds.

For the improvements visible in general and camp hospitals,
much is due to the labors of the Sanitary Commission.   By
the inspections and suggestions of its medical agents, many
evils resulting from inexperience and other causes have been
removed, and by the seasonable supplies of hospital stores it
has furnished, the sick and wounded have been greatly relieved.
The services rendered in the camps on the Peninsula, and on

the fields at Antietam, Fredericksburg and elsewhere, are
among the gratifying evidences of its usefulness as an auxiliary
to the Medical Bureau. At Antietam, the army was reached
by more than forty agents of the Commission, with supplies, at
an earlier hour than it was possible for the government to forward them, and within three days after the battle, they had
rendered relief, in some form, to eight thousand poor fellows
who had experienced the casualties of war. By their prompt
labors, hundreds of lives were doubtless saved, that otherwise
would have been lost. The same was true before Fredericksburg, where eighteen division hospitals had been organized.
The agents came laden with blankets, so much needed by the
wounded, exposed to a chilly night and to rain ; and welcome
were the changes of raiment they brought to those whose garments were stiff with dirt and gore. The value of such works
cannot be over-estimated, and a commission that carries them
so vigorously on, deserves the hearty and liberal support of the
patriotic and humane, whose spirit it so faithfully represents.
The relation it holds to the army is vital. Its experience in
everything pertaining to the sanitary welfare of the troops in
the field and in the hospital, is invaluable, and while the rebellion continues, will find ample scope for its disinterested
labors.

To the voluntary labors of such women (an honored word)
as Mrs. J. T. Fales, wife of Joseph T. Fales, Esq., of the Patent Office, Mrs. Chittenden, Mrs. Jillson, and others in Washington, who have so constantly visited local and camp hospitals,
great praise is also due. Their presence and sympathetic
words, even more than their gifts, have cheered thousands of
our wounded, whose sufferings, far from home, were making
them victims of despondency, and left an impression on grateful memories that will never be obliterated.

Of Mrs. Fales, it is no fulsome compliment to say she is a
Florence Nightingale of our army. She is from Iowa, and
when the rebellion broke out, entered upon her mission of

19*

mercy under the promptings of a noble patriotism. At Corinth, Pittsburg Landing, and elsewhere in the west, she was busy on the battle-field, ministering to wounded and dying soldiers. Last summer she was on the peninsula, dispensing to the sick and suffering, the refreshing contents of her ample trunk. A woman of sound judgment, of calm but energetic temperament, of warm maternal heart, practical in action, and uncompromising in her devotion to the Union, she enjoys the full confidence of the government, who have placed an ambulance and a driver at her command, and, thus appointed, she daily visits the hospitals, extending her drives often twenty miles distant from the capital.

The observations of one day prepare her for the details of the next. Whatever is lacking of clothing, stimulants or delicacies, she notes, and these, as far as in her power, are made the assortment of the following day. When at home, her practice is to visit the depots and steamboat landings, where she renders the aid in her power to the sick and friendless, sent from the army discharged, or destined to the government hospitals. A convenient tent, pitched in her front yard, has been a blessed home to many poor wayfarers, exhausted by disease, or destitute of means to procure food and lodging. To increase her usefulness, she corresponds extensively with individuals and associations, and whatever is sent to her for general or special distribution, is discreetly dispensed. Her interest embraces soldiers from every State, and many Rhode Island soldiers have been made glad by the kindnesses she has bestowed upon them.*

---

* An only son, Corporal Thomas H. B. Fales, of Co. K, 2d Rhode Island, was killed in the battle of Salem Heights, May 3d, at the age of twenty-one years. Of pure moral and christian character, and justly estimating the value of the Union, he heartily engaged in its defence. When Mr. Lincoln's election became known, and threats were made that he should never be inaugurated, young Fales joined a volunteer company in Washington, in which he served for several months, until disbanded. He then enlisted in the 2d Rhode Island regiment, and was with it in the bat-

In the history of this rebellion, a large chapter will be due to the loyal women of the country. To them, to a greater extent than has been acknowledged or generally realized, is the government indebted for the enduring patriotism of its army. The Rhode Island soldiers owe much to the Relief Associations in Providence and elsewhere, for remembrances that have revived flagging spirits, enlivened many a weary march, and cheered both camp and hospital.

> "Theirs are deeds which cannot pass away,
> And names that will not wither."

April 12. The civic amusements inaugurated on St. Patrick's Day, under the auspices of General Meagher, and culminating in the athletic entertainment given in honor of Gov. Curtin, under the sanction of Gen. Hooker, have been succeeded by military galas, honored by the presence of the President, Mrs. Lincoln, Master Lincoln and Attorney General Bates. These distinguished guests reached Acquia Landing in a fierce snow storm, on Saturday evening, 4th instant. They remained on board the steamer until the next morning, when they proceeded to Falmouth Station, where they were received by Gen. Butterfield, and thence escorted by a squadron of lancers to Gen. Hooker's head-quarters.

The storm of Saturday night, the snow drifts piled up about the camps, the sharp winds of Sunday, the mud of Monday, and the examination of encampments and hospitals on succeeding days, must have given the Presidential party a better idea

---

tle of Bull Run, and also in all its subsequent engagements. Brave, faithful in the discharge of his duty, and ever displaying generous, manly traits, he engaged the respect and esteem of his companions in arms. In the heat of the battle above mentioned, he was severely wounded, but refused to go to the rear. Soon after, a second shot pierced his breast, and he fell dead, and was buried on the field. An unsuccessful effort was made to recover his body, the rebel general refusing permission to enter his lines to search for the grave.

of the vicissitudes of a soldier's life than could have been derived from official reports. During the President's sojourn
here, every corps of the army, infantry, cavalry and artillery,
passed in review before him.

Ladies are always welcome visitors to the camp, and never
fail to be received with the courtesy due to their sex ; and the
presence of Mrs. Lincoln gratified the respectful curiosity of
the thousands who had never before seen a President's wife.
A tent was fitted up for her use, less sumptuous than the arrangements of the White House, but neat and comfortable.
At the reviews, she occupied a carriage, and appeared to take
a warm interest in the passing scenes. Of the President, a
characteristic anecdote is related. After the review, last
Wednesday, (8th,) an ardent admirer of the regulars, in dis-
paragement of volunteers, called his attention to the more
exact discipline of the former, inasmuch as they stood statue-
like without moving the head, when he passed, while the latter
almost universally dressed to the left, that they might keep him
in view along the entire line. He did not, however, take the
impression intended to be given, and simply replied, " I do n't
care how much my soldiers turn their heads if they do n't turn
their backs." He returned to Washington day before yesterday, and all is again quiet.

Some time ago, communication between the rebel pickets
and our own was interdicted, but gradually, after a short period, the old and somewhat familiar relations were resumed, and
good-natured jokes bandied across the river. The rebels have
been very free in expressing their opinions of the war, and
some of them, if reported, would hardly be accepted as complimentary to Mr. Jefferson Davis. From the pickets on our
side, they often get a sharp criticism, which is usually good-
naturedly received. The charm of Abydos to Leander was
scarcely stronger than is the affection of thirsty secesh for
Federal coffee. To obtain a luxury so rare, they often propose
a suspension of hostilities, that they may come over and par-

take of Union hospitality. Recently, half a dozen of them stacked arms and crossed the river. They wished the war over, and thought if their leaders were out of the way, the difficulties could easily be adjusted. After spending an hour, two of their number concluded to remain. The others returned. How they accounted for the absence of their companions without criminating themselves has not been reported. The Butternuts, however, are good at a dodge, and no doubt came off clear. The rebel army is still in full force at Fredericksburg. At the present time, they will hardly risk to weaken themselves at this point, however much they may desire to send troops elsewhere.

April 18. The New York papers have put us in possession of Culpepper and Gordonsville, consummations "devoutly to be wished," but the record, I am sorry to say, is not supported by facts. The statements probably grew out of a demonstration made by a body of Gen. Stoneman's cavalry and a support of infantry, at Kelly's Ford on Tuesday last, the account of which, before reaching New York, assumed the proportions of an important success. Whether Gen. S. designed anything more than a reconnoissance in force is unknown, but crossing the river and driving the rebels from their stronghold remains a work for the future.

The army, or at least portions of it, has been, for a week, under light marching orders, with eight days' rations kept constantly on hand. As usual, when a movement is in contemplation on the Rappahannock, the elements seemed to be in sympathy with the rebels. A severe rain storm on Wednesday last, has vetoed operations for a few days, and desire for active service is held in abeyance by that cardinal virtue, patience. The temporary absence on leave, of Capt. Martin, has devolved the duties of chief of artillery on Capt. Waterman. Ten days ago, battery C was withdrawn from the position in which it had been placed, to watch the enemy, and has since been in park, ready to hitch up at a moment's warning.

In some way the rebels had been apprised of the stir in our camps, and it is said, immediately sent reinforcements to guard the various fords. Of what is to be attempted or done by our forces, it is premature to speak. A week of fair weather will put the roads in a more passable condition, when large bodies can move with greater certainty of carrying their point. When again in motion, the wires will chronicle their deeds.

Gen. Fogliardi, a Swiss military celebrity, has been, for a short time, enjoying the hospitality of Gen. Hooker. He is accompanied by Col. Repetti and Lieut. Lubin, the latter acting as interpreter. The object of this visit is to obtain a knowledge of the character and efficiency of our army. To this end, he has favored with reviews and inspections. These, it is understood, have elicited warm encomiums.

Among the welcome personages seen among us since the President's visit, have been the paymaster and allotment commissioner Amsbury. To many of the regiments and batteries, five months' pay was due, and settling up has lighted a multitude of faces with smiles. The clergyman who thought he could preach better for having a V or an X in his pocket, differed little from his brethren of the human family, whose weapons of warfare are less spiritual; and no doubt when the word forward is heard, the step will be all the more elastic for a reasonable supply of green-backs. The allotment arrangement is an admirable one for safety, and numbers improved the presence of the commissioner to make remittances to their families or parents. I am informed that nearly half a million of dollars has passed through this channel from Rhode Island soldiers since the system was organized, and not a dollar has failed to reach its destination.

April 27. Gen. Stoneman's advance, mentioned under a previous date, appears to have been the signal for a general movement of the army; but since the return of the President and his party to Washington, the elements have been unpropitious, and little more than patient waiting could be done. For upwards of two weeks, in the apparent absence of the chief of the Zodiac, Aquarius usurped the rule, and exercised his peculiar functions without stint. The floods were poured; the Rappahannock increased its proportions; the little streams filled to repletion, and the roads rivalled their condition in the memorable mud expedition of January. Of course, this usurpation could not long be quietly submitted to, and by an adroit flank push, and a vigorous charge in front, Taurus regained the position from which he had been unceremoniously ejected, "and all the clouds that lower'd upon our house " were rolled behind the distant horizon, or " vanished into thin air," leaving Sol and Boreas full power to repair damages. By their joint industry, the ways have been so far improved that, to-day, under the inspiration of a balmy atmosphere and smiling skies, the army has commenced motion. Our battery moved at 11 A. M. Others will follow soon. We had but three hours notice, and in that time eight days' rations were drawn, three of them were cooked, and the battery was on the march. Large bodies of infantry are in motion, giving an animating appearance to the scene in every direction. Stirring events may be expected soon. We leave our old encampment with pleasant recollections of the comforts it afforded; but while we shall miss our commodious huts and the conveniences ingenuity contrived, we shall be well content to dispense with them, if this movement issues in success.

LETTER XXXI.

The Battle of Chancellorville—Part taken by the 2d Rhode Island, and five Rhode Island batteries—Stoneman's raid—Army recross the Rappahannock.

CAMP NEAR POTOMAC CREEK, VA., }
May 9, 1863.   }

For ten days the valley of the Rappahannock, and all the country between Fredericksburg and Richmond, have been in intense commotion. My date of the 27th ultimo announced that the Federal army was in motion. I now resume the narrative then interrupted, giving such particulars as have fallen under personal observation, and as have been hastily gleaned by inquiry.

If the reader looks at the map of Virginia, and makes a dot at Port Conway, some twenty miles below Fredericksburg, and then makes another dot at Kelly's Ford, twenty-five miles above, a clear view will be obtained of the extent of our line in the primary operations. This, however, was soon contracted. At Port Conway, a feint of crossing with a large body of our troops was made, which drew down Jackson, with 60,000 men, to oppose it. While thus diverting attention, the First, Third and Sixth corps, under Generals Reynolds, Sickles and Sedgwick, were massed at Franklin's old crossing. A portion of the troops were thrown over, driving the rebels from their rifle pits, and holding the bank, without advancing. The residue, including the 2d Rhode Island, remained encamped on this side until Friday, in plain sight of the rebel pickets, who had two pieces of artillery in position at an inconvenient nearness, with more of the same sort planted on the hills in their rear, overlooking and commanding the plain stretching back from the river, and extending towards Fredericksburg. They did not molest our troops, however, lest it might prematurely bring on an engagement, or perhaps prove a signal for an opening upon the city by two Federal batteries in front.

In the movement on the right, the Eleventh corps, under Gen. Howard, led off, followed by the Twelfth, Gen. Slocum, and Fifth, Gen. Meade, to which battery C is attached. They all took the direction of Kelly's Ford, but by different roads, leaving desolate the camps so recently the scenes of drills, reviews and athletic sports. The day was warm, and the men, burdened with rations, heavy knapsacks and overcoats, soon felt the pressure of the heat, and, before night, large numbers had cast aside every encumbrance but the contents of their haversacks, to be gathered up and brought on by the baggage teams, or to furnish a rich harvest of gleanings for the farmers on the route, or other *chiffonniers*, following in the wake of an army. By this injudicious act, (to which weary limbs and aching shoulders are easily provoked,) they deprived themselves of the protection, so soon needed, from evening chills and rain.

On the first day, (Monday,) our battery marched nine miles. On the second, we made eight miles, over roads in many places in very bad condition, and camped at Mount Holly Church. The third day, (Wednesday,) at 10 o'clock A. M., we reached Kelly's Ford. In this vicinity, General Stoneman's cavalry had lingered since the 13th April, when a contemplated raid towards Richmond was cut short by heavy rains. The pontoons were seasonably at the Ford, and speedily laid, and before night of the 29th, the army had crossed the Rappahannock, and Stoneman's cavalry was flying on its important mission. Our division took the direction of Ely's Ford, on the Rapidan, where we encamped for the night, having, in the meantime, captured over one hundred rebels. The next morning, (30th April,) we forded the Rapidan, which here is about seventy yards wide and three or four feet deep, and marched in the rain to Chancellorsville, ten miles in the rear of Fredericksburg. The Eleventh and Twelfth corps crossed the river at Germania Mills, and after a smart brush with the rebels, resulting in taking a considerable number of prisoners, formed a junction with

20

us. To gain time for this, and to confuse the enemy, immediately after our arrival, we made a feint off to the left towards Banks's Ford, on the Rappahannock. We went out with the 1st brigade, 1st division. Subsequently, the 2d brigade came up to reinforce us. We did not need their aid, and fell back to Chancellorsville and bivouacked for the night.

Chancellorsville is a one-house post-town, seventy-six miles northwest of Richmond. The house stands in the centre of a moderate sized clearing, is built of brick, and occupied as a tavern by its owner, from whom the locality derives its name. From this point radiate four roads, one leading to Fredericksburg, one to Gordonsville, one to Spottsylvania, and one to Ely's Ford. There is nothing particularly attractive in the spot or its surroundings, and at this time it was of consequence chiefly in a military point of view, bringing us within supporting distance of forces in different directions. For a short time, General Hooker made his head-quarters here. It was a very exposed situation, but better than any other that offered, from which to observe the field, receive information and communicate orders. The house was soon an object of attraction to the rebels, who made it an unsafe abode. While standing near a post on the piazza, General Hooker was struck senseless by a splinter thrown off by a cannon shot, and remained in that condition for nearly half an hour. This casualty may have seriously affected the fortunes of the battle. The house was subsequently burned.

On Friday, the 1st instant, our line of battle was as follows: Gen. Meade's, Fifth corps, on the left; then the Second corps, Gen. Couch, next on the right; then Slocum's, Twelfth; then Howard's, Eleventh, on the extreme right, with Sickles's, Third, in reserve. During the day, considerable cannonading and some sharp fighting occurred. At 10 A. M., our battery broke camp, and with the 1st and 2d brigades, marched off on the road leading to Fredericksburg. At 3 P. M., we countermarched and returned to Chancellorsville, and went into position, and so remained all night. Late in the afternoon, the enemy felt our entire line, and received some solid tokens of Federal disapprobation. Saturday morning, at 4 o'clock, the battery was relieved, and fell back a mile or so. Here it went into position again, while rifle pits were dug, and trees felled to strengthen our defence. Four pieces, Lieut. Lee's and Lieut. Fiske's sections, under Capt. Waterman, went down the road to the left of the centre of our lines, a mile or more, and took position. Lieut. Sackett remained at this point with his section. Up to near 5 o'clock P. M., all the movements of the day had been satisfactory. From the position of the different corps, it seemed the object of Gen. Hooker to induce the rebels to follow him here, where he was prepared to give them a crushing blow. But in his plans he was doomed to disappointment. Gen. Howard's corps had been pushed forward to support the right flank, and was doing a successful work, when suddenly, upon a heavy and vigorous charge by the rebels, two German regiments, in Gen. Schurz's division, broke and ran towards the rear, and in every direction, like flocks of frightened sheep, causing confusion, and carrying consternation wherever they went. Gen. Howard and Gen. Sickles exerted themselves with great energy to remedy the evil, but with only partial success.

The disaster necessitated a new line of battle, which General Hooker set about promptly. All night the generals of corps and divisions were incessantly at work. Old positions were abandoned and new ones taken up. The Fifth corps blended its strength with the Second; and the Eleventh, re-formed, took the old position of the Fifth. The line of Gen. Sickles was thrice fiercely assailed, and as often the rebels were beaten back. Birney pushed ahead with great vigor, and with Randolph's battery, soon sent to the rear, as prisoners of war, the entire remnant of the 23d Georgia regiment, numbering over four hundred officers and men.

During the afternoon of Sunday, the enemy made several attempts to force our lines, particularly at the apex of our position, near the Chancellor House, but Capt. Weed had massed a large quantity of artillery in such a position as to repulse, with great loss, everything placed within its range. The enemy tried several batteries and regiments at that point, at different times during the afternoon, and they were literally destroyed by the fire of our terrible guns. Nothing could live within their range.

[The storming of Marye's Heights, one of the most prominent and bloody events of the battle, was accomplished with heavy loss. "As Gen. Gibbon went to the right, the enemy's men were sent in that direction to meet him. As they had the shortest lines, the same men could be employed at whatever point we might threaten. Thus, ten thousand men should have been equal to at least fifty thousand, and we did not have more than fifteen thousand on the field. On the front, where Gen. Gibbon commanded, the 10th Massachusetts skirmished toward the enemy's pits, and the fire demonstrated that there were men there as well as cannon. Away on the left, Howe did just what Gibbon did on the right, and Newton did the same in the centre; yet, with all, though men were killed and wounded plentifully, there was nothing done. Every battle has these periods of indefinite endeavor, from which some one fact eventually shapes itself out, and becomes the fact of the occasion. So it was here; and while, in every direction, the artillery— Butler's battery, Hexamer's, McCartney's, Harris's, Hazard's, Adams's, and some others—thundered at the enemy, while Howe felt for a chance on the left, and Gibbon found every point equally difficult on the right, a plan of assault was determined upon, to be made by the 3d and 8th divisions under Gen. Newton, against the enemy's centre. Attempts to storm were to be made simultaneously by Gibbon, on the right, Howe, on the left, and Newton, on the centre, and were so made; but

inasmuch as Newton's was the successful attempt—as he was
the first to penetrate the line, and as when the line was once
penetrated at one point it was no longer tenable anywhere—
Newton's assault appears to deserve the especial honor. It
was made on the centre against Marye's Hill. The right
column was formed of the 61st Pennsylvania regiment, Col.
Spear, and the 43d New York, Col. Baker. It was supported,
as we have said, by two regiments in line, the 1st Long Island,
Col. Nelson Cross, and the 82d Pennsylvania, Major Bassett.
These two regiments were part of Shaler's brigade, and Shaler
went with them. The left column of attack was formed of the
7th Massachusetts, Col. Johns, and the 36th New York, Lieut.
Colonel Welsh. This column was supported by two regiments
in line of battle and a regiment of skirmishers in the open field
to the left. These skirmishers were the 43d New York. The
regiments in line were the 6th Maine and the 5th Wisconsin.
These two columns and their supports numbered in all about
8,000 men. They moved out of the town, to the assault, at
about eleven A. M. As soon as they came well into the enemy's field of fire, the terrible fusilade began. Colonel Spear,
at the head of his regiment, was one of the first hit, and his fall
affected his men, so that they wavered and fell into confusion
and disorder, and communicated it to the 43d, behind them,
and much of the ground already gained was lost. For this
column, it was so far a fair repulse. But in this critical juncture, Colonel Shaler, with magnificent gallantry, rallied the
column, brought it up to the work once more, and took it on
up the hill.' Meantime, in the left column, matters were somewhat the same. The Colonel of the Massachusetts 7th, was
hit, and his regiment faltered also, but was rallied handsomely
by Col. Walsh, of the 36th New York, and with those glorious
fellows it went on once more. The supports in the open plain
drew the enemy's fire heavily ; but they went on steadily, from
the first, and went into the work with the rest. Many of the
enemy's men were slain in their places, in the pits where they

20*

stood till the last moment, and resisted even as our men clambered over the walls. Col. Spear, of the 61st Pennsylvania volunteers; Major Bassett, of the 82d Pennsylvania volunteers; Major Faxon, of the 36th New York; Major Haycock, of the 6th Maine, with Captains Billings, Young and Gray, of that regiment, were killed in this assault. Col. Johns, of the 7th Massachusetts, was wounded here. By this success, the place was ours; the enemy's line gave way precipitately; our men entered at several points at once, and we captured eight guns and from eight hundred to a thousand prisoners."

The fierceness with which the battle raged may be judged by the fact, that the entire loss of General Sedgwick, who was in chief command, amounted, in killed and wounded, to six thousand. The heights were held until Monday, when assailed by a superior force, his rear threatened to be cut off, he retired across Banks's Ford.

The share of the 2d Rhode Island in this terrible conflict, is thus related by participants: " We took the Heights of Fredericksburg by storm. The flag of the 36th New York was first planted there. Then how they poured up. Hill after hill was taken — the grey-backs everywhere fled at sight. Many prisoners were taken. A sharp pursuit was instituted. Our division, under Gen. Wheaton, and the three other divisions of the Sixth corps, took the road to the southwestward. The rebels turned at bay several times, but gave way immediately. Towards night they made a formidable stand, driving in our troops in confusion. The 1st and 2d divisions were repulsed, and the other two brigades of our 3d division broke and fled through our lines. We were ordered up. The 37th Massachusetts on the left of the pike, and the 10th and 7th Massachusetts and the 2d Rhode Island on the right. The rebels broke from the woods, charging upon the fleeing New Jersey brigade, cheering as they came. The second brigade was quickly formed, and, on the double quick, passed the battery the rebels aimed at—down hill and up—excited by the presence of Generals Newton and Wheaton, commanding the Sixth corps and our division (the 3d). Capt. Young (2d Rhode Island,) Brigade Assistant Adjutant General, volunteer Aide to Colonel Browne, (36th New York,) commanding the brigade, and 1st Lieutenant Bradford, Adjutant 2d Rhode Island, acting as Aide to Gen. Wheaton, actively assisted in leading on.

" The 7th, 10th and 2d halted by a house on top of the hill, and poured a withering storm of Minies upon the elated line of rebels, swiftly advancing from the woods. Such firing, men say that heard it, and that have known what heavy firing is, they never heard before. The rebels halted, crouched, hesitated, yielded, turned and fled, every man for himself, seeking the cover of the woods. It was hot work. Every man fought as if all depended on his individual exertion.

" Our loss was heavy at the house. 1st Sergeant Greene of company I, and 1st Sergeant Nichols of company B, fell at the first fire. Lieut. Bates was here wounded in the thigh. Our men cheered as Gen. Newton and Gen. Wheaton showed themselves under fire. The latter praised their conduct, and said they did well. He said they had saved the corps, and prevented another Bull Run. It looked so. The rebels had fled. That was well. But again we went on. Gen. Newton had ordered Col. Rogers to take his regiment to the woods and save the corps, as all depended on this effort, and to the woods we went—down hill on the double quick and the run, across a little brook and up the opposite slope—halting to form, and advancing to the woods under a heavy front and flank fire from the enemy. The 10th and 7th Massachusetts, and three companies (F. E and I,) of the 2d Rhode Island, faced the latter. The other seven companies of the 2d Rhode Island, led by Col. Rogers in person, who thrice seized the colors and cheered on and rallied his men, entered the woods. At last, firing ceased. The regiment reformed on the edge of the woods, and in good order retired to the house aforesaid and took post, the right and left on slight elevations, and the centre in a depression between.

Lieut. Col. S. B. M. Read and Major Henry C. Jencks, behaved with great gallantry. Sergeant Edmund F. Prentiss received the commendation of his superior officers for good conduct on the field. Corporals Kelly and Flyer gallantly carried our colors through the entire battle. All the officers and men behaved bravely.

Under a tree, directly in the rear of the regiment, the dead were buried. Our loss was 7 killed, 68 wounded and 8 missing. Capt. Turner, of Co. G, belonging in Newport, was wounded while exciting his men to deeds of daring. Our wounded were mostly brought across the river in safety. It was late in the afternoon that the fighting took place. That night we slept on the field. It was rainy and cold. Morning opened foggy, but cleared up. No fighting, except occasionally on other parts of the field, till 3 P. M. Then rapid discharges of grape and canister, and cries and cheers on the centre and left, in the direction of Fredericksburg, announced some fighting. Long dark columns soon approached, rapidly crossing the fields to the rear, but whether of our troops fleeing or enemy pursuing, we could not tell. Unhealthy rumors and camp stories retailed by stupid or malicious persons, had made most anxious. The most improbable stories found ready believers. Night drew on fast. Some misunderstanding about the withdrawal of a regiment, all the pickets in front covering the flank of the army, for we occupied the extreme right, caused some croaking, but the appearance of Generals Sedgwick and Newton inspired all with fresh confidence. At last we had orders to withdraw. All night, till ten minutes of four in the morning, we marched up hill and down, across muddy plains and over fences, under fire of rebel batteries, and in the thick fog and darkness, to the bridges at Banks's Ford, where we crossed. Our regiment was one of the last to leave the field. Co. K, Captain John P. Shaw, was detailed as rear guard, and was among the last to recross the river. Yesterday was extremely hot. Many were affected. Among others, Captains Sears, Shaw and Foy, and Lieut. Bowen."]

In this battle, Colonel Tompkins, of the artillery, gave direction to fifty-four guns. Of their work at Marye's Heights, Salem Chapel and Salem Heights, he had reason to be proud. At the battle of the latter place, on Sunday, (3d,) he narrowly escaped being taken prisoner, and was saved by his self-possession and the color of the corduroys he wore. On that day, the Sixth corps (Sedgwick's) was in a precarious condition. General Hooker having fallen back from Chancellorsville, left General Lee at liberty to mass his entire army against this one corps, already decimated by the two severe engagements of the day before. The only line of retreat was by Banks's Ford, before referred to, where the Federals had two pontoon bridges. To cover this point, General Sedgwick was obliged to form his line upon nearly three sides of a square, with the river for the fourth. About 5 o'clock P. M., the enemy having massed a very heavy column against General S., attacked his left in great force, and for a time were successful. They were finally, however, checked and driven back. At the time this attack was made, Colonel Tompkins was on another part of the line, but seeing that more artillery was needed, he took a 12-pounder battery to the point threatened, and added it to that of the batteries already in position there. The fight raged furiously until after dark, and ended in checking the advancing enemy. Colonel T. then set out to ride back to where he had left General Sedgwick in the afternoon. The moon shone bright, but the road was shaded by trees so as to obscure the way far in advance. He had nearly reached the spot where he parted from the General, when he became aware that no troops were visible. He rode from under the shade of the trees, into the open field, but could not, with the aid of a glass, discover any living man. Only the dead lay scattered about. On turning his tired horse to make his way back to the left, a lively skir-

mish commenced in that direction; and by the flashing of the
guns, he perceived that he was in the rear of the enemy's
skirmishers. He then endeavored to make his way across the
fields to the river. He had gone about a mile and was approaching the river, through some scrub oaks, when he suddenly came upon a company of rebels, going in the same
direction. With great presence of mind, he followed behind
them, taking the precaution to throw open his coat so as to
display his corduroys, which, in the moonlight, looked grey—
the rebel uniform. After marching in this way two or three
hundred yards, they turned through the bushes, while he kept
straight on for a short distance, when he stopped to take an
observation. Just as he had decided upon his course, another
company of rebels came out of the bushes directly in his rear,
when he deliberately rode on at their head, they supposing him
to be field or staff officer of theirs. They soon turned aside,
and putting spurs to his horse, he made a wide detour through
a deep ravine, and reached the river, to which the forces had
fallen back preparatory to crossing.

Five Rhode Island batteries renewed their acquaintance with
the forces of Lee. Battery E was under the immediate command of Lieutenant Jastram, Captain Randolph, as chief of
artillery, being in every part of the field. It had a sanguinary
fight, and dealt death discharges with fatal effect. Subjected to
a galling enfilading fire, it lost two men killed, sixteen wounded,
and twenty-four horses killed, wounded and missing. Capt. Randolph narrowly escaped. While giving orders, a cannon ball
struck his horse in the rear and passed directly through him,
coming out at the breast, killing him instantly. A Minie ball cut
a sleeve button from Captain R.'s wrist, but inflicted no wound.
In the evening, while searching on the field for guns and caissons, that the great destruction of horses prevented being withdrawn, he unconsciously rode outside the Federal lines, when
he was discovered by a rebel officer, who attempted to inter-

cept his return ; but a fleet horse distanced his pursuer, and he arrived in camp without further molestation.

Battery G, Captain Adams, also in the hottest of the battle, was handled with great skill. It was early sent forward to an exposed position to silence a battery about six hundred yards distant, which it succeeded in doing. During the operation, it was subjected to a heavy and fatal cross fire from a rebel battery on the right. The casualties were twenty-four men killed and wounded, sixteen horses lost, and a gun carriage badly damaged. Among the wounded were Lieutenants Benjamin E. Kelley, O. L. Torslow, (not severely,) and Crawford Allen, (slightly.) Lieutenant Kelley's wound was caused by a shell, and proved mortal. He was conveyed to the Lacy House, where he lingered until Monday morning, (4th May,) and then passed peacefully away.* Lieutenant Torslow's horse was killed.

Battery A, Captain Arnold, participated in the battle. It

---

* Lieutenant Benjamin E. Kelley was the son of the late Captain Ebenezer Kelley, of Providence. When the rebellion first broke out, he was pursuing his studies in the High School; but aroused with patriotic indignation at the attempt to overthrow the Union he enlisted in the 1st Rhode Island regiment of three months volunteers, and at Bull Run was in the company of sharpshooters under Captain Goddard. On his return home, he felt it his duty to devote himself to the service of his country, and having a preference for the artillery arm, entered at once upon a preparatory course of study. He joined battery G, under a sergeant's warrant, and was promoted second lieutenant, November 18, 1862. He was with the army of the Potomac on the Peninsula, and in its subsequent campaigns, and in all scenes of action exhibited the spirit of undoubted courage. In one battle, his horse was shot. His prompt attention to duty, correct habits, and elevated moral qualities, gained him universal esteem. After being removed to the Lacy House, he received every attention that friendship and surgical skill could render, but all was unavailing. He was fully aware of his situation, and met his fate with the calmness of Christian trust. His remains were brought to Providence, and buried at Swan Point, May 9th. He died at the age of 22 years. A life full of promise, thus suddenly terminated, cast a deep shadow of sorrow upon a wide circle of friends.

crossed the river on Thursday, was engaged about two hours on Friday, went into position on Saturday, though not called to engage, and on Sunday went to the front, but experienced no disaster.

In the temporary absence of Captain Hazard, on account of sickness, battery B was commanded by Lieutenant T. Frederick Brown. Placed on a hill at point blank range opposite a rebel work, it had hardly got into position when it was sharply opened upon from that quarter. To this attention, it responded in a vigorous and effective manner. It was supported by the 2d Rhode Island.

Battery C, Captain Waterman, was under heavy fire, which it returned with spirit. Its position, one of great importance, was becomingly sustained. The casualties were, Sergeant Augustus S. Hanna and Frederick T. Moies, killed, and Lieutenant Sackett, Charles Jenkins and Patrick J. May, wounded. Hanna was shot in the neck with a Minie, and lived until the following afternoon. Moies was shot in the side with cannister, and died instantly. The day after the battle, the battery recrossed the Rappahannock at United States Ford, and day before yesterday, at 1 o'clock P. M., reached its old camp, after nine days hard service.

The mission of General Stoneman's cavalry, just mentioned, was a coöperative expedition, made in three columns. One, under General Averill, including the 1st Rhode Island cavalry, crossed the Rappahannock at Kelly's Ford, and advanced to Brandy Station, where it drove back the rebel pickets. It then proceeded to Culpepper Court House, and having captured a quantity of flour, pursued the retreating enemy to Rapidan Station, where he had a sharp encounter and took thirty-one prisoners. His object was to destroy the bridge, but in this was anticipated by the panic stricken foe. After marching to Orange Court House, he rejoined the main army at Chancellorsville. A second column, under General Buford, proceeded directly to Gordonsville, and there broke the connection on the Central Railroad, between that place and Richmond.

With his principal column, General Stoneman pushed towards Richmond, for the purpose of destroying the rebel railroad communications, and preventing a retreat. He traversed a great extent of the peninsula, destroying bridges, tearing up railroads and canal locks, seizing horses and military stores, and approached within a few miles of the rebel capital, awakening, on every hand, the liveliest alarm. It was a more brilliant affair than Stuart's celebrated gallop round our army, and quite as bold. But, unfortunately, communication not being kept up between him and General Hooker, neither understood the exact position of the other, and consequently the main benefits anticipated from the operation failed to be realized.

On the first and second days of the battle, the advantage appeared so decidedly with us, that General Hooker issued a congratulatory general order announcing to the army that the enemy were where they "must ingloriously fly, or come out from behind their defences, and give us battle on our own ground, where certain destruction awaits him." But this declaration proved premature. The current of events turned. The breaking of the Eleventh corps, at a critical moment, had not been anticipated, while the separation of our army by a vigorous and adroit movement of Lee, was like the reversing of the engine to a train of cars. General Hooker could, indeed, have continued to hold his position in the rear of Chancellorsville, where quantities of artillery were massed, but only to incur unwarrantable risks. The new disposition of the rebel forces, which their greatly augmented numbers enabled Lee to make, the derangement of plans caused by the stampede of the German regiments, the near exhaustion of our eight days' rations, the danger of being separated from the base of supplies, and other prudential considerations, determined the falling back of our forces in season to escape a possible fatality. This was done, without opposition, the rebels being too much

21

crippled and exhausted to follow and harass us. Our troops
fought with a bravery never excelled ; the rebels, as in former
battles, with the desperation of a last hope. The carnage, on
both sides, exceeded any former battle. Our losses are estimated from ten to eighteen thousand, in killed, wounded and
missing ; the rebel loss is much greater.* Their greatest general, next to Lee, Stonewall Jackson, is mortally wounded.†
In some places their dead lay in heaps, the effect of our artillery fire. We have taken five thousand prisoners, seven pieces
of cannon, and fifteen stands of colors. The rebels have captured some guns and a considerable number of men, but the
balance is largely in our favor. The scenes on the field were
essentially repetitions of those described in other battles. In a
location known as the Wilderness, heavily wooded and having
a thick undergrowth, lay many of the dead and wounded of
both sides. Much of the forest was dry timber, and this being set on fire by the bursting shells, numbers of the wounded,
unable to drag themselves from the spot, perished in the flames.
Tales of horror might be multiplied almost indefinitely. Let
the imagination have free scope, and the picture it draws will
hardly be an exaggeration of the reality. The army has again
tasted the bitter cup of disappointment, but Hope, at the bottom, speaks bravely of a future to be tried.

---

* Among our dead, we mourn the loss of Major General Hiram G.
Berry, who was killed in the action of Sunday. He entered the service
as Colonel of the 4th Maine volunteers, and in March last, was appointed
to the command of the 2d division of the Third army corps, under General Sickles. He was a brave and valuable officer. Of officers wounded,
are Generals Whipple, (since dead,) Brooks, Devens and Mott. Many
hair-breadths escapes among the general officers occurred. Generals
Couch, Hancock, Griffin and French, each had a horse shot under them.

† The Richmond Enquirer states that General Jackson, "through a
cruel mistake, in the confusion, received two balls from some of his own
men." He was shot through the left arm, which was amputated, and a
bullet passed through his right hand. He died on the 10th May, aged 37
years.

LETTER XXXII.

Encampments and their arrangements.

Camp near Falmouth, Va.,
May 16th, 1863.

By the date of this letter, it will be seen that we have changed our position. A second time we have made our *congé* to our comfortable huts, and advanced our camp about three miles, and are now parked about two miles from Falmouth, in a pleasant location, with a dozen other batteries in near proximity. The 2d Rhode Island volunteers are encamped about a mile from us. By a recent consolidating arrangement, the artillery assigned to each corps will constitute a brigade, under the command of a chief of artillery of the corps, who will be responsible for its efficiency and administration, to the chief of artillery of the army. And now that my pen is running on camps, I will answer, in brief, the accumulated questions concerning them, propounded by the uninitiated, and which, in the absence of fresh incident or interesting rumor, may serve as the material of a letter.

To one who has never seen an encampment on a large scale, a visit to the canvas homes of a division or a *corps d'armeé* will be fraught with interest. The visitor will be impressed with the order and regularity that prevails, and wonder that so much life can be provided for in so small a space. Of the general arrangements of an infantry encampment, a simple plan of a regimental camp will probably give a tolerable idea, remembering, always, in thinking of the army of the Potomac, to multiply it by one hundred or more. Take the following representation, made up of printer's types, and employ the imagination in creating a perspective, and you have the whole thing before you.

REGIMENTAL CAMP.

Surgeon.		Lieut. Colonel.	Colonel.	Major.	Quartermaster
O	O	O	O	O	O O

Company Officers Tents.

A	B	C	D	E	F	G	H	I	K
O	O	O	O	O	O	O	O	O	O

Men's Tents.

Λ Λ Λ Λ Λ Λ Λ Λ Λ Λ

Λ Λ Λ Λ Λ Λ Λ Λ Λ Λ

Λ Λ Λ Λ Λ Λ Λ Λ Λ· Λ

Λ Λ Λ Λ Λ Λ Λ Λ Λ Λ

Λ Λ Λ Λ Λ Λ Λ Λ Λ Λ

Λ Λ Λ Λ Λ Λ Λ Λ Λ Λ

Wagons.

— — — — — — — —

Sutler.

The Colonel of the regiment, as will be seen, occupies the centre, with the tents of the several companies in front. On his right are the tents of the Lieut. Colonel and Surgeon, and on the left those of the Major and the Quartermaster. The tent of the Chaplain has its appropriate place, as does the hospital tent and the regimental kitchen. The hospital tent is usually on the extreme left, in line with that of the Colonel, the latter on the extreme right of the camp, and all within guard lines. These do not, however, invariably occupy the positions here indicated, but may be varied according to the nature of the ground or other governing circumstances.

An entire army, like that of the Potomac, is never encamped in a solid or unbroken mass. Convenience, as well as sanitary considerations, require a suitable space between the several divisions, and also between the different regiments of a division, and hence an army of an hundred thousand men may be scattered over an extent of ten or fifteen miles. In a full encampment, the regimental hospital is usually merged in that of a brigade or division. When a camp has been properly laid out, the street of each company is commonly designated by a letter of the alphabet, or some favorite name: and when established for a time, a fine taste and much skill is often displayed, both in embellishing the grounds and securing tent comforts. The 2d Rhode Island have been noted for this.

In a campaign, an artillery camp is sufficiently near to the infantry, to be protected by it, in case of a sudden attack, and, at the same time, to aid in defending the camp should an assault be made. It embraces the files of tents for the privates and non-commissioned officers, with streets of suitable width, and gutters or drains to lead off the water during rains; separate tents for the captain, lieutenants, the quartermaster sergeant's department; a suitable spot for parking the battery; the picket ropes for the horses, and last, though not least, the kitchen. This latter, as often as otherwise, is a simple enclosure open to the weather, within which the functions of the cook are exercised.

If the camp is to be occupied for some time, and lumber can be obtained, a shanty may be erected to protect this important personage and his assistants from storms. According to strict military rule, the kitchen should be twenty-five paces in front of the front rank of tents, and the park opposite the centre of the camp, forty paces in rear of the officers' tents; but the nature of the ground does not always admit of exact conformity to the regulations, and then the nearest approach possible is adopted. On a march, where encampments are made for a single night, and often for a few hours only, a kitchen cannot easily be established, and generally every man cooks for himself in a very primitive manner. In marching through an open country, where dry fuel is not plenty, it is not uncommon to see men towards night armed with a fragment of a rail, foraged

21*

by the way, with which to cook their rasher of bacon or salt pork, and make their coffee or tea after bivouac.

. The tents in common use are the wall, (principally occupied by officers,) the wedge, or A, Sibley, and shelter. The wall tent is, in many respects, the most convenient, and resembles the upper story of a cottage house. The wedge, as its name imports, has the form of an inverted V, (thus, Λ.) and as it is designed to crowd the largest quantity of human flesh into the smallest given space, is scarcely high enough at the ridge to permit an inmate to stand erect, and entirely destitute of proper ventilation. It is poorly adapted to health or comfort. The Sibley takes its name from the inventor, Major H. H. Sibley, of the 2d United States dragoons. It is conical, easily pitched, has a ventilating arrangement, and in every respect, is vastly preferable to the wedge, or A. In winter encampments, both the wedge and Sibley are often mounted on a stockade base or frame of logs, thus constituting a roof to a convenient hut, warmed by a portable sheet iron stove, or a California fire-place, an affair that bears no resemblance to the fire-place of home, but that economizes fuel, and answers very well the purpose for which it was contrived.

The *tente d'abri*, or shelter tent, comes to us from the French, by whom it has been in use since 1837. Scott calls it " a most precious invention," for the reason, I suppose, of its convenience on a march. With us, it is simply two rubber blankets buttoned together, stretched over a pole resting on a couple of crotched stakes, and the sides fastened to the ground with pegs. Such a tent will accommodate two men. Its chief merit is, that it diminishes the bulk of baggage, is quickly pitched, and for temporary purposes, affords shelter from vertical rains and night dews. With it, an army on a short expedition, like our late nine days' campaign, resembles the independent Mollusca, carrying their habitations upon their backs. Except for the purpose mentioned, it is but little better than a dog kennel, which it somewhat resembles. On a larger scale, in a battery,

tarpaulins are used, which accommodate from six to ten men.
Tent furniture, of course, is limited, and a soldier's service of
plate is usually comprehended in a tin cup, tin plate, knife and
fork and spoon. While the army is in motion, tables and camp
chairs are out of the question ; straw is not always to be had,
and if the hungry soldier does not find a convenient stump, log
or fence, upon which to rest while disposing of his grub, he is
quite content to take it in oriental fashion on the ground.

The camp life of a battery is diversified with a variety of
calls, sounded by bugle. First comes reveille, announcing
what is not always the fact, that " tired nature's sweet restorer"
has done all the night work craved. But the voice is inexora-
ble, and the half-wakened sleeper tumbles out, wondering at
the hasty departure of the sable goddess, and breathing a wish
that " sweet forgetfulness of life " could have been protracted
another hour. Then follow feed call, breakfast, water, stable,
sick, drill, dinner and supper calls, all of which suggest their
several explanations. To these may be added roll call and
guard mounting.

As night approaches, the retreat sounds, to which supper
succeeds. At 9 o'clock, tattoo is sounded, and the men retire
to their quarters. Taps soon follow, when lights are extin-
guished, mirthful voices are silent, and sleepers go off to dream-
land, or spend a wakeful hour first, in speculations on what the
morrow will bring forth.

Neither the excitements of the march, the inspiration of the
battle, nor the quiet of an agreeable camp, make the soldier
forgetful of home ; and after an absence of a year or more, he
greets with no ordinary pleasure, the furlough that grants him
the privilege of visiting scenes familiar and dear. The form of
this coveted instrument is as follows :

To ALL WHOM IT MAY CONCERN.

The bearer hereof————————a sergeant [corporal or private,
as the case may be,] of Captain——————company, [giving the
letter, A, B, C, &c.,]————Regiment of [Infantry or Artillery, as

the case may be,] Volunteers; aged——years, ——feet——inches high, ——complexion, ——eyes, ——hair, and by profession a —————————; born in the State of—————, and enlisted at—————, in the State of—————, on the——day of —————, eighteen hundred and—————, to serve for the period of—————, is hereby permitted to go to—————, in the county of—————, State of—————, he having a furlough from the——day of—————, 186—, to the——day of—————186— at which period he will rejoin his company or regiment at—————, or wherever it then may be, or be considered a deserter.

Subsistence has been furnished to said——————to the—— day of—————, 186—, and pay to the——day of—————186—, both inclusive.

Given under my hand at—————this——day of—————, 186—.

　　　　　—————, Captain, Commanding—————.

The instrument is endorsed by the Captain, recommending the furlough, specifying the number of days to be allowed, and also the reasons therefor. This is approved by the brigade commander, and again by the General commanding division, when it goes to head-quarters, where it is granted by the General-in-Chief, countersigned by the Assistant Adjutant General. With these high autographs, the paper comes back to the company, the dates are filled out, and the happy possessor loses no time in starting for his destination.

As a visitor wanders through a camp, he meets officers of different grades, and unacquainted with the marks of distinction, is perplexed to discriminate. How shall he know their official positions? Attention to the following particulars will give him the desired information:

The shoulder straps of a Major General bear two silver embroidered stars, one on each end of the strap; a Brigadier General has one silver star only; a Colonel has a silver embroidered spread eagle; a Lieutenant Colonel has two silver embroidered leaves, one on each end of the strap; a Major has two embroidered leaves similarly placed. A Captain has two gold bars at each end of the strap; a First Lieutenant, one gold bar at each end; and a Second Lieutenant, no bars at all.

The cloth of the strap, by its color, distinguishes the arm of the service. For general and staff officers, it is dark blue; for artillery, scarlet; for infantry, sky blue; for riflemen, green, and for cavalry, orange color.

Non-commissioned officers are indicated by chevrons or stripes on the coat sleeve, in the form of a letter V. Corporals wear two stripes; Sergeants, three. Orderly Sergeants have a lozenge, or diamond shaped figure, within the angle of the chevrons. Sergeant Majors have the three stripes of a Sergeant completed into a triangle, base uppermost.

The kitchen of a camp holds an important place in the details of daily experience. Here, as in a well-regulated household, it is a power to win or repel—to stimulate the genial virtues, or to frictionize the animal nature. It is not to be assumed, or supposed, from anything here said, that soldiers, more than all other men, are given to appetite, or that they are principally occupied in devising methods of gratifying it. Still, they are not indifferent—nor should they be—to a capable administration of the culinary department. This need deserves more consideration than it has hitherto received, and if a brief plea for reform in the camp kitchen, shall arrest attention in the proper quarter, this page will have accomplished its object. Two years of observation and inquiry have furnished satisfactory evidence that the government could render no better service to the army than by providing for each regiment a chief cook who is master of his art. The health and good nature of an army is inseparably connected with its kitchen. To keep soldiers in good heart, and ready for anything in the line of active duty, they must be well fed; and good feeding depends on the skill of the cooks. The difference between rations properly cooked and otherwise, is the difference between robust health, good nature and economy on the one hand, and wastefulness, grumbling, indigestion and other forms of disease on the other. An accomplished cook will make poor rations (and sometimes they are poor) palatable, while one possessing neither skill, genius nor good taste, will spoil the best. A company or regiment having cooks who understand their business, can seldom consume all their rations, and will frequently have a barrel of beef or pork to dispose of for little matters that give pleasant variety to the primitive table of a soldier.

It was the boast of Guignart, the famous monarch of Rothschild's kitchen, that he could cook an egg six hundred different ways, and make soups in endless variety. Now, such extraordinary skill is not necessary in an army cook. Eggs are not set down among the common rations of a soldier. If he obtains them, they will probably be drawn from some quarter other than the commissary department; and even were they a part of his daily allowance, the ordinary methods of serving them would be quite satisfactory. But in the matter of meats, it is otherwise. It is not needful, indeed, that a cook should be able to prepare twenty choice dishes from a rump or round of beef, or be capable of concocting three hundred and sixty-five different kinds of soup, as was demanded of his *chef* by the great banker; but it is important that he knows the difference between soup and slush, and that he be competent to make two or three varieties, according to the quality of his meat, and make them well. Many an extemporized cook,—one who perhaps could not tell a hock from an aitch bone,—for want of practical knowledge, has wasted his time, spoiled the dinner, provoked the ire of hungry expectants, and served nobody satisfactorily, except the sutler, who is sure of a brisk custom after every badly cooked meal. Under the hand and eye of a cook who understands his business, even the "old horse" and "mule" that often defies mastication, could be relieved of their offensive qualities. In the arrangements for dealing summarily with contractors who impose stale provisions on the army, the government did a good thing. Let one more step be taken, and military kitchens be organized in keeping with the civilization of the age, and such as an army of intelligent men will appreciate. So much for camps and their adjuncts. Many details in regard to sinks, policing, drills, reviews, inspections, and other matters are omitted. Enough has been explained to gratify reasonable curiosity.

LETTER XXXIII.

Camp of Battery C removed—Presentation of the Kearny Cross—Picket intercourse—Piscatory amusements—Raid of the 8th Illinois cavalry—Ball—Sword presentation.

ARMY OF THE POTOMAC, CAMP OF BATTERY C., }
June 6, 1863. }

For some little time after the return of the army from its nine days' campaign, changes were made in the location of encampments, prompted by sanitary considerations. Many of the camps have been tastefully arranged, and with an eye to comfort. That of the 2d Rhode Island is formed about one-fourth of a mile from its old one. It is neatly laid out, and ornamented with trees. Our camp was moved last week, 27th ultimo. We are on new ground, not far from Gen. Hooker's head-quarters, and about six miles from our last winter home. But war assures "no constancy in earthly things," and judging from the past, as well as present signs, we may look upon our abode as temporary. At this season, the valley of the Rappahannock is clad in picturesque garments, though showing many unseemly rents. From Acquia Landing to Falmouth, the woodman's axe had spared but little of the forests with which the country had been heavily covered. Except here and there a clump of trees, or a large grove, countless stumps alone tell of the deep shades that, in the heat of last summer, were the pleasant retreats of feathered and animal tribes.

Last Wednesday, (27th ultimo,) was a day of pleasurable excitement to General Birney's division of the Third corps. Between four hundred and five hundred non-commissioned officers and privates were presented with the Kearny cross, in recognition of meritorious services in the battle of Chancellorsville. The distribution was preceded by a spirited address by General Sickles. Among the recipients were four members of Rhode Island battery E, viz.: William Turpey, John M'Aldes, Martin Harvey, and Albert N. Colwell. The ceremony took place in the presence of several general officers with their staffs, presenting a brilliant spectacle. The medal is a Maltese cross of bronze, inscribed on one side with the name of "Kearny," and on the other with the motto, "*Dulce et decorum est pro patria mori.*" It was struck in commemoration of the brave soldier whose name it bears, and will be to the members of the division who fought under him, what the decoration of honor was to the veterans of Napoleon—the pride of future days, when, to young listeners, the wondrous tale of battles shall be repeated, and with or without crutch, the winning of bloody fields described.

The rebel and Federal pickets keep up lively conversations across the river, and bandy jokes like old acquaintances, as indeed many of them are. At one of the posts lately, the former cried out,—"Where is Joe Hooker now?" "Gone to the funeral of Stonewall Jackson," was the quick response. The answer was deemed sufficient, and no further questions were asked. At another post, a few days ago, men of both sides, while bathing, met in the middle of the river and shook hands with the familiar exclamation, "How are you, old fellow?" In sportive mood, they agreed to exchange positions on shore, and personate each other, which they accordingly did. Then followed the calls, "How are you, secesh?" "How are you, pork and molasses?—when are you going to pitch into us again?" and a string of similar interrogatories. After amusing themselves in this manner awhile, they resumed their stations as representatives of hostile armies. In a week, these men may meet in deadly strife, and use the bayonet as freely as they have exchanged good natured sallies. This kind of intercourse, and sudden transition from the spirit of fierce contention to fraternal intercourse, is an anomaly in modern warfare, and to the moral and intellectual philosopher opens a curious field for psychological investigation. The Cooper of another generation will find in the story of picket life in our army, rich tints with which to finish up his glowing romance.

For a month past, the Rappahannock has afforded piscatory attractions, and, for a short time, rebel and Federal pickets improved their opportunities for varying their rations. Suddenly, sundry citizens of Falmouth were smitten with a desire for the scaly luxury, and repaired with suspicious frequency to the river, ostensibly to make purchases, but really, as believed, to communicate intelligence to the rebels. This led to an order prohibiting angling on the part of our pickets, and a notice to the rebels that if they persisted in the practice, they would be fired upon. So ended all displays of Waltonian skill, and no longer, unless by stealth, does the ichthyous family "greedily suck in the twining bait" of Federal or secesh.

The 8th Illinois cavalry, under Colonel Clendenin, comprising five hundred men, have lately returned to their encampment, after an extensive and successful foraging expedition of two weeks duration. They advanced to King George Court House, and there dividing into three columns, swept over the entire neck of the peninsula, exploring every nook and corner, seizing the goods, boats, and other material substance of smugglers, destroying a large quantity of provisions that could not well be removed, and confiscating to Federal use, horses, mules, and whatever else could be turned to good account. The spoils with which they returned were as varied as ever seen in the triumphal procession of an ancient conqueror. Of equine and

22

mongrel animals, a string of five hundred came in very seasonably to supply needs in the cavalry, and in the transportation department. With these, came oxen, carts, wagons, carriages—top and topless,—about one hundred prisoners, and upwards of eight hundred contrabands, including mammas and pickaninnies, who voluntarily abandoned their masters, and sought the advantages of the emancipation act. Of this number, three hundred are reputed able-bodied men, and with such pay as the government allows, will be able to support themselves and families very comfortably. The value of property destroyed is estimated at more than one million of dollars, the loss falling heavily on those engaged in contraband trade.

The success of this raid is a very satisfactory offset to some of the sharp practice of Stuart, and adds to the reputation for smartness which the 8th Illinois has already gained. An order has been issued, authorizing a clean sweep to be made of horses belonging to disloyal persons resident in any part of the country, as a species of property contraband of war, and available, while in the hands of its owners, to guerrillas and others engaged in the rebel interests. Should the order be strictly carried out, the inhabitants of the Rappahannock valley, of secesh proclivities, will pay dearly for the aid they have rendered to rebel spies and agents, while our army has been encamped among them, besides securing to the use of the government a better class of animals than is usually obtained by purchase.

Last Wednesday evening, the camp of General Howe's division was the scene of a festivity at which Terpsichore presided. A spacious dancing hall was erected of pine trees, and covered with branches; and when illuminated by candles blazing from rustic chandeliers, presented the appearance of a fairy bower. A number of ladies, wives of officers, graced the occasion, and those favored with an invitation to participate in the agreeable excitements of the evening, pronounce the whole thing *recherche*. In the Second army corps, General French, whose brilliant charge in the battle of Chancellorsville received, on the field, the warm encomiums of General Howard, has been made the recipient of an elegant dress sword, the gift of the 14th Indiana volunteers. These episodes in camp life break the monotony of daily drills and parades, and give healthful play to the social element.

For a few days, it has been evident that whatever the rebels might be about, something of importance on our side was soon to take place. Yesterday, speculation was brought to a focus. A reconnoissance in force on our left was ordered, and at this moment a large body of the Sixth army corps hold position on the other side of the river, having, as reported, taken two hundred prisoners. There was a smart cannonading last night. Our battery is under orders to be in readiness to march with three days rations, in what direction is not yet made known.

LETTER XXXIV.

Lee invades Pennsylvania—Federal army in motion—General Hooker relieved—Succeeded by General Meade—Battle of Gettysburg—Lee defeated and retreats—Pursuit—Sanitary and Christian Commission—Hospitals and the field.

CAMP NEAR FAIRFAX COURT HOUSE, VA.,
June 21, 1863.

For two weeks past, the eyes of the whole country have been fixed with anxious gaze upon the two opposing armies, separated by the Rappahannock. Watching each other with the mutual consciousness of having an able foe to deal with, movements and counter-movements have been made, without materially changing their relations. Since the battle of Chancellorsville, the rebel General Lee has more than once indicated a disposition to cross the river and demolish his Federal antagonist. But disposition and ability were not, in his case, united, and while the former was intense, the latter was unequal to the task.   The results of the late battle were not such as to warrant a direct assault upon our lines, nor could he longer remain in comparative quiet, and satisfy popular expectations in Secessia.   Necessity was laid upon him to act, and he conceived the bold and dangerous plan of invading Pennsylvania, at the same time threatening Maryland, Western Virginia and Ohio.   By suddenly throwing the bulk of his army into Pennsylvania, seizing the capital, and possibly Philadelphia, subsisting his forces at Federal expense from the rich fields and plentiful granaries of the valley of the Susquehanna, he would show a dash, daring and self-reliance calculated to inspire confidence throughout the confederate States, and supply material for a graphic and effective picture in Europe. A success of this sort would be a more powerful auxilliary to the confederate agents in London and Paris, than any verbal or written arguments they could present to the governments from whom they were seeking the recognition of nationality.

[Some of the objects and purposes of this invasion are thus stated by General Lee, in his report made to General Cooper, at Richmond, July 31st:

"The position occupied by the enemy opposite Fredericksburgh being one in which he could not be attacked to advantage, it was determined to draw him from it. The execution of this purpose embraced the relief of the Shenandoah valley from the troops that had occupied the lower part of it during the winter and spring, and, if practicable, the transfer of the scene of hostilities north of the Potomac.

"It was thought that the corresponding movement on the part of the enemy, to which those contemplated by us could probably give rise, might offer a fair opportunity to strike a blow at the army therein commanded by Gen. Hooker, and that, in any event, that army would be compelled to leave Virginia, and possibly to draw to its support troops designed to operate against other parts of the country. In this way, it was supposed that the enemy's plan of campaign for the summer would be broken up, and part of the season of active operations be consumed in the formation of new combinations and the preparations that they would require.

"In addition to these advantages, it was hoped that other valuable results might be attained by military success."

The first movement towards the invasion of Pennsylvania was opened soon after the battle of Chancellorsville, by a cavalry movement, which was met and quashed at Brandy Station by General Pleasanton, about the 1st of June. On the 13th, General Milroy was attacked at Winchester, by the advance of Lee's army, under General Ewell, and retreated, after a short conflict, to Harper's Ferry, abandoning all his stores and cannon to the rebels. This opened the way for the advance of the foe across the Potomac. Another force of its cavalry crossed the upper Potomac on the 15th, causing great consternation in Maryland and lower Pennsylvania. It entered Chambersburg and Mercersburg in the evening. The alarm caused by this raid was unnecessarily great, for the main army of Lee had not yet reached the south side of the Potomac. The Union garrison at Frederick, Md., fell back to the Relay House, on the 16th. A detachment of the enemy attacked Harper Ferry the same day, but was shelled back by General Tyler, from Maryland Heights. Ten thousand rebel infantry crossed the Potomac at Williamsburg, in the night, beginning in earnest the great invasion which was now fully shown to be intended. Fights took place at Aldie, on the 18th and 19th, between General Pleasanton's and a body of the enemy's cavalry. More rebels constantly poured across the Potomac, and on the 19th, Ewell's entire division occupied Sharpsburg, in Maryland. By this time, Pennsylvania, New York, and New Jersey began their great effort to repel Lee's advance, from the North. Meanwhile, General Couch had commenced the organization

22*

of a militia force at Gettysburg to check the twenty thousand men under Ewell, who were raiding like banditti through the country. The main rebel army was entirely across the Potomac, below Williamsburg, on the 26th, moved northward via McConnellsburg and Chambersburg, and began, in partially scattered columns, its advance through Pennsylvania, in the direction of Philadelphia and Baltimore.

Forty thousand rebel troops and a hundred pieces of rebel artillery passed through Chambersburg on the 27th. On Sunday, York was occupied by General Early, who made his famous levy on its citizens. Harrisburg, long threatened, was not yet attacked.

The reason for changing his purpose to proceed at once to Harrisburg, is thus given by General Lee :

" Preparations were now made to advance upon Harrisburg ; but, on the night of the 29th, information was received from a scout, that the Federal army, having crossed the Potomac, was advancing northwards, and that the head of the column had reached the South Mountain. As our communications with the Potomac were thus menaced, it was resolved to prevent his further progress in that direction by concentrating our army on the east side of the mountains. Accordingly, Longstreet and Hill were directed to proceed from Chambersburg to Gettysburg, to which point Gen. Ewell was also instructed to march from Carlisle.

" Gen. Stuart continued to follow the movements of the Federal army south of the Potomac after our own had entered Maryland, and, in his efforts to impede its progress, advanced as far eastward as Fairfax Court House. Finding himself unable to delay the enemy materially, he crossed the river at Seneca, and marched through Westminster to Carlisle, where he arrived after Gen. Ewell had left for Gettysburg. By the route he pursued, the Federal army was interposed between his command and our main body, preventing any communication with him until his arrival at Carlisle.

" The march towards Gettysburg was conducted more slowly than it would have been had the movements of the Federal army been known."

Having thus anticipated a portion of the narrative, and put the enemy on the field where he is to be by and by found, we turn back to Federal action in the premises.]

When it became certain that Lee's army was in motion, it only remained to follow his example, ascertain his design, and thwart his purpose, or do the better thing — conquer him. Preparatory to leaving our position in front of Fredericksburg, the sick and wounded, numbering about 10,000, were transferred to the hospitals in Washington, and the army stores not needed for immediate use, secured on board transports. Materials not worth removing were destroyed, so that the village of government buildings at Acquia Landing, and the whole region lately teeming with busy life and gleaming with weapons of war, suddenly became desolate as " the wide waste of all devouring years."

On the 14th, Gen. Hooker removed his head-quarters from Falmouth to Fairfax Court House, accompanied by two divisions of the Second army corps and two divisions of the Sixth. The Twelfth corps had preceded him to this place. The Third, Fifth and Eleventh corps had also taken up their line of march. As soon as circumstances permitted, the entire army was in motion. The tale of battery C, in the departure from the Rappahannock, is brief and soon told. From the 6th to the 14th instant, the battery was on picket, two miles below Fredericksburg, at or very near the spot where Franklin crossed last December. A portion of the Sixth corps, including the 2d Rhode Island volunteers, were on the other side of the river, where they had dug rifle pits, thrown up a large breastwork with embrasures for Parrott guns, and had a masked battery of 24-pounders in position. Our line on that side was in the form of a semi-circle, either flank resting on the river.

The diagram below will, perhaps serve in the place of a more particular description.

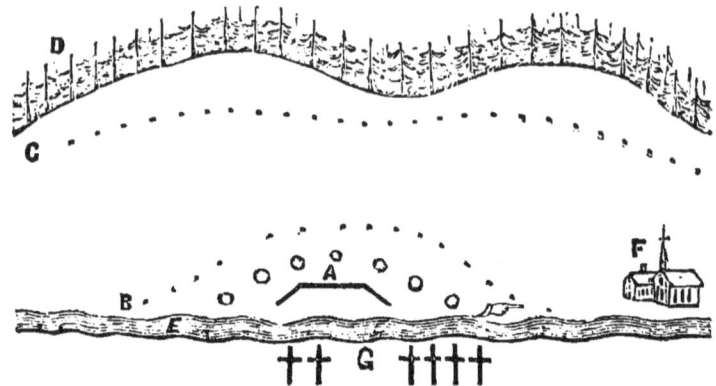

A. Federal rifle pits and redoubts.
B. Federal pickets.
C. Rebel pickets.
D. Hill, dense woods filled with rebels.
E. River.
F. Fredericksburg.
☞ 2 miles to Fredericksburg.
G. Position of Battery C.

The position of our battery, as will be seen, was on this side of the river, and, during the term of picketing, was temporarily attached to the Sixth corps. Subsequently, the assignment was made permanent, as was also the case with battery G, and under this arrangement we are no longer in the former artillery reserve. We have been supplied with new armament, and our park now consists of six 10-pounder Parrotts. There is something painful in breaking up old associations, and separating from those with whom we have for nearly two years shared the fortunes of war ; but the corps to which we have gone has won a noble reputation,—its chief holds a first rank among the generals of the army of the Potomac, and regrets are mitigated by the thought that we are to share in the good name which the honorable record of the past has secured.

On the afternoon of the 14th, the battery moved from its position and marched to Stafford Court House, where it arrived at 5 P. M. The place consists of a court house, jail, a

few outbuildings, and perhaps half a dozen rusty looking
dwellings, and presents nothing in appearance interesting or
attractive. At 10 o'clock P. M., we started for Dumfries, and
marched all night, through a thinly populated region. A century ago, this town was of some importance in a business point
of view. At present it is a dirty looking place, inhabited by
" poor white trash." On the 16th, we broke camp at daylight
and marched to near Fairfax Station, and, on the 18th, proceeded to Fairfax Court House, and went into camp one mile
beyond. This makes our third visit to this place within fifteen
months. The march from the Rappahannock was hot and
dusty, and the travel over old corduroy roads very fatiguing. .

Hyattstown, Md., June 28. Day before yesterday, at 3
o'clock A. M., battery C broke camp at Fairfax Court House,
and with the Sixth army corps, took up the line of march for
the future field of action. We advanced fifteen miles in a
drizzly rain, passed through Drainsville, and made camp one
mile beyond. Yesterday, we crossed the Potomac on a pontoon bridge at Edward's Ferry and camped, having marched
ten miles. To-day, we advanced eighteen miles, passing
through Poolesville, and halted for the night at this place, a
little post village, situated on Bennet's creek, 36 miles north-
west of Washington. The day has been signalized by the
transfer of the command of the army from General Hooker to
General Meade. This was announced in the following general
orders :

HEAD-QUARTERS, ARMY OF THE POTOMAC, }
Frederick, Md., June 28, 1863. }

GENERAL ORDER, No. 65. In conformity with the orders of the
War Department, dated June 27, 1863, I relinquish the command of
the Army of the Potomac. It is transferred to Major General George
G. Meade, a brave and accomplished officer, who has nobly earned
the confidence and esteem of the army, on many a well-fought field.
Impressed with the belief that my usefulness as the commander of the
Army of the Potomac is impaired, I part from it, yet not without the

deepest emotion. The sorrow of parting with the comrades of so many battles is relieved by the conviction that the courage and devotion of this army will never cease nor fail; that it will yield to my successor, as it has to me, a willing and hearty support. With the earnest prayer that the triumph of its arms may bring successes worthy of it and the nation, I bid it farewell.

JOSEPH HOOKER, Major General.

S. F. BARSTOW, Acting Adjutant General.

GEN. MEADE'S ADDRESS ON TAKING COMMAND.

HEAD-QUARTERS OF THE ARMY OF THE POTOMAC,
June 28, 1863.

GENERAL ORDER, No. 66. By direction of the President of the United States, I hereby assume command of the Army of the Potomac. As a soldier, in obeying this order, an order totally unexpected and unsolicited, I have no promises or pledges to make. The country looks to this army to relieve it from the devastation and disgrace of a hostile invasion. Whatever fatigues and sacrifices we may be called upon to undergo, let us have in view constantly the magnitude of the interests involved, and let each man determine to do his duty, leaving to an all-controlling Providence the decision of the contest. It is with just diffidence, that I relieve, in the command of this army, an eminent and accomplished soldier, whose name must ever appear conspicuous in the history of its achievements; but I rely upon the hearty support of my companions in arms, to assist me in the discharge of the duties of the important trust which has been confided to me.

GEORGE G. MEADE,
Major General Commanding.

S. F. BARSTOW, Assistant Adjutant General.

This change gives to the army of the Potomac its sixth commander. General Meade comes to his new command under trying circumstances, but with a record that gives assurance of ability equal to the demands of the hour.

Near Gettysburg, July 5. By rapid marches, such as must convince the sceptical that the army of the Potomac has legs, it reached this place in season to gain position and offer battle to the confederates. On the 29th ultimo, battery C left Hyattstown at 5 o'clock A. M., taking its course through Monrovia, New Market, Ridgeville and Mount Airy, and after marching 25 miles, camped at Sam's creek, at 7½ o'clock. The next day an advance of 15 miles was made, and passing through Westminster, which had been ransacked by rebel cavalry the night before, went into camp near Manchester. The entire night of the 1st instant was occupied in marching, and, on the 2d, passing through Uniontown and Littlestown, the battery went into park near Gettysburg, as a part of the reserve, which is the position of General Sedgwick's corps. The march was not marked by much incident. Foraging was practiced as opportunity offered. At and around Fairfax Court House, and until we reached the Maryland line, the secesh spirit was quite prevalent, but as we advanced, the Union feeling became more apparent. The women, generally, were prompt to contribute whatever they could to the comfort of the soldiers. At almost every house they were baking bread for the thousands of hungry passers. A lady told me she had baked up two barrels of flour, and distributed it without charge. A few, however, bent on making a penny, demanded fifty cents to one dollar per loaf for their bread.

Gettysburg is situated at the head of a beautiful valley lying between the Cacoctin and South Mountains, from which issue roads to nearly every point of compass. There is nothing in the place or the neighboring country, to invite the presence of war. Its seat of learning, its school of the prophets, its beautiful cemetery, and the calm of its rural scenery, all suggest quiet and peaceful pursuits. As already seen, it appears not to have been Lee's original design to deliver battle here, but the necessity was forced upon him by his inability to proceed directly to Harrisburg. It was good judgment in him to thus use his necessity. On some other field, he might have been flanked, and, in case of disaster, his retreat wholly or in part cut off. But here, the danger of either was hardly manifest. From a flank movement on the south, he was secure, while his rear was sufficiently open to escape, to warrant the risk of a general battle.

The preliminary manœuvres on both sides for position having been made, the battle was opened on the 1st by General Reynolds, and continued through the day. It was severely fought, and terminated at night in a mutual heavy loss. General Reynolds was mortally wounded while examining the field for an advantageous disposition of his men, and the command of the corps devolved on General Doubleday. Early on the morning of the 2d, the battle line was formed, the Second and Third corps being on the left, resting on Round Top Hill, the First and Eleventh on the right, and the centre occupying the heights near the cemetery. The entire line extended nearly two miles.

The head-quarters of General Meade were established at a small house on the south side of the road leading to Taneytown, and directly in the rear of his centre. It was a dangerous spot, but convenient for observing operations and sending orders to the right and left. But the General was bound to share the risks of his centre, and the heavy fire it sustained was watched with a coolness that inspired the confidence of the officers about his person.

The battles of the first and second day determined nothing. If the first day gained anything to the Federal side, as much was lost. The second day's fight was even more death-dealing than the first. The rebels hurled a heavy force against our left, only to be beaten back with immense slaughter. Ewell tried a similar experiment on our right, and after a short, doubtful state of things, was repulsed with heavy loss. The centre was in like manner assailed, but with no better success. The battle continued until 8½ o'clock P. M., and terminated with a bad record for the rebels. The advantage was with Meade. Friday, the 3d, was the great battle day, and developed the full power and skill of the opposing armies. Which, now, was to be master of the position, Meade or Lee? A few hours would and did decide. The stake with Lee was the Confederacy—with Meade, the salvation of Pennsylvania and the preservation of Baltimore and Washington. The former lost, the two latter, to human appearance, must be, and then Maryland. No wonder that both braced themselves, as mighty giants, for the struggles of the day. And when they met, what a concussion of forces! Language is feeble to describe it. The charge and the repulse; the rally and the charge repeated; the surging of heavy rebel columns against the impenetrable walls of Federal artillery and infantry; the rush of cavalry, and the shouts of moving masses, formed a succession of pictures intensely exciting; while the steady roll of musketry and the thunderings of three hundred cannon, rending the skies and shaking the earth to its centre, seemed like the outburst of a dozen volcanoes. Lee struggled like one hanging between life and death. His generals fought their men with the fierce recklessness displayed at Malvern Hill. But Victory refused them her banner; and abandoning all hope, they commenced a retreat, leaving thousands of their dead to be buried by Federal hands, and ten thousand of their wounded to be cared for in Federal hospitals. Lee's estimated loss, from all causes, was between thirty and forty thousand. As though apprehensive of defeat, his wagon trains were put in motion towards the Potomac while the battle was going on, and the continuance of the fight on Friday may have been, in part, to gain time for their safe departure. Soon as the retreat became known, Sedgwick's reserve was brought to the front and put in pursuit. The Federal advance continually threatened the rebel rear, exciting constant alarm, and keeping them on the alert to ensure escape. Upwards of 500 of their wagons were destroyed.

The position and conduct of the Rhode Island troops in this battle sustained, with honor, the reputation already gained. The 2d Rhode Island, of Sedgwick's reserve, though not directly engaged, was led by Colonel Rogers, under a storm of shells, to different parts of the field, in support of points hardly

23

pressed. Colonel Tompkins, commanding the artillery brigade of the same corps, met his responsibilities handsomely in the direction of forty-eight guns. Battery C was held in constant readiness for action, but was required only once to go to the front as a relief. It experienced no disaster. Battery G was engaged on Friday, and expended one hundred and sixty-two rounds.

Captain John G. Hazard, chief of the artillery brigade in Howard's (Second) corps, had five batteries in the field, which fought bravely. In the midst of a hot fire, his horse was shot under him. His Adjutant, Lieutenant G. L. Dwight, met with a similar casualty. The two Rhode Island batteries in Captain Hazard's brigade, (A and B,) were severely cut up. The former, Captain Arnold, had position on a hill, and was subjected to a destructive artillery fire, which it returned with great spirit. Captain Arnold's loss was five killed, twenty-three wounded,— among them Lieutenant Jacob H. Lamb, Sergeant B. H. Child, and Corporals Wesley B. Calder, William H. Rider and Edwin Shaw,—and one missing. Thirty horses were also lost. Battery B went into action under Lieutenant T. F. Brown, and came out of a fiery ordeal with a heavy loss of horses, four men killed, and twenty-three wounded and missing. Lieutenant Brown was wounded in the neck. Lieutenant Joseph H. Milne, who had been detailed to United States battery A, received a mortal wound. Sergeants John T. Blake and Edwin A. Chace were each wounded in the wrist. Lieutenant A. H. Cushing, a brave officer commanding United States battery A, was killed.

Captain George E. Randolph, commanding the artillery brigade in Sickles's (Third) corps, had five batteries of his own brigade and three from the artillery reserve, in the battle, which were finely handled. Early in the action, he was wounded in the shoulder by a Minie, but continued on the field, directing the movements of his command. His Adjutant, Lieutenant Jastram, was very active, and rendered important aid in the varied duties of the day. Battery E was taken into battle by Lieutenant John K. Bucklyn. It was posted on the road from Gettysburg to Emmettsburg, near the Peach Orchard that formed the angle of our lines. The rebels concentrated upon it a heavy fire of shot and shell, causing a loss of twenty-nine men killed and wounded, and forty horses killed and disabled. Lieutenant Bucklyn was severely wounded in the breast while removing a caisson whose horses were shot. Lieutenants Benjamin Freeborn and Charles B. Winslow were slightly wounded, as were Sergeant Hargraves and Corporals Farmer and Alexander. The men, no less than officers, in the several batteries, deserve warm commendation for coolness and vigorous work under the hottest exposure. None could have done better.

One year ago, the army of the Potomac, exhausted by the fatigue and the excitement of its seven days' battles, was reposing at Harrison's Landing. The brightness of the national anniversary was then shadowed by disappointment, in prospect of being withdrawn from the Peninsula without gaining the prize almost within our grasp. Yesterday, the anniversary returned, enlivened by brilliant deeds, and witnessing to a success long delayed. In a spirit becoming the event, General Meade issued the following address:

HEAD-QUARTERS, ARMY OF POTOMAC, }
Near Gettysburg, July 4, 1863. }

GENERAL ORDERS, No. 68. The Commanding General, in behalf of the country, thanks the army of the Potomac for the glorious result of the recent operations. Our enemy, superior in numbers, and flushed with the pride of successful invasion, attempted to overcome or destroy this army. Baffled and defeated, he has now withdrawn from the contest. The privations and fatigues the army has endured, and the heroic courage and gallantry it displayed, will be matters of history to be ever remembered.

Our task is not yet accomplished, and the Commanding General looks to the army for greater efforts to drive from our soil every vestige of the presence of the invader.

It is right and proper that we should, on suitable occasions, return our grateful thanks to the Almighty Disposer of events, that in the goodness of His providence, He has thought fit to give victory to the cause of the just.

By command of Major General Meade.

S. WILLIAMS, A. A. G.

Throughout the three days' fighting, the coöperation of the several corps was hearty and complete. Orders were promptly communicated from head-quarters and as promptly obeyed. Generals Sickles, Barnes, Gibbon, Doubleday, Howard, Hancock, Sedgwick, Slocum, Webb, Shurtz, Wadsworth, Howe, Pleasanton, Kilpatrick, Bufford, and the many others not named, exerted themselves to the utmost in carrying out the plans of the Commander-in-Chief, and the officers of every grade, as well as the privates of every regiment, conducted with a bravery never excelled. To General Meade, the victory was costly. With the immense amount of artillery pitted against him, and the strength of an hundred thousand infantry and cavalry thrown furiously upon his lines, it could not be otherwise. If the sacrifice exceeded all former example, its fruit was victory —on this field clear and decisive—and victory, at any price, in such a crisis, became a joy. Of Generals killed, besides Reynolds, were Zook, Shired, Paul and Weed, the latter lately an able chief of artillery. Of the wounded, were Generals Sickles, (leg amputated,) Merideth, Graham, Hancock, Gibbon, Warren, Hunt, Butterfield, Barlow, and Doubleday. Defeat, to the rebels, was still more costly. Two of their Generals were killed, (Barksdale and Garnet,) and thirteen wounded, three mortally. General Archer was taken prisoner.

The field, after the battle, exhibited all the terrible features of Antietam intensified. In no previous battle had the number of killed and wounded been so great. Over an area of many miles lay thickly mingled, wounded and dead men, wounded and dead horses, broken caissons, disabled guns, muskets, havcrsacks, and other appurtenances of war. Cemetery Hill, where the fight had raged with hurricane violence, was strewn with the dead and dying, and the cemetery itself filled with dead men and horses, the fragments of shattered monuments, broken gravestones, damaged caissons and exploded shells. The field hospitals, and Gettysburgh, which had become one vast hospital, were crowded with Federal and rebel wounded, taxing to the utmost the services of surgeons and nurses.

[To describe the scenes here, would be but to repeat in words of stronger emphasis, the ghastly tales of Savage's Station, Malvern Hill, Antietam and Fredericksburg. One who visited the hospitals, writes: " In the court house, in the very heart of Gettysburgh, we found our own soldiers lying on the bare floor, covered with blood, and dirt, and vermin, *entirely naked* having perhaps only a newspaper to protect their festering wounds from the flies! Their wounds were very severe. Some of them were disfigured beyond the possibility of recognition. Oh! it is impossible to describe these mangled and marred fragments of humanity. One we saw with a great cavern in his side, from which the lungs protruded several inches. Another unfortunate, whose eyes had been shot out whilst trying to creep to a fence for shelter, was struck in the body five times! Of the number above named, eighty-three were shot in the body; seventy-seven were cases of amputation; the rest were wounded mostly in the lower limbs. And this may be regarded as a fair average exhibit.

" Riding on over muddy roads, and through swollen streams, we came to the camp hospital of the Third army corps, against whose undaunted front Longstreet had hurled his legions, only to be crushed and driven back. The large number of their wounded attested the valor with which this corps had fought. Language fails to depict the misery which was here present. Scarcely had one man out of nearly three thousand anything to lie on but the ground, covered by an old blanket or oil-cloth, and hundreds had undergone amputation since the battle. The surgeons were still busily engaged in cutting off arms and legs. The several limbs were piled up at different tables. Gangs of men were employed all the time as grave-diggers, and the dead lay on stretchers, or on the ground, waiting for burial."

Another adds:

"The sad scenes and sights of the wounded, the sick, the bereaved, hang up pictures in the halls of memory and imagination that will never be taken down. Here is a poor rebel with both legs off below the knee, waving a long wisp of straw to keep the flies off, and the freight cars must be a hard bed for him to lie on in a jolting journey of eighty miles. Here is one with a spot on his back, the place of a severe wound, perfectly black with the flies which have lighted on his shirt. Here is a man with a hole in the top of his head. Here a poor boy is minus an arm. Here a confederate, wounded, has a shirt as black as the chimney, which has, apparently, not touched water since the fall of Fort Sumter. For, with all that is done, and it is a benevolence computed only by billions, much that still remains undone would attract the quick eye and pain the gentle heart of woman. But men rough it through somehow; God and their good angels only know how. But we saw little complaint, heard no angry words. If women can bear terrible wounds, sickness, and anguish more patiently than did these victims of Gettysburg, they must be largely compounded of angel and divinity." And now, as messengers of humanity, came the agents of the Sanitary and Christian Commissions, to do the needed work at the moment of pressing demand. With the forecast and energy displayed at Antietam and Fredericksburg, the Sanitary Commission pushed forward, in wagons, large quantities of hospital supplies, to meet the deficiencies in the stores of the surgeons, shortly before the battle commenced; and after the battle, eleven wagon loads of special supplies were distributed to the corps hospitals and to scattering groups of wounded found in the field, before any supplies arrived by railroad. What was done by this noble organization, during the ten days following the battle, may be learned from the following incomplete statement of the quantities of the principal articles distributed : The perishable articles, (amounting to over 60 tons,) were taken to the ground in refrigerating cars. A considerable quantity of the same articles, purchased from or contributed by the farmers about Gettysburg, is not included under this statement.

Of drawers, shirts and other hospital body-clothing, 39,884 pieces, being equal to full suits of clean bed-clothing for ten thousand wounded men.

Of beds, sheets, blankets, comforts, pillows, cushions for wounded limbs, and mosquito nets, 11,700 pieces, being equivalent to a complete bed equipment for eighteen hundred men, severely wounded.

Of bed utensils......................................728
Of towels and napkins.........................10,000
Of sponges...2,300
Of combs.. 1,500
Of buckets 200
Of soap, Castile...............................250 pounds.
Of old silk..300 yards.
Of tin basins, cups, etc.........................7,000
Of old linen, bandages, etc.....................110 barrels.
Of water tanks......................................7
Of water coolers................................. 46
Of bay rum and Cologne water.....................100 bottles.
Of fans..3,500
Of chloride of lime...............................11 barrels.
Of shoes and slippers...........................4,000 pairs.
Of crutches.......................................1,200 "
Of lanterns.......................................180
Of candles..350 pounds.
Of canvas...300 sq. yds.

OF ARTICLES OF SUSTENANCE, VIZ. :

Fresh poultry and mutton ....11,000 pounds.
Fresh butter ....6,100 "

Fresh eggs, (chiefly collected for the occasion at farm-
    houses in Pennsylvania and New Jersey)........8,500 dozens.
Fresh garden vegetables.........................675 bushels.
Fresh berries.....................................48   "
Fresh bread ....10,300 loaves.
Ice... 20,000 pounds.
Concentrated beef soup........................3,800   "
Concentrated milk 12,500   "
Prepared farinaceous food.....................7,000   "
Dried fruit...................................3,500   "
Jellies and conserves 2,000   "
Tamarinds...................................·750 gallons.
Lemons.................................... 116 boxes.
Oranges 46   "
Coffee ....850 pounds.
Tea 426   "
White sugar................................6,800   "
Syrups, (lemon, etc.) ....785 bottles.
Brandy 1,250   "
Whisky....................................1,160   "
Wine.....................................1,148   "
Ale.......................................600 gallons.
Biscuit, crackers and rusk ....134 barrels.
Preserved meats.............................500 pounds.
Preserved fish..............................3,600   "
Pickles...................................400 gallons.
Tobacco..................................100 pounds.
Tobacco pipes.............................1,000

The service of the Commission has never been more honorable to those engaged in it than in this campaign. The fact
that four of its agents were taken prisoners of war, while en-
deavoring to push forward supplies ; that in performing assigned
duties, several of them placed their lives in imminent jeopardy,
while others, forgetful of self, labored continuously during successive days and nights; and that, while there were many
critical points in the arrangements of the service, nothing of
consequence failed to be found at the time and place demanded,
testify to the courage, zeal and industry, no less than to the

patience and good discipline exercised. More than double the usual number of persons were employed; nearly all those added to the force having been formerly in the service of the Commission, and volunteering their assistance for the emergency. Without this prompt and munificent aid, the sufferings of the wounded must have been inconceivably increased.]

When the army commenced the pursuit of Lee, there was a general impression that he would be compelled to give battle at Hagerstown, Williamsport, or possibly on the old field of Antietam, in which event it was believed he would be bagged sure. But he had a quick eye and a becoming respect for lines of retreat; and having made provision for the safety of his baggage trains, nimble legs carried him and his broken army across the Potomac, and saved him from a general engagement. At one moment, while but a portion of his army had crossed, appearances favored the expectation of a battle, and the men on our side were in high spirits. But they were doomed to disappointment, which, it is but truth to say, the tidings of the victory at Vicksburg and Port Hudson assisted them to bear with tolerable equanimity. There were doubtless military reasons why Gen. Meade yielded his understood wish for an immediate attack, to the adverse opinions of the majority of his generals in council. Nothing would have been more gratifying to the army of the Potomac than to have finished the work begun at Gettysburg, on either of the aforementioned fields, as the crown stone of the southwestern triumphal arch; but it may be that the Almighty has another vial of wrath to pour out upon the Old Dominion, to consummate the evils she has invoked on herself, by striking hands with rebellion, dishonoring her patriotic antecedents, and insulting the memory of her Washington. If "things sweet to taste prove in digestion sour," this failure and defeat must be the most mortifying of General Lee's experiences since he assumed supreme command of the rebel army in Virginia. The prestige gained on other fields is under a deep shadow. He returns, not a conqueror, having dictated terms of peace, but a fugitive, driven back, shorn of one-third of his army. The charm of a northern invasion has been broken, and the experiment will hardly be repeated.

[The alarm created by the defeat of Lee was at once visible in the tone of the rebel newspapers. The most extraordinary efforts were made to conceal from the people, as long as possible, the disastrous results of his campaign. They were told that he had achieved a great victory, had annihilated the Federal army, had overburdened himself with prisoners, and that the deeds of the campaign transcended in glory those of all other battles! In future years, when the story of Gettysburg shall be read, it will appear incredible that the editor of the Richmond Enquirer, five days after the battle, with a full knowledge of the facts, wrote and published as follows:

" Gen. Lee's magnificent victory at Gettysburg has, doubtless, cost us very dear, as many of us will know too well when the sad details come in. At present, we have only the grand and glorious result—the greatest army of the Yankee nation swept away, trampled under foot, and all but annihilated upon its own soil ; the best part of Pennsylvania laid under contribution to sustain our army, and, in some small measure, make good our heavy losses ; the second city on the continent open to our armies, and already reckoning up the number of millions it must pay to ransom it from pillage and conflagration ; our own city of Baltimore, waiting its deliverance with a passionate but secret joy; and Washington, that foul den of thieves, expecting the righteous vengeance of Heaven for the hideous crimes that have been done within its walls. In Philadelphia, how the Quakers quake this day ! In Washington, how the whole brood of Lincoln and his rascal ministers turn pale—how their knees smite together, as they hear from afar off the roar of the grand Army of the Potomac rolled back in bloody rout and dismay, and see flashing through their guilty dreams the avenging bayonets of those they dared to call ' rebels ! ' Ha ! does their monstrous crime weigh heavy on their souls to-day ?· Mingling with the cheers that greeted the sweet perorations of their Fourth-of-July ' orators of the day,' do their ears hear the wail of the homeless and the fatherless whose houses they have lain in ashes, whose pride and strength they have laid low in the graves of a hundred battle-fields? Yes, they begin to feel that they were in the wrong; that there was some mistake somewhere; and, for the first time, they pray for peace.

"But this is only their first lesson. It is probable that our Peace Commissioners will have yet several other such to administer, before the enemy shall be perfectly satisfied that there is no possible peace for him until he withdraws every soldier from the soil of every State, including Missouri, Kentucky, Maryland and Delaware, and yield up to their lawful owners every town and fort he holds all around our borders. *Cincinnati, for example, would, we are assured, burn well.* It is the enlightened metropolis of strychnine whisky, the queen city of fat pork, peopled by as God-abandoned sons of Yankees as ever killed a hog. Our troops have now got a taste of northern viands, and their fine, healthy appetite grows by what it feeds on. Ohio also has silver and gold, and towns to ransom, and fertile plains to sweep of flocks and herds. As they *will* have war, let them have their fill of it, and that in its highest perfection and widest development. So, and not otherwise, will Peace spread her white wings, and cover all the land as the waters cover the sea.

"We are only at the beginning of our peace movement, and other such diplomatic protocols as that of Gettysburg will yet have to be formulated before the end comes. We hail with joy the inauguration of the new era, the opening of the true path to freedom and to peace. We are prouder than ever of our heroic army and of its illustrious General, of whom it is the highest praise to say that he is worthy of the troops he leads; firmer than ever in the belief that peace will come to us only in one way—by the edge of the sword."*

---

* It is still more incredible that General Lee should have written similar statements to the President of the Rebel Confederacy, from whom he could have had no justifiable motive in concealing the truth. Yet, according to the Richmond Enquirer, such was the fact. In its issue of July 11th, it says: "The President received a letter from Gen. Lee, on Saturday, which puts to rest all anxieties in relation to the situation of our army in Maryland, and confirms the statements which have been made, that our army has been uniformly victorious in its encounters with the enemy in Pennsylvania. The letter states, in effect, that the engagements at Gettysburg resulted in defeating the enemy completely, in killing and wounding a number far exceeding our own, and in the capture of a large number of prisoners; that the falling back of our army to Hagerstown

Of the cool assurance of this gasconade, it would be difficult to find a parallel.]

In the account now given of the most deadly battle in which the army of the Potomac has been engaged, many particulars of interest have necessarily been omitted. It would be pleasant to bring to notice instances of individual bravery; to speak of men in the ranks, whose good conduct deserves a perpetual record; to mention, by name, the wounded and the dead, who, with no ambition other than to do their duty, offered themselves voluntary sacrifices on the altar of their country's service; but such a record would of itself swell to a volume, and cannot here be made. But they will not be forgotten. Friends who mourn the departed, and rejoice in the surviving, will hold them in affectionate remembrance. A grateful country will honor their patriotism; and, in advancing years, one who can say,—" I fought at Gettysburg," will find his utterance a passport to generous sympathies ever enduring.

Camp near Warrenton, Va., July 27.   Twenty days have passed since battery C commenced its return march from Pennsylvania.   On the morning of the 7th instant, it left camp at Emmettsburg, and proceeding by the way of Middletown and Boonsboro, went into position on the 10th, in the neighborhood of Funkstown, Md., that place then being occupied by rebels. The next day, Lieutenant Rich advanced his section about fifteen hundred yards, and fired four rounds over the village, without drawing out a response.   The etymology of this rather

---

was a prudential move, not occasioned by any success on the part of the enemy, and not through any apprehension of contingencies arising which might insure his success at that point. The gist of the letter, in a few words, is that the enemy was even more thoroughly cut up and whipped than he ever has been upon southern soil, and that the occupation of Ha- gerstown was a movement dictated by strategy and prudence, as essential to the success of the campaign."

uneuphonic name rests in obscurity. For aught that appears
to the contrary, it may have been the homestead of the original
Peter, whose numerous progeny have obtained an unenviable
notoriety. However this may be, it is one of the principal
villages washed by Antietam creek, and boasts a population of
seven or eight hundred. Our march brought us within a few
miles of Hagerstown, which the rebels occupied immediately
after their retreat from Gettysburg. The roads over the Cumberland mountain were in a bad condition, and the marching
exceedingly fatiguing. Continuing our march, we proceeded
to Berlin, a post town eight miles below Harper's Ferry, where
we arrived on the 16th. There was little of interest to attract
the eye or excite the imagination, in this place, or its surroundings, and the order to break camp, on the morning of the 19th,
was a welcome sound. Marching through the town, we crossed
the Potomac on a pontoon bridge, and passing through Lovet-
ville, encamped at 3½ o'clock P. M., having marched twelve
miles. The 2d Rhode Island crossed the same day, on a similar bridge, thrown over below. We were now, once more,
after an absence of nearly six weeks, treading the soil of Secessia. Temporary absence had failed to clothe it with new
beauties, or to inspire reverence for its presiding spirit. Treason was as hideous as when its brazen trump first sounded
defiance to constitutional law, and sent a thrill of horror through
the land.

Pursuing our course, we camped at Rector's Cross Roads on
the 22d, and the next day passed Rectortown, the head-quarters of Gen. McClellan, last November, and Salem, a village
" beautiful for situation," but whose inhabitants cannot yet take
up the refrain, " now no more the drum provokes to arms."
Bloody months may pass before the soul of social life its name
imports, will be realized. On the 24th, at 11 o'clock A. M.,
the battery reached Manassas Gap, where the horses were fed,
watered and grazed. After three hours rest, we counter-
marched and took another road, when the march was continued

24

to Klum's creek, where we encamped for the night, having made twenty miles—a pretty good day's work. On Saturday, (25th,) a march of fifteen miles brought us to this place, near which, eight months ago, we paused on our march to what proved our winter quarters before Fredericksburg. The 2d Rhode Island, which took nearly the same route from Berlin, arrived the same day, and halted about two miles from Warrenton.

Here we pause. The close of the Pennsylvania campaign brings us to a period in the rebellion when we may look back and take counsel of the past, and forward, to divine the future. The fierce and sanguinary struggle of more than two years and a half duration, was entered upon by the Unionists with reluctance, and only from a conscientious sense of duty to the Government whose authority was defied, and to constitutional law, which interposed a barrier to the destructive sweep of anarchy. They were tender and forbearing—as events have shown, unwisely so. They shrank from violence, and especially from bloodshed, in restoring obedience to authority. Their pursuits were peaceful; they deprecated domestic broils, and were ready to accept quiet on any terms consistent with mutual rights, law and order. But they found themselves dealing with lawless revolutionists—men who had resolved to break up the Union, go out of it if they could not, or remain in it only on stipulations that would perpetuate in their hands a controlling power in the nation. It was really a question of freedom or bondage—of master or vassal—of life or death—and the friends of the Federal government were made sadly sensible, that personal rights could be ensured, and national life preserved, only at the price of blood; and blood has flowed in torrents, staining the fair inheritance purchased by sacrifice, with fratricidal gore.

The contest begun. Treason fired the first gun. But on

our part it was not a battle for sectional aggrandizement. Had
it been, not a regiment could have been raised in the North
for its prosecution. With the North, it was a war for peace;
for the restoration of harmony; for the vindication of a viola-
ted constitution; for the maintenance of civil government; for
the security of property, personal liberty, and that vital feature
in organized society—the inviolability of contracts. And more.
It was a war for the safety of nations. The principle assailed
by anarchists was the principle that underlies and upholds
nationalities. It was a battle for Europe no less than for
America; for the throne as for the republic; for England and
France as for the United States.

In this light, it was seen by the peace-loving and law-abiding millions of our own land, and by the intelligent and orderly
of all lands. It was natural to suppose, under such conditions,
that the government of the United States would receive the
sympathy of at least the two nations claiming to be the most
enlightened and honorable in their diplomacy of the nations of
the Old World. Of France, not so much was expected as of the
mother country; yet, even she, it was believed, would at least
preserve a strict neutrality. How she has met the expectation, her hobnobbing with rebel agents, and other equally offensive conduct, show. But of England—and, by England,
her government is meant — better things were believed.
Something was hoped from the influence of a community of
language, identity of interests, the kindly feeling supposed to
be well established towards us, and above all, her professed
detestation of human oppression. But painful has been the
disappointment. She has shown herself selfish when she
should have been generous; practicing duplicity when straight-
forward frankness was her duty; resorting to Machiavellian
arts when she should have been true to an honorable national
life. Her policy has lacked the element of principle. Her
Palmerstons have shuffled and bent the knee to Cotton, when

they should have borne themselves erect like high-minded
men.   In the face of all professions of friendship, and while
the princely hospitalities showered by our nation upon the heir
to her throne were yet fresh in memory, she insidiously struck
a blow at our national unity.   She dickered with treason.
She suffered her island ports to be made the rendezvous for
repairs and supplies, to an outlaw preying upon the commerce
of a country with which she was at peace.   She permitted to
enter, and protected in departure, from a chief commercial port,
a vessel whose flag, by the law of nations, was piratical, and
which she knew, as is believed, intended to capture, sink and
destroy all merchantmen sailing under the flag, and claiming
the protection of the United States, that crossed her corsair
path.   She knew, that in the shipyards of Liverpool, iron-clads
were building by her own subjects, ostensibly for China, but
really for the rebel confederates, yet chose not officially to see
the fact, until forced to by the moral sentiment of the world.
She knew privately, unofficially, that articles contraband of
war were daily exported, in British bottoms, from her own
ports, for the aid and comfort of rebellion in this nation, but
adopted no measures to prevent it.   And ignoring her West
India emancipation, and her long years boasting of superior
humanity, and with a will to do us harm, she has indirectly
encouraged rebellion, while professing to hate the thing that its
leaders avowed to be the corner-stone of the new nation they
are striving to rear!   England, then, scarcely less than the
South, is responsible for the present condition of our country.
Had she taken counsel of her Brights and her honest masses,
instead of her corrupt aristocracy; had she been just to her
position, and acted as she ought, rebellion had long since come
to an end.   Without foreign intervention, the cause of the
anarchists was utterly hopeless; and so long as England, by
covert measures, encouraged the hope of ultimate recognition,
she contributed to the protraction of this intestine war.   So the

pen of History will record, when it writes the dark, sad page of her national tergiversations.*

What, then, is the lesson taught by the past? It is, that in this contest, we are to hope for nothing from two powers of Europe with which we have been most intimate, on the score of principle or friendship. If anything is yielded, it will be the fruit of self-interest. We are to rely more on our inherent strength. We are to develop our material forces, with the vigor of a nation in earnest. We are to increase our naval arm of four hundred sail, if need be, until with its hundred iron clads, it can defy all haters of our republic. We are to culti-vate harmony of purpose; to stand by the government, with only this one thought—the Nation as a Unit.

When rebellion begun, it seemed a small thing, and expec-tation was common that it would come to a speedy termination. But expectation was destined to disappointment. The deep-seated character of the disease was imperfectly understood, even by the wisest. From the little thing it seemed, it swelled to enormous proportions, like the human body under mercurial treatment. But by processes sometimes heroic, and sometimes lenitive, its distorted features have been largely reduced, while the power of the Federal government to treat it successfully has correspondingly enlarged. When will the unnatural con-test cease? This question is often asked, coupled with another— What is to be the result? When will it cease? None but

---

* Since this page was written, a speech delivered by Lord John Russell, at Blairgowrie, Scotland, has been published, which may be regarded as a semi-official development of the future policy of the British government towards the United States. The policy indicated, from whatever cause the change, is much more conciliatory than the course pursued in an earlier stage of the rebellion. This is well. It is due, from what is known of Lord Russell, to believe that his speech is an honest expression of his private feelings; but as an explanation of, or an indirect apology for, the conduct of the English government in the past, it is exceedingly lame. There stand the facts, and no amount of reasoning can hide their moral obliquity.

the Omniscient can answer. Its end may be nearer than any suppose. Causes unseen may be at work to bring it to a speedy termination ; or, if the Infinite's plans are not yet ready for a final development, it may be protracted until the value of the sacred principle involved shall be so impressed on the national heart, as to ensure to it the strength of an undivided support. That there are still difficulties to be met, it were idle to deny. In some form, they will appear till the death throe. But the signs of encouragement are not to be overlooked, nor undervalued. These are many ; and among them, in the words of another, are "the great deliverance from the long strain and menace of invasion—the easy victory over anarchy at home, which some had thought to be our most formidable foe."

What is to be the result of this still uncompleted war ? That which has ever issued from the contestant forces of right and wrong—human good. Out of Waterloo, Victor Hugo tells us, grew liberty ; and the deadly struggles of Magenta and Solferino, helped to diffuse its spirit over the continent, to soften the hard features of despotism, to emancipate thought, and to call out the latent endowments of national manhood. And so, out of this contest with "the conspiracy of unscrupulous and traitorous men," will grow a higher form of national life—of purer humanity and Christian civilization.

APPENDIX.

In preparing the following sketches of the several regiments and batteries sent into service by Rhode Island, it has been the aim to seize upon salient points in the history of each, rather than to burden the narrative with minuteness of detail that would extend this volume far beyond prescribed limits. Though, for this reason, particulars of camp life, marches, picket and other experiences may be missed, that participants therein would like to see, it is believed that the omissions do not, in any degree, affect the integrity of the story, nor obscure the merits of the work accomplished. In the body of the volume, as will be seen by reference to the Index, many incidents of regiments and batteries are given, which it is unnecessary here to repeat.

FIRST REGIMENT RHODE ISLAND VOLUNTEERS.

Rev. Augustus Woodbury, pastor of the Westminster Congregational Church and Society, in Providence, has written an admirable and exhaustive history of the campaign of this first three months regiment from Rhode Island. To that volume the reader is referred, to learn how, in the hour of our country's peril, all classes and conditions of society, "rich and poor, native and foreigner, Protestant and Catholic, radical and conservative, republican and democrat, alike felt the mighty impulse" of loyalty, and sprang as one man to the rescue. The name of this regiment is introduced here, not for the purpose of writing its history anew, but to preserve its numerical relation to its successors in the war, and to add a testimony to the invaluable service it rendered the government by its prompt response to the call for 75,000 men.

The regiment departed from Providence in two detachments, on the 20th and 24th of April, 1861, the first under Colonel Ambrose E. Burnside, and the second under Lieutenant Colonel Joseph S. Pitman. Both left with the warm benedictions of the immense throngs that crowded to witness their departure. After a brief sojourn at the Patent Office in Washington, a beautiful encampment was provided about one mile north of the capitol, which received the name of Camp

Sprague. The battle of Bull Run was fought, in which the regiment made an honorable record; the term for which it enlisted had expired; and assured that the capital was safe, it returned home, bearing in its wounded, and in its tattered colors, the evidence of a bravery of which Rhode Island will ever be proud.

The regiment arrived in Providence on the morning of the 28th July, and the reception was a magnificent tribute of popular feeling to men who had distinguished themselves for martial qualities—withstanding a trial more fearful than any they could have anticipated, and found faithful beyond all they had promised. They came on the morning of the Sabbath, and, as if by concert, yet not by any mutual understanding, the houses of worship were closed, and the thousands of worshippers lined the streets, to greet with a spontaneous expression of sympathy and affection, men who had faced the raging storm of death. Yet a Sabbath morning never seemed more sacred, nor were its proprieties ever more becomingly preserved. At Fox Point, the regiment was formed in line, and the vast procession moved. First came the escort of fourteen companies belonging to Providence, Newport and Pawtucket, with Gilmore's & Shepard's Bands, together with a large number of citizens. Then followed the regiment, including the brass and drum band, at the head of which rode its gallant Colonel and staff, accompanied by Lieutenant Governor Arnold, Adjutant General Mauran and Captain Hoppin of his staff. As the extended column filed through various streets, the stillness of the hour was broken, again and again, by deep yet orderly outbursts of feeling. Handkerchiefs waved from every window. Colonel Burnside was fairly loaded down with boquets, and nearly every bayonet in the regiment was decked with flowers. The battle-torn flag was warmly greeted. At every point the soldiers were beset and crowded by hundreds who had acquaintances and relatives in the regiment, and who, when they discovered among the brown and sun-burned faces the one they sought, rushed up with demonstrative joy and words of welcome. There were a few that wandered about with sorrowful faces, and did not find those for whom they waited and hoped. The manly form of the Christian patriot, Lieutenant Henry A. Prescott, was missing, and the memory of his fall on the fatal field, cast a shadow upon many hearts.

In Railroad Hall, Messrs. L. H. Humphrey & Co. had laid an ample collation for about three thousand persons. To this, the soldiers were welcomed by Lieutenant Governor Arnold, followed in an earnest and appropriate address by Bishop Clark. "This day," he said, "is sacred. These men have been doing a sacred and solemn work. The greeting which we now tender them is appropriate to this hallowed season." He referred to the reports of valor that had come to him, and he thanked them all for what they had done. He added :

"You brought home with you, to-day, the sick and the wounded. May God heal them in His good time, and restore them to us sound in limb and firm in health. You have left others behind. We know not what may be the fate of some of them, but we pray God to have them in His keeping, and give them back to us in due season.

"You have left also the dead, and the soil of Virginia is now in a real sense sacred to us. Often, in the morning and in the evening, our thoughts have turned to that hallowed spot, as the Israelite turned toward Holy Jerusalem.

"We will embalm the names of the departed in our memories; we will write them on the tablets of fame, and Rhode Island shall raise a monument to their memories that shall tell to all coming generations how sacred she holds her heroic dead.

"I wish that our Governor were with us to-day; but, true to his nature, he remains not where honors await him, as they would have done if he had come home with you, but where his most solemn duty lies. He stays to succor those who are in want. And when he has done all the work that he can do for us there, then may God send him back to us and we will render him due honor. [Applause.]

"You have come back to us, as they say, from a defeat. I rejoice to say that Rhode Island comes back from a victory. You had achieved your triumph and won the battle before the tide turned, and if all the men in the field had been like you, and all the officers like Colonel Burnside, [Great applause] and all the leaders like Governor Sprague, [Renewed applause] the whole north would have been in a blaze of exultation to-day."

The scene in the hall was scarcely less exciting than that which had just preceded it in the streets. After the collation, the regiment was dismissed until the following Thursday, August 1st, when it met on Exchange place, for the last time, and listened to the farewell order of its beloved commander. The following is a list of the

FIELD AND STAFF OFFICERS,

(Commissioned and Non-commissioned.)

Colonel—AMBROSE E. BURNSIDE. Brigadier General of Volunteers, U. S. A., August 6th, 1861 ; Major General, March 18th, 1862. In command of the Department of North Carolina. Joined General McClellan on the Peninsula. Commander-in-Chief of the army of the Potomac, November 7, 1862. Relieved, and appointed to the command of the Department of the Ohio.

Lieutenant Colonel— JOSEPH S. PITMAN.

First Major—JOHN S. SLOCUM. Resigned, and appointed Colonel of 2d regiment R. I. V., May 8th, 1861.

First Major—JOSEPH P. BALCH. Promoted from Second Major, June 27, 1861.

Second Major—WILLIAM GODDARD, appointed June 27, 1861.

Surgeon—FRANCIS L. WHEATON. Resigned, and appointed Surgeon in 2d regiment R. I. V., June 6, 1861. Brigade Surgeon. Surgeon-in-Chief at Portsmouth Grove Hospital. Relieved, 1862.

Surgeon—HENRY W. RIVERS. Promoted from Assistant Surgeon, June 7th. Surgeon 4th regiment R. I. V. Promoted to Brigade Surgeon, March, 1862.

Assistant Surgeon—NATHANIEL MILLER.

Assistant Surgeon—GEORGE W. CARR. Appointed Assistant Surgeon in 2d regiment R. I. V., August 27, 1861.

Assistant Surgeon—JAMES HARRIS. Attached to 2d regiment R. I. V., July 1st, 1861 ; taken prisoner at the battle of Bull Run, July 21st, 1861 ; released, September, 1861. Appointed Superintendent United States Hospital, in Providence, April, 1862.

Adjutant—CHARLES H. MERRIMAN. Appointed Acting Assistant Adjutant General and Chief of Staff of Brigade. Major 10th regiment R. I. V., May 26th, 1862. Resigned, June, 1862.

Quartermaster—CYRUS G. DYER. Resigned, and Captain in 2d regiment R. I. V., June 5th, 1861.

Quartermaster—WILLIAM LLOYD BOWERS, June 5th, 1861; taken prisoner at Bull Run, July 21st; released and returned to Providence, January 25th, 1862.

Commissary—ALVAN COLE.

Paymaster—HENRY T. SISSON. Captain, December 20th, 1861. Major, 3d regiment R. I. H. A., February 5th, 1862. Colonel 5th regiment R. I. V., November 5th, 1862.

Chaplain—AUGUSTUS WOODBURY. Very active on the field as Aide to Colonel Burnside at the battle of Bull Run.

Assistant Chaplain—THOMAS QUINN. Appointed Chaplain 3d regiment R. I. H. A. Transferred to 1st regiment R. I. L. A. Discharged January 8th, 1862.

Engineer—HENRY A. DEWITT, May 31st, 1861. Planned Camp Sprague.

Sergeant Major—JOHN P. SHAW. Lieutenant 2d R. I. V., June 6, 1861. Captain, July 24, 1862.

Sergeant Major—JOHN S. ENGS, June 8th, 1861.

Quartermaster Sergeant—HENRY A. BARTLETT. Relieved, May 2d. Appointed Lieutenant United States Marine Corps.

Quartermaster Sergeant—ELIAS M. JENCKES.

Commissary Sergeant—WILLIAM L. HUNTER.

Ordnance Sergeant—JAMES W. LYON. Lieutenant 4th regiment R. I. V.

Drum Major—BENJAMIN G. WEST. Bugler in 3d regiment R. I. H. A.

Hospital Steward—JAMES H. TAYLOR. ·

The Captains of the several companies were Arthur F. Dexter, Nathaniel W. Brown, George W. Tew, William W. Brown, Nicholas Van Slyck, Stephen R. Bucklin, Charles W. H. Day, Peter Simpson, Henry C. Card, John T. Pitman.

The regiment was accompanied, throughout the campaign, by the Providence American Brass Band, under the leadership of Joseph C. Greene, one of the most accomplished performers on the bugle in the United States. In the camp and on the march, the music of the band had the charm of inspiration, while, on the field of battle, the humanity of its members was displayed in the care bestowed upon the wounded and dying. The names of the Band were Joseph C. Greene, Band Master, and afterwards occupying the same position in the 4th regiment R. I. V., Henry L. Dana, Alfred E. Dickenson, William L. Dunbar, Thomas P. Fenner, John C. Harrington, Willard Haskell, Augustus Heise, William W. Hall, Walter B. Kingsley, George E. Mason, William F. Marshall, Emory Paine, Abijah M. Pond, Edward L. Potter, Carroll J. Pullen, William Lee Reynolds, Beriah G. Reynolds, Samuel D. Spink, Stephen R. Sweet, Sylvester J. Sweet, William E. Whiting, Stephen G. Whittemore.

On the 10th of August, a public welcome was given to the Band in the Church of the Ministry at Large, in the presence of an audience crowding the house to its utmost capacity. The pulpit window was festooned with national flags, above which were the words,—"*American Brass Band Welcome*." After appropriate introductory services, the following original hymn was sung by the congregation with thrilling effect:

"1. Welcome, friends, to homes and kindred,—
   Welcome to this sacred fane:
Here accept our friendly greetings,
   As this day we meet again.
Mem'ries thickly gather round us,
   Paling joy with shades of woe;
Tears we drop for brothers fallen,—
   Tears that from deep fountains flow.

"2. From the scenes of war and carnage,
   You have come with wearied tread;
Where the charge—the raging conflict—
   Strewed the field with martyr dead;
Where, by Mercy's inspiration,
   Hearts were moved to deeds humane;
Where Samaria's proud example
   Shed its fragrance o'er the plain.

"3. Thanks we tender for the service
   You so nobly rendered there,
To the wounded and the dying,
   'Mid the lurid death-storm fire.
Never be that day forgotten;
   Ever bright that work of love;
May the meed of ' well done, faithful,'
   Crown life's close with joy above.

"4. Safe returned from march and peril,
   Faithful to Rhode Island's fame;
High on merit's scroll recorded,
   Shall be found your honored name.
Patriot Band! we once more greet you,—
   Welcome to this sacred fane;
Welcome to our heart-affections,
   As this day we meet again."

Addresses were then made by Rev. E. M. Stone and Hon. William M. Rodman, suggested by the passing hour. Mr. Stone reviewed the events of the preceding five months, culminating in the battle of Bull Run. He bade the band a fraternal welcome. It was fitting that the house of God should be the place of greeting. The service they had done was God's service. The spirit by which they had been actuated was the inspiration of the Almighty. He thanked them for their example of patriotism—for their self-forgetfulness and voluntary deeds of humanity on the battle field. It was his earnest prayer, that when life's last battle had been fought, they might be found enrolled in the innumerable army of the living God.

Mr. Rodman spoke of the condition of the country and the duties of the patriot. He made delicate allusion to Colonel Burnside, as a model christian commander, and referred tenderly to Slocum, Prescott and others, of the noble dead. He greeted the Band in well-chosen words, and closed with solemn reference to the end of life. He is the wise and true man, who, faithful to his country and his God, dies the good soldier of Jesus Christ.

To these addresses, the Band responded by playing, with touching pathos, " Home, Sweet Home." The exercises were closed by singing the national hymn—

" My country, 'tis of thee,"—

in which the suppressed feeling of a deeply moved congregation found full expression.

SECOND REGIMENT RHODE ISLAND VOLUNTEERS.

On the first call of the President of the United States, for additional men to serve for a period of three years, unless sooner discharged, Governor Sprague took prompt measures to organize a second regiment of infantry and a battery of artillery. On the 8th of June, 1861, an order to that effect was issued. The camp was established on the Dexter Training Ground, in Providence, and named Camp Burnside. Major John S. Slocum, of the 1st regiment, who had served with reputation in the Mexican War, was appointed Colonel. Colonel William Goddard, of the Governor's staff, was detailed to act temporarily as Lieutenant Colonel, and on being relieved, General Charles T. Robbins was appointed temporarily to that position. At the request of Colonel Slocum, Colonel Christopher Blanding assisted in drilling the regiment.

While making preparations for departure, the regiment received numerous tokens of interest and regard from friends, in'the form of articles designed for personal convenience. The citizens of Lonsdale made a liberal donation to the Hospital department, and the firm of A. & W. Sprague generously presented one thousand rubber blankets for the use of the men. Chaplain Jameson was made the recipient of handsome dress sword and a purse of $200. Many of the officers, for themselves, or for their companies, received substantial expressions or good will.

Shortly before leaving for Washington, an elegant stand of colors was presented to the regiment from a number of ladies of Providence, through Colonel Jabez C. Knight, Paymaster General. The regiment was drawn up in line, and the ceremony took place in the presence of an immense throng. To Colonel Knight's address, Colonel Slocum made a brief response, expressing his grateful sense of the kind remembrance, and giving assurance that the colors should be preserved from the stain of dishonor. Addresses were also made by Rev. Edward B. Hall, D. D., and Captain Cyrus G. Dyer. Company D,

Captain Nelson Viall, having been appointed to carry the colors, the beautiful American ensign of silk, with gold fringe and tassels, and having the name, "2d Regiment R. I. V.," inscribed in gold letters on the centre red stripe, was passed by Colonel Slocum to Lieutenant Ames. The regimental standard of blue, with gold fringe and tassels, and bearing on its folds the arms of Rhode Island, was passed to Lieutenant Monroe, of the artillery.

On the 19th of June, all things being in readiness, tents were struck at 2 o'clock P. M., and at $4\frac{1}{2}$ o'clock, the regiment, headed by the Governor and his staff, together with the Secretary of State, Paymaster General Knight, and several other prominent citizens, took up the line of march to Exchange place, where, in the presence of a large crowd of spectators, a short and spirited address was delivered by Bishop Thomas M. Clark, who also invoked the divine blessing. After these services, the march was resumed to Fox Point, where the regiment embarked on board the steamer State of Maine, and the battery, under Captain William H. Reynolds, on board the steamer Kill Von Kull. The regimental field and staff officers, as far as appointed, were as follows:

Colonel—John S. Slocum.
Lieutenant Colonel—Charles T. Robbins, (temporarily.)
Major—Sullivan Ballou.
Adjutant—Samuel J. Smith.
Quartermaster—James Aborn.
Commissary Sergeant—James T. Tate.
Surgeon—Francis L. Wheaton.
Hospital Steward—E. A. Calder.
Assistant Hospital Steward—W. L. Wheaton.
Chaplain—Thorndike C. Jameson.

The vacancies were not all filled until after the regiment reached Washington. The Captains of companies, in the regular order of their letters, were Cyrus G. Dyer, John Wright, Nelson Viall, William H. P. Steere, Isaac P. Rodman, Levi A. Tower, Nathan Goff, Jr., Charles W. Greene, Samuel J. Smith, Charles W. Turner.

Accompanied by Governor Sprague, Secretary Bartlett and Bishop Clark, the regiment arrived at Washington at 3 o'clock on Saturday morning, June 22d, and was warmly welcomed by its companions in arms, the Rhode Island 1st. It encamped in Gale's woods, near Camp Sprague, and the next three weeks were devoted to ordinary duties. On the 25th, both regiments, and the two batteries, under Captains Tompkins and Reynolds, paid their respects to President Lincoln, by whom they were reviewed. The scene, as they marched up New York and down Pennsylvania avenues, was exhilerating, and the drill, discipline, completeness of outfit and soldierly appearance, called forth universal commendation.

On the 21st July, came the battle of Bull Run, which Rev. Mr. Woodbury, in his interesting history, has graphically and accurately described. In that memorable action, Colonel Burnside commanded a brigade, comprising the 1st and 2d Rhode Island, Captain Reynolds's Rhode Island battery, the 71st New York and the 2d New

25

Hampshire. A battle had been for some days anticipated, and the order to move was received with lively expressions of satisfaction. On the march, Colonel Slocum had the advance, which he kept until the regiment reached the field. There, with Captain Reynolds's artillery, it was the first to engage, and fought the enemy forty-five minutes without support. In this sanguinary and disastrous battle, Colonel Slocum, Major Ballou and Captains Tower and Smith fell. The death of Colonel Slocum devolved the command of the regiment on Captain Frank Wheaton of the United States army, then acting Lieutenant Colonel. On the fall of Major Ballou, Captain Viall left his company in charge of Lieutenant Stanley, and assumed the duty of a field officer. It was unfortunate, as the result of the battle showed, that the brigades were not kept together on the march, or at least within supporting distance. The men of the 2d Rhode Island stood up bravely under a heavy fire from the rebel batteries, but to no purpose. Having exhausted their ammunition, they retired to the rear to replenish. The regiment was then ordered into line to support New York troops, to the south of its old position. At this time regiments were getting uneasy, some were broken and flying, and it became evident that the day was lost. The regiment retired in good order under fire, the panic which seized other troops leaving no other alternative than retreat. The loss in this battle was 28 killed, 56 wounded and 30 missing.* Governor Sprague identified himself with the fortunes of the two Rhode Island regiments. He joined Colonel Burnside's brigade as a volunteer, and was in the hottest of the fight, inspiring the men by his coolness and courage. His horse was killed under him. The death of Colonel Slocum, whose gallantry on the field was conspicuous, made a sad void in the hearts of the men he led. Major Ballou was a gentleman of amiable character and high culture, and showed himself among the bravest of the brave. Even after he fell, he continued to shout to the men to press forward. Captain Tower fell early in the battle, while boldly leading his men to the charge. He merely requested to be turned over, and died without a struggle. Captain Smith, after having led his company bravely through the strife, and performed all the duties of a gallant officer, was instantly killed by a ball from a masked battery, on the retreat. The colors of the regiment were completely riddled by balls, but the standard bearer, Sergeant John M. Durfee, of Captain Viall's company, stood manfully by them, and brought them from the field.

Upon the death of Colonel Slocum, Lieutenant Colonel Frank Wheaton succeeded to the command of the regiment, Captain William H. P. Steere was appointed Lieutenant Colonel, and Captain Nelson Viall, Major. On returning to Washington, from Bull Run, the quarters of the regiment were temporarily established at Camp Clark,

---

* The wounded of the 1st and 2d Rhode Island, not taken prisoners, were brought home at an early day. The remains of Colonel Slocum, Major Ballou and Captain Tower were buried on the field. They were subsequently exhumed, brought home and entombed with military honors. The indignities practiced by the rebels upon the Union dead who fell into their hands, would have been disgraceful to savages.

so named in honor of the Bishop. Subsequently, they were moved to Camp Sprague, but finally a favorable spot was selected by Col. Wheaton, on the farm of a Mr. Ray, about four miles northeast from Washington, and near the United States Soldier's Home, to which was given the name of Camp Brightwood. Here the regiment remained until March, 1862, perfecting itself in drill, performing picket service, clearing away forests, and throwing up a defence to guard an approach to Washington, to which they gave the name of Fort Slocum—an honorable testimony to their cheerful industry, and a worthy monument to the memory of their first and revered commander. During the six months occupancy of Camp Brightwood, frequent visits of friends and constant arrivals of home remembrances, kept up a pleasant excitement that broke the monotony of military routine. With the 7th and 10th Massachusetts and the 36th New York, they constituted the brigade commanded by General Couch, in which, by proficiency in drill and other soldierly qualities, they held a first rank. On the 8th October, 1861, the regiment was visited by Governor Sprague, accompanied by President Lincoln and other distinguished gentlemen. On this occasion, they were presented with a flag sent to them by patriotic citizens of California. A brief address was made by the President, which was appropriately replied to by Colonel Wheaton. The 4th regiment Rhode Island volunteers was present. Both regiments were drawn up near each other, and were addressed by Bishop Clark, in an eloquent and stirring speech. The doxology was then sung, and the ceremonies concluded. It was a proud day for the regiment, and the men were highly complimented for their fine appearance.

On Wednesday, March 26th, the regiment took final leave of Camp Brightwood, and embarked at Washington, on board the steamer John Brooks, for the Peninsula. On reaching Fortress Monroe, March 28th, company F, Captain William B. Sears, was the first to debark. The regiment marched through Hampton, and encamped four miles from Newport News, where it remained a week, and then proceeded to Warwick Court House, which was reached April 5th. During the siege of Yorktown, it was constantly employed in picket and other duties, rendering important service. On the evacuation of that place by the rebels, it formed a part of Stoneman's advance ordered in pursuit, and, by hard marching, reached Williamsburg in season to participate in the capture of the enemy's fortifications there. The regiment arrived on Monday, at 3 o'clock P. M., and stood in line, in rain and mud, till daylight on Tuesday. It relieved and saved a regiment that had been badly cut up by unwisely drawing upon it the fire of Fort Magruder at eight hundred yards distance. Here, Captain Sears captured a small rebel flag. From Williamsburg the regiment took the advance under General Stoneman, which was kept during the operations on the Pamunky and Chickahominy rivers, and beyond, approaching, at times, almost within sight of the spires of Richmond. It was the first to take posession of White House. It took part in the battles at Mechanicsville and Seven Pines, experiencing considerable loss in killed and wounded. On arriving at Turkey Bend, it was detached with the 7th Massachusetts, to guard the Turkey Bend bridge, and remained there until Porter's corps crossed. Not being seasonably relieved, it was unable to participate in the battle of Malvern Hill. After that action, when the army fell back to Harrison's Landing, the regiment was assigned to the rear as a cover. On the 5th July, it was in position on the west side of James river, opposite City Point, busy in mud and water, throwing up a line of breastworks to cover batteries and infantry. A battle line extended three or four miles across the Point, with gunboats protecting the rear. A ditch and abattis rendered the approach difficult, and had the rebels made the trial, they would have met a reception hotter than the sun then pouring down his unrelenting rays. Such had been the exhaustive nature of its work after leaving Yorktown, that, on the 16th July, the regiment could number only 250 effective men.

On the withdrawal of the army of the Potomac from the Peninsula, the regiment proceeded to the vicinity of Yorktown, where it remained a week, occupied in destroying earthworks thrown up when the Federal army lay in front. On the 29th August, it embarked for Alexandria, where it landed, September 1st, and proceeded to Germantown, to the support of Kearny. After sharing the fortunes of Pope's Bull Run campaign, it returned to Alexandria, proceeded thence on board the steamer Nelly Baker, to Georgetown, debarked and crossed Chain Bridge to Fort Ethan Allen, and continued its march to Elk Mountain, where it held position during the battle of Antietam. The following day, it came to the front, and was occupied in guarding the river. Subsequently, it marched to Williamsport to prevent the crossing of Stuart. Afterwards, it proceeded to Poolsville, and then to Warrenton and New Baltimore, and finally to the front of Fredericksburg. In the battle of December 14th, it crossed the river in advance of all Franklin's corps, and took a captain and two privates of the Georgia 19th, prisoners. Company F, Captain Sears, had two men slightly wounded by the fragment of a shell. Here, Colonel Wheaton having been appointed to the command of a brigade, the command of the regiment was assumed by Colonel Nelson Viall, who received his commission on the field. All the duty assigned it during this battle was discharged with a spirit and efficiency that gained for it warm commendation.

The men of the regiment were strongly attached to Colonel (now General) Wheaton, and were unwilling to part from him without some suitable expression of their feelings. After the battle and their return to their encampment, arrangements to that effect, already begun, were completed, by a committee consisting of the first sergeants of each company, assisted by Colonel Viall and Lieutenant Colonel Goff. Four hundred dollars were contributed by the enlisted men, with which was purchased a superb sword, belt and silver spurs. These were formally presented to the General, in behalf of the contributors, by Sergeant Edmund F. Prentiss, of company C, chairman of the committee. In a few words, the General acknowledged the gratifying testimonial, and subsequently, more at length in a written communication, in which he spoke of his long and pleasant connection with the regiment, and of the deep interest he should always take in its future success. "Never forget," he said, in conclusion, "that you have a reputation to sustain. Your dear old flags bear many proofs of that. Remember that you are descended from those noble patriots who were pronounced by Washington, when he reviewed his troops at Cambridge, to be the 'flower of the American army.' The precious inheritance those few words gave you must be sacred in your hands. Our native State that sent you out to battle for her principles, in this our second war for independence, has confidence in your ability to prove honorable sons of those who conquered for her in the first. Go, then, to gallant deeds, and remember, each one of you, that Rhode Island's name and fame is in your keeping. Preserve it as your fathers did ; and when the war is over,—when those who would destroy our liberties shall be themselves destroyed ; when the flag our fathers gave us shall be the only one to float secure in all of this broad land ; when liberty and law shall prove too strong for traitors,—then, but not till then, may we think of peace, or of the joyous welcome that waits us at our homes."

Not long after the first battle of Fredericksburg, Colonel Viall resigned, and the temporary command of the regiment devolved on Lieutenant Colonel Nathan Goff, Jr., an able and highly esteemed officer. He was succeeded by Colonel Horatio Rogers, Jr., transferred from the 11th Rhode Island volunteers, then stationed at Miner's Hill. In the second expedition of General Burnside, which, as already mentioned, a violent storm and other causes rendered abortive, the regiment endured the fatigue and discomforts of the march with soldierly patience. Winter life followed, relieved of irksomeness by a full share of picket duty. February and March passed with only such occurrences as were common to other camps ; but when the third attack of Fredericksburg was decided on, the order to march came to the 2d Rhode Island as a welcome sound.

The part taken by the regiment in the storming of the heights of that city has been shown on page 234. To the account there given, a few particulars may be added. After recrossing the Rappahannock at Banks's Ford, on Tuesday, May 5th, it performed picket duty at the Ford, and guarded the pontoon train until Friday, the 8th, when it marched to the neighborhood of its old camp. In eleven days campaigning, the regiment did four and a half days picket duty, and fought two battles. Its casualties, as already mentioned, were heavy. Nothing could surpass the determination with which the men advanced to the extreme front when a regiment was flying panic-stricken through their ranks ; the gallantry with which they drove the rebels back ; the pertinacity with which they held their ground until support could come up ; and the excellent order and spirits with which they retired when ordered back. This regiment, as much or more than any other, contributed towards checking the enemy when our forces were being driven on the right. It saved a New Jersey regiment, hotly pressed in the woods, from annihilation and probable capture.

After about four weeks rest, the regiment was again in motion. On the 6th June, it crossed the Rappahannock, and took part in a demonstration below Fredericksburg, to keep the enemy's troops in that neighborhood. On the night of the 13th, it recrossed the river, and began its march northward with the rest of the Sixth corps, via Dumfries, Fairfax Court House, Centreville, Edwards's Ferry,

25*

Poolesville, Newmarket and Westminster, halting here and there a day or two. About 9 o'clock of the evening of July 1st, while in bivouac near Manchester, the regiment was hurriedly got into line, and marching all night and all the next day, up to four o'clock in the afternoon, it arrived near Gettysburg, a distance of about thirty miles. As it approached, the thunder of artillery and the rattling of musketry seemed nearer and nearer, and then came the stream of wounded and stragglers, sure signs of a battle going on somewhere close by. The whole corps was bivouacked for two or three hours, to rest after their long tramp, and then were put into position on the field of battle, on the extreme left, where they lay on their arms all night, being drawn up into three lines, the second brigade forming a part of the middle one. The next day, the day of the great battle, was a busy one for the regiment, for wherever the fighting was thickest, there the second brigade was sure to be sent to reinforce points hard pressed ; but though the regiment had to traverse that bloody, fatal field, through shot and shell, time and time again, first to the centre, then back again, then retrace its steps, then to the right, and so on, it was not called into direct action. The day after the battle, the regiment was on picket on the further edge of the battle field, and as it rained and the sun shone by turns, the stench was insufferable. The loss in this battle was one man killed and five wounded. In the pursuit of the rebels on their retreat, the regiment had a picket skirmish at Williamsburg, July 12th, in which three men were wounded. Continuing its march back into Virginia, it made camp near Warrenton, July 25th, having marched, going and returning, nearly three hundred miles.

It is a remarkable fact in the history of this regiment, that from the first battle of Bull Run to that of Chancellorsville, it has met the same rebel regiments on picket, and been opposed to the same on the field. So frequently had they met, that many of the men, on both sides, formed a familiar acquaintance. On the first picket service after a hard battle, the secesh would inquire, with apparent interest, after Federals not present. The scrupulous regard paid by the 2d Rhode Island to the order against picket firing, secured the respect and entire confidence of these opponents, and when the former took their posts, the latter would leave their rifle pits to which they had resorted for cover, stack arms, and enter into friendly conversation. From the beginning, the regiment has supported an honorable reputation for respecting private property in proximity to its encampments. The amount of hard labor it has performed has not been surpassed by any other regiment in the army of the Potomac ; but whether intrenching, clearing away forests, marching or fighting, it has maintained a uniform character for bravery and efficiency.

THIRD RHODE ISLAND REGIMENT.

FIELD AND STAFF OFFICERS,

(*Commissioned and Non-commissioned.*)

Colonel—Ashur R. Eddy, U. S. A. Resigned, September 17th, 1861.

Colonel—Nathaniel W. Brown, September 17th, 1861, Died at Port Royal, S. C., October 30th, 1862.

Colonel—Edwin Metcalf, Major, August 27th, 1861. Resigned, August 4th, 1862. Colonel, 11th regiment, September 15th, 1862. Colonel, 3d R. I. H. A., November 11th, 1862.

Lieutenant Colonel—Christopher Blanding, August 19th, 1861. Resigned, on account of ill health, October 14th, 1861. Appointed Major, 3d H. A., December 9th, 1861 ; resigned on account of failing health, September 2d, 1862. Captain Hospital Guards, Portsmouth Grove, October 17th, 1862.

Lieutenant Colonel—Stephen R. Bucklin, October 2d, 1861. Resigned, December 26th, 1862.

Lieutenant Colonel—John Frieze, 1st Lieutenant 3d H. A., February 11th, 1862. Major, 3d H. A., September 16th, 1862 ; Lieut. Colonel, January 14th, 1863.

Lieutenant Colonel—Horatio Rogers, Jr., 1st Lieutenant 3d H. A , August 27th, 1861 ; Captain, do., October 9th, 1861 ; Major do., August 18th, 1862 ; Colonel 11th regiment, December 27th, 1862. Colonel, 2d regiment.

Lieutenant Colonel—Charles R. Brayton, October, 1863.

Major—Charles W. H. Day. Promoted from Captain 3d H. A., November 28th, 1862.

Major—James E. Bailey. • Promoted from Captain, 3d H. A., August 27th, 1861.

Major—Henry T. Sisson. Promoted from Captain, 1st L. A., February 5th, 1861 ; resigned, August 6th, 1862 ; Colonel, 5th regiment, November 5th, 1862.

Major—William Ames. Captain, company G, 2d regiment, July 21st, 1862 ; promoted to Major, 3d H. A., January 2d, 1863. Post Commander at Fort Pulaski.

Major—George Metcalf. 2d Lieutenant 3d H. A., October 9th, 1861 ; 1st Lieutenant do., May 20th, 1862 ; Captain do., July 8th, 1862 ; on General Terry's staff on Morris Island ; Major 3d H. A., November, 1864.

Adjutant—Joseph J. Comstock, Jr. Captain, 3d H. A., March 11th, 1862. Major, 14th (colored) regiment.

Adjutant—James L. Richardson, March 11th, 1862 ; resigned, December 30th, 1862.

Quartermaster—William P. Martin, August 21st, 1861 ; resigned August 30th, 1862. Appointed by the President, Commissary of Subsistence.

Surgeon—Fenner H. Peckham, August 15th, 1861 ; resigned, February 22d, 1862.

Surgeon—Horatio G. Stickney. Promoted from Assistant, February 22d, 1862.

Surgeon—GEORGE S. BURTON. Promoted from Assistant, June 22d, 1863. On detached service at Morris Island.

Assistant Surgeon—JOB KENYON, August 28th, 1862; resigned, June 10th, 1863.

Assistant Surgeon—HORACE S. LAMSON, March, 1862.

Chaplain—THOMAS QUINN, August 15th, 1861; Chaplain, 1st light artillery, November 7th, 1861.

Chaplain—JAMES GUBBY, October 21st, 1861; resigned, September 26th, 1862.

Chaplain—FREDERICK DENNISON, 1st cavalry, November 7th, 1861; 3d H. A., January 20th, 1863.

Quartermaster Sergeant—J. B. MINER, September, 1861; discharged for disability, September 4th, 1862.

Quartermaster Sergeant—BABCOCK W. ALLEN, May 13th, 1863.

Commissary Sergeant—SAMUEL A. FISKE, October 12th, 1861.

Hospital Steward—EDWIN S. THURBER, August 21st, 1861.

Hospital Steward—FENNER H. PECKHAM, Jr., November 6th, 1861.

Hospital Steward—FRANK H. GOULD, December 1st, 1862.

Band Master—WILLIAM F. MARSHALL.

MUSICIANS.

Nelson H. Arnold, Thomas Buckley, John Buckley, James Burrows, Samuel Booth, James Bedford, John F. Kavanagh, James Doran, Thomas Fetherstone, Albert C. Greene, Peter Macnamara, John Roe, John P. Smith, Robert Siela, Daniel Shea, Hugh Showcross, W. A. Welch, Richard Welch, Thomas Whitworth, John Walker, Giles Waterhouse.

On the departure of the regiment, the Captains were John Daily, Libteus C. Tourtellot, Thomas B. Briggs, James E. Bailey, John H. Gould, Pardon Mason, Charles W. H. Day, Hugh Hammell, William E. Peck, Richard G. Shaw, ——Labin and Simon S. Rankin, Lieutenant commanding.

On the 12th August, 1861, Governor Sprague issued an order for organizing a third regiment of infantry. General Charles T. Robbins was appointed acting Colonel, and Colonel Christopher Blanding acting Lieutenant Colonel. These gentlemen, with Majors Balch and Sinnot were constituted a board to examine those recommended by companies for commission. Drs. Rivers and Miller were assigned to the duty of medical examiners. An encampment was formed on Spring Green Farm, on the Old Warwick road, which received the name of Camp Ames. On the 19th August, Captain Ashur R. Eddy, U. S. A., was appointed Colonel of the regiment. Lieutenant Colonel Blanding also received a commission as second in command. For several weeks, the discipline and drill of the regiment was principally in the hands of the latter.

On the afternoon of the 7th September, the regiment left Camp Ames, and marched to Providence, to embark on board the steamer Commodore for the camp on Long Island, which was under command of General W. T. Sherman. They were a hardy body of men, and possessed largely the fighting qualities that secured to them the high reputation they subsequently won. The regiment reached Providence between five and six o'clock, and wheeled into Exchange Place. Here, a hollow square was formed, when the troops were addressed by Rev. A. H. Clapp and the Chaplain, Father Quinn. They then defiled into Westminster street, and passing to the steamer moored at Smith's wharf, at 10½ o'clock took their departure. On arriving at Fort Hamilton, N. Y., an encampment was assigned the regiment, which immediately commenced a thorough course of light and heavy artillery drill, under the direction of Lieutenant Colonel Blanding. This was continued by him until the 14th October, when, on account of ill health, he resigned and returned home. His departure was deeply regretted by the officers of the regiment, who appreciated his skill as an instructor, his tact as a disciplinarian, and his courtesy as a commander, in token of which, they presented him with a valuable gold headed cane, accompanied by a complimentary letter, signed by them all.

Colonel Eddy having resigned, he was succeeded by Colonel Nathaniel W. Brown, who continued the daily drills until the embarkation of the regiment for Fortress Munroe, October 12th, where it arrived on the 14th, and encamped about one mile beyond, towards Hampton. While here, a gift of colors from the ladies of Providence, camp colors from Mrs. Manton, of New London, and seasonable articles of comfort for the sick, from Mrs. Bucklin and other ladies of Pawtucket, were received. On the 23d October, the regiment embarked with the expedition under General Sherman and Admiral Dupont, destined to Port Royal, S. C. The fleet arrived off that place, November 4th, after a boisterous passage. Without attempting an extended account of the services of the regiment, the following synopsis of its field history is given.* It was present at the naval action at Port Royal, November 7th, 1861, landed two companies the same day, and the balance the next, and was assigned to the charge of Fort Welles. Subsequently, Fort Seward, at Bay Point, the entrenchments at Hilton Head, the entrenchments at Beaufort, and Fort Mitchell, on Skull Creek, were garrisoned by detachments from it. In December, 1861, company C, Captain Day, made a successful reconnoissance up Broad river to Beaufort. Company I, Captain Strahan, held a small battery on Otter Island, from December, 1861, to May, 1862. In June following, Lieutenant Colonel Blanding, with a small party, made a surprise of the White House on the main land, near Pinckney Island, where the rebels had been quite busy. The house and outbuildings were destroyed. Companies E and G mounted the guns and manned the batteries erected on Jones's Island in the Savannah river, in February and March, 1862. On the 15th February, four rebel gunboats attacked the batteries, then commanded by Captain Gould, and after an engagement of an hour, were driven off without loss on the Federal side. In the bombardment of Fort Pulaski, April 11th and 12th, companies B, F and H assisted, and after

---

* February 17th, 1862, by general order, the name of the regiment was changed to " 3d regiment Rhode Island Heavy Artillery," with authority to increase it to twelve companies of 156 men each.

the capture of the Fort, company G formed a part of its garrison. In the movement on Charleston, in June, 1862, by way of John and James Islands, companies B, E, F, H, I, K, and one section of C (mounted) were included. On 16th June, in the engagement on James Island, the principal part of the battalion acted as infantry. Companies B, F and K were deployed as skirmishers, under the direction of Major Sisson. The fire of the enemy was very severe. The Federal loss was 7 killed, 30 wounded and 8 missing.

Major Edwin Metcalf, who commanded the battalion in this battle, received special commendation from the brigade commander, Colonel Robert Williams, for " courage and soldierly conduct." In his report to Governor Sprague, he says, "It is my belief that no officers or men could have behaved better under fire than they did, and certainly, no officer could have led his command with more skill and bravery than did Major Metcalf." The Major, in his report, speaks in the highest terms of the coolness, steadiness and courage displayed by his men, and, in conclusion, says, " I take great pleasure in speaking of the Adjutant of the battalion, First Lieutenant J. Lanahan, of company I, always prompt and cool, and sustaining me in every difficulty by his good judgment and long experience as a soldier. First Lieutenant A. E. Green, commanding company B, was especially energetic and active. Second Lieutenant E. S. Bartholomew, of company E, nobly proved himself deserving the commission he had received since our departure from Hilton Head, falling mortally wounded while cheering on his men into the thicket from which the enemy so severely annoyed us. Captain H. Rogers, Jr., and First Lieutenant C. R. Brayton, of company II, were untiring in their exertions, and zealously supported me. First Lieutenant A. W. Colwell, of company F, and Second Lieutenant D. B. Churchill, of company K, particularly attracted my notice by their coolness and energy. I am pleased to name First Sergeant G. W. Greene and Sergeant J. B. Batchelder, of company B, First Sergeant O. A. Thompson, of company E, and First Sergeant W. Wheeler, Jr., of company K, as distinguished for gallant conduct. I shall feel justified in recommending them to the Governor of Rhode Island for promotion."*

Company M assisted in transporting and working two boat howitzers at the affair of Pocotaligo Bridge, in October, 1862, and companies E, K and L formed part of the force, but were not engaged.†

---

* In the battle on James Island, Captain Benjamin Church, son of Colonel Peter Church, of Bristol, R. I., was killed, receiving a shot through the head, when near the foot of the parapet of the enemy's breastworks. He commanded a company in the 8th Michigan, which was badly cut up. Daniel Lyman Arnold, youngest son of the late Governor Lemuel H. Arnold, of Rhode Island, was killed in the same battle, serving honorably in the ranks.

† Lieutenant Jabez B. Blanding was badly wounded in the left arm, in this action. In a reconnoitering trip through the Coosaw river, on the 8th April, 1863, on board the gunboat George Washington, he narrowly escaped with his life, by the explosion of her magazine, caused by a rebel shell.

Companies B, D, F, I, K, L and M sailed for Stono Inlet, April 2d, 1863, to take part in the second movement on Charleston, but returned to Hilton Head, on the 12th. In an expedition up the Cohambee, on the 1st of June, 1863, under Colonel Montgomery, a section of battery C, commanded by Captain Brayton, participated. He captured many horses, mules and cattle, destroyed rice mills and store houses containing cotton and rice, and brought off all the negroes within hailing distance. Companies B, C, D, H, I and M are now, (October 29th, 1863,) with General Gilmore on Morris Island, having batteries of 20, 30, 100 and 200-pounder Parrott guns and also mortars. In the first attack on Morris Island, they received praise from the General for the manner in which they worked their guns. Light company C is also there, doing excellent service. In the attack on Fort Sumter, company M lost a valuable officer in Lieutenant Henry Holbrook, who was struck in the breast by a fragment of a shell, and died shortly after being removed to the hospital. During the progress of the siege, Captain Charles R. Brayton received promotion as Lieutenant Colonel of the regiment, and Captain Joseph J. Comstock, Jr., was appointed Major of the 14th Rhode Island. Other Captains in command of batteries are Strahan, Shaw and Colwell. Both officers and men have made a proud position for themselves.

Not long after the arrival of the regiment at Hilton Head, Lieutenant Asa A. Ellis returned to Providence to obtain additional men. Colonel Blanding having accepted the position of Major, superintended the recruiting. On the 19th February, 1862, he sailed from New York on board the United States steamer Oriental, with 225 men, and arrived at Hilton Head, March 23d. On the passage, a gale was experienced, and off Charleston harbor the steamer was mistaken, in the night, for a blockade runner, and was brought to by the United States gunboat Florida, which fired several guns. Shortly after parting with the Florida, the steamer was discovered to be on fire. It was quickly subdued without exciting alarm. This was fortunate, as there were 450 tons of ammunition on board. The Colonel and his recruits were warmly welcomed, and the regiment, now increased to twelve companies, was in good condition for active service. The day following his arrival, he was ordered to the entrenchments (then occupied by companies B, C and K,) extending about two miles, and mounted with forty pieces of heavy artillery. As an outwork of the post, the position was honorable, the duties arduous and satisfactorily performed. Major Metcalf had previously been stationed here.

Among other duties, Colonel Blanding was directed to examine all the approaches to the works ; and taking with him a sergeant of the regiment, mounted, he thoroughly explored every part of the island, making a map of all the roads leading from the outside to the entrenchments. The knowledge thus acquired was of great service whenever it became necessary to strengthen and extend outlaying pickets, or to post them in a manner best to prevent surprise, though it was the occasion of many extra hours in the saddle. At one time, when an attack was daily expected, the pickets were so much extended, that it required a ride of ninety miles to visit them. This was repeatedly done in twenty-four hours by Colonel Blanding, viz., in the morning, to post them ; in the afternoon, to give them the countersign and instructions for the night, and in the night to see that all was right. An impaired constitution, however, was not equal to such unremitting field labors, and, with the intense heat of summer and the night exposure to the malaria of a swampy country, brought on a fever that seriously threatened his life. By counsel of the surgeon, he again reluctantly resigned. On recovery, after reaching home, he was appointed Captain of the Hospital Guards at Portsmouth Grove.

Many particulars of Port Royal, Port Royal Ferry, Beaufort, Hilton Head, Daufuskie, Tybee and Otter Island, together with other localities, would furnish a chapter of exceeding interest, but except in this general allusion, they must be passed. The services of the regiment, as will be seen, were very miscellaneous, its companies being almost constantly scattered. This added not a little to the cares and anxieties of its commander, and to the pressure of which his constitution began to yield. In the summer of 1862, worn by constant duties and the effect of climate, Colonel Brown came home on a brief leave of absence, to obtain the benefit of a northern atmosphere. He spent a few weeks in the bosom of his family, and returned to Hilton Head, where he arrived on the 15th September, apparently in improved health, and in excellent spirits. His return was the signal for a spontaneous expression of the respect and good will he had gained from both officers and men. His reception was enthusiastic in the extreme. But this delight was of short duration. On Saturday, October 25th, he was seized with a virulent fever that baffled the best medical skill, and, on the morning of the 30th, expired, at the age of fifty-one years. His sudden and unexpected decease cast a gloom over the regiment, and his loss was sincerely mourned. The funeral obsequies were conducted by Rev. H. L. Wayland, chaplain of the 7th Connecticut regiment, and Chaplain Hudson, of the Volunteer Engineers. The remains of the deceased were borne to the grave on an ambulance, festooned with the national flag, and drawn by six grey horses. The horse he usually rode, led in the procession by a servant, and the long cortege that followed, imparted to the occasion a deep solemnity. Of Colonel Brown, Chaplain Wayland writes:—
"On the morning of the battle of Pocotaligo, I saw him at Mackay's Landing, superintending the debarkation of the artillery. He greeted me cordially, as he always did. I little anticipated that it was the last greeting I should exchange with him. During the day, he was twelve hours in the saddle, and underwent both on that day and during the night previous, and the night and day following, very great fatigue. Either he had already imbibed the virus of the prevailing disease, or returned exhausted, his system was not able to resist it, and he began to fail soon after reaching camp..... We laid his mortal remains in the Pine Grove Cemetery, but a little way from the intrenchments which he, with his noble corps, have guarded long and faithfully..... I never saw any one look more thoroughly the soldier and leader than he did on the morning of the 22d, when, for the last time, I saw him mounted and eager for the advance..... He had a high sense of the value of religion and religious observances. But a few days before the action of Pocotaligo, he expressed his desire that I would come and preach to the regiment on the first Sunday when I could command the time. Colonel Brown was much interested in

the establishment of religious worship near head-quarters at the post, and was a regular attendant until his sickness." Lieutenant Walter B. Manton, a valuable and highly esteemed officer, died of the same disease, five days before Colonel Brown, and General Mitchell, at Beaufort, the day after. Lieutenant Manton was acting Quartermaster of the regiment.

Colonel Brown, son of Isaac Brown, was a native of Providence, and, for many years, engaged in manufacturing. He was a member of the well known firm of Jacob Dunnell & Co. When the rebellion broke out, he was among the first to tender his services in defence of his country, was appointed Captain in the 1st Rhode Island regiment, and at Bull Run displayed extraordinary coolness and courage. In command of the 3d Rhode Island, he displayed the fine qualities essential to success as an officer. He was a thorough disciplinarian,— prompt and decided in action, and ever watchful of the interests of his men. He possessed to perfection one great virtue of a soldier,— strict temperance; and what he practiced, he encouraged in others. A few weeks before his death, he was placed on the staff of General Mitchell, as chief of artillery, and in the fight near the Charleston and Savannah Railroad, where he took command of the entire artillery, it was said by eye-witnesses of that thrilling scene, that his conduct was of a noble type. If it was not permitted him to fall on the battle-field, his memory, as a brave and faithful officer, will be none the less honored, and his name will be inscribed on the roll of the sons of Rhode Island who gave their lives for their country *

The 3d Rhode Island Heavy Artillery was probably more widely known in the Department of the South than any other regiment, and contributed as much for the advancement of the cause as any other troops. It was looked upon, both by General Hunter and General Mitchell, as among the most reliable of their forces. For three months previous to the surrender of Fort Pulaski, the detachment serving in the investment, slept every night alongside their guns in flat boats, in swamps and in entrenchments, and received commendation from Brigadier General Viele for their "patriotic and sturdy endurance." In nearly or quite every engagement or skirmish that occurred, one or more of its companies participated; and in the siege of Charleston, the hard toil in the trenches, the cheerful endurance

---

* January 27th, 1863, the remains of Colonel Brown and of Lieutenant Manton were brought to Providence, in charge of Major John B. Frieze. The funeral of the former was solemnized on Friday, 30th, in the presence of a large concourse, including the Governor and members of his personal staff, and other military gentlemen. The pall bearers were Colonel William W. Brown, Colonel William Goddard, Colonel James Shaw, Colonel Nicholas Van Slyck, Major Joseph Balch and Lieutenant Colonel S. R. Knight. The religious services were conducted by Rev. Dr. Edward B. Hall, Rev. Augustus Woodbury and Rev. Mr. LeBaron. The remains were conveyed to the North Burial Ground.

The funeral of Lieutenant Manton took place January 31st, and was attended by a large number of friends, Rev. A. H. Clapp officiating. The pall bearers were Francis M. Smith, Henry Rhoades, Albert C. Greene and C. A. P. Mason. The remains were interred in the Swan Point Cemetery.

of exposure to an insalubrious climate, and the brave handling of seige guns, by its representative companies, earned for it a deserved fame.

NOTE.—BOMBARDMENT OF FORT PULASKI, PAGE 207. A few details are here given that were omitted in their proper place in the narrative:—

In March, the 3d regiment, as already mentioned, having been changed into heavy artillery by an order from the War Department, companies L and M were sent out from Rhode Island, and recruits for the other companies, so that they were increased to from 110 to 140 men each. The regiment was moved, with the exception of company A, Captain Briggs, from Fort Wells about a mile out on the island, where field works had been erected, about a mile and three-quarters in length, and served as the garrison of those works. Companies F and H went to Tybee Island. There, with the 7th Connecticut and 46th New York, they were engaged in doing picket duty, digging earthworks, building magazines and hauling ordnance two miles from where it was landed to the batteries. Much of this was night-work, and very trying to the strength of the men. The engineering was principally done by three companies of Snell's New York volunteer engineers. On the 10th of April, at 7½ o'clock A. M, the signal for commencing the bombardment was given from battery Sigel, and the batteries opened fire. Captain Horatio Rogers, Jr., Company H, commanded battery McClellan, composed of two 84 and two 64 pounder James' rifle guns, sometimes called 42 and 32 pounders, because that would be their calibre with round shot. The charge used for the former was eight pounds of No. 5 powder, and for the latter, six pounds; for the shell, from one pound to one pound and a half of musket powder. From 8 o'clock till dark, Captain Rogers kept up a well-directed fire from his battery, and recommenced at 5½ o'clock the next morning, and continued till 2½ P. M., when the rebels hauled down their flag and hoisted a white one. The James' guns were very effective, and their work fully realized the expectations that had been entertained of them. On the first day, the battery fired 383 solid shot and 20 shell; on the second day, 187 solid shot and 203 shell. Very few of the shell tumbled, as was the case with the Parrott guns, but went true point first The firing of the largest guns was at an elevation of 4¼ ° and 4½ °; the smaller at 4 and 5 °. The recoil on sanded rails was from 3½ to 4¼ feet. The battery was very highly complimented by General Gilmore, for its precision and effectiveness. His first words on landing, after receiving the surrender of the fort, as he saw the James' projectile lying everywhere inside, "Tell Captain Rogers the 42-pounders did it" Colonel Olmstead, the rebel commander, declared that but for the James' guns he should not have surrendered, and that their penetrating force was overwhelming.

In this assault, Captain Mason, company F, had battery Scott, composed of three 10-inch and one 8-inch columbiad guns, which were handled with great vigor and success. Captain Tourtellot, Company B, had two batteries about two miles distant from Pulaski. His guns were served with telling effect, and the firing received the commendation of Generals Hunter and Benham. Battery McClellan was 1620 yards from the wall of Pulaski, at which the firing was directed, and 1689 yards from the flag staff. Battery Scott was about 40 yards further off. The work in the trenches was very hard and disagreeable, the light sand sifting into everything. Twice, battery McClellan, against which the rebels concentrated all the guns they could bring to bear, came near being blown up. Once, a shell burst directly over the entrance to the magazine, into which Captain Rogers had just stepped, blowing it to pieces and burying him up with sand and splinters, without serious injury however, and slightly wounding two men. At another time, a 10-inch columbiad solid shot struck the front of the magazine, carrying off the sand covering and baring the boards beneath. One man, James Campbell, of Valley Falls, R. I., was killed by a shell. He was the first man in the regiment killed in action, and the only one killed on the Federal side in this affair. In working the battery, Captain Rogers was ably sustained by Lieutenants Brayton and Barney; and the men, witnessing the effect of their shots, were enthusiastic about their favorite guns. Captains Bailey and Gould, with their respective commands, bore an honorable part in the contest.

FOURTH REGIMENT RHODE ISLAND VOLUNTEERS.

FIELD AND STAFF OFFICERS,

(*Commissioned and Non-commissioned.*)

Colonel—Justus I. McCarty. Commission revoked, October, 1861.

Colonel—Isaac P. Rodman, Captain 2d regiment, June 1st, 1861 ; Lieutenant Colonel 4th regiment, October 19th, 1861; Colonel 4th regiment, October 30th, 1861 ; Brigadier General, April 28th, 1862 ; mortally wounded at the battle of Antietam, September 17th, 1862.

Colonel—William H. P. Steere. Captain 2d regiment, June 1st, 1861 ; Lieutenant Colonel 2d regiment, July 22d, 1861 ; Colonel 4th regiment, June 12th, 1862. Acting Brigadier General, 1863.

Lieutenant Colonel— George W. Tew. Captain 1st R. I. detached militia, April 18th, 1861 ; Captain 4th regiment, October 2d, 1861 ; Major 4th regiment, October 11th, 1861 ; Lieutenant Colonel 4th regiment, November 20th, 1861 ; resigned, August 11th, 1862 ; Major 5th regiment, October 1st, 1862.

Lieutenant Colonel—Joseph B. Curtis. 2d Lieutenant and Adjutant 4th regiment, September 16th, 1861 ; 1st Lieutenant and Adjutant of same, October 2d, 1861 ; Assistant Adjutant General, General Rodman's Staff, June 9th, 1862 ; Lieutenant Colonel 4th regiment, August 11th, 1862 ; killed in the battle of Fredericksburg, Va., December 13th, 1862.

Lieutenant Colonel—Martin P. Buffum. 1st Lieutenant 4th regiment, October 2d, 1861 ; Captain of same, October 11th, 1861 ; Major of same, October 10th, 1862 ; Lieutenant Colonel of same, December 24th, 1862.

Major—Levi E. Kent. Captain 4th regiment, October 2d, 1861 ; Major of same, August 11th, 1862 ; resigned, September 26th, 1862.

Major—James T. P. Bucklin. 2d Lieutenant 4th regiment, October 2d, 1861 ; 1st Lieutenant do., November 20th, 1861 ; Captain do., April 30th, 1862 ; Major do., January, 1863.

Surgeon—Henry W. Rivers. August 27th, 1861. Division Surgeon, 1863.

Assistant Surgeon—Robert Miller. August 27th, 1861.

Adjutant—Henry J. Spooner. 2d Lieutenant and Adjutant 4th

regiment, August 27th, 1862; 1st Lieutenant and Adjutant of same, October 1st, 1862.

Quartermaster—SIDNEY C. SMITH. 2d Lieutenant and Quartermaster, September 16th, 1861; 1st Lieutenant 4th regiment, October 2d, 1861; resigned, August 11th, 1862.

Quartermaster—BRAYTON KNIGHT. 2d Lieutenant and Quartermaster, 4th regiment, August 11th, 1862; 1st Lieutenant and Quartermaster of same, November 25th, 1862.

Sergeant Major—JABEZ S. SMITH. 2d Lieutenant 4th regiment, November 20th, 1861; resigned, August 11th, 1862.

Quartermaster Sergeant—ZERAH B. SMITH. 2d Lieutenant, 4th regiment, November 20th, 1861; resigned, February 24th, 1862.

Hospital Steward—THOMAS J. GRIFFIN, Jr.

Assistant Hospital Steward—GEORGE F. WATERMAN.

Chaplain—ALONZO B. FLANDERS. Resigned, October 31st, 1862.

Chaplain—SILAS S. CUMMINGS. Resigned, October, 1863.

Leader and Director of Band—JOSEPH C. GREENE.

Drum Major——————MURDOCK.

MUSICIANS.

Edward G. Bishop, Isaac H. Barrows, James Gough, C. E. Coggeshall, E. M. Churchill, D. P. Gladding, David Hudson, Joseph G. Jenison, John Guinness, James McCormick, William Naydan, William H. Johnson, William T. Nichols, Calixa Lavalla, George Lavalla, Orrin G. Shaw, John Leach, Charles F. Folger, Jabez Butterfield, Jacob Butterfield.

The commanding officers of companies, when the regiment departed, were Captains George W. Tew, John A. Allen, Henry Simon, Levi E. Kent, Nelson Kenyon, and Lieutenants Erastus E. Lapham, James T. P. Bucklin, Martin P. Buffum, Charles Tillinghast, William C. Wood.

The Fourth Regiment of Rhode Island Volunteers was organized by Colonel Justus I. McCarty, of the regular army, and who had seen service in Mexico under General Scott. At the time of his appointment, he held a commission as Major of an independent battalion. On the 5th of September, 1861, the first detachment, in charge of Captain Topliff, went into camp between Olneyville and Apponaug, west of the railroad, on the ground subsequently named "Camp Greene," in honor of General Nathaniel Greene, of Revolutionary fame. Two days after, a second detachment was added. The enthusiasm of the State was still fresh; recruits poured in faster than was convenient to properly equip them, and before the close of the month, the regiment was reported full. It was the determination of the Colonel to secure the greatest possible efficiency to his command, and to that end, most of the officers were required to prove their capacity by drilling men in squads, and in companies, before being recommended for commission. Men were taken from the ranks for non-commissioned officers, and tested in the various duties of their positions. In his manner, an unusual activity was aroused, and the best military talent developed. The camp, laid out with military exactness, was a model of neatness. The grounds were well adapted to drills and parades, and the work of perfecting the regiment in a knowledge of the manual was pushed with great vigor. After less than a month of practice, the regiment was reviewed by Governor Sprague, in the presence of General Burnside and many State military officers ; and the soldierly appearance of the men, as well as the accuracy of their evolutions, excited gratifying surprise. Like the regiments that preceded it, the members of the 4th received frequent substantial tokens of interest from personal friends, while, in its organized capacity, it was patriotically remembered by the gift of two elegant stands of colors, from ladies of Providence. The first was presented through Mrs. R. M. Bates and E. A. Winn, and the second through Mrs. Philip Allen, Jr. Both were warmly acknowledged by Colonel Mc-Carty, in behalf of the regiment.

Orders having been issued for the regiment to proceed to Washington, it took its departure on board the steamer Commodore, October 2d, amid the thundering of cannon and the mingled cheers and tears of kindred and friends. On the march from the camp to the place of embarkation, in Providence, the regiment was accompanied by Governor Sprague, Colonel Sprague, of his staff, Adjutant General Mauran, with Captain Hoppin, his Aide, Paymaster General Knight, Colonel Charles H. Tompkins and Lieutenant Colonel William H. Reynolds. The Providence Horse Guards, under Colonel George W. Hallett, performed escort duty. Governor Sprague, Colonel Tompkins and Major Sanford met the regiment at New York, and accompanied it to Washington, where it arrived October 6th, and took temporary quarters at Camp Sprague. The day following, it marched back to the city, and went into camp in tents. Soon after, it shifted to a better position on Capitol Hill. Subsequently, it made an encampment, known as "Camp Casey," near Bladensburg, where it had the advantage of a fine grove, to break the sharp rays of an autumn sun, and of a broad level field, for drills, parades and reviews.

On the 16th October, Colonel McCarty, at the head of the regiment, paid his respects to the President, at the White House, and on the day following, the regiment was reviewed by General Casey. A pleasant visit to Brightwood, to witness the presentation of a stand of colors from California to the 2d Rhode Island, diversified the next week ; and on the following week, October 25th, the regiment composed part of the military cortege that followed the remains of the lamented Colonel Baker, who had just fallen at Ball's Bluff, to the grave. Among the dirges played while the funeral train was moving, was the "Dead March in Saul," by the band of the Fourth. It added greatly to the solemnity of the occasion, and was repeated twice by request. On the 28th, the regiment, in connection with ten others, was reviewed by General McClellan. Soon after, Colonel McCarty's commission was revoked, and Captain Isaac P. Rodman was appointed to fill his place.

The first heavy marching experience of the regiment, was to Lower Marlboro, Md., where it was ordered during a State election, to preserve the peace, and ensure to all electors their rights at the ballotbox. This delicate mission was successfully accomplished by Colonel

26*

Rodman, and the discreet conduct of his men, left a very favorable impression going and returning. A march of one hundred miles over a muddy road was made in four days alike, fatiguing and amusing. One who participated in the expedition thus writes :—"Through mud and water knee deep, and obliged to use, at almost every step our full strength to extract our legs therefrom, we went, carrying our blankets, guns, forty rounds of ball cartridge, and two days rations in our haversacks. The Colonel and some other officers had mercy on some of us, and carried our guns and blankets. One cadaverous looking individual, with elongated features, was mounted on the Chaplain's horse, while the latter trudged on by the side of a Pennsylvania 45th, carrying his gun." The experience was but a dim foreshadowing of that in reserve. At Camp Casey, the regiment was brigaded with the 81st Pennsylvania, 61st New York and the 5th New Hampshire, under the command of Brigadier General O. O. Howard. The latter took the place of the 45th. On the 30th October, the 4th was mustered into the service of the United States, and fairly launched upon the stormy sea of rebellion.

Skirmish, battalion and other complicated drills occupied the month spent at Camp Casey. The Chaplain was active in the discharge of his varied duties, and found encouragement in his work. On the 28th November, the regiment passed into Virginia, over Long Bridge, to the strains of "Dixie," from Captain Greene's bugle ; and on the 29th, pitched its tents at Camp California, under the guns of Fort Worth, in the neighborhood of Fairfax Seminary. There was much in this vicinity to interest the lover of nature, or the curious in localities. The ancient church in Alexandria, where Washington worshipped, the Marshall House, where the gallant Ellsworth was murdered, were attractive spots, and from the beds of scilified wood, not far from the camp, the devotee of science could soon load himself with sparkling geological specimens.

On the 14th December, the regiment proceeded to Edsall's Hill, where it made its first acquaintance with picket life, diversified with occasional scouting and foraging expeditions. Returning to camp, the holidays came with their athletic sports. The ladies of Rhode Island remembered the soldiers, as timely donations of mittens and socks testified. Colonel Rodman was made the recipient of a handsome testimonial of regard from his officers, giving birth to a neat presentation speech from the Chaplain, and calling forth a feeling reply ; and on New Year day, the regiment was addressed by General Howard, and Hon. George H. Browne, then member of Congress from the second Rhode Island congressional district, the latter lifting the curtain slightly and partially revealing the work of its early future. The famous Burnside Expedition loomed up in the distance, the dangers and glory of which the Fourth was destined to share.

The day of departure came. Winter quarters, half-finished, were abandoned ; General Howard said a few farewell words, commendatory of the past and prophesying an honorable future for the Fourth, and the regiment took up the line of march for Washington, where the muskets of the men were exchanged for newly-imported Belgium rifles. A night at the Soldier's Rest, and a tedious ride of thirty-seven miles in the government cars, the next day, occupying eleven hours, brought the regiment to Annapolis, where its tents were pitched on the grounds of the Naval Academy, in the midst of a driving snow storm. But plenty of straw made all inside comfortable, and the sight of many home faces, recognized in the 5th Rhode Island, which arrived a few days previous, gave cheerfulness to the hour in defiance of snow and wintry cold.

While waiting the departure of the expedition gathering at Annapolis, the regiment was brigaded with the 8th and 11th Connecticut regiments and the 5th Rhode Island battalion, which, together, constituted the third brigade of the Coast Division. Pastimes of various kinds filled the spare hours. Occasionally, some returning from the city to the camp, would appear suspiciously corpulent, a condition that close examination and careful manipulation were able speedily to reduce. One poor fellow of this class, naturally slender, who suddenly gave indications of a bad case of *ascites*, received at once the compassionate attention of his captain, who, after relieving him of twelve "original packages," restored him to his customary condition !

On the 7th January, 1862, the regiment embarked on board the Eastern Queen, and sailed for Fortress Monroe, and thence with the fleet gathered there, for Roanoke. The Burnside Expedition, at the time of its organization and departure, though not so large as the one subsequently fitted out against New Orleans, was formidable for that period. Some idea of its magnitude may be gained from the fact, that within one week after the fleet began to arrive at the rendezvous in Hatteras Inlet, upwards of one hundred vessels of various tonage were lying at anchor over the bar. The land forces consisted of eleven regiments and one battalion of infantry and one light battery, in all probably ten thousand men. Add to this a force of five thousand sailors, and it gave a total land and naval force of fifteen thousand men. The rumors as to the destination of the expedition were various, but a few weeks revealed both its destination and purpose.

In the objects and success of this expedition Governor Sprague heartily sympathized, and, on the eve of its departure, issued an appropriate and inspiring address to the Rhode Island troops attached to it. "I regret," he said, "that I cannot accompany you in the new work to which you are called; but I am assured you will be cared for, and I can safely assure you that you will be remembered. The heart of the State will go with you, and many prayers will ascend for your triumph in every struggle, and your safe return to your hearth-stones. In whatever situation you may be placed, Rhode Island will do all in her power to promote your well being. She sends you this her cheerful good-bye, and earnest God speed."

In the very outset, disaster threatened the enterprise. With what terrific power the storm raged when the fleet was approaching its destination ; how steamers fouled each other for the want of sea room ; how vessels dragged their anchors, and crashed into each other; how the Eastern Queen was driven on shore ; how the splendid ocean steamer New York, laden with ammunition, stranded on the beach and went to pieces ; how the gunboat Zouave went down, and was a total loss ; how the Pocahontas, an unseaworthy steamer, was beached three or four miles north of Hatteras Light, with the loss of all the horses belonging to the 4th R. I. ; how the men suffered for want of fresh water and food ; all these, and many more thrilling incidents, have been made the subjects of such minute description, as to render their repetition here unnecessary. But while the winds lashed the ocean into foaming madness, and the ocean spent its mighty force on the seemingly doomed Armada, its leader was calm, apparently, as when directing its preliminary arrangements at Annapolis ; and his quick eye made him, on the instant, master of the situation. General Burnside rose in strength with the perils of the hour. He was seen every where. On a little tug, that went puffing and struggling through the angry waves like a faithful Newfoundland climbing out of the trough of the sea, and shaking off the briny envelope when threatened to be engulphed, the General would appear when and where most needed, while his clear, ringing voice, would be heard above the fury of the storm, imparting his own fortitude to officers and men, bringing order out of confusion, and safety out of apparent inevitable ruin. It was a nobler triumph than the winning of a field.

But the storm ceased, the troops were landed, and the battle of Roanoke Island fought. The attack was made on the morning of February 7th, and continued on the 8th, by the naval and military forces of the expedition, which resulted in the capture of six forts, forty guns, over two thousand prisoners, and three thousand small arms. Among the prisoners were Colonel Shaw, the commander of the Island, and Colonel O. Jennings Wise, commander of the Wise Legion, and son of Hon. Henry A. Wise, of Virginia. The latter was mortally wounded, and soon after died. The Federal loss, as reported by the commanding general, was thirty-five killed and two hundred wounded. In this battle the regiment passed through its first experience under fire. It occupied various important positions during the day, and conducted with the promptness and coolness of veterans. It was the first to plant the Union colors on the captured Fort Bartow, and the beautiful banner received from the ladies of Providence, announced to the fleet that victory had been achieved. Colonel Rodman and Lieutenant Colonel Tew led their men with great bravery, and General Parke, in his official report, particularly commended Lieutenant Joseph B. Curtis, Adjutant of the regiment, for being " conspicuous in conducting and cheering on the men." The regiment bivouacked the night of the 8th in the rear of Fort Bartow, many occupying the quarters of the rebels. Soon after it went into camp at " Camp Parke," where it remained for a month recruiting its strength. While here, Quartermaster Smith was detailed to act for the brigade and Captain Jeremiah Brown was detailed to enclose the burial ground adjacent to the camp, which he did in a very neat and satisfactory manner.

The next conspicuous action of the regiment was at Newbern, which was captured March 14th, by the combined land and naval forces under General Burnside and Commodore Goldsborough, with a loss on the rebel side of 46 siege guns, 3 field batteries, about 300 prisoners, 3000 small arms, and 500 men killed and wounded. The Federal losses were 91 killed and 466 wounded. In this expedition the regiment embarked on the Eastern Queen the 9th of March, proceeding to the Neuse River, and landed near the mouth of Slocum's creek. The troops of the several regiments were formed on their colors as fast as they reached the shore, and were soon on the march up the right bank of the river. The rain had rendered the roads very muddy, and the march to the point of action was wearisome. In the battle, General Parke's brigade, consisting of the 4th and 5th R. I., 8th and 11th Connecticut, was held for a support. The General having discovered an uncovered point in the enemy's works, the duty of charging and turning his flank was assigned to Colonel Rodman. This was done. "Forward Fourth Rhode Island," said the Colonel, and the regiment marched up the railroad, passing an abandoned rifle pit, and exposed to a fire from the front and both flanks, The order "On the right into line, march!" was given. Then came the order to charge, and with a stentorian shout it was made. The rebels fled, throwing away muskets, equipments, blankets, and whatever else impeded their retreat, and those who were not taken prisoners, or overtaken by some leaden messenger, rushed through the woods in the rear. One trophy of this charge was the battle flag of Latham's battery, whose guns were also taken. The casualties in the regiment were 8 killed and 22 wounded. Of the former, were Captain Charles Tillinghast, and Sergeant George H. Church, Jr. Both fell in the charge made in support of General Reno's brigade. Captain Tillinghast was the son of the late Dr. George H. Tillinghast, of Providence. He was a brave and energetic officer, and greatly beloved by his men. Sergeant Church was the son of Dr. Church, of Wickford, R. I. He died in the faithful discharge of his duty. Captain William S. Chace, son of the late Major John B. Chace, of Providence, was severely wounded in the neck. Lieutenant George E, Curtis, of Providence, was wounded in the shoulder.

Following the fall of Newbern was the investment and reduction of Fort Macon. The investment was perfected on the 25th of April, and on the following day, after a bombardment of ten hours, the fort surrendered. In the meantime, companies A and E occupied Morehead City for the purpose of cutting communication with the fort. On the 25th, company A, Captain Brown, and company B, Captain Buffum, both under command of Major John A. Allen, crossed over to Beaufort, and took formal possession of the town. Major Allen was declared Military Governor, and Captain Buffum Provost Marshal. Besides the two companies in Beaufort and one in Carolina City, seven were on the Banks, working in the trenches. The labor of those on the Banks was very arduous, and was cheerfully performed. Five companies of the 4th alternately relieved the 8th Ct. and 5th R. I. Battalion in the trenches for fifteen days, exposed through the day to the fire of the enemy, during which time the siege batteries were planted. Not a day passed that the enemy did not open upon them, firing from thirty to fifty shell, none of which injured any of the regiment.

The 5th R. I. Battalion, being on duty in the trenches at the time of the surrender, received their arms, and five companies of the 4th regiment relieved Major Wright, guarding the prisoners until they were shipped off.

The fort was much damaged, and some twenty-six guns rendered unfit for service. The day following the surrender, Colonel Rodman was ordered to cross with his command to Beaufort, where it was assigned provost duty. On the 1st of May the Colonel was appointed Military Governor, and Major Allen Provost Marshal for the entire district. Having been appointed Brigadier General, the Colonel took leave of the immediate command of his regiment June 2d, in an affectionate general order. The feeling expressed was reciprocal, and the men parted with him with sincere regret. Lieutenant Colonel Tew assumed the command. Lieutenant Joseph B. Curtis was appointed on General Rodman's staff.

The brilliant success with which the North Carolina Expedition had thus far been conducted, created among the troops the most unbounded confidence in their Chief, and throughout the country increased his already popular reputation as an energetic and skillful commander. In this universal homage, Rhode Island warmly participated. Upon the recommendation of Governor Sprague, the General Assembly unanimously directed him to procure, and cause to be presented to General Burnside an elegant sword, in testimony of the appreciation of his eminent services at Roanoke. The sword was manufactured by Tiffany & Co., of New York city, from a design prepared by Captain Augustus Hoppin, A. A. General. General Edward C. Mauran was selected by the Governor to present the sword in person to General Burnside, and on the afternoon of June 20th the ceremony took place at Newbern, in the presence of 16,000 troops, together with a large and brilliant staff. The escort duty was performed by the 4th and 5th Rhode Island, and the salute, as the General appeared on the field, was fired by R. I. battery F., Captain Belger. The fine appearance and good conduct of the 4th on the occasion, was complimented by Lieutenant Colonel Tew, in a general order the next day. On the morning of presentation day, both regiments had a dress parade in front of General Burnside's quarters, which drew from him expressions of entire satisfaction. In his report of the presentation, General Mauran says, "The deafening cheers which went up throughout the entire lines, combined with the presence of so large a body of well disciplined troops, presented a scene to be remembered." Of the marches, bivouacs, reconnoissances, picket and other services, or the varied movements in battle which filled up the experience of the Fourth Rhode Island, during its connection with the army of North Carolina, it is impossible here to give a minute description. Suffice it to say, they were such as characterize the life of a hard working regiment in an active campaign, and whether exposed to the perils of rebel bullets, or to the insidious influence of a debilitating climate, their obligations were met with cheerful alacrity. Many of their number nobly fell on North Carolina soil, in vindication of human rights, and more still live, who will bear to their graves the honorable scars of a devoted patriotism.

The Anniversary of our National Independence was celebrated by the 4th and 5th R. I., with a zest quickened by a dispatch received on the 3d of July, announcing the capture of Richmond, a statement soon after contradicted. The two regiments were formed in a square, the Declaration of Independence was read by Captain Buffum, a prayer offered by the Chaplain, the band poured forth patriotic strains, the men gave nine hearty cheers, and the ceremonies ended. The rest of the day was spent in festivity.

But now, the Fourth was destined to act in another field of duty. General Burnside was called to join General McClellan on the Peninsula, and the regiment followed his fortunes. On the 6th of July it embarked on board the Empire City, and sailed for Fortress Monroe, where it arrived on the afternoon of Tuesday, July 8th, and debarked the troops at Newport News Point. On the same day, Colonel William P. Steere, who had been appointed from the 2d Rhode Island, arrived and joined the command. On various fields he has proved himself a brave and able commander, and under his administration the regiment has maintained an honorable reputation for harmony and discipline. Lieutenant Colonel Tew, having resigned August 11th, Adjutant Curtis, of General Rodman's Staff, was appointed to succeed him.

The troops from North Carolina were organized into the Ninth army corps, under General Burnside. The third division was commanded by General Parke, and the second brigade, composed of the 4th Rhode Island and the 8th and 11th Connecticut, was commanded by the senior Colonel Harland. Lieutenant George F. Crowningshield, of the 4th Rhode Island, was appointed acting Aide on his staff. Surgeon Rivers was made division surgeon on the staff of General Parke. The regiment did not reach the Peninsula in season to actively engage in the operations there. It proceeded with General Burnside to Fredericksburg, to supply the place of McDowell, who had been sent to the aid of Pope. Gen. Parke being made chief of General Burnside's staff, General Rodman was assigned to the command of the division. Pope's retreat rendered the evacuation of Fredericksburg necessary, and after the destruction of the government depot of supplies at Acquia Creek, on the 31st August, the Fourth, with the rest of General Burnside's command, proceeded to Washington and joined McClellan to drive Lee out of Maryland. Marching on to the scene of action, it formed a part of the forces that made a triumphal entrance into the city of Frederick, and was with its noble chief in the battle of South Mountain, September 14th, where, under the gallant lead of Colonel Steere, it sustained the honor won in North Carolina. A member of the Fourth, present in the action, thus describes the scene at one period of the day: "The battle was now terrific. The enemy had thrown his whole force upon the Union lines, but the men of the north had been unshaken. Side by side, and shoulder to shoulder, had they stood. Fearful gaps had been made in their ranks, but the shock of the enemy had been broken. But the gallant Reno had fallen. 'Many a better man than I will fall to-day,' he had said in the morning; and now he had fought his last fight. Deep was the sorrow of the Fourth, as they saw the form of that brave leader borne by. But still the battle raged. The rattle of musketry was incessant; bullets were thickly showered; and as fast as the powder-begrimmed cannoneers could load their pieces, 'from rank to rank their vollied thunder flew.' In the valley below and on the hillside beyond, the continuous flash of rifles showed the opposing line of battle. For a few minutes an ominous silence would reign, and then the storm would burst forth again in all its fury, as with the last expiring energies of the foe, they dashed again and again on the Federal lines, only to fall back repulsed, bleeding and broken. While

in this position, Colonel Steere found Colonel Ferero, whose brigade
he was ordered to support, and the latter, conducting the Fourth,
moved into position. The road, for at least three-quarters of a mile,
as an officer remarked, ' was strewn with dead, lying like cord wood.'
Upwards of thirty bodies lay in one spot not sixty feet square, and
two were hanging from the fence they had strode, never to reach the
other side. Forming in line of battle, the regiment marched to the
front and took position on the left of the 51st New York." Victory
rewarded the Federals in this fierce contest. Night came, and most
of its hours were laboriously employed by Assistant Surgeon Smalley,
in rendering service to the wounded, Surgeon Miller being detailed
at the general hospital. The casualties of the Fourth were three men
wounded.

On the 17th September, the Fourth shared the dangers and helped
to gain the glory of the bloody field of Antietam. The battle and its
results have already been described, pages 146–155. On the left wing
with Burnside, the Fourth showed an activity second to no other
regiment engaged, and both officers and men were nerved by a common sentiment of valor. The exposures of the day are well attested
by the record of ninety-eight killed and wounded. In the midst of
the battle, and while changing the position of the regiment, Colonel
Steere was struck in the left thigh by a rifle bullet, but made no remark, and still attempted to lead on his men. Fainting, however,
from loss of blood, he was carried to the division hospital, to which
he had been preceded by the lamented General Rodman and his Aide,
Lieutenant Robert H. Ives. Everything possible was done by Surgeon Miller to render them comfortable.* The Major being sick, and
having then no Adjutant, it was left to Lieutenant Colonel Curtis and
one other field officer to handle the regiment, in consequence of
which, at one time, under a very severe fire it broke, but was soon
reformed. The color bearer, Corporal Thomas B. Tanner, was killed
upon a hill, having carried his flag, supported by Lieutenants George
E. Curtis and George H. Watts, within twenty feet of the enemy.
It was saved by Lieutenant Curtis. The officers wounded besides
Colonel Steere were Captain Caleb T. Bowen, taken prisoner and pa-
roled, Lieutenants Watts, severely, George P. Clark, dangerously, and acting Lieutenant George R. Buffum, mortally. In his report
to the Governor of Rhode Island, Lieutenant Colonel Curtis says :—
"Throughout the day I never saw an officer but that he was encouraging and directing his men," and he makes special mention of
the bravery of Lieutenants Watts and Curtis, Sergeants Wilson, Coon,
and Morris, Corporals Leonard and Farley, and privates McCann and
Peck.†

---

* Colonel Steere was taken to Hagerstown, and thence to Philadelphia,
where, in the hospitable family of Colonel Peter Fritz, he was under the
care of Dr. Paul B. Goddard Forty-seven days elapsed before the ball
was extracted. He joined the regiment in May, having been taken from
duty nearly ten months.

† In the battle of Blackwater, October 3d, 1862, Corporal James H.
Burbank, Company K, Rhode Island 4th, detailed on board the Commodore Perry, distinguished himself for gallantry and was recommended for
promotion by acting Rear Admiral S. P. Lee.

November found the army of the Potomac in front of Fredericksburg, with General Burnside in command. The story of its march, and of its sanguinary battle of December 13th, has been told, pages 171 to 192. In the fatigue and excitements of that march, the 4th Rhode Island shared. With the perils of that battle, it was identified. Colonel Steere still disabled from service on the field by his wound, Lieutenant Colonel Curtis was yet in command. On the 12th, the regiment crossed the river to Fredericksburg, and reported to Colonel Hawkins for picket duty. Before daylight on the 13th, it was relieved by the 9th New York, and after being held till 8 o'clock, in reserve, it joined its brigade, then lying on the river bank, and all the morning listened to the music of shells fired by both friends and foes, which occasionally burst overhead. At sunset, the regiment was ordered forward with its brigade to the support of Colonel Hawkins, and soon reached where the 9th New York were lying on the ground in support of a battery. Here, while Lieutenant Colonel Curtis was reforming the line, which had become somewhat broken by the nature of the ground passed over, a ball from a shrapnell shell, which exploded immediately in front, struck him in the head and he fell dead. Major Buffum, who had, until the day the Fourth crossed the river, been Provost Marshal of the division, and who, at his earnest request, was relieved of that duty that he might be with his regiment, now assumed the command and held his position for the night. On the night of the 15th, he recrossed the river. The casualties, besides the death of the commander, were Lieutenant George E Curtis, Corporal Hiram Freeborn, and seven privates, wounded. Seven days after the battle, Dr. Lloyd Morton, commissioner appointed to examine into the physical condition of the Rhode Island troops in Virginia and around Washington, visited the regiment and found 448 men reported for duty. The hospital department was in good condition, and on the 21st January following, only eight men were requiring its care.

Lieutenant Colonel Curtis was the son of George Curtis, Esq., of New York, and grandson of Hon. Samuel W. Bridgham, the first Mayor of Providence. No officer could have been more sincerely mourned. " Young, thoughtful and earnest," one writes, " at the very outset of the war, he gave his manifold talents and attainments to the cause of his country. Animated with the highest patriotism, he labored earnestly and arduously in his new career, and though the rebellion maintained a longer existence and assumed more gigantic proportions than ever he anticipated, yet he never flagged in his endeavors, and never doubted for a moment but that the cause of the nation would be crowned with ultimate and complete success." His remains were brought to Providence, and lay in state, with those of Lieutenant Colonel Welcome B. Sayles, of the 7th Rhode Island, in the Representatives Hall, under a spacious marquee formed of mourning drapery. Lieutenant Colonel Sayles was buried December 20th, in Grace Church Cemetery, with masonic and State military honors. Lieutenant Colonel Curtis was buried in the North Burying Ground, where religious services were conducted by Rev. Dr. Edward B. Hall. At the instance of his friends, the funeral was private.

December 24th, Major Buffum was commissioned Lieutenant Colonel, and Captain James T. P. Bucklin, Major. The regiment was

27

detached from Colonel Harland's brigade, and with the 13th New Hampshire and 25th New Jersey, formed into a new brigade under Colonel Dutton of the 21st Connecticut. Lieutenant George F. Crowninshield was appointed on Colonel Dutton's staff. On the 8th February, 1863, the regiment, with the Ninth army corps, embarked at Acquia Creek for Fortress Monroe. The early days of a pleasant encampment at Newport News were made more pleasant by the receipt of a generous supply of fresh vegetables, a portion of the cargo of the Helen and Elizabeth, sent by considerate friends at home. Shortly after encamping at this place, the regiment was honored with a handsome national flag and guidons, presented by a few friends in Providence, through Mrs. Sarah M. Hall. The flag was inscribed with the names of the victories in which the Fourth had nobly borne its part—Roanoke Island, Newbern, Fort Macon, South Mountain and Antietam—with the words, " Fourth Rhode Island Volunteers," in the centre. The gift was appropriately acknowledged by Lieutenant Colonel Buffum, who referred to the fidelity with which the the regiment had defended its first banner, as the best assurance of the manner in which the second would be cherished. On the 13th of March, the regiment made its camp near Suffolk, Va. On the 16th April, six companies were in support of Fort Dix, two companies in support of Simpson's battery, two companies in the rifle-pits, and Lieutenant Field, with twenty men, in support of Fort Halleck. On the 3d of May, the Fourth had a sharp brush with the rebels at Hill's Point, across the Nansemond river, driving in their pickets and occupying their rifle pits and earthworks, losing, in the conflict, Corporal James Grinod killed, and Lieutenant George F. Waterman, Corporal George W. Allen and privates George Erwin and Joseph A. Griffiths, wounded. In advancing up the hill to examine the ground and judge of the enemy's force, Colonel Buffum and Major Bucklin were exposed to the fire of their sharpshooters, but fortunately escaped injury. May 22d, Colonel Buffum made a reconnoissance in the Dismal Swamp, down the Jericho canal ; and on the 24th, another with a detail of sixty men, to Drummond Lake. On the afternoon of the same day, the balance of the regiment, with Corcoran's Legion and most of the 3d division of the Ninth corps, made a reconnoissance on the Edenton road, encountering the enemy and capturing their first line of breastworks.

Among the marked features of the summer, was the building of Fort Rodman, one of the most important in the cordon of defences designed to stretch from the West Branch of Elizabeth river to Dismal Swamp, and an expedition by the way of Yorktown and White House, to near Hanover Court House, from which the regiment returned July 13th, having had a fatiguing march over bad roads, under a burning sun, that tested to the utmost the endurance of both officers and men. In July, it was transferred from the Ninth to the Seventh corps, second division, third brigade, under General Naglee. In the same month, Colonel Steere became acting Brigadier General of the third brigade of Getty's division of the Eighteenth army corps, leaving Lieutenant Colonel Buffum in command of the regiment

From the date of departure from Providence to September 9th, 1863, the Fourth broke camp eighty-five times, made heavy marches in three rebel States, and went within eight miles of Richmond. In the same period, besides the part taken in the battles of Roanoke, Newbern, Fort Macon, South Mountain, Antietam and Fredericksburg, it had two skirmishes on the Nansemond river and two at Suffolk. It entered the field with 890 men. On the date referred to, it had 581, including 175 recruits. Up to the same time, it had lost 295 in killed, wounded and by disease. Patriotism and fidelity is the sum of its honorable record.

On the 31st October, Chaplain Flanders was compelled by sickness, to resign. He had been with the regiment from its organization, and by his judicious and faithful ministrations, obtained the confidence and esteem of both officers and privates. His departure awakened general regret.

FIFTH REGIMENT RHODE ISLAND VOLUNTEERS.

[First organized as a battalion, and after the taking of Fort Macon, recruited to a full regiment. In 1863, changed to heavy artillery.]

FIELD AND STAFF OFFICERS,

(Commissioned and Non-commissioned.)

Colonel—HENRY T. SISSON, November 5th, 1862.

Lieutenant Colonel—JON ARNOLD. Captain, 5th R. I., November 30th, 1861; Lieutenant Colonel, 7th R. I.

Lieutenant Colonel—GEORGE W. TEW. Promoted from Major of 4th R. I., 1862.

Major—JOHN WRIGHT. Captain, 2d R. I., June 1st, 1861; Major, 4th battalion, November 7th, 1861. Resigned, July 25th, 1862.

Major—THORNDIKE C. JAMESON, December 13th, 1862.

Adjutant—CHARLES H. CHAPMAN, Resigned, 1862.

Adjutant—JAMES M. WHEATON, (1st Lieutenant,) June 9th, 1862.

Chaplain—Rev. WALTER M. NOYES. Resigned, August 15th, 1862.

Chaplain—HENRY S. WHITE.

Surgeon—EPHRAIM L. WARREN, December 10th, 1862.

Assistant Surgeon—ALBERT POTTER, October 10th, 1861.

Assistant Surgeon—JEROME B. GREENE.

Hospital Steward—FRANK GLADDING, 1st Lieutenant.

Quartermaster—MUNRO H. GLADDING, (1st Lieutenant,) November 30th, 1861. Died at Beaufort, N. C., November 2d, 1862.

Quartermaster—WILLIAM W. PROUTY. Promoted from Quartermaster Sergeant.

Commissary Sergeant—CHARLES E. BEERS. Promoted to 2d Lieutenant.

Sergeant Major—JOSEPH J. HALLINGER. Appointed Lieutenant 14th R. I.

Sergeant Major—JOSHUA C. DROWN.

Captains when the battalion left Providence, Jonathan M. Wheeler, Allen G. Wright, James M. Eddy, George H. Grant, Job Arnold. Captains, October 3d, 1863—Isaac M. Potter, James Gregg, William W. Douglas, James Moran, George G. Hopkins, William R. Landers, John H Robinson, Henry B. Landers, John Aigan, Emilius Di Meulen, Charles Taft.

The Fifth Battalion Rhode Island Volunteers was recruited under authority received by General Burnside, from the Secretary of War, to raise a division for coast service, to be commanded by himself, and denominated the "Coast Division." It was organized at Camp Greene, in October, 1861, from which it was transferred to Camp Slocum, on the Dexter Training Ground, in Providence. In the commencement of the enlistment, it was expected to act, in times of need, as marines, and was to be armed with Burnside rifles and short boarding swords. It was drilled, however, with muskets, and has never used any other small arm. The battalion consisted of five companies, with the ultimate design of being made a full regiment. To serve under General Burnside, and to be identified with his fortunes, was, to many, independent of other considerations, an inducement to enlist; and, though the 4th Rhode Island had so recently filled its ranks and departed, leaving the field less favorable to rapid enrollment for the next comer, in about seven weeks the enlistments had reached the required numbers.

On the 27th December, 1861, the battalion departed for Annapolis, to join the Expedition to North Carolina. The morning was spent in preparations. At 3 o'clock, P. M., it was reviewed by Governor Sprague, and exhibited a commendable discipline. After the review, the line was thrown into column and marched to the depot, where a train was in waiting. At 4½ o'clock, amid the cheers of the multitude assembled to witness the departure, the cars moved off, and the battalion bore with it, to its future field of service, the best wishes and earnest prayers of numerous friends. Nothing occurred on the journey to damp the cheerful spirit in which the troops left home. Duty beckoned them onward. Patriotism found range in the expectations of coming days; and the vision of glory to be won under a noble chieftain made welcome the active duties to which they were hastening. At Annapolis Junction, a delay of three hours, enabled the lovers of nature to enjoy delightful autumn scenery resting in the lap of winter, under a bright sun that permeated the atmosphere with an almost summer warmth. The camp of a western regiment was located there, and to the Fifth an opportunity was afforded of witnessing, and with admiration, the perfection of its drill. The delay ended, the battalion soon reached its immediate destination.

At Annapolis, all was bustle and methodical activity. Transport vessels were constantly arriving and getting in readiness for their living freight; troops were daily pouring in; and General Burnside, the soul of the movement, was everywhere present, perfecting the arrangements. His staff, in this expedition, was as follows:—

Assistant Adjutant General—Captain LEWIS RICHMOND.
Division Quartermaster—Captain HERMAN BRIGGS.

Assistant Quartermaster—Captain WILLIAM CUTTING.

Assistant Division Commissary—Captain E. R. GOODRICH.

Aides-de-Camp—Lieutenant DUNCAN C. PELL and Lieutenant GEORGE R. FEARING.

Medical Director and Acting Division Surgeon—Major W. H. CHURCH, M. D.

Naval Officer—Commander S. F. HAZARD, U. S. N.

At length all was complete. On Thursday, January 9th, 1862, the Fifth left Annapolis, on board the transport ship, Kitty Simpson, and sailed for Fortress Monroe, where she arrived on the 11th, and there found a large fleet of sailing and steam vessels. With this fleet, the voyage to Hatteras Inlet was continued. Off Cape Henry, the pilot left the transport, taking charge of two hundred and fifty letters homeward bound. On reaching the Inlet, the draft of the vessel was found to be only six inches less than the depth of water covering the bar. Casting anchor, three days were devoted to lightening ship, and then the propeller Virginia attempted, by aid of a hawser, to help her over. But the swell of the waves only lifted her up to plunge her, with greater violence, into the sand, when the hawser parted, and for a time she was left by the tug to her fate. In this perilous position she remained about six hours, rising and falling with the regularity of a trip-hammer. At each thump, a shiver, as if foreboding certain destruction, was felt from stem to stern, with the only offsetting encouragement that, at each rise, the force of the waves impelled her forward a few feet. Late in the afternoon, while struggling with the elements that had proved so disastrous to some, and threatened so violently to engulph all, the Kitty Simpson was relieved by the steam tug Eagle, who connecting by hawser and favored by a rising tide, succeeded in drawing her over the bar into safer moorings. To those on board the scene was one of intense excitement.

After laying inside the bar for about three weeks, all was made ready for an assault upon Roanoke Island. The Fifth, making a part of the 3d brigade, under General Parke, had been shifted to the steamer S. R. Spaulding, General Burnside's head-quarters, and moved towards its destination.

The day before the battle, Lieutenant Andrews, of the New York 9th, but acting as General Burnside's Aide, with a detachment of the 5th Rhode Island, made a boat reconnoissance for a suitable place to land. Having sounded out a good channel, and just as the boat reached the shore, the crew was fired upon by a rebel squad, wounding, in the jaw, Charles Viall, of Providence, thus giving to Rhode Island the honor of having shed the first blood in the enterprise. The action between the Federal fleet and the rebel gunboats begun on the 7th February. That afternoon and night—the night dark and rainy—about 11,000 troops landed. As the small steamers in which they were taken came only within 400 feet of the shore, the men were compelled to wade through water and deep mud. The next morning, at an early hour, the enemy fired on the Union pickets and drove them in. Generals Foster, Reno and Parke soon had their brigades in motion. The advance was supported by six howitzers, commanded by Midshipmen Porter and Hammond, and manned, in part, from the

27*

fleet. After fording a creek, General Foster's force came up with the
enemy's pickets, who fired their pieces and retreated. Striking the
main road, the brigade pushed on, and after marching a mile and a
half, came in sight of the enemy's position. In the mean time, the
Fifth was ordered to seek and take possession of a house for a hospital, which was done ; but beyond being brought under a heavy fire in
consequence of taking a wrong road, the guard duty to which it was
assigned prevented contact with the rebels, and no casualties were
suffered. In the front the battle was now raging violently. The
Massachusetts, Connecticut, New York, New Jersey and Pennsylvania troops behaved handsomely. General Parke came up with the
4th Rhode Island, 8th Connecticut and 9th New York, and gave
timely and gallant support to the 23d and 27th Massachusetts. Fort
after fort was taken. The rebels fled from before the impetuosity of
the Federals, and General Foster having kept up a pursuit for five or
six miles, was met by a flag of truce borne by Colonel Pool of the 8th
North Carolina, seeking terms of capitulation. These were unconditional surrender, which, after a little delay, were accepted. In the
course of a few days, Elizabeth city and Edenton were taken possession of by Commodore Goldsborough. The victory by sea and land
was complete, giving to the Union forces entire possession of all the
inland waters of North Carolina.

The news of the fall of Roanoke was received in Rhode Island with
the liveliest demonstrations of joy. In Providence, the 1st New England regiment of cavalry paraded in honor of the event ; it was made
the subject of a special address by the Governor to the General Assembly ; the chimes of Grace Church pealed out the Star Spangled
Banner and other patriotic airs : a national salute was fired in the
afternoon, another at sundown, and in the evening one hundred guns
were fired by a detachment of the Providence Artillery.

Nearly a month was spent at Roanoke, after the battle, during
which time General Burnside was preparing for an advance upon the
rebels. The days were enlivened by drills and common camp duties.
In the manual of the rifle, the battalion made great proficiency, for
which, and for the neatness of its encampment, credit was given at
head-quarters.

In the expedition against Newbern, captured March 14th, the Fifth
was transported to the landing at the mouth of Slocum's creek, by the
steam tugs Eagle and Curlew.. On the morning of the 13th, the landing was effected under cover of the naval fleet commanded by Commodore Rowan, and after a hard march in mud and rain, bivouacked
at night, unconsciously, near the enemy. Fortunately, its camp fires
did not attract attention. At 6 o'clock, the next morning, the line was
formed, and two hours later the heavy firing on the advance announced that the work had begun. Soon the order. " Forward ! "
was passed along the eager lines, and the Fifth was in motion for the
field. "As we filed by General Burnside," writes one engaged in the
action, " we glanced at his noble countenance, and caught from his
look a new inspiration for the conflict before us. Silently we deployed into the thick woods, all intent upon the new sounds of musketry and artillery in full play upon our position. One shell came
screaming through the trees, cutting the branches in its course, passed

near the General, and exploded far off behind. Then, as if at a signal, the woods on our right resounded with the reports of heavy guns
and musketry, like rain upon a seething sea. We advanced, halting
now and then, and obeying the order to lie down while showers of
lead whizzed by our ears and brought down twigs and branches from
every tree. Not a few, too, clipped almost musically by, in close
proximity to our heads and limbs; but here, fortunately, no one was
struck. I was most agreeably surprised to see our men steadily advance at the word, nor make the least motion backwards. At last
we came to a deep ravine, or rather a series of hills and gullies thrown
together in inextricable confusion, and were told that the great battery of the enemy had been taken by part of the Massachusetts 21st,
but could not be held by the small number who entered, and was
consequently retaken by the enemy. We were ordered to fall in behind the 4th Rhode Island and the 8th Connecticut; but the 8th
halted and allowed us to take our position next the 4th. Then—
'Charge, Rhode Island!' was the cry, and on we ran, over stumps
and fences, up a steep bank, across an open space, the bullets all the
time keeping time to our steps and whistling close to our ears, and
halted only inside the breastworks, with the 4th in advance inside the
main battery—the enemy in retreat. The fire from the left of our position still continued, and after forming line under it to repel an expected charge, we were ordered to turn to the left, take up a position
under the brow of a small sand ridge, covered, as the whole battle-
field was, with tall trees and thick underbrush. Here, after having
crossed the hot fire from the rebel rifle pits and battery beyond the
railroad twice, we fired our first volley—advancing to the brow of the
hill, taking aim, firing, and then retiring a few steps to load. That
volley, the prisoners told us afterwards, killed fifteen men. We
slackened the fire of the enemy at that point three times, but were
interrupted by a rumor that we were firing into our own men. The
fog and smoke and dense wood prevented us from seeing anything for
a while, but as a puff of wind for a moment cleared the view in front,
we saw, with joy, that we were firing at the grey coats and caps of
real enemies. Now, the 4th, who had been doing good service somewhere near the centre of the enemy, beyond the large battery, were
ordered to support us, and to advance with their flag, as we had none.
They filed past on our left, and scattering through the woods in our
front, rushed down over the railroad, across rifle pits and gullies, and
with one shout, carried the concealed battery beyond, and decided the
victory. Our advance was now undisputed and triumphant. The
railroad and the turnpike led us straight into Newbern. We took
two camps in which the fires were still burning, and the bread left in
the mixing troughs. The 4th was stationed in one and the 5th in
another. Just as our tired limbs were warning us that they could
not carry us much farther, the news was brought us, 'our gunboats
are at the wharf in Newbern.' We arrived at our camp in time to
eat the warm bread baked by the enemy."

The loss of the Fifth, in this battle, was four killed, and seven
wounded. Of the killed, the battalion mourned the loss of Lieutenant Henry R. Pierce, of company D, who fell, shot through the heart,
while enthusiastically encouraging his men to action. Lieutenant

Pierce had been, for several years, the successful Principal of the High School in Woonsocket, R. I., and entered the service of his country from a conscientious sense of duty. Into his new profession he carried the ardor that distinguished him as a teacher, and his soldierly qualities, not less than his social and moral traits, secured for him a warm place in the affections of his brother officers. His remains were brought to Woonsocket, and on the 29th April, deposited in Oak Hill Cemetery, with military honors and appropriate religious ceremonies, amidst the tears of the wide circle to whom he was endeared as the patriot soldier, faithful teacher and sincere christian.

Whatever may have been the feeling of the white population of Newbern, on the entry of the Union forces, there was nothing equivocal in the conduct or language of the slaves. Many of them welcomed, with almost frantic joy, the day of deliverance, as they regarded it, and "Bless de Lord, I'm free," was uttered with an unction that showed how highly they prized the boon. After the battle, the Fifth had its camp near Newport city, and for a time was engaged in guarding part of the railroad from that place to Beaufort, and in repairing the damage done to it by the retreating enemy. A bridge 180 feet long, essential to the transport of supplies in the investment of Fort Macon, had been destroyed. This was rebuilt in five days, under the direction of Major Wright, and the cars running over it.

The investment of Fort Macon, owing to the difficulties in transporting siege materials, was a slow and somewhat difficult undertaking; but the marshy shore and yielding sand bluffs of Bogue Island, as well as other obstacles, were finally overcome, and on the morning of April 26th, the bombardment commenced. The Federal gunners attained great precision in firing. Out of fourteen hundred shells fired, four hundred and fourteen were thrown within the walls. The rebels also showed accuracy in the aim of their guns. Captain Pell, who rendered valuable assistance in the working of a 10-inch mortar battery, narrowly escaped death from one of their projectiles. While looking over the parapet, he perceived a shot coming, and immediately "ducked" into the pit. The shot, a 32-pounder, struck and passed through the embankment within three inches of his head, burying him up in the sand. Other hair breadth escapes occurred. A conference with the rebels under a flag of truce terminated in an unconditional surrender, they solemnly promising not to bear arms against the United States until regularly exchanged. Fifteen guns had been dismounted, seven men killed and fourteen wounded. The prisoners numbered upwards of three hundred and fifty, and among the spoils were fifty-two cannon, thirty thousand pounds of powder, thirty thousand cartridges, and a large quantity of military stores. The rebels fired 250 thirty-two pound shells, 200 ten inch shells, 150 eight inch shells, 4 percussion shells, (rifled,) 150 twenty-four pound shells, 800 solid shot, and about 9000 pounds of powder.. Yet the Federal loss, remarkable to say, was only one man killed and two wounded. The man killed, William Dart, of 3d N. Y. artillery, was standing up on the parapet of the 10-inch mortar battery, driving home a pointed stake, and disregarding the warning to "duck" by one who saw the flash of the rebel gun—which was the last fired before flag of truce came out—he was hit by the fragment of a shell bursting near him, which lacerated his body in a shocking manner.

To the Fifth Rhode Island was assigned the honor of taking possession of the Fort. A few days previous, two beautiful colors, inscribed with the names of "Roanoke" and "Newbern," had been received, the gift of ladies in Providence, but no time had offered for their formal reception; and now opened a providential occasion for the ceremony. Lieutenant Douglas, at his request, was permitted to return for them to camp, where they had been left, and with a speedy gallop they were soon brought on the ground. The battalion was formed in line. The colors were taken by General Burnside, who unfurled and handed them to Major Wright. He passed them to the color bearer, who took his place at the head of the column, and the procession moved in the following order : General Burnside, General Parke, Captains Biggs and King, Major Wright, Color Bearer, Fifth Rhode Island, Staff, members of the press present. Entering the fort, the battalion ascended to the ramparts, and marched once around; and while Captain Joe Greene pealed forth "The Star Spangled Banner," and "The Red, White, and Blue," the stars and stripes of the 5th were firmly planted in the sight of surrounding thousands, and the inspiring ceremony of taking possession ended. That night the Fifth returned to its encampment, and the Fourth R. I. occupied the Fort.

In May, after the fall of Fort Macon, the camp of the Fifth was on Bogue Banks, near by. The situation, in many particulars, resembled Newport. It had the some bracing sea air, the same hard beach, and the same opportunities for surf bathing. Scup were plenty, sea fowl in abundance, and it only wanted the presence of a bevy of sea nymphs, with their red bloomers and bewitching straw hats, with a corresponding number of male admirers, doing the dutiful in the briny sports, to make the illusion complete. The Fifth remained here until General Burnside was called to the aid of General McClellan on the Peninsula, when it went to Beaufort, where Major Wright became military commandant, and Lieutenant Douglas was appointed Provost Marshal of the District, the duties of which delicate and often perplexing office, he discharged with firmness and excellent judgment. In the imposing pageant of the Sword Presentation, which occurred at Newbern, June 20th, as already described, the Fifth participated with the Fourth in performing escort duty. It was a proud privilege, and the honor thus conferred upon them by their beloved chief was most gratifying. Nature joined man in imparting glory to the occasion. At the moment a shower was falling in the distance, and as the General rode into the area where the ceremony was to be performed, a beautiful rainbow spanned the heavens, forming a triumphal arch of gorgeous splendor over the uncovered head of the hero, and giving as it were a divine brilliancy to the scene.

If, up to this period, fewer decided indications of Unionism among the leading inhabitants of North Carolina were visible than had been anticipated, the reason, perhaps, might be found in their distrust of permanent protection, should they unequivocally avow themselves. While the army of General Burnside, if kept in a body, might be sufficient to overpower the rebels at any given point, it was evident that, to keep the advantages gained as he proceeded, he must leave garrisons behind at almost every step, and thus in a short time reduce his strength too much to penetrate the State, and hold important interior positions. Should they, under such circumstances, take a decided stand, and the Union army fail to be reinforced sufficiently to hold the State against any subsequent rebel operations, it might terminate in confiscation of property to the confederacy, if not in death as an additional penalty, without any benefit inuring to the Union as an equivalent for the sacrifice. Had it been possible to have given General Burnside at the outset, fifty thousand instead of fifteen thousand troops, with which to have put the entire State practically and at once under military rule, the Union feeling believed to exist, would probably have been manifested with a strength that would have saved the old North State from the entanglement of a reluctant alliance with rebellion.

Major Sisson received his appointment of Colonel of the Fifth, November 5th, 1862, but did not arrive out to take command until January 9th, 1863. He was received in a flattering manner, and complimented with a regimental parade and review, under the direction of Major Tew, which displayed the men to fine advantage. A collation followed, and a pleasant hour was spent in friendly greetings. In the evening, Colonel Sisson received his officers at the Gaston House, which he made his quarters.

In the beginning of March, 1863, the rebels conceived and attempted to execute a plan for the capture of Newbern. In this, by timely and judicious countermovements on the part of the Union forces, they were foiled. Shortly after, Lieutenant Colonel Job Arnold dissolved his connection with the Fifth to join the Seventh Rhode Island. Colonel Arnold had been identified with the regiment from its organization, had shared with it the dangers of the sea-storm at Hatteras, the fatigues of numerous marches, and the risks of battle. In all positions of danger he had shown himself brave; prompt to act, but not injudiciously impulsive; a thorough soldier without pretence; self forgetful, and always thinking of the interests of his men; in his intercourse with brother officers, governed by the most delicate sense of honor, and ready to yield a personal advantage rather than stand in the way of another's advancement. These, with a happy and sympathetic nature, had greatly endeared him to both officers and men, and the separation caused sincere regret. Before leaving, the officers of the line presented him with an elegant sash and field glass, as a slight token of their regard. An affectionate note, signed by every non-commissioned officer and private in the regiment, was also addressed to him, giving assurance of their united best wishes for his future success and welfare.

The climate, not less than the fatigues and exposures of active campaigning, had early severely affected the health of Chaplain Noyes, and by sickness he was finally taken off from the duties to which he had been faithfully devoted. He resigned August 15th, 1862. In his successor, Rev. Henry S. White, the regiment was singularly fortunate. Genial and practical, quick to see, and sensitive to feel the soldier's needs, the welfare of the men was kept constantly in view, and his usefulness was made apparent in other than merely professional ways. On a visit to Rhode Island in May, 1863, his earnest appeals in behalf of the regiment, secured contributions in money of nearly fifteen hundred dollars, besides numerous miscellaneous donations of substantial and convenient articles for camp and hospital use. With the money, a varied cargo, including one hundred tons of ice, was purchased, which reached Newbern on the afternoon of July 3d, in season to enhance the enjoyments of the National anniversary. To the men, these evidences of interest had no ordinary charm. They felt that amid the poisoning miasma, and under the scorching sun of their remote field of duty, they were still remembered. Home, with many of its long missed comforts, seemed to have come to them, and words of gratitude found free and full expression.

Rahl's Mills, Kinston, Whitehall, Tarboro' and Goldsboro', are representative names of military operations subsequent to the capture of Fort Macon.

But among the military adventures of the Fifth, the raising of the siege of Washington, N. C., must ever occupy the most prominent place as a hazardous and brilliant achievement. Immediately after the capture of Newbern, it was occupied by the national forces. Early in April, 1863, the garrison there consisted of the 27th and 44th Massachusetts volunteers, and one company of the 3d New York Cavalry. These, with about one hundred armed negroes, numbered but little more than 1300 men. Three gunboats, the Louisiana, Ceres and Commodore Hull, lay in the stream. General Foster, commanding the Department of North Carolina, had gone to Washington to inspect the garrison and defences there, and suddenly found himself besieged by the rebel General Hill, with a force variously estimated at from 10,000 to 16,000. The enemy had also taken possession of Rodman's, Hill's, and Swan's Points, where they planted strong batteries, and for a distance of seven miles held the entire command of the river, rendering an approach by water a seeming impossibility. The land forces made a complete cordon around the town, so that escape was out of the question. General Foster made the best possible disposition of his little band, and for sixteen days stood up bravely against the bombardment, opened and continued by his formidable foe. Provisions now were short, the pinchings of hunger felt, and, to the besieged, starvation or surrender seemed the only alternative. Still they held out, and answered the shrill voices of rebel shells with the thunder of their heavy guns. If surrender must come, it would be only when the last meagre ration was consumed, and the power to resist totally exhausted.

When the tidings of General Foster's situation reached Newbern, immediate steps were taken for his relief. On the third day of the siege, General Spinola, with his brigade, was sent by water, with several gunboats, to co-operate in the operation. The attempt failed. The gunboats ascended to within range of Hill's Point battery, and opened fire, but the response was such as to forbid an attempt to run by, and they retired with two holes in one of their paddle boxes. Another expedition overland, by General Spinola, was attended by no better success. Matters now looked more serious than ever. Aid must speedily be rendered, or the hard pressed garrison must yield. At this juncture, Colonel Sisson, with the Fifth Rhode Island, was ordered by General Palmer to proceed to Washington. Rev. Edward H. Hall, Chaplain of the 44th Massachusetts, who had been to Newbern on business, joined the expedition and participated in its dangers. On Friday, 10th April, the Colonel, accompanied by General Palmer, embarked his command on board the transport steamer Escort, and proceeded up to Maul's Point, on the Pamlico river, ten miles below Washington. Here he found a fleet of gunboats, and some transports loaded with provisions, ammunition and forage. But the hindrances to proceeding further were no less formidable than those from which the gunboats with General Spinola's brigade recoiled. These were the three batteries of heavy guns before mentioned. That at Rodman's Point, commanding the river and city, and those at Hill's and Swan's Point, nearly opposite each other, threatening to blow into atoms any craft that should attempt to run the gauntlet. Besides these, a triple row of piles extended across the river, with the exception of a passage about one hundred feet wide and four hundred feet from the shore, and directly under the guns of the battery. To increase the difficulty in finding the crooked channel, the enemy had removed all the buoys in the river. A reconnoissance by Captain W. W. Douglas and Lieutenant Dutee Johnson, with fifty volunteers from the regiment, and which was very successfully conducted, discovered three rebel batteries on the west bank of Blunt's Creek, which would prevent an approach to Washington by land. To most, the case now seemed hopeless. To Colonel Sisson it did not. He believed Washington could be reached, and he resolved, if permitted, to make the attempt to go there. He dispatched Major Jameson to General Palmer, on board the Southfield, to volunteer his command to attempt the passage of the blockade. From the perilous and uncertain nature of the enterprise, the General did not feel warranted in ordering it, but gave the Colonel discretionary power to act as in his judgment might be practicable. This was enough. He decided that the object of the expedition was of sufficient importance to demand the risk. Calling his men around him, he told them that he had resolved upon his course after deliberate consultation with his officers ; that General Foster must be relieved, and the 44th Massachusetts, part of their own brigade, must be rescued from danger. If the 44th were in their place, he knew they would go through. Would they do less ? The response was hearty and unanimous, and preparations were made at once for the passage. The machinery and pilot house were protected as thickly as possible with hay bales : the ammunition, [some twenty tons of which had been put on board,] shifted to the safest part of the boat, where the soldiers threw themselves upon it to protect it still more ; all lights were put out, and every one except the officers on duty, and a company of sharp-shooters, were ordered below decks.

" So in silence and darkness, [Monday, 13th,] the Escort began her perilous voyage. Pushing slowly up to the sunken piles, with the gunboats at a respectful distance behind, she felt her way through the narrow passage. Once she struck upon the piles, and hearts beat fast at the thought of sticking fast, unable to move, right under the rebel battery. But it was only for a moment. Backing slowly down the stream, she tried once more, pushed through just as the rebel gunners seemed to discover her, and putting on a full head of steam, soon ran out of reach of the shot that were sent whizzing after her. Rodman's battery, however, was still to be passed, an even more formidable task, for the channel runs close in to shore, and for two miles the Escort was in range of their heavy guns. All along the banks of the river, volleys of musketry were poured in upon the boat; but as she approached the batteries, the storm burst upon her with relentless fury. But courage and heroism carried a charmed life. The Escort was not to suffer that night. Pressing on the steam again, she ran safely by the batteries without the loss of a man. Then, when the danger was past, and the great success achieved, the suppressed emotion of those three long hours found eloquent vent. The Rhode Island boys sent the glad cheers ringing through the town, carrying the first promise of hope and relief to the worn but stout-hearted soldiers in the trenches."*

On Wednesday night, 15th, the rebels supposing General Foster to have received a large reinforcement, evacuated their works under cover of a heavy fire which they opened upon the town, and left the Federal forces in undisputed possession of the post. In his report of this expedition, made to Adjutant General Mauran, Colonel Sisson says :—
"I cannot close before mentioning the gallant conduct of my officers and men, during the period of suspense through which we passed. Their self-possession and ready obedience were extremely gratifying to me, and justify a confidence that they will never prove recreant in the hour of danger.

" I would speak particularly of Lieutenant Colonel Tew and Major Jameson, whose advice and support materially aided me in the conception and execution of our undertaking; of Captain William W. Douglas, who, during the reconnoissance of Monday morning, displayed great coolness and bravery in proceeding, in company with Sergeant Major J. J. Hathinger, in advance of his men, directly under the enemy's guns, to prepare an accurate sketch of their position. Captains H. B. Landers and Isaac M. Potter, Lieutenant Thomas Allen and Sergeants Mott and Conger, were at their posts on deck, and ably performed their respective duties."†

Lieutenant Colonel Tew, with five companies of the Fifth, took possession of Rodman's Point, where the following note was found :

"YANKEES ! ! !— We leave you, not because we cannot take Washington, but the fact is, it's not worth taking ; and, besides, the climate is not agreeable. A man must be amphibious to inhabit it. We leave you a few bursted guns, some stray solid shots, and a man and brother rescued from the waves, to which some fray among his equals

---

* Letter of Rev. Edward H. Hall.

† The General Assembly of Rhode Island, at its May Session, 1863, passed a resolution of thanks to Colonel Sisson and the officers and men of the 5th Rhode Island regiment, " for the gallantry and heroism which they displayed in running the gauntlet of the enemy's batteries on the Pamlico river, under circumstances of extraordinary peril."

consigned him. But this tribute we pay you, you have acted with much gallantry during this brief siege. We salute the pilot of the Escort.

"Co. K, 32 N. C. Vols."

The pilot of the Escort referred to, was killed, on her return passage down the river, with General Foster on board, he being obliged to take an early departure after the enemy withdrew. By his orders, Assistant Adjutant General Hoffman presented to Colonel Sisson and the officers and men under him, thanks "for the energy, perseverance and courage displayed in running the gauntlet of the enemy's batteries."

The Massachusetts 44th felt deeply the important service thus rendered, and on the 25th April, Colonel Francis L. Lee communicated to Colonel Sisson a series of resolutions, thanking him and the regiment for an act of valor that raised the siege and brought the much needed succor at a critical moment, and expressing the desire, if it met the wishes of the Fifth, to present it with a set of colors bearing a device commemorative of the act of gallantry. This was subsequently done. On the return of the 44th, from its nine months term of duty, an elegant banner was procured and placed in the hands of Rev. Henry S. White, Chaplain of the Fifth, he then being in Boston, to be presented by him to the regiment. The ceremony of presentation took place at Newbern, August 3d. Chaplain White made an appropriate address, referring to the unity of the two States represented in the gift, and bidding his compatriots, as they looked upon it, to "remember the duties of the future as interpreted by the history of the past." Lieutenant Colonel Tew, in the absence of Colonel Sisson, received the flag, and responded in behalf of the regiment in a patriotic and spirited address. When the 44th returned home, Colonel Sisson accompanied them; and on the occasion of a subsequent visit to Boston, the lady friends of the regiment presented him with an elegant sword, sash and belt, together with two massive pieces of silver, in token of their appreciation of his services in the rescue.

In the several campaigns of North Carolina, the 5th Rhode Island maintains an honorable position. A hard working regiment, ever doing with promptness and spirit whatever duties were assigned it, the good name it has achieved is held among the choice treasures of the State.

SIXTH REGIMENT RHODE ISLAND VOLUNTEERS.

This was intended to be a colored regiment, and the order, directing its formation, was issued August 4th, 1862. Owing to causes mentioned in the introduction of this volume, it was not organized.

SEVENTH REGIMENT RHODE ISLAND VOLUNTEERS.

FIELD AND STAFF OFFICERS,

(Commissioned and Non-commissioned.)

Colonel—ZENAS R. BLISS.

Lieutenant Colonel—WELCOME B. SAYLES. Killed in battle, Fredericksburg, Va., December 13th, 1862.

Lieutenant Colonel—JOB ARNOLD. From 5th Rhode Island, 1863.

Major—JACOB BABBITT. Mortally wounded at battle of Fredericksburg, Va., December 13th, 1862.

Major—THOMAS F. TOBEY. 1st Lieutenant and Adjutant, 10th Rhode Island, May 26th, 1862.

Adjutant—CHARLES F. PAGE. 1st Lieutenant, September 4th, 1862.

Adjutant—JOHN SULLIVAN.

Quartermaster—DEAN S. LINNELL. Quartermaster Sergeant, 10th Rhode Island.

Quartermaster—JOHN R. STANHOPE. Quartermaster and 1st Lieutenant, November 3d, 1862.

Surgeon—JAMES HARRIS.

Assistant Surgeon—WILLIAM A. GAYLORD.

Assistant Surgeon—ALBERT G. SPRAGUE. August 29th, 1862.

Assistant Surgeon—CHARLES G. COREY.

Chaplain—HARRIS HOWARD.

Sergeant Major—J. S. MANCHESTER. 1862.

Quartermaster Sergeant—STEDMAN CLARK. 1862.

Commissary Sergeant—JOHN R. STANHOPE, Jr. 1862.

Hospital Steward—STEPHEN F. PECKHAM.

Captains, September 10th, 1862—Lewis Leavens, Theodore Winn, George E. Church, William H. Joyce, (Lieutenant commanding, since Captain,) Thomas F. Tobey, Lyman M. Bennett, Rowland G. Rodman, James H. Remington, Thomas B. Carr, George N. Durfee. Captains, August 8th, 1863, not mentioned above—Alfred M. Channell, Percy Daniel, James N. Potter, Thomas Greene, Ethan A. Jenks, George A. Wilbur, Edward T. Allen, George N. Stone.

The Seventh Regiment of Rhode Island Volunteers was organized under a general order dated May 22d, 1862, to serve during the war. Circumstances were less favorable for rapidly filling it up, than had surrounded its predecessors. But the officers and agents, to whom the duty of obtaining enlistments was assigned, prosecuted their work with unwearied diligence, and early in September the regiment had nearly reached its maximum number. The camp, known as "Camp Bliss," was established in a pleasant locality near the shore of the Bay, in South Providence, and the summer was devoted to drill in the manual, and the formation of soldierly habits, in preparation for the fatigues of the march and the conflict of the field, that were subsequently to become an experience. The commander, Colonel Zenas R. Bliss, was an accomplished officer, transferred from the regular United States service. A thorough tactician and disciplinarian, and with a careful eye to the comfort and health of the men, he was eminently fitted to secure their efficiency.

On Wednesday, September 10th, the regiment broke camp and marched to Mashapaug station, where it took the cars for Washington. The night on the Sound was pleasant to wakeful eyes, and the moon shed her mild lustre as a halo of glory upon the embryo patriots, as they watched from the deck of the Commonwealth the motion of the silvery waters through which she ploughed. The departure from New York, the next morning, called forth friendly demonstrations from the shipping in the harbor. At Philadelphia, a hospitable entertainment at the Volunteer Refreshment Saloon awaited the regiment. As it marched through the streets, shouts and cheers for Rhode Island and Pennsylvania rent the air; flags and handkerchiefs were waved on every side; officers and men shook hands with the ladies and gentlemen thronging the sidewalks, and even little children claimed a kiss or made other demonstrations of affection; and the regiment carried with it pleasant memories of the city of Brotherly Love, lasting as life. At Baltimore, another bountiful collation awaited it, but no greeting voice was heard in the streets. The Monumental City had not yet recovered the full freedom that had been violently wrenched from her loyal citizens by the strong hand of rebel sympathizers, and Unionism prudently held its peace. But a better day came, and Baltimore, in its municipal rule, ceased to be to the country, the impersonation of secession.

A slight injury to the Drum Major, William H. Hopkins, near the Relay House, was the only incident of exciting interest that occurred between Baltimore and Washington, where the regiment arrived on the 12th, and encamped on Capitol Hill. On the 16th, the camp was moved across the Potomac to Arlington Heights, and the Seventh was assigned to the command of General Paul, of the second brigade of Casey's division, when drills for field service again occupied the time. Leaving this encampment about the 1st of October, the regiment proceeded by the way of Frederick, Md., to Sandy Hook, near Harper's Ferry, where it arrived on the 3d, and marching up the steep side of Maryland Heights, a distance of half a mile, encamped at the foot of the main mountain. From this point the skirts of the field of Antietam could be discerned, quickening the blood of patriotism; and in the far distance, a rebel flag waving defiantly in the breeze. On the 6th, the encampment was removed to the valley below, where the regiment was visited by General Burnside, who was welcomed with hearty cheers. Moving with the army of the Potomac, in November, the Seventh found itself in its appointed place before Fredericksburg, on the 13th December, and engaged with veteran coolness in that hard-fought field. To describe this battle would be only to repeat the tale already told; but it should be said, that throughout that sanguinary day, and under the most trying circumstances, the regiment exhibited the most unflinching bravery. It marched over or held its position on the hottest part of the field in good order; expended all its ammunition, and used more procured from the dead and wounded, and from other regiments; and after this expenditure of ammunition, remained on the field with fixed bayonets until ordered off, at 7½ o'clock in the evening. The flag of the regiment was pierced by sixteen bullets and a fragment of a shell. The casualties of the day fell with severity upon both officers and men. Lieutenant Colonel Sayles was instantly killed by the fragment of a shell, while lying on the ground with the regiment, under fire. Major Jacob Babbitt was mortally wounded. Adjutant C. F. Paige was wounded in the forehead. Captain Rowland G. Rodman received a wound in the right shoulder. Captain James H. Remmington had his jaw broken. Captain Lewis Leavens was bruised by fragments of a shell. Lieutenant George A Wilbur was shot through the leg. Lieutenant David R. Kenyon was wounded slightly. Sergeant Major J. S. Manchester lost his right arm. Colonel Bliss was constantly exposed during the day, and had several narrow escapes. At one time, when the regiment was advancing, he moved towards an opening in a fence—a sort of shell road through the palings—and before he reached the gap five men had fallen there before the unerring fire of the rebel sharpshooters. He then passed the barrier unhurt. The shell that killed Lieutenant Colonel Sayles ricocheted over the head of the Colonel, covering him with bood; and subsequently the Adjutant fell bleeding upon his left arm. The entire list of the wounded, officers and privates, was reported to be 140.

The remains of Lieutenant Colonel Sayles were brought to Providence, and buried from the State House, December 20th, as already described, with military and masonic honors. Colonel Sayles was a native of Bellingham, Mass. He was well known not only in Rhode Island, but throughout the country. He was for eight years Postmaster in Providence, having been appointed by President Polk, and re-appointed by President Pierce, and discharged the duties of that office with great efficiency. He was one of the founders, and for several years the chief editor of the *Providence Post*, and displayed no small ability in the conduct of that paper. He had long been a conspicuous leader in the Democratic party in Rhode Island, and by his energy, ability and fearlessness, wielded a large influence. His executive ability was uncommon. He had the chief supervision of the organization of the Seventh regiment, and addressed himself to his new duties with characteristic vigor. At the age of fifty years, he fell in this its first battle, leaving a wife and several children to mourn his loss.

Major Babbitt was a prominent citizen of Bristol, R. I., and President of the Commercial Bank in that town. His body was brought home and buried January 1st, 1863, with military honors. The funeral was attended by a large concourse of citizens. Governor Sprague, and Colonel Gardner of his personal staff, Adjutant General Mauran and Quartermaster General Cooke, were in attendance upon the services, which were conducted at the house of the deceased by Rev. Dr. Thomas Shepard, and in the church by Rev. Mr. Stowe. Flags were displayed at half-mast on public and private buildings, the bells of the churches were tolled during the moving of the procession, and minute guns were fired by a detachment of the Artillery.

28*

After the battle of Fredericksburg, the regiment remained at its old camp near Falmouth until the 9th of February, when the whole corps were ordered to Newport News, Va. While doing picket duty along the Rappahannock, February 6th, the rebel pickets communicated this intelligence to the Federals, and also repeated the orders to which the regiment had listened at dress parade the day before, showing the presence of spies, or of rebel sympathizers. Indeed, little was done in the Union encampments that was not immediately known on the opposite side of the river. The 7th suffered severely from the effects of the malarious character of the atmosphere in the vicinity of the Rappahannock, and lost many of its members by death, and more by transfer to the various hospitals of the North. Moving by rail to Acquia Creek, and from thence in transports, it reached Newport News February 11th. On the 14th, the camp was enlivened by the arrival of the Elizabeth and Helen, with a donation of vegetables, and about 300 boxes of personal comforts, sent as mementos of home. Here the regiment remained until the night of March 25th, having that afternoon been paid off for the first time since entering the service.

The health, as well as discipline of the regiment, had materially improved during its stay at Newport News, and all started in good spirits for Kentucky, General Burnside having been assigned to the command of the ' Department of the Ohio," and taking the 9th corps with him. The Seventh reached Cincinnati March 29th, and left same afternoon for Lexington, Ky., at which place it arrived and encamped near the Fair Ground on 31st. Staying here only sufficient time to rest the men from the fatigues of the journey, it left for Winchester on April the 8th. This was the severest march the men had ever encountered. The weather was very warm, the roads made of Limestone retained the heat, and when they reached camp at about 9, P. M., not an officer or man but what complained of blistered feet. The distance—twenty-three miles—on the men who, since their first arrival at Falmouth November 17th, 1862, had made no single march of over three miles, was telling in its effects, and all were completely exhausted. Lieutenant Colonel Job Arnold, appointed from the 5th R. I., joined the regiment in the West, and participated in its subsequent fatigues and exposures, winning, by private and professional worth, the confidence and esteem of his command.

During April and May the regiment encamped at Richmond, Paint Lick, Lancaster, and Crab Orchard. At Richmond, the camp ground at the hour for dress parade, became the frequent resort of people of the vicinity, and on May-day was enlivened with the presence of a number of ladies, accompanied by General Nagle and his staff. Besides the attraction of neat and well drilled soldiers, the dress parade presented that of fine music from a band, whose energy and perseverance have made them very good performers. On the first of June, while at Crab Orchard, the regiment was ordered to the front towards Cumberland Gap, with eight days rations, sending all surplus baggage and winter clothing of the men to Hickman's Bridge, Ky., for storage. It had hardly completed the arrangements for moving, when these orders were countermanded, and it was ordered to start at once to join the army of the Tennessee in front of Vicksburg, Miss. June

4th, the regiment marched to Nicholasville, a distance of thirty-six miles, in two days, took cars for Cairo, Ill., via Cincinnati, there embarked on steamboats for Vicksburg, and reached Sherman's Landing, nearly opposite that city, June 4th ; disembarked here, and encamped in a swamp surrounded by Contraband camps. Early the 15th, the regiment made an effort to join General Grant's army, in the rear of Vicksburg, but hardly reached the river before it was ordered to Snyder's Bluff, on Yazoo River, to assist in defending Grant from an attack by Johnston. Taking small steamboats for this place, it arrived and encamped on the 17th, remaining until the 23d. On this day, the brigade to which the seventh was attached, started for the front towards Big Black, camping near Neely's for a week, making in the time, one reconnoissance in force, crossing the Big Bear Creek.

July 4th, news of the surrender of Vicksburg reached camp, and was published in the afternoon of the same day. The troops started towards Jackson in pursuit of Johnson and his force. He retreated into Jackson. The Union forces reached that city July 10th. It was cn this march, that, in passing a plantation of Jefferson Davis, the house of a Mr. Cox, formerly his steward, was searched, and the library, and a large amount of the rebel President's private correspondence discovered and seized, according to inclination, as trophies of war. The correspondence, largely political, extended over many years, and the portions preserved revealed almost every shade of opinion and purpose on the part of the writers in regard to public affairs, from radical State rights views to positive secession. To the future historian of the Rebellion, this correspondence will be of great use, as a help in explaining some of the mysteries of political combinations issuing in treason.

On the afternoon and evening of July 11th, the regiment, with a portion of the 6th New Hampshire, both under command of Colonel Bliss, proceeded to the Mobile and Ohio Railroad, and destroyed some 500 yards of the track, burning the ties and bending the rails, rendering them unfit for use. The telegraph was also cut, and the wire burned.

On 12th, the regiment supported the 35th Massachusetts, doing front picket duty. 13th relieved them, and skirmished with the enemy the entire day, losing Lieutenant Adjutant Sullivan, and Lieutenant Fuller Dingley prisoners, two men killed, and nine wounded. In this affair, which really assumed the proportions of a battle, officers and men behaved with the greatest gallantry. Adjutant Sullivan particularly distinguished himself by advancing in front of the Union lines, and bringing off the body of a Sergeant who had been shot early in the morning ; and when taken prisoner he had just posted a company sent by Colonel Bliss to reinforce the line. The men killed were Sergeant John K. Hull, of South Kingstown, R. I., and private Jonathan R. Clark, of Charlestown, R. I., both highly respected by their officers.

The regiment left Jackson July 20th, and arrived at Snyder's Bluff, 24th. Here, writes a member of the 7th, "The campaign of the 9th Army Corps, in Mississippi has ended, and with it that of the 7th R. I. It has been the most arduous of any in which we have been engaged, compared with which, our last fall's campaign in Virginia was comfortable, and our spring visit to Kentucky a mere pastime. While in Mississippi, we have truly learned that the duties of a soldier's life may be arduous in the extreme, but throughout the whole we have accomplished all that has been asked of us, both as men and soldiers ; have received the compliments and thanks of both department and corps commanders, while we have won, I trust, the friendship and respect of the north-western troops, with whom we have been brought in contact. Such appreciation may seem of small moment, and may offer but little consolation to those who have been brought low by sickness, but to those who are spared, the hearty grasp and welcome of our western brothers are very pleasing.

From July 4th to July 24th, a period of not less than three weeks, the regiment marched from Kneely's station to Jackson and returned to Mill Dale, a distance of a little more than one hundred miles. During the time, scarce a night passed when they were not under arms. When in the vicinity of Jackson, they were often in line twice during the same night. Such continued interruptions of the hours of repose, together with their arduous duties and the continued heat of the climate, were severely felt in their influence upon the health of the men. After the evacuation of Jackson, but a few days were allowed us for rest, when we were subjected to the severest trials of all—the return march to Mill Dale. This march, a distance of fifty miles, was accomplished in eighty hours, including all halts. Many of the men were without shoes ; many had substituted drawers for pants, and others had arrayed themselves in various articles of apparel found at Jackson. A motley crowd were we, and I often heard the wish expressed that Westminster street might have been on our line of march. Added to the excessive fatigue of our marches was the want of complete rations. An Adjutant General said on the last morning, "I am without my breakfast—the niggers stole all my hard tack last night—I'll give fifty cents for one of Uncle Sam's pies this morning." A march of thirty-two miles, from Jackson to the Big Black, in two days, and a halt at night. The last beeve in the coral is killed and eaten for breakfast, while this pleasing dilemma demands consideration—to remain is to starve, to go on is to tax our weary limbs to their utmost point of endurance. A dinner of green corn and salt is provided, with a little tea, (the sugar was gone two days before,) upon which we march at four o'clock. We cross the Big Black river and encounter a thunder storm, through which we march, while wet to the skin, eleven miles. For supper we take tea, and sleep on wet blankets. We breakfast on the anticipation of some hard tack at Mill Dale, and march seven miles. At noon on the 14th, all feasted on hard tack."

Colonel Bliss, in his report of the operations of the regiment after leaving Kentucky, says : "The conduct of the regiment during the expedition has been praiseworthy, and credit is due them for their gallantry in repelling the sortie of the enemy, and for the soldierlike manner in which they have submitted to the many privations and fatigues they have been obliged to undergo. Several nights in succession they were turned out, and remained in readiness to repel the attacks of the enemy. They have suffered severely from the intense heat, and debilitating effects of the elements. Some of the marches were long, with but little water, and many of the men were bare-footed and without proper clothing, and at times all were on less than half rations."

August 8th, the brigade embarked on steamboats for Cairo. They had not proceeded far before they run aground in the Yazoo River, and in attempting to get off, the boat containing the 7th broke the rudder, and they were obliged to remain in the river until Sunday afternoon 10th. The effect of this delay was soon perceptible in the men. Drinking the water from the swamp, many of them were taken sick with the Yazoo fever, and during the trip up the Mississippi, three died, and were buried on the shore. The troops arrived at Cincinnati August 20th, crossed the river, and encamped in Coving-ton. From Covington they proceeded to Nicholasville, Ky., stopping there two weeks, during which time one Lieutenant and six men were buried.

The campaign in Mississippi, honorable alike to officers and men, was disastrous in its effects on the regiment. Its results were, in-cluding the two killed at Jackson, a loss of 35 by death, to October 1st, besides many subsequently discharged or transferred to the In-valid Corps.* On the 7th September, the regiment was ordered to join the army of General Burnside, in Tennessee; but on representa-tion of its condition, it was sent to Lexington, Ky., to do provost duty. By steadiness in battle, cheerful endurance of long marches and scanty fare, and fidelity in the discharge of every duty assigned it, the 7th Rhode Island has shown that the praise awarded by its commander was merited.

One writing from the army of the Cumberland, has said, "To go to Charleston is a frolic; but to go to Chattanooga is sober earnest;" and a similar statement might be made in regard to the long and tire-some marches of the 7th Rhode Island. To go to Cincinnati by rail was pleasant recreation, but to march hither and thither, in Missis-sippi, under a scorching sun, and inhale the miasma of its swamps; to bivouac with little or no shelter from drenching rains; to do the work of soldiers on poor rations and deficient in quantity, or to slake a raging thirst from stagnant pools from which horses refused to drink; to do and endure all this and more, as the routine of daily life, without expectation of applause, was to do the sober, earnest, but

---

* July 1, 1863, at Camp Neelys, Warren county, Miss., 119 men were reported absent from the regiment sick. The returns, November 1st, reported the number of the regiment to be 32 officers and 516 men. Lieutenant Colonel Arnold, who then commanded the regiment, had been untiring in his endeavors to develop to the utmost the qualities of the gentleman and the soldier, in those over whom he was placed. By orders adapted to the end, a spirit of emulation among the members of the companies, in regard to neatness of dress and equipments, and sol-dierly bearing, was stimulated. These requisites of a good soldier, at all times to be fostered and cherished, and for which the regiment had often been complimented, were particularly to be encouraged at this time when it represented the government in a city of high importance, which num-bered, among its inhabitants, many whose wavering loyalty depended upon the conduct of those who were its defenders.

prosaic work of patriotism, stripped of all poetic charm. It was to test soldierly virtues in no ordinary manner; and that the men neither faltered nor lost their buoyant spirit, redounded more to their honor than would a victory achieved under the stimulus of a glorious name to be won.

EIGHTH REGIMENT RHODE ISLAND VOLUNTEERS.

This, like the 9th and 10th regiments, and under the same call, was intended to be composed of three months volunteers for the emergency; but not being required for that brief service, it was not organized.

NINTH REGIMENT RHODE ISLAND VOLUNTEERS.

FIELD AND STAFF OFFICERS,

(Commissioned and Non-commissioned.)

Colonel—CHARLES T. ROBBINS, temporarily.

Colonel—JOHN T. PITMAN, July 3d, 1862. Major of same, May 29th, 1862; Lieutenant Colonel of same, June 9th, 1862; Lieutenant Colonel of 11th R. I., September 16th, 1862.

Lieutenant Colonel—NICHOLAS VAN SLYCK, temporarily.

Lieutenant Colonel—JOHN HARE POWELL, July 3d, 1862. Captain of same, May 26th, 1862; Major of same, June 9th, 1862.

Major—GEORGE LEWIS COOKE, July 3d, 1862. Promoted from 1st Lieutenant and Quartermaster; Major, 12th regiment, October 13th, 1862; Lieutenant Colonel of same, October 22d, 1862, temporarily.

Adjutant—ALBERT C. EDDY, temporarily.

Adjutant—HENRY C. BROWN.

Quartermaster—WILLIAM McCREADY, Jr., May 26th, 1862. 2d Lieutenant and Quartermaster, 2d cavalry, November 12th, 1862.

Surgeon—LLOYD MORTON.

Assistant Surgeon—HENRY KING; do., 12th R. I., October 19th, 1862.

Chaplain—N. W. TAYLOR ROOT.

Sergeant Major—ROBERT FESSENDEN. 2d Lieutenant and Adjutant, 11th R. I., October 1st, 1862.

Commissary Sergeant—G. MILLAR.

Quartermaster Sergeant—ALFRED O. TILDEN.

Hospital Steward—HENRY E. TYLER.

Principal Musician—CHARLES GREENE.

Captains—Charles L. Watson, Robert McCloy, John M. Taylor, Samuel Pierce, Henry F. Jenckes, James R. Holden, Henry C. Card, John A. Bowen, —— Place, —— Slocum, —— McKinly.

The Ninth and Tenth Rhode Island regiments were organized for an emergency under the same general order, and may properly be spoken of together in their incipient state. In May, 1862, Washington was menaced, and more men were needed in the field. The Secretary of War called for supplies of three months volunteers, and Rhode Island again showed herself among the first to respond. The tidings of the peril and the need came on Sunday at midnight, (25th) and "as the news flashed along the wires, men leaped from their beds, and hastened to the places of rendezvous, to march at once to the South." The excitement and enthusiasm was intense as when the integrity of the nation was first threatened, and affected alike all classes. "Men hurried again from their counting rooms; students dropped their books and fell into the ranks; citizens of high social position, who had filled important offices of trust in executive and other departments of State, patriotically came forward, and threw the weight of their example into the scale of duty; mothers, who had already sent sons to the war, heroically bade their other sons God speed; brides parted tearfully but bravely with their husbands; and the sorriest and saddest men were those who could not go." The two regiments, as well as a battery of Artillery, were made up mostly of the National Guards, and with such rapidity were the ranks filled, and such the activity of the Adjutant General's and Quartermaster General's Departments, that in four days the Ninth and Tenth regiments were completed, equipped, and forwarded to the seat of War.

The Ninth Rhode Island was organized by Colonel Charles T. Robbins, and left Providence in two detachments, the second of which took its departure May 28th, and proceeded directly to Washington. Nothing occurred on the route to mar the enjoyment or cool the ardor of the men. To many, it was more than an ordinary trial. They had not had the advantage of a few weeks of camp life and discipline to prepare them for the rough experience of soldiers; but coming from studies, or other peaceful pursuits, they were required to adopt at once habits differing widely from accustomed modes of living, testing severely natures the most robust. On arriving at Washington, the regiment marched to Tennallytown and formed an encampment, which subsequently received the name of "Camp Frieze." Here a month was spent in thorough attention to drill, and to all other duties essential as preparations for any service to which it was liable to be called. During this month it was regarded as a part of the force for the defence of the Capitol, and with other regiments encamped in its vicinity, did constant picket duty in the neighborhood of, or beyond Chain Bridge. On the 1st of July the regiment moved, via Washington and Long Bridge into Virginia, and encamped near Fairfax Seminary. It remained there only two days, however, going from thence by the river to Washington, and out across the eastern branch of the Potomac to the line of fortifications, which extends from nearly opposite Alexandria to a point opposite Georgetown. Here it relieved the 99th Pennsylvania, which joined

McClellan on the Peninsula. These were veteran troops, and after-ward did good service. For the remainder of its term of service, the regiment performed garrison duty in this chain of forts, its head-quarters being at Fort Baker.

The distribution of the companies was as follows:

Company A. Captain McCloy, at Fort Greeble.
" F. " Taylor, " " Carroll.
" D. " McKinly, " " Snyder.
" I. " Pearce, " " Stanton.
" C. " Bowen, " " Ricketts.
" H. " Jenks, " " Wagner.
" E. " Place, " " Baker.
" K. " Holden, " " "
" G. " Watson, " " Dupont.
" B. " Card, " " Meigs.
" L. " Slocum " " Davis.

The total number of guns on both branches of the Potomac, cover-ing the approaches to Washington, was 213. Life at the forts was unavoidably monotonous. The separation of the companies limited social intercourse, and the spare hours between the regular daily ar-tillery drills, were occupied with such amusements as each man was inclined to, or by home correspondence. The readiness to improve opportunities for the latter, is shown by the fact that, during the few weeks the regiment was at Camp Frieze, about ten thousand let-ters were written and posted, while quite the same number were re-ceived, keeping home affections warm, and home influences exerting their steady and useful power. The chaplain, according to custom, acted as Postmaster, and in other ways interested himself in the wel-fare of the men. For the reason above assigned, general religious services were impossible. At the close of each day's drill, a brief exercise, terminating with the doxology and benediction, was given, and on Sunday evenings, at dress parade, at headquarters, a sermon was delivered. The duties of the chaplain were very faithfully and satisfactorily performed.

The health of the regiment was generally good. During the three months absence, but two deaths occurred. The first death was that of Sylvester B. Arnold, son of George Arnold, of North Kingstown, aged 21 years. He belonged to Company K, Captain Holden, was a good soldier and cheerful companion. His remains were sent to Rhode Island, to be buried among kindred and friends, but before they were taken from camp, received full military honors, the burial service being first read.

The history of the Ninth is necessarily brief and uneventful. It is not identified with brilliant deeds, such as attract the gaze, and call forth expressions of wonder or admiration. It cannot point to hard fought battles, and exhibit a long list of casualties, as evidence of its prowess. But if destitute of these features, history will nevertheless give it a deserved recognition as a reserved power. Important, but not dazzling, duties were assigned it, and these were faithfully per-formed. In every respect, it was a credit to the State, and worthy of being had in honorable remembrance. At the expiration of the term of enlistment, the regiment returned home. It reached Providence in the steamer Bay State, August 31st, and was escorted by the 10th regiment through various streets to Exchange Place, where it was dismissed. With one exception, the companies belonged in other towns, and left the city, in the earliest trains, for their respective homes. Companies A and H, of Pawtucket, were handsomely received there, and a bountiful collation provided. A similar reception was given to company I, in Warren, and a speech of welcome made by A. M. Gammell, Esq. A few days after, the regiment assembled in Providence, was paid off, and mustered out of service.

TENTH REGIMENT RHODE ISLAND VOLUNTEERS.

FIELD AND STAFF OFFICERS,

(Commissioned and Non-commissioned.)

Colonel—ZENAS R. BLISS. Colonel, 7th R. I., August 8th, 1862.
Colonel—JAMES SHAW. Jr. Promoted from Lieutenant Colonel, August 11th, 1862; Lieutenant Colonel, 12th R. I.; Colonel, colored regiment in Maryland, 1863.
Lieutenant Colonel—WILLIAM M. HALE. Promoted from Captain, August 11th, 1862.
Major—CHARLES H. MERRIMAN, temporarily.
Major—JACOB BABBITT. See 7th R. I.
Adjutant—BENJAMIN F. THURSTON, temporarily.
Adjutant—JOHN F. TOBEY.
Quartermaster—JAMES H. ARMINGTON. 2d Lieutenant; 1st Lieutenant, June 9th, 1862; resigned July 19th, 1862.
Quartermaster—CHARLES W. ANGELL. 2d Lieutenant, July 25th, 1862.
Surgeon—GEORGE D. WILCOX.
Assistant Surgeon—ALBERT C. SPRAGUE, Jr.
Chaplain—A. HUNTINGTON CLAPP.
Sergeant Major—EDWARD R. GREENE.
Commissary Sergeant—JAMES O SWAN.
Quartermaster Sergeant—DEAN S. LINNELL.
Principal Musician—GEORGE LEWIS.

Captains—Ex-Governor, Elisha Dyer, Hopkins B. Cady, A. Crawford Greene, William E. Taber, William M. Hale, Benjamin W. Harris, Jeremiah M. Vose, Christopher Duckworth, G. Frank Low, William S. Smith, Samuel H. Thomas, Charles H. Dunham, temporarily.

On the 23d of May, 1862, a special order was issued for the commandants of the several military companies of the State " to assemble their respective commands at their usual places of rendezvous, and report one company, minimum standard, from each organization, to the office of the Adjutant General, for three months service at Washington." At a meeting of the officers composing the 1st Rhode Island regiment National Guards, Hon. Elisha Dyer presiding, it was resolved, "that Colonel James Shaw, Jr., be and is hereby requested to offer to His Excellency, the Governor, the services of the organization known as the 1st Rhode Island regiment National Guards, as now officered and organized, in response to the call and service made by him." The offer was accepted. On the night of May 25th, a despatch announced the defeat of General Banks, and the utmost haste to reach the Capital seemed necessary. At i o'clock A. M., an order was received by Colonel Shaw, from the Executive, to immediately organize the National Guard. The companies were ordered to meet at their respective armories, at 9 o'clock A. M., and at 7 o'clock P. M., of the same day, 613 men were reported to the Governor, ready for duty. These were at once organized as the 10th Rhode Island volunteers, and at the request of Colonel Shaw, Captain Zenas R. Bliss, an experienced officer of the United States army, was appointed its commander. On the following day, (27th,) the regiment departed for Washington in the midst of a pouring rain.

Nothing of special importance occurred on the journey. At Philadelphia, the regiment was provided with a bountiful collation, and received other courteous attentions that enlivened the hour, and that are still gratefully recollected. Passing through Baltimore, the regiment arrived in Washington on the 29th, and took quarters in the barracks near the depot, for the night. The next morning, the line of march was taken up for Tenallytown, where a site for a camp was selected, just beyond the village, and in the midst of a cold, drenching rain, the tents were pitched. This was named "Camp Frieze," in honor of the Quartermaster General of Rhode Island. The regiment was attached to the brigade commanded by General Sturgis, and on the 9th of June was mustered into the service of the United States. The usual routine of camp life now commenced, with its daily drills and detail for guard and picket duty. The camp was pleasantly located, but lacked the convenience of suitable ground for parade. Religious services were held every evening, and on the Sabbath, while together, the Ninth united with the Tenth in the principal service of the day, the Chaplains officiating alternately. The Tenth found in Rev. Mr. Clapp, a true, sympathetic friend and faithful spiritual adviser, who both by official and unofficial services, greatly endeared himself to the men.

If picket post had its serious side, it also furnished amusing incidents, that relieved the tedium of "the sentinel's lonely beat." On Saturday evening, May 31st, the first night duty of this kind was performed by Captain Harris, of Company F. and a small squad of men. Sunday evening, from indications that seemed to require greater precaution, Captain Dyer, of Company B., was ordered "to select thirty privates, with ten rounds of ball cartridges each, and post himself at such place and distance, on the middle road, (leading to Frederic, Md.) as he thought most advisable, and to report at Headquarters at sunrise next morning." The night was excessively dark, and a severe thunder storm was raging. The men, with coats or blankets to protect them, water in their canteens, and hard biscuit in their haversacks, were in line at nine o'clock, P. M. Ammunition was distributed, strictest caution and silence enjoined, and the detachment left camp. Captain Dyer, (accompanied by his 1st Lieutenant, J. Frank Low, and three Sergeants.) was, as also his command, ignorant of the road or country. Picking their way as best they could, with the vivid flashes of lightning, and subsequent impenetrable darkness, drenched before leaving camp, in the heavy continuous rain ; the "picket squad" were halted between one and two miles from camp, by the roadside, while the Captain and Lieutenant knocked at the door of what appeared a large farm-house. No one answering, and lights being seen, the knock was repeated. Stillness was again the response. The other side of the house was traced by following the boards, &c., and dispensing with any formality, the outside door was opened into a large room, in which the family of two males, three or four females and children, were gathered. "I want quarters for my men for the night," says Captain D. "We have no room," was the answer. "You must make some ; my men are wet through ; the night is boisterous ; we want no beds or furniture, but room ; we do not leave here." "But there's no room in the house." "Then show us the barn. We are coming in under cover somewhere, with your leave if we get it, without it if we don't." "You can go into the wagon-shop." "Very well, show us the wagon-shop." Light in hand, father and son came out, and their courtesy and locomotion was essentially quickened, by the sight of a larger number of well armed guests than he supposed were honoring them. The wagon-shop was soon cleared—as was necessary—seats were arranged, a large Kerosene oil lamp brought in, with a stone jug of water, the way to the spring pointed out, and "if we wanted anything in the night, come for it." The beginning, and the end of the host's welcome were very different. It was afterwards ascertained that the family were rank secessionists, having at that time two sons in the rebel army. But as long as picket duty was performed by the 9th or 10th regiments at "Camp Frieze," so long was the wagon-shop of —— —— its headquarters. The picket guard of that night were posted in advance of the command, relieved every two hours, and reported themselves, as ordered, at sunrise, fully satisfied with their first night's experience of a soldier's life. There were several starts during the night. Market wagons were searched for "things contraband of war," and a gay Lothario, returning from Rockville at midnight, passed the night in the wagon-shop, as he foolishly undertook to pass the picket on horse-back, not knowing any countersign but what had been exchanged at Rockville. Colonel Robbins, sympathizing in the abrupt annihilation of his pleasures, dismissed him, as the Captain led him next morning, to head-quarters, with the advice, "to do his courting earlier, or get the countersign."

On the 26th of June the regiment passed into Virginia, over Long Bridge, and made its encampment near Fort Ward, in the neighborhood of Fairfax Seminary. The march of about eighteen miles, was performed in six hours, and the regiment marched into their new camp with every man in line, and as in good order as if on parade. All the forces south of the Potomac not garrisoning fortifications, were now formed into one division, consisting of two brigades, the

first under command of General Cook, and the second under Colonel
Bliss, which comprised batteries I, 2d N. Y. C, 1st N. Y., 16th
Indiana, 2d Excelsior, 9th and 10th R. I., 32d Massachusetts volunteers, and 12th Pennsylvania Cavalry. The camp was finely situated
on a large plain, well adapted to battalion drill and evolutions of the
line, and anticipations were awakened, that opportunity for becoming
perfected in these would be afforded. But in this there was disappointment. On the 29th orders were received to take possession of
the forts then garrisoned by the 59th New York. On the 30th, the
regiment embarked at Alexandria for Washington, then marched to
Tennallytown, and bivouacked for the night, and on the 1st of July,
the companies were distributed as follows :

Company B. Captain Dyer, Fort Pennsylvania.
"   K.   "   Low,   "   "
"   D.   "   Smith, "   DeRussey.
"   A.   "   Taber, "   Franklin.
"   E.   "   Cady, "   Alexander.
"   I.   "   Hale, "   "
"   F.   "   Harris, " Ripley.
"   H.   "   Duckworth, Battery Vermont, and Martin
                              Scott.
Company C.   "   Vose, Fort Cameron.
"   G.   "   Greene, " Gaines.
"   L.   "   Gallup, Light Battery, encamped near Fort
                              Pennsylvania.

These forts and batteries, mounting 52 guns, 20, 24, 32 and 42
pounders, extended over a space of six or eight miles, from Battery
Cameron on the left, near Georgetown and the Potomac, and Fort
De Russey on the right, near Rock Creek, and commanding the
Potomac at and near Chain Bridge, and all the roads leading to Harper's Ferry and Rockville. The transfer from the camp to garrison
duty was anything but agreeable to the regiment. By this, it was
compelled to forego all hopes of perfecting itself in infantry tactics,
and to commence with the rudiments of artillery, with which it was
entirely unacquainted. Instructors were furnished from the 112th
Pennsylvania, 2d Artillery, and very commendable progress was soon
made in the use of the new arms, but extended, as the regiment was
over so long a line of fortifications, the garrison at each post was
necessarily very small, and the duties severe. In many cases, the
turns for guard duty came every other day. In addition to other duties, a detail of forty men from the regiment was required to report
daily, at Battery Vermont, to complete the extension of that work.

The interest of the National Anniversary at Fort Franklin, was
enhanced by the presentation of a flag to Company A, Captain Taber,
the gift of the ladies of the Fifth Ward, in Providence. It had been
the intention that the presentation should be made by the Chaplain,
but in consequence of illness he was unable to be present, and in his
place Mr. W. P. Hood, a student of Brown University, made the
presentation address, which was responded to by Captain Taber.
The flag was then hoisted to the head of the staff by Lieutenants Bennett and Belcher, amid the cheers of all present. Refreshments followed, and the ceremonies were closed with renewed cheers for the

flag, and for the donors. On the 28th of July, Company G, Captain Greene, had a flag raising at Fort Gaines, which called forth patriotic speeches from Chaplain Clapp, Adjutant Tobey, Captains Gallup and Duckworth, Lieutenants Allen and Pierce, Dr. King, Sergeant A. J Manchester, (Principal of the Prospect Street Grammar School, Providence,) and others. The stars and stripes floated over the fort for the first time, and were flung to the breeze amid reiterated cheers.

About the 1st of August, an epidemic fever broke out at Fort De Russey, and twenty-two men from Company D. were at one time on the sick list. As the fever decreased at this post, it appeared at Fort Pennsylvania, and in companies B and K, for some time after the details of the day were made, not half a dozen men from both could be mustered for company drill. On the 6th of August, Colonel Bliss having been ordered home to take command of the 7th regiment, took leave of the Tenth in a general order, in which he tendered his thanks to the officers and enlisted men for the cheerful faithfulness with which they had discharged all the duties required of them, and giving assurances of his entire satisfaction with their conduct while under his command. On the departure of Colonel Bliss, Lieutenant Colonel Shaw assumed the command, and on the 22d received a commission as Colonel of the regiment, Captain Hale being also commissioned Lieutenant Colonel. Colonel Shaw was a valuable officer, and discharged his duties with spirit. Ever watchful for the comfort of his men, one of his earliest acts was to apply to General Sturgis for a release of his regiment from the daily details of laborers for Battery Vermont, on the ground that the hard work and exposure to the sun, with the thermometer ranging from 100° to 130°, was daily increasing his already large sick list. A verbal reply to this application, through Lieutenant Colonel Haskin, was, in substance, that a requisition for "contrabands" had been made, but as they had not been obtained, the regiment must do all the work it was able. The details were therefore continued until it was ordered home. The task was a thankless one, which the men justly felt that idle hands in Washington might have better been employed to do. To dig, they were not ashamed. To endure any needful hardship and exposure, they were always ready; but they could not see the reasonableness or propriety of being taken daily from their duties as soldiers, and put to the service of common laborers, when there were hundreds of contrabands lounging idly about the streets in Washington, living at public charge, and rendering no return for what they received, who could have performed this same labor without detriment to their health, and with decided advantage to their morals. However, grumbling was no part of their desire, whatever may have been their sense of injustice; the orders to toil in the trenches were still promptly obeyed, and a large amount of work performed.

It was a pleasant circumstance, in this short campaign, that the regiment was officered by gentlemen well known as citizens to the rank and file. Their previous social and military acquaintance engendered a mutual regard that greatly facilitated discipline, and ensured order and becoming courtesy in camp. And while justice accords an honorable testimony to all the officers, for the manner in which they discharged their duties, it will not be invidious to refer

29*

particularly to one of their number, whose former position, as the chief magistrate of the State, gave increased value to the service now rendered. At the very commencement of our national troubles, Ex-Governor Dyer took a strong and decided stand in support of the government, and by personal effort as well as by earnest appeals, did much to arouse the spirit that burst into a patriotic flame all over the State. In the organization of the National Guard, he actively engaged, and was chosen Captain of the Fourth Ward company, which, under his command, was brought into fine discipline. In volunteering without hesitation or delay, to meet a crisis which was then believed to involve the serious consequences of the battle-field, he set a meritorious example widely appreciated, and that, in its beneficial effects, was immediately visible. As soon as it was known that he had done so, the ranks of his company were filled, including fifty-nine young men from Brown University and the upper classes of the Providence High School. With a just comprehension of the obligations of an officer, and with a deep sense of the more than ordinary responsibilities that rested upon him, he maintained towards the men under his command the relations of an interested friend. By timely counsel to the inexperienced, by watchful care of their health, and by manly moral courage in sustaining their rights, he secured universal confidence and respect; and among the recollections of three months, by no means free from vexations and trials, the intercourse between the commander and the privates of company B will ever be preserved by the latter in grateful memories.

Reference has already been made to the Chaplain, whose duties were so varied and so usefully performed. It is due to those with whom he was associated, to add, that his situation was rendered exceedingly pleasant by the cordial and hearty support given him by every officer in the regiment; and though attendance upon Sabbath worship was never coerced, the congregations were uniformly large, the hearing attentive, and the direct and indirect effect, in the highest degree, satisfactory. The beneficial results were seen not merely on the Lord's day, in the quiet of the camp, and in other external signs of respect for holy time, but in the vocabulary of the week day, and the homelike manner of passing the hours when not on duty. At the close of the day, instead of gathering in knots for the indulgence of boisterous vulgarity, or paining sensitive ears with obscene songs, groups might often be seen, as the evening twilight gathered, blending their voices in some favorite hymn, or filling the air with patriotic strains. The fruits of the Chaplain's labors demonstrated the fact, that with the office properly filled, and the sympathetic support of officers who understand the value of the moral element in the discipline and effectiveness of a regiment, it is possible to maintain as high a standard of character in the camp as is found among a corresponding number of persons exposed to the temptations of civic life. But without such chaplains and such officers, results like these are impossible.

The term for which the Tenth volunteered had now nearly expired, and on the 21st of August, Colonel Shaw received a note from Lieutenant Colonel Haskin, A. D. C., asking if the regiment would be willing to be sworn in for an extra term of from two to four weeks, until it could be relieved by another regiment, and that one be instructed in the heavy artillery drill. To this a negative answer was given, the reasons for which the following letter explains :

HEAD-QUARTERS 10TH R I, VOLS.,
Fort Pa., Aug. 22, 1862.

COLONEL:—Yours of the 21st, requesting the regiment to remain two or three weeks or one month after the expiration of their term of service, is received, and has been laid before the regiment. I regret to say that it has not met their approbation, though, when all the circumstances are considered, I am not surprised at the result.

You will remember that the regiment started from Rhode Island at twenty-four hours' notice, coming only for the emergency, and expecting to be relieved within a month. Many of them left important business matters and permanent situations that they feel must be attended to. They will have staid, on the 26th instant, the longest time, as they understood it when they left home, that would possibly be required of them, and have made their arrangements expecting to be at home at that time. We have many amongst us, who are expecting positions in the regiments to be sent from our State, and many that are now being offered by many of the towns. These all wish to go. The epidemic fever which now prevails at Fort Pennsylvania, has a great influence. Sick men always wish to go home. Under these circumstances, I trust you will do the regiment the justice to believe that its disinclination to stay is not from any lack of patriotism, or desire to comply with every wish of the government. So much we think was manifested by the readiness with which they volunteered for what then appeared immediate, active service, and the cheerfulness with which they have served through the longest time mentioned as the limit of our stay. I trust our reply, when thus explained, will meet the approbation of General Barnard.

I am, sir, very respectfully,
Your obedient servant,

(Signed,)   JAMES SHAW, JR.,
Lieut. Col. Commanding.

To Lieut. Colonel Haskin, A. D. C.

This reply was perfectly satisfactory to Colonel Haskin, who said that he did not think the regiment should have been called upon to stay, and that, had General Barnard (who had just assumed the command) understood the circumstances, he would not have made the request.

But though these reasons were entirely sufficient in the sight of military men on the spot, who perfectly understood the case, there were those who persisted in continuing to ask, and often in a cynical spirit, " Why did you not stay ?" " How is it that you come home just now ?" These questions were answered by the Chaplain, and his reply is here quoted : " They came home because their work was done. They went out to defend the Capital for three months, and so far as God gave them the ability, they did it. It was all they had to do. It was everything they were called to do. The regiment did its work, and received the commendations of those who had its direction. It went where it was ordered, and did what it was ordered, nobly and soldierly. That the regiment did not go into battle was not its fault. It was placed where the exigencies of the service required, and the labors performed were not mere sportive recreations. It was not the kind of work they had expected. But, nevertheless, without saying what they liked or disliked, they did it cheerfully; and cheerful and ready obedience are the true qualifications of the soldier. It is easy to criticise. Let those who do so, go and see if they can do better." For vindication, if such be necessary, this is sufficient.

On the 24th of August, the 113th New York took their post at the several forts and batteries, and on the 25th, the 10th Rhode Island and the 10th battery started for home, passing through Baltimore, Harrisburg and Easton to Elizabethport. There, a steamer was taken for Providence, where the regiment and battery arrived on the morning of the 28th. A pleasant reception awaited them from expectant friends. A salute of thirty-four guns was fired by a section of battery H, under command of Lieutenant Thomas S. Anthony. The First Ward Light Guard, Captain Nathan J. Smith, performed escort duty, and accompanied by the Marine Artillery, the regiment marched to Exchange Place, where they were dismissed to their several armories, to partake of generous hospitalities. They were mustered out of service September 1st. The regiment returned with 674 men, twenty-five reported as unfit for duty, and three left behind in hospitals sick. Two died, viz., Frederick Atwood, of Providence, at the hospital in Georgetown, July 30th, of typhoid fever; and Matthew M. Meggett, of Pawtucket, at Fort Pennsylvania, of the fever then prevailing. The remains of both were brought home. Both of the deceased were good men, faithful soldiers, and highly esteemed. Mr. Meggett had been a student in Brown University, and intended, when his studies were completed, to prepare himself for the christian ministry. His sickness was borne with christian fortitude, and his departure peaceful.

In his final report to the Governor, Colonel Shaw says: "Of the character and conduct of the regiment, I cannot speak in too high praise. It was all that could be asked. The guard-house was an almost useless institution. We were permitted to perform but an humble part in the great struggle for all that we hold most dear; but I hope that that part was well done, and that it will meet your approval and the approval of the citizens of our honored State."

ELEVENTH REGIMENT RHODE ISLAND VOLUNTEERS.

FIELD AND STAFF OFFICERS,

(Commissioned and Non-commissioned.)

Colonel—EDWIN METCALF. Colonel, 3d H. A., November 11th, 1862.
Colonel—HORATIO ROGERS, Jr.
Colonel—GEORGE E. CHURCH, 1862.
Lieutenant Colonel—JOHN T. PITMAN.

Major—NATHAN F. Moss. Promoted from Captain, November 5th, 1862.

Adjutant—ROBERT FESSENDEN.

Quartermaster—JOHN L. CLARK. 1st Lieutenant, 11th R. I.; resigned, October 1st, 1862; 1st Lieutenant and Quartermaster, 12th R. I. regiment, October 9th, 1862.

Quartermaster—HENRY S. OLNEY. 1st Lieutenant, 3d H. A., January 29th, 1862; resigned, August 6th, 1862; Quartermaster, 11th R. I., October 1st, 1862.

Surgeon—THOMAS W. PERRY.

Assistant Surgeons—GEORGE H. TAFT, JOSEPH W. GROSVENOR.

Chaplain—JOHN B. GOULD.

Sergeant Major—JOHN PITMAN.

Quartermaster Sergeant—SAMUEL W. TILLINGHAST.

Commissary Sergeant—JAMES ZIMMERMAN.

Hospital Steward—JACOB S. PERVEAR, Jr.

Captains —William H. Ayer, Charles W. Thrasher, Charles H. Parkhurst, Thomas W. Gorton, Jr., Hopkins B. Cady, Edward Taft, Amos G. Thomas, Nathan F. Moss, Joseph H. Kendrick, William A. Mowry, Joel Metcalf.

Various causes combined to promote enlistments for the nine months' regiments, in the summer and fall of 1862.* The disastrous issue of McClellan's campaign on the Peninsula had impressed on every loyal mind the need of new sacrifices and of more strenuous efforts. Still under the delusion that the failures of the Army of the Potomac were caused by inadequacy of force, the North believed that overwhelming numbers of troops must be at once mustered to prevent yet more fatal calamities. The timid gladly offered exhortations and money, in order to hasten volunteering which was to avoid the necessity of a draft. The short term of service attracted many whom duties at home and unwarlike tastes forbade to enter, for the longer period, on the duties of the soldier, while the enormous bounties offered by States, towns, and even individuals, rendered a brief devotion to the country not pecuniarily unprofitable.

The 11th regiment was enlisted during the month of September, amidst unusual demonstrations of patriotic enthusiasm. Meetings of citizens were held almost daily, at which men of all professions, disdaining the common exhortation—Go, came forward to urge the more effectual plea—Come. As the companies were filled, they went into camp on the Dexter Training Ground, in Providence. Here they learned their first military lessons, amidst a throng of friends who crowded the grounds, to cheer with every form of sympathy, the last few days the soldiers were to spend at home. From respect to the memory of General Stevens, then recently killed in battle, this camp was named " Camp Stevens." The regiment was organized by Captain A. C. Eddy, a staff officer of the State militia, and delivered to Colonel Edwin Metcalf, early in October. The appointment of this

---

* This sketch was furnished by a member of the regiment.

accomplished officer to command the 11th was very popular with the whole regiment. Every private and every officer learned to regard him with affection ; and it was with sincere regret that we parted with him, when, after commanding the regiment a little more than a month, he left it to fill a more important position. Lieutenant Colonel John T. Pitman remained with us during the entire nine months, and won, to a rare degree, our respect and confidence.

The regiment was recruited, almost wholly, in Providence and the immediate vicinity. Two companies, B and F, were furnished mostly by Pawtucket and Central Falls. Of the city companies, two, I and K, were recruited under the auspices of the Young Men's Christian Association. The quotas of the several wards of the city were distributed among the remaining companies. Of the general character of the men composing the regiment, it may be said, that it was fully equal to that of the average of regiments in our army. Whatever intellectual superiority may be inferred from an extraordinary amount of letter-writing, may be attributed, in large measure, to the men of the 11th Rhode Island.

Shortly before the departure of the Eleventh, a handsome regulation national flag was presented to it by the ladies of Providence, through Hon. William M. Rodman, who represented the donors in a neat and appropriate speech, and to which a suitable reply was made by Lieutenant J. T. Edwards. The flag bore on the field the motto, "God and the Constitution," and on the centre stripe, the name of the regiment.

On the evening of the 6th of October, the regiment left Providence by a special train, on the Stonington railroad. It arrived in Washington on the evening of the 8th. That night we spread our blankets on the filthy floor of the barracks, near the depot, and slept soundly, after the fatigues of our tedious journey. Before the order came to fall in, the next morning, almost every man had found an opportunity to tell, in a letter to his friends at home, how cruelly the government provides for the transportation of its brave defenders. From this pleasing occupation, we were roused by the order to prepare to march. We moved to a dusty plain on East Capitol Hill, and there pitched our tents. The regiment remained here until Saturday, when we broke camp and began a new march. Passing through Washington and Georgetown, we marched up the Potomac, across Chain Bridge, to a spot near Fort Ethan Allen, where we bivouacked for the night. On Sunday morning, we moved to a beautiful camping-ground, in an orchard, about a mile from the fort, where we pitched our second camp. After little more than a week pleasantly spent here, in drilling, we struck our tents and packed our baggage for a new change of position, on the 21st. Having camped for a single night in a field near its destination, the regiment took its position on Miner's Hill, on Wednesday, the 22d.

In these three weeks, the raw recruits of the Eleventh had wonderfully enlarged their experience. They had learned the wholesome lesson that the individual soldier moves in an infinitesimally small orbit, and that his importance is an inappreciable element in the events he witnesses. At home, he had relations of more or less complexity with society and the State. Here, he was cut off from all possibility of exerting large influences, and stood to his neighbor in no deeper relation than that of file-leader. To " cover square " was his duty to his fellow-man. The raw recruit had been marched into a field late on a chilly evening, and told that he might sleep there that night. He had found that this was easy to do, and that it did not give him an asthma or an influenza. This increased his self-respect. It was a manly, soldierly feat to scorn a roof and sleep under the stars, amid the falling dews. He had lain in dust and dirt, and had learned that this is not so really bad as it is unbecoming. The recruit had not simply entered into new hardships ; he had gotten rid of innumerable old ones. With a minimum of responsibility to bear, no forethought to exercise, no need to use his accumulated knowledge, he gave his mental faculties a genuine vacation, and exulted in the development of his bodily strength and endurance.

At Miner's Hill, the regiment was brigaded with the 40th Massachusetts, 141st New York, 22d Connecticut, a Virginia regiment, and a battery of light artillery. These camps were in near proximity to each other, the 11th occupying the highest ground on the summit of the hill. The brigade was commanded by General Robert Cowdin, formerly Colonel of the 1st Massachusetts, at this time a nominee of the President to the office of Brigadier General, and who subsequently failed of confirmation by the Senate. None of the men in General Cowdin's command were able to appreciate the motives which weighed with the senators in their rejection of this officer.

Miner's Hill was one of the military positions that constituted the defences of Washington. It is situated just at the North-west corner of the square area formerly embraced within the District of Columbia. The duties of the brigade stationed here were, besides the regular drill and guard duty, to picket its portion of the front of the defences, and to be on the alert to repel any raid which the enemy might suddenly make towards the Capitol. The turn for both picket and guard duties came to each company once in about eight or ten days. An abundance of time was thus left for drill, which our commanders did not fail to improve. In the forenoon, special hours were assigned for the instruction of the companies in the bayonet exercise, and in skirmishing, and in the afternoon, long and rapid battalion drills inured us to the fatigue of bearing arms. During the months of November and December, the regiment attained a proficiency in military exercises which no subsequent practice ever enabled it to surpass. The picket duty at this position was devoid of danger and excitement. Now and then a deserter from the Army of the Potomac, far beyond us at the front, was arrested in his vain attempt to reach his home, but no collision with the enemy occurred while the regiment remained in this camp. About 12 o'clock on the night of Sunday, the 28th of December, we heard, for the first time, the *long roll* In consequence of an alarm, occasioned by the approach of a body of rebel cavalry, a movement was made, in the vain hope of cutting off their retreat Three regiments, including the 11th, of Cowdin's brigade, made a midnight march of four or five miles to the front, remained under arms the next day at a spot known as Mill's Cross Roads, and in the evening were counter-marched back to camp.

Early in November, Lieutenant Colonel Pitman succeeded to the command of the regiment, in consequence of the departure of Colonel Metcalf, who went to Hilton Head, S. C., to take command of the 3d regiment Heavy Artillery. The vacant Majorship was filled by the promotion of Captain Moss, of Company II.

As the cold season advanced, the men learned the various shifts by which comfort is secured, even by dwellers in tents, in a country abounding in rain and mud. The neighboring pines yielded the material for stockading the tents, and even for building huts, which, well plastered with the adhesive *Sacred*, were proof against water, air and light. Numerous packages of creature comforts from the thoughtful friends at home, reproduced for us, as far as was possible, a New England Thanksgiving, and enlivened the winter holidays with pleasant cheer.

Although Miner's Hill had become somewhat of a home for us, yet, on the morning of the 14th of January, the regiment fell into line with alacrity, under orders to move to a new camp, there to perform new duties. The monotonous, unheroic, unsoldierly work of guarding a convalescent camp, was destined to be its service for the next three months. Picket duty was no longer performed; drill, except the scantiest, was of necessity neglected, and the military spirit of the men sadly declined. Far from the front, within the defences of Washington, it was almost as remote from any possibility of collision with the enemy, as the citizens of the Capitol itself. Veterans of the Army of the Potomac, old Campaigners of the Peninsula, as we afterwards found, envied us such a safe, snug birth. But we, being young in the service, and still afflicted with the verdant folly of military enthusiasm, had set our hearts on seeing the *front*.

The Convalescent Camp lies on the London and Hampshire Railroad, three or four miles from Alexandria, and about as far from Washington. Fort Richardson, and one or two other fortifications, overlook the valley in which it is situated. In January, 1863, it consisted of a vast number of tents of all kinds, covering many acres of ground, and disposed apparently without regularity. The place reeked with filth and vile odors. A great quadrangle of barrack buildings, fifty in number, was, at this time approaching completion, but had not yet been occupied by troops. In this loathsome camp were congregated soldiers of all regiments, just discharged from hospitals, awaiting complete recovery, in order to be sent again into the field. Their numbers varied greatly from day to day, reaching sometimes as high as six or eight thousand.

The authorities of the Convalescent Camp had found difficulty in its management, from the reluctance of the men to be sent to their regiments in the field. Men would absent themselves from camp in order to avoid the roll-call, which would include them in the squad ready to go forward to the front. Coercion therefore became necessary. A guard must be put around the convalescent patriots to secure their presence in camp. This was the service assigned to the Eleventh. For this purpose the regiment was detached from Cowdin's brigade, and placed as guards under command of Lieutenant Colonel McKelesy, an officer of General Heintzelman's staff, in charge of the Convalescent Camp. In this position, it was included within the command of Brigadier General Slough, military governor of Alexandria.

So long was the line of sentinels required to surround this vast camp, that one-half of the regiment was required to do guard duty each day. The work naturally became tedious. The deep mud and slush, and the horrid camp filth, rendered the operation of posting guards in the night formidable in no slight degree. The onerous duty fell to the soldier every alternate day. The sarcastic convalescents soon learned all the circumstances pertaining to their guards which were most convenient for jeers and gibes. The short term of service which, in their sober moods, they confessed they envied us, and the large premiums offered for even this short term, were made the theme for every form of taunt and insult, and flung into the teeth of our patient sentinels. The only heroic features in our position were, that we obeyed orders—the highest duty of the soldier—and honestly longed to be out of the odious service to which it had been our ill fortune to be assigned.

On the 23d of January, Colonel Horatio Rogers, formerly Major in the 3d Heavy Artillery, arrived in camp, and took command of the regiment. Though Colonel Rogers remained with us less than a fortnight, yet, in this brief time, he made an excellent impression on officers and men, and, by his enthusiasm for military enterprise, and his decided disgust with the work he found us doing, inspired some hopes that we might be marched away from the stench, filth, and obscenity of the Convalescent Camp, to the clear air of the camps on the Rappahannock. But before we fairly knew him, our second colonel left us, as the first had done, to command a veteran regiment in a more honorable field.

By a general order of Colonel Rogers, our camp received the popular designation of Camp Metcalf.

On the 3d of February, Companies C and K were ordered to the Camp of Distribution, near Fairfax Seminary. Though breaking camp in winter is by no means an enviable task, yet these companies gained, on the whole, by the change. The Camp of Distribution was, at that time, situated on the Leesburg Turnpike, a mile or two from Alexandria. Its site was elevated and healthful. The purpose subserved by this camp was, the distribution of the men discharged from hospitals, and the numerous stragglers, gathered from all parts of the country, to their respective regiments. On the 18th of March, the Camp of Distribution having been removed to the immediate vicinity of the Convalescent Camp, companies C and K rejoined the regiment.

At Camp Metcalf, the regiment enjoyed the comfort of Sibley tents, well stockaded and floored. The requisite lumber was procured from Washington, at the expense of the men themselves. By strictly enforcing the performance of police duties, a good degree of comeliness and neatness had been attained in camp. A fine brass band, composed of members of the regiment, was here organized, and after due time spent in the work of preparation, made its appearance at dress parade in the last days of winter. This band always remained an object of pride to the regiment, and did very much to relieve the tedium of its unexciting duties. Passes to Washington and Alexandria, both for officers and men, were not difficult to obtain. Our three months at Camp Metcalf were therefore passed in comparative luxury. But in justice to the regiment as a whole, it should be stated, that the prevailing spirit among the men was dissatisfaction with their duties at this position.

On the 20th of March, Colonel George E. Church took command of the regiment, and continued with it till the expiration of its term of service.

On Sunday, the 12th of April, orders were issued which at once produced a commotion, quite unprecedented at Camp Metcalf. Marching orders—to go we knew not whither—seven days rations to be taken, baggage to be cut down to a *minimum*,—these were startling innovations in the monotony of our guard duties. Sunday, and the two following days were spent in packing, for transportation to Rhode Island, all of our accumulated baggage which could not be carried on a march, and in vainly conjecturing what could be the destination of so many troops as we knew were ordered from the city of Washington. Less than three months now remained of the term for which we had entered the service. As yet, we had not seen the enemy, and had almost despaired of being gratified with that pleasant spectacle. Now, we were confident, our aspirations were to be realized. The regiment therefore fell cheerfully into line in the midst of an April rain, on the morning of the 15th, and bade a hearty and noisy farewell to the Convalescent Camp, of unblessed memory. The satisfaction of the men at quitting the ignoble service they had performed for three months, prevented much regret on giving up to others the winter quarters which they had taken so much pains to construct.

It was quite agreeable, on the wet and muddy morning, to be taken to Alexandria by railroad. Here we found several steamers at the wharves, and the bustle of embarkation of a considerable number of troops. The 11th was marched aboard the ancient steamer "Hero." On this venerable relic, we had the usual luck of troops aboard transports, crowded amid filth and wet, but were nevertheless abundantly jovial, indulging our last jokes on the Convalescent Camp. An afternoon's sail brought us to Matthias Point, off which the Hero lay at anchor during the night. Thursday was occupied in steaming down the Chesapeake. Other boats, carrying soldiers in the same direction, were constantly in sight. At sunset we rounded Old Point Comfort, and stopped a few minutes off Fort Monroe, to send a messenger ashore. Thence, during twilight and early evening, we proceeded up Hampton Roads and the Elizabeth River, to Norfolk, arriving about nine o'clock. After disembarking and waiting several hours for transportation, the regiment took a train on the Norfolk and Petersburg railroad, and early the next morning found itself in Suffolk.

Suffolk, commanding from its position two important railways of the South, had been occupied and fort'fied by the Federal Government, as the key of the important port of Norfolk. Its importance was well understood by the rebel leaders, and its defences had been established on a scale commensurate with the probabilities of an attempt to repossess it. It had been garrisoned during the winter by Federal troops, who had erected extensive fortifications, and mounted many heavy guns. We found the town completely surrounded by earthworks, consisting of numerous forts and batteries, which were connected by breast-works and rifle-pits.

About a fortnight before our arrival, a large rebel force under Longstreet had appeared before Suffolk, to attempt its recapture. Foiled in his endeavors to surprise the garrison, the rebel general had, as far as possible, invested the town, and commenced the construction of formidable works, apparently with a view to a siege. The complete investment of Suffolk was however impossible, because our gunboats had control of the Nansemond river, and the Dismal Swamp constituted, on the side towards Norfolk, a very effectual defence. Communication with Norfolk was, therefore, at no period of the operations, cut off, and reinforcements were easily and rapidly brought by rail to the very spot where they were needed. The necessity of securing the position against the large show of rebel force, was the reason why so many regiments had been ordered from the vicinity of Washington down the Chesapeake.

At Suffolk, the Eleventh was annexed to the brigade of General Terry, who commanded the western front of the defences. A camping-ground was assigned to it near the head-quarters of Major General Peck, not far from the bridge over the Nansemond, known as the Drawbridge. Here the regiment pitched, for the first time, its shelter tents. These tents had been furnished to the men at Miner's Hill, but had never before come into requisition. Stockaded with lumber obtained from houses destroyed in the town, they formed very pleasand healthful summer quarters. Our camp-ground was almost surrounded with valleys through which flowed brooks, furnishing abundant facilities for washing and bathing.

By an order of the Colonel, this camp received its name from the regimental surgeon, and was henceforth known as "Camp Perry."

Like all other towns of Virginia which have come within the operations of the contending armies, Suffolk presented a very desolate and repulsive appearance. Before the war, it had evidently been a dilapidated place, containing hardly a single building that showed signs of thrift and enterprise. Now all the activity in its streets was military. Very many of the houses and nearly all the public buildings were occupied as hospitals, quartermasters' storehouses, or as head-quarters of generals. Except the negroes, very few of the original inhabitants remained, and these few were mostly women and children. A large number of negroes had gathered here, many of them refugees from points further west and south, whose labor was usefully employed on the works which were in process of construction.

Our first impressions of Suffolk were wholly novel. Hardly had we stepped from the cars before we perceived, from the reports of artillery and musketry, that the enemy was not far distant. While we pitched our camp, a neighboring battery was keeping up a constant fire. By looking carefully into the edge of the woods which skirted the fields beyond the river, we could see the grey-coats themselves.

The regiment was at once set about duties wholly different from anything it had done before. At night, large details were made to work with the spade and the pick on fortifications whose exposed positions prevented all operations on their exterior by day. A detail of several companies was made each night, to lie under arms in the batteries, ready to repel an attack. All drill was necessarily omitted, the men needing the day to recover from the fatigue of the night. Frequently the regiment was ordered into line on some sudden apprehension of an attack, but as often broke ranks and returned to quarters. Except an abundance of fatigue duty, constructing and strengthening breastworks and garrisoning batteries at night, the regiment had little to do until the enemy withdrew his forces.

On Sunday, the 3d of May, a reconnoissance in force was made beyond the Nansemond, to ascertain if the enemy was still present in force. The Eleventh received orders to be ready to march, and confidently expected to meet the enemy. The regiment remained under arms during the entire day. From our camp, we saw the troops pass over the drawbridge and form line of battle in the fields beyond the river, while the skirmishers deployed, and, advancing towards the woods, soon drew the rebel fire. A scattering fire of musketry, with some artillery practice, was kept up till night. A considerable number of killed and wounded, brought in on the ambulances, showed that there had been serious work at the front. As the day waned, and no orders came for us to cross the river, we saw that it was as *reserve* that we had been acting, and that we should not participate in the action. At sunset, the regiment was marched to a line of breastworks on our own side of the river, and there spent the night without alarm. The next day it was ascertained that, during the night, the enemy had retired beyond the Blackwater, and that Suffolk was no longer invested.

After the retirement of the enemy, the duties of the regiment became somewhat different. Fatigue work still remained to be done. A line of strong earth-works which the enemy had constructed, four or five miles from the town, was to be demolished. The fortifications of the town itself were to be strengthened. But daily drills were now established, and the regiment advanced once more in military precision and discipline. Its dress parades were especial commendations. Details were sent out on picket on the road leading to the town.

On the 16th of May, the regiment was ordered to join a large force which had been sent out a few days before, for the purpose of taking up the rails on the Norfolk and Petersburg and the Seaboard and Roanoke Railroads. As the rebels had no military posts east of the Blackwater, a considerable portion of each of these roads was open to the operations of our army. Considering the immense value of railroad iron to the Southern Confederacy, the deprivation of so large a quantity of it was thought to be a serious blow. On this expedition, the regiment was absent from camp eleven days, bivouacking at various points near the railroads, and acting, with many other regiments, as guard to the working party. Once, during this time, our picket companies were attacked by a force of the enemy on the road leading to Zuni, and succeeded, after a sharp skirmish, in forcing them to fall back.

The term of service of the regiment was now drawing to a close; but its severest duty yet remained to be performed. On the 12th of June, a large force of infantry, artillery and cavalry, including the Eleventh, left Suffolk under command of Brigadier General Corcoran, and took its march eastward toward the Blackwater. During the next six days, these troops marched a distance averaging nearly twenty miles a day. The most plausible conjecture as to the object of this movement seems to be that it was a reconnoissance in force, preparatory to the evacuation of Suffolk, which shortly afterwards took place. The troops were halted and formed in line of battle,—once in the vicinity of South Quay; once near Zuni, and twice in the neighborhood of Franklin. On these occasions the artillery threw shell into the enemy works, but without eliciting any reply. At Franklin, a collision between our cavalry and the rebel pickets resulted in a few casualties. The manner in which this march was conducted seemed to be the one most adapted to weaken and disable the men, and weaken their confidence in their commander. General Corcoran frequently did not begin his day's march till nearly noon, and then continued it, with only the briefest halts, till late in the evening. Such toil, under the burdens which the soldier has to carry, and in the torrid June sun of South Virginia, was painful in the extreme. Under a judicious and skillful leader, a distance of twenty miles a day, for several days, may be accomplished, even under a burning sun, without greatly injuring the efficiency of the troops. But the regiments which General Corcoran led to the Blackwater returned to Suffolk on the 18th, straggling, exhausted and disgusted.

Arriving in Camp Perry, we found orders to be ready to break camp immediately, to move again, we knew not whither. One night was allowed for rest, and on the morning of the 19th, we left Suffolk in the cars. At Norfolk the regiment was transferred to the steamer Maple Leaf. We awoke the next morning off Yorktown. After disembarkation, we pitched a camp a short distance below the town, near the banks of the York river, outside of the fortifications. While at this position, we were intensely interested to visit the famous works constructed by McClellan, at the outset of the Peninsular campaign. But far more memorable were the traces of that other siege of Yorktown, from which the hostile general could not escape, and which honorably closed a long war, instead of commencing a series of disasters.

The evident object of the movement to the Peninsula was to threaten an attack on Richmond from that quarter, and thereby effect a diversion in favor of Hooker who was, at that time, manœuvring to prevent Lee from crossing into Pennsylvania. Most of the force which had garrisoned Suffolk was withdrawn for this purpose After a day of rest on Sunday, the Eleventh marched on the morning of the 22d, with many other regiments, to Williamsburg. That night we bivouacked near the battle-field. On Tuesday, we saw our companions continue their march up the Peninsula, while we, on account of the near expiration of our term of service, were distributed among the forts and redoubts of Williamsburg. Here the regiment remained till the evening of the 30th, when it was relieved and commenced its march towards Yorktown. After marching all night, it reached its camp at sunrise on the morning of the 1st of July.

At Miner's Hill, the religious needs of the regiment were among the earliest provided for. A large and convenient log building was erected for a chapel, and occupied for Sabbath exercises, and also for weekly social conferences, which were freely participated in by officers and men. The meetings on the Sabbath were usually well attended, and the influences of a primitive worship beneficial. During the entire term of service, devotional exercises were held by the Chaplain at dress parade, except when the weather or the separated condition of the regiment prevented. At Suffolk, meetings of much interest were often held in the open air.

Relieved from active duty, we now waited only for transportation, to embark for home. On the evening of the 2d, we broke camp and marched down to the wharf, where the propeller John Rice was already taking aboard the baggage. After resting all night on the sand of the beach, we embarked in the morning, and soon were steaming out of the Chesapeake into the open sea. On the evening of Saturday, the 4th, we entered New York Harbor, and anchored for the night in North River. During Sunday night, we lay at anchor near the eastern end of the Sound. Starting again on Monday morning, we reached Providence at noon, and disembarked among a crowd of friends, who had gathered to welcome us home. Colonel Paine's regiment of militia escorted the Eleventh to Railroad Hall, where, after partaking of a generous collation, we broke ranks ; and, in a few days thereafter, were mustered out of the service.

TWELFTH REGIMENT RHODE ISLAND VOLUNTEERS.

FIELD AND STAFF OFFICERS,

(Commissioned and Non-commissioned.)

Colonel—GEORGE H. BROWNE.
Lieutenant Colonel—JOSEPH P. BALCH, temporarily.
Lieutenant Colonel—GEORGE LEWIS COOKE, temporarily.
Lieutenant Colonel—JAMES SHAW. Jr. December 31st, 1862.
Major—GEORGE LEWIS COOKE, temporarily.
Major—CYRUS G. DYER.
Adjutant—JOHN TURNER. 1st Lieutenant ; resigned, December 25th, 1862.
Adjutant—OSCAR LAPHAM. 1st Lieutenant; promoted to Captain.
Adjutant—MATTHEW N. CHAPPELL.
Surgeon—BENONI CARPENTER.
Assistant Surgeon—HENRY KING ; resigned.
Assistant Surgeon—PROSPER K. HUTCHINSON ; resigned.
Assistant Surgeon—SAMUEL M. FLETCHER.
Chaplain—SAMUEL W. FIELD.
Quartermaster—JOHN L. CLARKE.
Sergeant Major—JOHN P. ABBOTT. Promoted.
Sergeant Major—DANIEL R. BALLOU. Promoted.

Sergeant Major—CHARLES POTTER. Promoted.
Sergeant Major—WILLIAM H. LINDSEY. Promoted.
Sergeant Major—JOHN F. DOWNES.
Quartermaster Sergeant—PARDON E. TILLINGHAST.
Commissary Sergeant—AMASA F. EDDY.
Hospital Steward—FRANK H. CARPENTER.

Captains—Edward S. Cheney, (resigned,) Christopher H. Alexander, James M. Longstreet, James H. Allen, George C. Almy, (resigned,) John P. Abbott, 1st Lieutenant George H. Taber, (acting Captain,) John J. Phillips, William E. Hubbard, William C. Rogers, Oliver H. Perry, George A. Spink, 1st Lieutenant Edmund Fales, (acting Captain,) Oscar Lapham.

On the 18th day of September, 1862, George H. Browne was appointed and commissioned as Colonel of the 12th regiment Rhode Island volunteers. On the 13th of October following, the regiment was mustered into the United States service, having been recruited and organized in less than four weeks. On the 21st of the same month, the Colonel, in obedience to orders, left with his command for Washington, D. C. Owing to a disagreement between the State authorities and the soldiers, relative to the bounty promised them, all did not leave that day; but those remaining behind joined it soon after its arrival at Washington. The command proceeded by way of New York city, Harrisburg and Baltimore, and through Washington to Camp Chase, a little south-westerly of Arlington Heights. Before they had completed the pitching of their tents, a furious storm of wind and rain set in, lasting two days and nights, and rendering their *debut* into military life anything but agreeable. Here they were brigaded under Colonel Wright in Casey's division of the army of the defences of Washington. Here, too, they were armed, receiving the old Springfield smooth-bores. At the end of a week they removed camp to Fairfax Seminary, some six miles distant, where they were assured they would remain during the winter. This incited them to make their camp as neat and comfortable as possible, in which they succeeded admirably. Their duty consisted in drill and picket, which was fast preparing them for the severe service subsequently demanded of them. There was no force between them and the enemy; consequently they must be on the alert, and General Casey is sure that all under his command practice his tactics. But this pleasant service did not last long. On the 1st of December, 1862, several brigades, including the one to which the 12th was attached, were put in motion for Fredericksburg. The march, which was one of uncommon severity and privation, was through Washington, down the east side of the Potomac, to Liverpool Landing, crossing to Acquia Creek, and thence to Falmouth. But five wagons to a regiment were allowed. In these were to be transported all the camp equipage, baggage, hospital stores, ammunition and rations of more than a thousand men, for about ninety miles. The inevitable consequence was that the regiment was out of rations long before reaching its destination. The first four days were pleasant, and though blistered feet, and legs and backs weary of their burdens, called forth many complaints and mal-

edictions against those who compelled them to take this toilsome
journey, when they might have embarked at Alexandria on some of
the many transports lying idle there, and been landed at Acquia in a
few hours ; yet nothing more serious resulted from it. Few men who
have not been in actual service have any definite idea of a real march.
They do not reflect, that the soldier must lug his arms, equipments,
always forty—and sometimes eighty—rounds of ammunition, from
three to five days' rations in his haversack, his canteen filled with
water, his knapsack stuffed with great-coat, dress-coat and change of
under clothing, his woolen and rubber blankets, an extra pair of
shoes, his cup and plate, and lastly, his tent— all told, no light or
convenient outfit. And cold or hot, shine or rain, strong or weak,
fresh or weary, and sometimes well or sick, these, though worse to
support than the " old man of the mountain," must be borne. The
rations, it is true, grow lighter day by day, but what if they give out,
as they did on this march ?

The sight, at the close of their third day's march, was a grand one.
The two brigades that had thus far preceded, were overtaken. They
had encamped on the southern or farther side hills of Pircutaway
Valley, and we on the northern. The whole formed a sort of Amphi-
theatre. When all had fairly got into position, at once camp fires
blazed up in every direction. The night was very dark, and this im-
provised illumination lighted up the objects around with a singularly
distinct and startling effect. The whole was heightened by the hur-
rahs and shouts of the men. The rabbits, which abound in this region, were constantly being routed from their hiding places, and in
their terror and attempts to escape, would run from one squad, or company, or regiment, to another ; and the men, forgetting their weariness and blisters, would put chase with a hurrah and shout, that
echoed among the hills till it seemed as if Pandemonium were let
loose. The darkness of the night, the fitful flash of the thousands of
camp-fires, the rushing to and fro of the soldiers in the chase, and the
echoed shouts, all produced a scene of grand confusion and brilliancy
rarely seen, and which will never be forgotten by those who witnessed it.

The fifth day opened rainy, and the roads became first slippery and
then muddy. Before nightfall, few had anything in their haversacks. The teams were unable to keep up. Lame, foot-sore, weary,
hungry, and wet through, the whole command were obliged to make
their bed on the wet ground in the woods. Late in the evening, the
snow fell to the depth of two or three inches, and before morning
it became cold, and ice formed to the thickness of half an inch. Sleep
under such circumstances was not, of course, particularly sound or
refreshing. But, even in misery, there are some silver-lined clouds.
Reveille wakened the stiffened and sore marchers, to admire one of
the most beautiful winter scenes ever beheld. The feathery snow had
adhered to the wet trees and shrubs, and been fastened there ornamented by frost work, so that when the sun rose bright and clear, the
prospect in every direction resembled some fairy land. All, for a
moment, in admiration of the scene, forgot their woes. But what
was to be done ? On inquiry it was found that there was no supply
train, and the Quartermaster's stores had been used up. His feeble

mules and five wagons over such roads, made but a poor show in dragging, besides their other load, rations for a thousand men. After much delay, the Quartermaster obtained from another regiment—which had the same number of wagons, but not near as many men—a breakfast, which, hastily devoured, all fall into line and are off, though their load seems to have grown heavier during the night. This day's march, however, though one of intense suffering, was not a long one. After about two hours groping through the bended trees, the whole force found itself on a high plain, raked by the piercing winds from the bay, here about four miles wide. Here they halted, waiting impatiently enough their turn for crossing. The morning sun had melted the snow, but by one o'clock, P. M., it began to freeze. The Brigade commander refused permission to use any of the surrounding wood for fires, till it became evident the men must perish without. The 12th were the first to take the responsibility, and vote fires on that occasion a "military necessity." All the other regiments soon followed, but even then so exposed was the situation, that they suffered intensely. About dark, part of the 12th succeeded in getting on board an open Ferry boat, and started for Acquia. The wind seemed fresh from the glaciers of Iceland, but the hope of obtaining shelter and food on the other side encouraged them, and they endured in silence. What was their disappointment on arriving at Acquia! The so called wharf was narrow, shackly, and covered with ice; not a building was there; the place was low and swampy, and exposed to the blast, and the few stationed there in tents seemed but little disposed to turn out in the night, even to feed and direct a thousand starving men.

At last, after earnest and somewhat angry remonstrances, rations were procured and loaded upon the cars, ready to be sent to whatever camping-ground might be selected. To discover a suitable spot, get the regiment off the swampy banks of the creek, and thread the way safely along the railroad track, with engines constantly switching and backing, and this at 10 o'clock of a dark night, was not an easy task. But it was finally accomplished. After a tedious search, the Colonel found a brook, and near by, on a side hill, a space where the trees had been felled and some cut up. This was good luck, for there were but two axes with the command, and the trains were on the other side of the river. The regiment was speedily brought up and pushed, by companies, in among the fallen timber. The snow was nearly six inches deep. But the hill, in a measure, broke the wind, and in a few minutes the hillside was luminous with camp fires. About eleven P. M., the train, with rations, reached the spot where the command left the track, and details brought them to camp. There was little sleep in camp that night, and one day's rations disappeared at a single meal. The bill for fuel, had it ever been presented to the Auditor, would have astonished that worthy gentleman. The smoke eddied and whirled and circled round and round, clinging to the hill side till it almost suffocated the poor fellows, but it was better than freezing. This spot was ever after known by the soubriquet of "Camp Smoke."

In this trying experience, the Colonel fared even worse than the men. While he succeeded in procuring food for them, he failed to obtain any for himself. With considerable difficulty, he succeeded in securing shelter for the night, on board a steamboat at the wharf, but was compelled to hold his fast for twenty-four hours, when some of the soldiers shared their meal with him.

Here the regiment remained three days, when, with the brigade, it was again in motion for Fredericksburg, in front of which it arrived the night before the battle, and bivouacked on the snow. Through the solicitation of Lieutenant Colonel Welcome B. Sayles, of the 7th, the 12th was, in the distribution of regiments, brigaded with the 7th in the first brigade, General Nagle, second division, General Sturgis, of the Ninth army corps, General French, General Sumner's grand division. But the 12th had hardly stacked arms, before an order came to be in readiness to cross the Rappahannock, the next morning at daylight, to attack the enemy in his works. To weary, lame, foot-sore men, this was rather severe; but the order was blithely obeyed. Ammunition secured and rations cooked, the men, at a late hour, sought brief repose; but soon the roar of artillery aroused them from sleep, and springing up and hastily swallowing a cup of coffee, they were soon in line, and on their way to the field.

The crossing, however, was not made until the next morning. The general plan of the battle, and the position of the enemy in the rear of Fredericksburg, has been described in another part of this volume. Once over the Rappahannock, the regiment, according to orders, pushed rapidly through Fredericksburg, and soon reached a position within fair range of the enemy's rifles. They had halted but a short time, when word came down from the right of their line, that another order had been given to advance. The 48th Pennsylvania was now withdrawn, and held as a reserve; and the 2d Maryland, which was in front of the left wing, after some delay, pushed forward to and across the railroad, and took refuge under the steep bank formed by the railroad cutting through the side hill. Passing the word along the line, the Twelfth hurried on at double quick, through the brick-yard and on to the railroad, in good order. Here General Nagle appeared, and gave the word "Forward," and the right wing, having a smooth field before them, pushed on under the Captains to the extreme front of the Federal lines, and within seventy yards of the rebel lines. No Lieutenant Colonel of the Twelfth had been appointed at this time, and Major Dyer, who had charge of the right wing, was disabled soon after arriving at the railroad, and was taken to the rear, leaving the Colonel without the aid of a single field officer. Meanwhile the left wing of the Twelfth, except the two extreme left companies, which were round the hill so far as to be partially hidden, being unable to pass in line over the regiment that preceded them and up the steep bank, moved by the right flank and filing left, went up a place in the bank less steep than the rest, and reached a partly level tract on the hill, where, again forming hastily in line, they advanced rapidly till they encountered a cut in the hill about forty feet deep and nearly an eighth of a mile long, running diagonally across their line of march. Following the example of the Colonel, they successively jumped into this as they reached it, and attempted to climb the opposite bank and reach the smooth field beyond. But it was too steep forsuch a movement, and the companies, in jumping down and attempting to climb the opposite side, became disordered and broken

up. The enemy, too, opened a most horrid fire upon them from an enfilading battery, with shell and grape and canister, as soon as they jumped
into the cut. After some little delay, the Colonel formed them in the
bottom of the cut and marched them by the flank down to its inter-
section with the railroad, and then on the railroad to the place where
the right wing crossed. There forming in line, they pushed up and
planted the colors on the extreme front of the Union line. The two
companies on the extreme left, round the hill, had not, it seems, heard
the last order to advance; but finding the rest of the regiment had
gone forward, moved up the hill and across the plain, into the cut
before spoken of, and remained there exposed to the fire of the battery that enfiladed it till evening.

About an hour after the Twelfth reached the front of the Union
line, a New York regiment, in moving up over the hill and plain before spoken of, was fired upon by the enemy's batteries, and several
shells exploded directly in its ranks, making sad havoc. The men
threw themselves flat upon the ground, but soon sprung up, and mis-
taking the Union forces in the front for the enemy, discharged a volley directly among their friends, by which several were killed and
wounded. The Twelfth had one killed and three wounded by this
sad mistake. The Twelfth remained in this position till evening,
when having fired away all their ammunition, and the other regiments
having decided to withdraw, they filed into the rear of the retreating
column, and returned to the position they occupied the night previous,
on Sophia street. Here, before leaving, a hospital had been established in the African Church. It was sad enough to find it so completely filled with tenants, but too many of whom were from the ranks
of the Twelfth. The roll was called and reports made, when it appeared, that of those who, a few hours before, marched out with the
regiment, one hundred and nine were either killed or wounded.
Among them were the manly and brave Lieutenants, Briggs and Hopkins, who fell when they had nearly reached the front.

As a regiment, the men had stood up nobly, and but for the broken
and impracticable nature of the ground the left wing had to pass
over, all would have swept up in an unbroken line. Some few had
faltered, but the number was small, although it was their first experience on the field, and they were in the very centre and hottest part
of one of the most sanguinary battles of the war. Many of the officers and men distinguished themselves for coolness and daring in
the face of a murderous fire. Besides the two just named, the Colonel in his official report to General Nagle, particularly mentions Captains Cheney and Hubbard, Lieutenants Lawton, Roberts, Alexander,
Pendleton, Bucklin, Tabor and Abbott, Sergeant Major Potter, and
Serjeants Ballou, Cole and Pollard. General Nagle, in his report to
General Sturgis, commends the regiment for behaving well, and doing
"more service than was expected from raw troops." And he adds,
"Colonel Brown, who was the only field officer, (Major Dyer having
been disabled before going into action,) is entitled to much praise for
his personal conduct." The brigade to which the 12th was attached
lost 522 men, or one-fifth of the whole number.

Subsequent to the battle, the regiment remained in Fredericksburg
two days, and on Monday night, 15th of December, re-crossed the

river, the brigade covering the retreat of the centre. For several weeks after, the regiment suffered severely from want of suitable shelter, and a deficiency in food. The weather was inclement, fuel not easy to be obtained, and protection from the storms and piercing winds of the most miserable kind. To men in health, the situation was sufficiently trying, but to the sick and dying, it was heart rending. Only those who passed through the experience can fully comprehend the destitution and absolute horrors of those weeks. Men who suffered thus deserve well of their country.

On the 8th of January, 1863, Lieutenant Colonel James Shaw, Jr. joined the regiment, and through the residue of its term of service, showed that the appointing power had not misjudged his qualities as an officer. In the second advance on Fredericksburg, January 20th, the 12th was to have participated; but the storm setting in before called to move, it fortunately escaped the muddy experience to which other portions of the army were subjected. January passed, with the usual routine of picket and other duties, and on the 9th of February, the Ninth Army Corps, including the 12th Rhode Island, withdrew from the Rappahannock, and embarking at Acquia Creek, steamed to Newport News, and encamped on the banks of the James River. There was nothing in the memories of the past to awaken regret at the change. A miserable plain of alternate mire and frost had been given up for camps finely situated, pure air and good water. New "A" tents took the place of the poor concerns that were pervious alike to rain, snow and wind. The Corps gained by the operation in spirits and discipline, and in the advantage of both the 12th shared. The original destination of the 9th Corps was North Carolina; but when General Burnside was assigned to the Department of the Ohio, he insisted that his old corps should go with him. His wish was granted, and thus it became the fortune of the 12th and 7th Rhode Island to enter upon a wide field of duty in the West. On the 25th of March, the regiment proceeded by steamer to Baltimore, and thence by rail, via Pittsburg and Columbus, to Cincinnati, where it arrived on the evening of the 30th, and received a hospitable welcome. The same night it crossed the Ohio to Covington, and the next day reached Lexington. From the 1st to the 23d of April, the regiment made the acquaintance by marches of Winchester, Boonsboro', Richmond, Paint Lick, and Lancaster. From thence it moved to Crab Orchard, where preparations were made for an advance into Tennessee; but suddenly the orders were countermanded, and others issued, directing a post-haste march to Vicksburg. The route lay through Cincinnati. The march was begun, and passing through Lancaster, Nicholasville was reached, when the 12th was detached from the corps, and ordered to report to General Carter, at Somerset. For Somerset it started, and reached there June 9th, having marched 100 miles in six days, and when the arms were stacked and the roll called, every man answered,—a pretty good evidence of its locomotive ability. The sum of the succeeding months, was almost constant marching hither and thither, with the enemy often near, and a daily expectation of a battle. At Somerset it was detached, and sent to Jamestown, where it arrived June 23d. Here the regiment found itself in proximity to Morgan's guerrillas, and by various movements held them in check. Near Neatsville, a train of wagons under Quartermaster Clark, returning from Lebanon with supplies, was attacked by a rebel force of sixty-five men, but defeated, and driven off by the guard of twenty-eight men of the 7th Ohio. The enemy lost one killed, two wounded, and twelve taken prisoners. Subsequently Morgan made an incursion into Indiana and Ohio, threatening Cincinnati, and causing great consternation in those regions. On the 4th of July, at day-break, the regiment was called to arms, the enemy being reported as approaching on several roads; but they altered their course, and passed through Columbia to Lebanon, pursued by the Union Cavalry. At a later hour, the regiment started on its return to Somerset with 20 prisoners, including one Captain. The 9th found it at Crab Orchard again, and the 10th at Dick river, and the 11th at Hickman's Bridge. But one day now remained of the nine months since the regiment was mustered into service, and its steps were turned towards home. Arriving in Cincinnati on the night of the 12th of July, it remained, at the request of General Burnside, for special duty until the 19th, enjoying again the generous hospitality of the citizens, when a final move for Providence was made. It arrived there on the 22d, and was warmly received. A salute was fired by the Marine Artillery; the streets were lined with waiting friends, flags were hung out all along the line of march, handkerchiefs were waving everywhere, and boquets and wreaths were scattered with liberal hand. Escort duty was performed by the 4th and 6th regiments of Rhode Island militia, the former under Colonel Nelson Viall, and the latter under Colonel James H. Armington. The procession marched to Exchange Place; the men stacked arms, and repaired to Howard Hall, where an ample collation had been provided and served up by L. H. Humphreys. A blessing upon the repast was invoked by Rev. Dr. Swain. Governor Smith gave a warm welcome to the regiment, and thanked officers and men for the services they had rendered on the field. Colonel Brown responded in an admirable speech, describing briefly the work the regiment had done, and predicting the re-union of "a mighty nation, whose arms will be more a shield for every citizen than was ever Rome in her proudest days." The repast over, the men were dismissed until the following week, when they were mustered out of service.

The Chaplain's office, as in other regiments, was of manifold character. Besides performing his spiritual duties, he acted as postmaster to the regiment, an important and highly responsible labor; and as he was supposed to know everything, and to possess ability to command anything wanted, an endless variety of questions were to be answered, all descriptions of articles to be supplied, and all sorts of service to be rendered; now distributing comforts from home, addressed to his care; now writing, or superscribing letters for the men; now supplying yarn to some provident enough to darn their stockings, and now hunting up a nail wanted for some tent arrangement; and all going to smooth out wrinkles, neutralize excess of bile, increase content, and serve the interests of the country. The government can have no better class of helpers in the army than chaplains, whose hearts are full of sympathy, and whose hands are full of good works.

31

During the term of nine months, the regiment travelled 3500 miles, 500 of which were on foot. Its record will compare favorably with any other nine months regiment which has been in the service during the war. Previously to its leaving Cincinnati, General Burnside issued the following commendatory order: "On the departure of the 12th Regiment Rhode Island volunteers, at the expiration of their term of enlistment, the Commanding General wishes to express his regret at taking leave of soldiers, who, in their brief service, have become veterans. After passing through experiences of great hardship and danger, they will return with the proud satisfaction that, in the ranks of their country's defenders, the reputation of their State has not suffered in their hands."

THIRTEENTH REGIMENT RHODE ISLAND VOLUNTEERS.

This regiment was ordered by the Governor, for six months service, June 16th, 1863. Enlistments were commenced, and "Camp Smith" established on the Dexter Training Ground, Providence. August 18th, the order was revoked, and the enlisted men transferred to other regiments.

FOURTEENTH REGIMENT RHODE ISLAND VOLUNTEERS.

[This colored regiment was organized as heavy artillery, and numbers 1800 men. The commissioned officers are white; the non-commissioned, colored.]

FIELD AND STAFF OFFICERS,*

(Commissioned and Non-commissioned.)

Colonel—NELSON VIALL. 1st Lieutenant, 1st regiment R. I. detached militia, April 18th, 1861; Captain, 2d R. I. regiment, June 1st, 1861; Major of same, July 22d 1861; Lieutenant Colonel of same, June 12th, 1862; Colonel of same, December 13th, 1862; resigned.

Lieutenant Colonel—RICHARD SHAW.

Major—JOSEPH J. COMSTOCK, Jr. Promoted from Captain in 3d R. I. H A.

Adjutant—JOSEPH C. WHITING, Jr. 1st Lieutenant, November 9th, 1863.

---

* The list of officers was incomplete at the time this page was printed. All the appointees had not then presented themselves for examination.

Quartermaster—JOHN B. PIERCE. 1st Lieutenant, October 27th, 1863.
Surgeon—BENONI CARPENTER.
Assistant Surgeon—JOSEPH R. DRAPER.

Captains –Joel Metcalf, Jr., Thomas W. Fry, George Bucklin, George W. Cole, Henry Simon.

First Lieutenants—Thomas B. Briggs, John B. Pierce, (Quartermaster,) Phanuel E. Bishop, Joseph C. Whiting, Jr., (Adjutant,) Zephaniah Brown, Charles H. Case, Charles H. Mumford, A. H. Barker.

Second Lieutenants—E. F. Aborn, Charles H. Potter, George Weeden, Rowland R. Hazard, George H. Burnham, Walter F. Wheeler, Daniel J. Viall, Charles P. Gay.

This regiment of 1800 men was organized under a general order of Governor Smith, by Colonel Nelson Viall.* The enlistments begun in August, 1863, and on the 28th of the same month the first company was mustered in "Camp Fremont," on the Dexter Training Ground, Providence. In the course of a few weeks a battalion was enlisted, which was subsequently expanded to a regiment. In September, four companies were transferred to "Camp Bailey," on Dutch Island, and from time to time, were followed by others, where they were thoroughly drilled in company, battalion and regimental movements. Here, too, as mentioned in the introduction, daily details were employed in working upon the fortifications, which the State was erecting under the authority of the general government, for the protection of Narragansett Bay. With the exception of about seventy-five drafted men, the regiment is composed of volunteers, and its general material may be judged of by the small number of deaths (four) and desertions (eleven), from the commencement of its organization up to December 3d. The nativity of the men is as varied as the shades of their complexion, representing eight States of the Union, besides several rebel States, Cuba, Hayti, and the isles of the Carribean Sea. The average height of the first six companies. as ascertained by measurement, is a little over five feet seven inches, and the average age of the same men is a fraction more than twenty-four years. They are

---

* Colonel Viall served as a private in the Mexican War, under his personal friend, the late Colonel Slocum, then Captain. and was promoted successively to corporal and sergeant in the regular service. At the breaking out of the rebellion, he was Lieutenant Colonel of the Providence Artillery. Upon the call of the President for 75,000 men, he raised a company, the command of which he declined. hoping to keep all the officers as they stood in the militia. which was done. He was appointed First Lieutenant in company B, Captain Nicholas Van Slyck, and served until the second regiment of volunteers was ordered to be raised, when, in accordance with the wish of Colonel Slocum, he was commissioned Captain of Company D. He was successively commissioned Major, Lieutenant Colonel and Colonel of the regiment. After the battle of Fredericksburg he resigned, and when the colored regiment was organized, he was placed n command.

i

well formed, with strong and compact frames, quick to learn, yielding ready obedience to orders, and in all respects giving promise of great power in the field. For the success with which the experiment of organizing and preparing for service the first colored regiment sent from Rhode Island, since 1776, has been attended, great credit is due to Colonel Viall, who, from its inception, devoted himself untiringly to the work.

Among the agreeable incidents of the island life of the regiment was a flag presentation, which occurred November 19th. A cloudless sky and a genial, autumnal atmosphere, heightened the enjoyments of the occasion to those who, by invitation of His Excellency Governor Smith, were permitted to witness the scene.

The visitors numbered not less than three hundred, and comprised His Excellency the Governor, and the gentlemen of his personal and the general staff, (including Colonel J. H. Almy of New York,) His Honor the Lieutenant Governor, a portion of the staff of the Major General, the Brigadier Generals and members of their staffs, several Colonels of the State militia, the Provost Marshal of the First District, members of the General Assembly and of the city governments of Providence and Newport, the President of Brown University, a number of our city Clergy, and a few other invited guests. The excellent American Brass Band was also on board, and contributed much to the pleasure of the occasion.

The Montpelier left her wharf in Providence about 10 o'clock, and proceeded down the Bay, touching at Portsmouth Grove and Newport for a few moments, to receive additions to the already large number of distinguished persons on board. Leaving the latter place, the party proceeded around Beaver Tail, and as the steamer approached the landing at Dutch Island, the Third Cavalry, under Lieutenant Colonel Parkhurst, were observed in line on the opposite hill-side of Conanicut. The bright sabres flashed in the sunlight as they were brought to a salute, when the distinguished party were nearest to the thither shore. About 1 o'clock the boat reached the wharf at Dutch Island, and the Governor received the usual salute of fifteen guns, fired under the direction of Major Comstock. Lieutenant Charles H. Potter, (officer of the day) was stationed at the landing in command of a company detailed to receive the visitors. Colonel Viall came on board, and welcomed His Excellency and those accompanying him to the Island, after which the landing was made in the following order:

Commander-in-Chief and Staff, Major General's Staff, Brigadier Generals and Staffs, Adjutant General and Staff, Quartermaster General and Staff, Paymaster General and Staff, Members of the Legislature, Invited Guests.

Upon moving to the hill, which forms an admirable parade ground, the regiment was seen formed in line. When the Colonel had taken his position in the centre of the column, one company was taken from the flank at right shoulder shift in column of platoon, field music in front, followed by the band. This company proceeded to the Colonel's Headquarters, and came up left into line. The Color Bearer, preceded by a Lieutenant and followed by a Sergeant, received the color, and returned, followed by the Lieutenant and Sergeant, the Company presenting arms on his appearance, and the drums beating "to the color." The Company wheeled into column of platoon at shoulder arms, and marched in quick time, directing their march to a point 150 paces in front of the right flank of the regiment, and then on a line parallel with the Regiment, until opposite the centre, when the head of the column turned to the left, guide right (directing flank on a line with centre of Regiment) and halted twenty paces in front of the Colonel. The Color bearer passed by the right flank, and presented Colors to the Governor. The Company retired by the left and rear to its position in line, the Band remaining with the Governor. The Governor then presented the standard to Colonel Viall, accompanied by the following brief address :

Colonel Viall, Officers and Men of the Fourteenth :

It affords me much pleasure to present to your regiment, our Fourteenth "Corps d'Afrique," this flag, and I feel confident it will be entrusted to as brave men as ever entered the service in defence of our country and its liberties. And I feel assured that but one thought will occupy the mind of every man in the regiment, and that thought is, *our country.* Let this flag be your beacon light, its stars ever to shine. I now surrender it to your keeping. Let its history be Rhode Island's history.

Colonel Viall, in behalf of the Fourteenth, expressed his thanks for the beautiful stand of colors, and promised that it should be preserved from dishonor or disgrace. The flag would be a perpetual reminder of His Excellency, and his zealous and untiring efforts to promote the welfare of the regiment, and would incite to noble deeds wherever in the battle's front it might be unfurled.

After the reception of the colors by the Colonel, and the passage of the same to the color bearer, the Colonel ordered "Present Arms," the music playing "to the Color," while the Sergeant took his post in line. The Color Company is under the command of Captain Bucklin, and the Color Sergeant is John Van Slyke.

The Governor then introduced to the regiment Hon. H. B. Anthony, as "the man to whom you have got to look for your increased pay."

Senator Anthony then addressed the men in an earnest and patriotic strain, expressing his gratification with their excellent appearance, and intimating that he should fulfil his duty in the matter touching the pay of the colored soldiers. He spoke of the colored regiment raised by Rhode Island in the War of the Revolution, that under Colonel Christopher Greene, received and merited the praise of General Washington. He thought he risked nothing in saying that this regiment would receive equal justice from the President and the Federal Government. The man who wore the uniform of the United States, who followed the stars and stripes to the field of battle, could never become a slave, but throughout our broad land, every man made in the image of his Creator, would stand forth in the liberty with which his Creator had endowed him.

Senator Anthony was followed by the Right Reverend Bishop Clark, Rev. Dr. Edward B. Hill, Rev. Dr. Barnas Sears, President of Brown University, and Rev. Dr. Leonard Swain, in brief and eloquent speeches, setting forth the mission of the colored race in this war, the value of time to a soldier, the practical issues of the great

31*

struggle, watched by the whole civilized world, and the great principle of inalienable rights set forth in the Declaration of Independence, which the ceremony of the hour re-affirmed.

The regiment then broke into column and passed in review before the Governor, making a very gratifying appearance, and receiving hearty applause from the spectators as they passed by. A half hour more was spent in looking over the grounds, calling upon the various officers of the regiment, and inspecting the progress of the fortifications, which was quite satisfactory. The Governor, for the nonce, became an artillerist, and sent a few shells and solid shot across the harbor, giving evidence of his ability in that direction, and the effectiveness of the works to resist a hostile invasion of our soil.

At 4 o'clock the steamer's whistle summoned the visitors on board, where many found, to their surprise and gratification, that the last item necessary to make the day one of the most pleasant in all their experience, had been attended to. This was a generous and ample collation got up under the direction of the well known caterer, Mr. L. H. Humphreys. While the visitors were discussing the contents of the tables, the boat put off, going around the North end of Conanicut, and down to Newport. On her return, she passed near the ships occupied by the Naval School, the members of which gave hearty cheers, which were returned from the decks of the Montpelier with interest. In the outer harbor, she passed under the stern of the captured blockade runner, Robert E. Lee, which put in for coal, while on the way to Boston in charge of a prize crew. After cheering the gallant tars, and receiving a suitable response, the boat turned her prow homeward, (stopping a few moments at Portsmouth Grove) and arrived in the city about seven o'clock. A detachment of the Marine Artillery, stationed on the Fall River Company's Wharf, under command of Major General Pierce, greeted the arrival of the distinguished party by a salute of fifteen guns.

On the 7th December, a battalion of the regiment, numbering 600 men, left the island under Major Comstock, came up to Providence, and went temporarily into camp at "Camp Fremont," preparatory to proceeding to New Orleans. On Wednesday, December 9th, the colored ladies of Providence presented the battalion with a handsome flag of yellow silk, bearing the artillery symbol, cross cannons, surmounted by the letters, "U. S.," and below the regimental designation, "14th Regiment R. I. H. A." Governor Smith, Lieutenant Governor Padelford, Major General Robbins, Adjutant General Mauran, His Honor Mayor Knight, and a large concourse of spectators were present. The presentation address was made by Mr. John T. Waugh, a colored native of Virginia, in which he spoke of the condition and capabilities of his race, and the opportunity now afforded for its vindication. "You are expected," he said, "to do your utmost to wipe out the foulest blot which stains our land. See to it that history writes that you nobly sustained the honor of the flag."

The speaker then handed the banner to Sergeant John Jenkins, of company A, who briefly and handsomely responded. He, in turn, handed it to Major Comstock, who, on receiving it, thanked the ladies for the gift, and expressed himself proud to be an officer in a colored regiment.

The officers of this regiment were passed upon by the Board of Examiners for officers in the United States army, established in Washington, at the head of which is General Silas Casey, a native of Rhode Island. The portion of the regiment left at Dutch Island was included in the assignment to New Orleans, and soon followed the advance led by Major Comstock.

·

FIRST REGIMENT RHODE ISLAND CAVALRY.

FIELD AND STAFF OFFICERS,

(Commissioned and Non-commissioned.)

Colonel—ROBERT B. LAWTON. Dismissed July 1st, 1862.
Colonel—ALFRED N. DUFFIE. Promoted to be Brigadier General, June 24th, 1863.
Colonel—JOHN L. THOMPSON, (acting,) 1863.
Lieutenant Colonel—WILLARD SAYLES. Resigned July 7th, 1862.
Lieutenant Colonel—JOHN L. THOMPSON. Promoted from Major, July 11th, 1862.
Major—WILLARD SAYLES. Promoted to Lieutenant Colonel, February 21st, 1862.
Major—ROBERT C. ANTHONY. Promoted from Captain, February 21st, 1862; resigned, July 7th, 1862.
Major—EDMUND C. BURT. Promoted from troop B, July 11th, 1862; mustered out of service, August 7th, 1862.
Major—STEPHEN R. SWEET. Resigned, April 7th, 1863.
Major—WILLIAM SANFORD. Resigned, June 14th, 1862.
Major- JOHN WHIPPLE, Jr. Promoted from Captain, June 27th, 1862; resigned February 17th, 1863.
Major—WILLIAM H. TURNER. Promoted from Captain, March 1st, 1863; on detached service, August, 1863.
Major—PRESTON M. FARRINGTON, July 11th, 1862.
Adjutant—JOHN WHIPPLE, Jr.
Adjutant—AUGUSTUS W. CORLISS.
Adjutant—CHARLES S. TREAT. From 1st Lieutenant, August 1st, 1862; resigned, November 30th, 1862.
Adjutant—EZRA B. PARKER, since June 18th, 1863. In Libby Prison, Richmond, Va.
Quartermaster—CHARLES A. LEONARD.
Commissary—LEONARD B. PRATT.
Surgeon—TIMOTHY NEWELL. Resigned, May 23d, 1862.
Surgeon—JAMES B. GREELEY. Promoted from Assistant, June 1st, 1862; wounded, September, 1862; honorably discharged.
Surgeon—WILLIAM H. WILBUR.
Assistant Surgeon—JAMES B. GREELEY. Promoted.

Assistant Surgeon—AUGUSTUS A. MANN. Taken prisoner, June 18th, 1863; exchanged.
Assistant Surgeon—NATHAN B. STANTON. September 18th, 1862.
Assistant Surgeon—ALBERT UTTER. January 16th, 1863.
Chaplain—FREDERICK DENNISON. Resigned, January 19th, 1863.
Chaplain—ETHAN R. CLARK. February 5th, 1863.
Sergeant Major—ALFRED S. CHILDS. Promoted to 2d Lieutenant, December 6th, 1862.
Sergeant Major—JOSEPH W. DEWEY. January 1st, 1863.
Quartermaster Sergeant—CHARLES E. ELLISON.
Commissary Sergeant—ELI E. MARSH.
Hospital Steward—EDWARD C. CAPWELL. March 10th, 1863.
Chief Buglers—EDWARD H. GURNEY, discharged for debility, February 25th, 1863; JOHN W. DAY.

Captains—Joseph I. Gould, E. C. Burt, Lycurgus Sayles, Robert C. Anthony, John Whipple, Jr., Charles N. Manchester, Augustus H. Bixby, P. M. Farrington, John Rogers, J. B. Wood, Joseph J. Gould, Frank Allen, William H. Turner, Jr., Edward E. Chase, Stephen R. Sweet, Lorenzo D. Gove, John L. Thompson, Arnold Wyman, John J. Prentice, William P. Ainsworth, Willis C. Capron, George H. Rhodes.

FIRST BATTALION.

Quartermaster—Leonard B. Pratt.
Sergeant Major—Edward E. Chase.
Quartermaster Sergeant—Benjamin Weaver.
Commissary Sergeant—Samuel P. Mason, James P. Taylor.
Hospital Steward—Nathaniel G. Stanton.
Saddle Sergeant—Frederic Ocherhausen.
Veterinary Sergeant—William Spooner.

SECOND BATTALION.

Sergeant Major—James M. Henry.
Quartermaster Sergeant—Thomas Manchester.
Commissary Sergeant—Ira Wakefield.
Hospital Steward—Joseph A. Chedell.

THIRD BATTALION.

Adjutant—George T. Cram.
Sergeant Major—Charles C. Harris, Eugene M. Bowman.
Quartermaster Sergeant—Jacob B. Cooke, Henry E. Newton.
Commissary Sergeant—Eli C. Marsh.
Hospital Steward—Edwin D. White.
Veterinary Sergeant—Edward Brown.

The First Rhode Island Cavalry was organized in the Autumn of 1861. Its camp was established at Pawtucket, where it passed the winter. In the work of enlistment, Major Willard Sayles, Major William Sanford, General Gould, and others, were actively engaged. October 7th, Colonel George Hallet was appointed temporarily to the command of the regiment, and directed to "establish a system of drill with swords and carbines, dismounted." November 4th, he was appointed Chief of Cavalry in Rhode Island, and Captain Robert B. Lawton, late of the U. S. Army, was appointed Colonel of the regiment.

On the 12th of March, 1862, a battalion under Major Sanford left Providence for Washington. In a few days the rest of the regiment followed. Uniting there, it proceeded to "Camp Mud," at Warrenton Junction, and for a time was constantly engaged in picket duty, scouting and reconnoissances, with an occasional skirmish. From there it went over into the Shenandoah. A battalion of 100 men was sent forward to Front Royal in advance column, to save bridges, and do any other work circumstances might require. They entered Front Royal just as the 12th Georgia Infantry was setting fire to the bridge on the opposite side. Putting spurs to their horses, the cavalry charged upon them with great impetuosity, taking 117 prisoners and recapturing twenty men and two officers of the 1st Vermont Cavalry. Captain William P. Ainsworth and seven men were killed, and seven wounded. Captain Ainsworth belonged to Nashua, N. H. He was a brave officer, and universally esteemed.

From this service, the battalion went to Manassas in July. Colonel Alfred N. Duffie, an accomplished French officer, succeeded Colonel Lawton in the command. Colonel Duffie immediately commenced a thorough course of drilling, which greatly increased the efficiency of the regiment. In August it moved to Rappahannock village, thence to Raccoon Ford, and thence to Cedar Mountain, when the rebels were encountered, and a sharp fight ensued. Major John Whipple and Lieutenant Barker had their horses shot. Lieutenant Richard Waterman lost one man killed and one missing out of his command. Six other men were killed, and several horses lost. The conduct of the regiment was complimented by General Banks. On the 22d of August, at the same place, it was in line of battle all day. At Groveton, August 29th, and at Bull Run August 31st, it was under fire. At Chantilly, September 1st, it drew the fire of the enemy, and engaged in the fight, losing two men wounded, and two horses. On a scout between Leesburg and Aldie, in October, Captain Gove encountered a superior force of the enemy, and was killed, together with several privates. In an affair at Beverly Ford, two men were killed.

December 19th the regiment received a handsome flag from the ladies of Providence, through Governor Sprague. The presentation by Colonel Tristam Burges gave unusual animation to dress parade, and the acceptable token of remembrance was received with hearty cheers. In a severe battle at Kelly's Ford, March 15th, 1863, great gallantry was displayed. The regiment charged across the river, repulsed the enemy, and took 24 prisoners. It also lost heavily in men taken prisoners, and killed and wounded. Here the accomplished Assistant Adjutant General of the regiment, Lieutenant Nathaniel Bowditch, received a mortal wound. Major Farrington, a brave and skillful officer, received a wound in the neck. Captain Allen Baker, Lieutenants George H. Thompson and George W. Easterbrook, Sergeant James E. Bennett and Corporal James W. Vincent, were among the wounded. Lieutenant Henry L. Nicolai, Sergeant Jeremiah

Fitzgerald, and private Joseph Gardner, were killed. The whole number of killed and wounded was 21 ; missing 18.

On the 17th of June, Colonel Duffie made a reconnoissance in force to Middleburg, where he encountered a vastly superior rebel force, and a severe fight ensued. On the following day he was attacked on both flanks, and in danger of being surrounded, but bravely cut his way through, and escaped by Hopewell Gap. Major Farrington, with 2 officers and 23 men, was for a time cut off from the rest of the regiment and after remaining twenty-four hours within the rebel lines, succeeded in bringing his party safely in. Sergeant Palmer and 12 men were also cut off, but rejoined the regiment without loss. The casualties were 5 killed and 9 wounded. Of the former was Lieutenant Joseph A. Chedell, a promising young officer, and universally esteemed for high moral qualities. He belonged in Barrington, R. I. Of the latter, were Captain A. H. Bixby, Lieutenants Barnard Ellis and Simeon Brown, Sergeant George H. Steele, and Corporals George W. Gorton, George S. Bennett, and Lawrence Cronan. Captain Briggs had a narrow escape from a bullet, which struck his sabre, held in advance while rallying to the charge. Surgeon Augustus A. Mann showed great coolness and courage in volunteering to assist in rallying the men, and leading a command to the charge. He was taken prisoner to Richmond, and released in November, 1863. In this action, Sergeant George A. Robbins, having charge of the flag, was taken prisoner, but made his escape after about a week of captivity. He saved the flag from falling into the hands of the rebels, by taking it from the staff and concealing it about his person. For this, and for meritorious conduct in the battle, he was promoted to be First Lieutenant.

The duties of Chaplain were very faithfully performed by Rev. Charles Dennison, while connected with the regiment. He resigned January 19th, 1863, and was succeeded February 5th by Rev. Ethan R. Clark. Mr. Dennison was subsequently appointed Chaplain of the 5th R. I. Heavy Artillery, and joined that portion of it on Morris Island engaged in the siege of Charleston.

Colonel Duffie having received the appointment of Brigadier General, Lieutenant Colonel John L. Thompson succeeded to the command of the regiment. He was a lawyer in Chicago, and at the breaking out of the rebellion enlisted as a private in the three months light battery that went from that city. He subsequently joined the 1st R. I. Cavalry as Lieutenant, and by merit rose to the command.

From the nature of the service, the regiment has often been long separated from the base of supplies, and subjected to meagre fare. Its marches have been frequent and fatiguing, and its spirit and conduct have given it an honorable rank in the Cavalry arm of the Army of the Potomac.

SECOND REGIMENT RHODE ISLAND CAVALRY.

FIELD AND STAFF OFFICERS,

(Commissioned and Non-commissioned.)

Colonel—AUGUSTUS W. CORLISS, (acting.)
Lieutenant Colonel—AUGUSTUS W. CORLISS. Promoted from Major, January 15th, 1863; resigned, and honorably discharged.
Major—AUGUSTUS W. CORLISS.
Major—ROBERT C. ANTHONY. March 25th, 1863.
Major—C. N. MANCHESTER. January 13th, 1863.
Assistant Surgeon—H. W. KING. Resigned.
Adjutant—EDWIN A. HARDY. Promoted to Captain, January 15th, 1863.
Adjutant—WELCOME FENNER.
Adjutant—WALTER M. JACKSON. Promoted to 1st Lieutenant, April. 4th, 1863.
Adjutant—C. E. BRIGHAM.
Quartermaster—WILLIAM McCREADY, Jr.
Sergeant Major—HENRY STEBBINS.
Hospital Steward—NATHANIEL G. STANTON. Promoted to Assistant Surgeon, April 23d, 1863.

Captains—Robert C. Anthony, George A. Smith, William H. Stevens, George W. Beach, Edwin A. Hardy, Peter Brucker, William W. B. Greene, George Henry Getchell, William J. McCall, Henry C. Filts.

August 31st, 1862, orders were issued by the War Department for raising the first battalion, 2d regiment, Rhode Island cavalry, to be under the command of Major Augustus W. Corliss, of the 7th squadron Rhode Island cavalry, (three months.) November 15th, orders were issued to make it a full regiment of three battalions. The first battalion was full December 24th; the second battalion, January 19th, 1863; and Major Corliss was promoted to be Lieutenant Colonel. The two battalions were ordered to join General Banks, and had all arrived in New Orleans in season to take part in the first advance on Port Hudson, March 14th, 1863. During this expedition, Captain William H. Stevens was wounded and taken prisoner, with three men of his company. The regiment was part of the force engaged in the Teche Expedition, during which it was engaged in the battles of Bisland and Franklin. The expedition proceeded to Alexandria, La., on Red river, and then to Port Hudson. During the siege of Port Hudson, the regiment was actively employed in scouting and foraging. On the 20th June, it contributed to a force sent out to protect a forage train between Clinton and Jackson, La. The force consisted of the 2d Massachusetts regiment, (250 men,) one section of artillery, 122 Rhode Island cavalrymen, and 250 men of the 6th and 7th Illinois cavalry. They were attacked by two Arkansas regiments, a heavy cavalry force and two pieces of artillery. Colonel Corliss was in the advance, and held the enemy in check, while he sent three times for the artillery to come up. He then went and brought it up himself, • and fired twenty rounds of spherical case shot, killing one of the enemy and wounding seven. He also captured four prisoners.

The cavalry lost David Goodman and Alexander Brenno, company A, taken prisoners. Lieutenant E. C. Pomroy, company A, was severely, but not dangerously, wounded in the neck and mouth. Frank Brucker, company A, was wounded in the shoulder slightly. In the fight at Springfield Landing, July 2d, the regiment lost one man killed, four severely wounded and thirteen taken prisoners, ten of whom were parolled. Those held were Lieutenants J. H. Whitney and Welcome Fenner and private John Graf. When the rebels took Brashear city, they captured Major Anthony and about 20 new recruits.

Like most cavalry regiments, this one lost more men on picket duty and skirmishes than in large battles. Hard marches and climate also aided greatly to diminish its numbers. Reduced below the minimum allowed, it was consolidated, by general order, July 1st, 1863, into one battalion of four companies, and united with the 1st Louisiana cavalry. The field and staff, consisting of Lieutenant Colonel A. W. Corliss, Major C. W. Manchester, Surgeon H. W. King, Adjutant C. E. Brigham, and Quartermaster William McCready, Jr., resigned and were honorably discharged. The officers retained were Captains William J. McCall, Henry C. Filts, George W. Beach and E. A. Hardy; First Lieutenants, J. N. Whitney, Charles W. Turner, John D. Hanning, Walter M. Jackson; Second Lieutenant, Frank Hays. All other officers were mustered out of the service. The battalion was finally united with the 3d Rhode Island cavalry, at New Orleans.

THIRD REGIMENT RHODE ISLAND CAVALRY.

Enlistments for this regiment were commenced in July, 1863, and a camp established at Mashapaug. August 18th, the recruits, 150 in number, were transferred to "Camp Meade," in Jamestown, on Conanicut Island. Recruiting offices were kept open in Providence, and Captain A. T. Bushee, formerly of the 1st New York Chasseurs, engaged actively in procuring enlistments in the country. On the 4th of December, 376 men had been enlisted. The field and staff officers were then as follows :

Colonel—WILLARD SAYLES.
Lieutenant Colonel—CHARLES H. PARKHURST.
Major—EDWARD STANLEY.
Adjutant—LIVINGSTON SCOTT.
Surgeon—JOHN C. BUDLONG.
Quartermaster—STAFFORD MOWRY.
Commissary—WILLIAM SANFORD.

At the above date, the roster of officers had not been completed. The destination of the regiment was New Orleans, to join the forces of General Banks, for which place it left the latter part of December.

FIRST REGIMENT RHODE ISLAND LIGHT ARTILLERY.

The importance attached to the artillery arm of the service, at the commencement of the rebellion, by the Executive of Rhode Island, has been attested by the work the batteries sent into the field have done. In long and wearisome marches, in picket and reconnoissance duties, and in the heavy sacrifice of life and limbs they have made, they have shown the prime qualities of soldiers,—promptness, endurance and courage. So much of their story has been related in preceding pages that brevity here will seem to be demanded.

STAFF AND FIELD OFFICERS.

Colonel—CHARLES H. TOMPKINS. September 13th, 1861; Chief of artillery brigade, sixth army corps.

Lieutenant Colonel—WILLIAM H. REYNOLDS. Resigned, June 26th, 1862.

Lieutenant Colonel—JOHN ALBERT MUNROE. December 4th, 1862; in command of Camp Barry, Washington, D. C.

Major—CHARLES H. TOMPKINS. Promoted to Colonel.

Major—ALEXANDER S. WEBB. Resigned, October 9th, 1862.

Major—JOHN ALBERT MUNROE. Promoted to Lieutenant Colonel.

Major—JOHN A. TOMPKINS. Promoted from Captain, battery A, December 4th, 1862.

Major—SAMUEL P. SANFORD.

Adjutant—JEFFREY HAZARD. Promoted to Captain, battery H.

Adjutant—CRAWFORD ALLEN, Jr.

Quartermaster—CHARLES H. J. HAMLIN.

Surgeon—WILLIAM T. THURSTON. Honorably discharged, April 6th, 1863.

Assistant Surgeon—FRANCIS S. BRADFORD. Resigned, July 18th, 1862.

Assistant Surgeon—JOHN H. MERRILL.

Chaplain—JOHN A. PERRY.

Hospital Steward—JOHN GIDEON HAZARD.

BATTERY A.

(Mustered into service June 6th, 1861.)

Captains—William H. Reynolds, promoted to Lieutenant Colonel 1st regiment R. I. L. A.; John A. Tompkins, promoted to Major do.; William A. Arnold, promoted from 1st Lieutenant battery E, December 6th, 1862.

Lieutenants—Thomas F. Vaughan, John A. Munroe, John A. Tompkins, John G. Hazard, Charles F. Mason, Gamaliel Lyman Dwight, John Albert Munroe, Charles D. Owen, Peter Hunt.

Battery A left Providence June 19th, 1861, William H. Reynolds, Captain, Thomas F. Vaughan, John A. Munroe, John A. Tompkins and William B. Weeden, Lieutenants, and 151 men. It arrived in Washington, June 22d, and was attached to Burnside's brigade, Hunter's division, McDowell's army corps. It opened the attack on the right in the battle of Bull Run, July 21st, losing 5 guns, and 2 men killed and 14 wounded, as related by Rev. Mr. Woodbury, in his history of that battle. The gun saved was under the command of Lieutenant Tompkins. On the 28th July, the company left Washington for Sandy Hook, where it relieved the 1st battery (three months men) R. I. detached militia, Captain Charles H. Tompkins. On the 11th August, one section, under Lieutenant Tompkins, was sent to Berlin, Md., and did picket duty on the Potomac until September 3d, when the battery was once more together at Darnestown, Md. On the 13th September, Lieutenant Tompkins assumed the command, Captain Reynolds having been promoted to be Lieutenant Colonel. On the 16th, Captain Tompkins proceeded, with two guns, to Harper's Ferry, and on the 16th, was engaged in the fight at Bolivar Heights, Va. On the 20th, he marched for Edward's Ferry, where he found the rest of the battery; and on the 26th October, marched to Muddy Branch, Md. The battery wintered at Poolsville, Md.; and, in March, 1862, after the operations against Winchester, shared the fortunes of McClellan's army on the Peninsula. It was engaged before Yorktown, at Fair Oaks, Peach Orchard, Savage's Station, Charles City Court House and Malvern Hill, and was the last battery to leave the hill when the army fell back to Harrison's Landing. After leaving the Peninsula, the battery was in the reserve at Chantilly, and on the 2d September, two guns engaged in a skirmish with the enemy. Another skirmish occurred at Hyattstown, Md., on the 11th September. At Antietam, on the 17th, the battery was engaged for nearly four hours within 300 yards of the enemy's line of battle, and repelled, with great loss to the rebels, a charge made upon it. The battery had 4 men killed, 15 wounded, and 10 horses lost. Lieutenants Mason and Hazard bravely worked at the guns for the want of men. The battery proceeded with the army to Falmouth. December 4th, 1862, Captain Tompkins was promoted to be Major, and Captain William A. Arnold, promoted from 1st Lieutenant of battery E, took the command, and participated in the battle of Fredericksburg, as mentioned on page 188. In the operations of December 12th to 15th, Major Tompkins was in command of the artillery on the right of the Lacy House, opposite Fredericksburg. In April following, he was assigned to the command of the artillery brigade in Brooks' division, consisting of Rhode Island batteries C and D, McCartney's Massachusetts, Hexamer's New Jersey and Rigby's Maryland. The brigade was hotly engaged at Marye's Heights, Fredericksburg and Salem Church. In May, Major Tompkins was ordered to the artillery reserve, to reorganize the volunteer batteries, some twenty-three in number. Upon the completion of that work, he was appointed Assistant Inspector and Chief of Staff of Reserve. In the official reports of Generals Sedgwick and Sumner, he was recommended for promotion for " meritorious conduct and bravery," and after the battles of

May 3d and 4th, was highly complimented by Generals Brooks and Sedgwick.

Since taking command of battery A, Captain Arnold has gained an honorable reputation for bravery and skill. In the sanguinary battle of Gettysburg, (see page 266,) the battery was fought with great energy and effect, until nearly cut to pieces, and there, and in the more recent operations on the Rappahannock and Rapidan, Captain Arnold and his command won deserved praise.

BATTERY B.

(Mustered into service August 13th, 1861.)

Captains—Thomas F. Vaughan, resigned December 11th, 1861; Walter O. Bartlett, January 24th 1862, resigned August 19th, 1862; John G. Hazard.

Lieutenants—Raymond H. Perry, George W. Adams, Horace S. Bloodgood, Francis A. Smith, John A. Tompkins, William B. Weeden, George E. Randolph, Henry Newton, Jeffrey Hazard, Thomas Frederic Brown, Jacob H. Lamb, James P. Rhodes, William S. Perrin, Charles A. Brown, Gamaliel L. Dwight, Joseph H. Milne.

Battery B was enlisted and organized under the active supervision of Colonel William H. Parkhurst, who was also appointed its Captain, which circumstances compelled him reluctantly to decline. It was composed of able-bodied men, capable of doing good service. On the 13th of August it left Providence for Washington. At Philadelphia it was received with marked attention, and partook of bountiful refreshments provided by the Union and Cooper Refreshment Committee. After arriving at Washington, the battery was assigned to General Stone's command, afterwards Sedgwick's Corps Army of the Potomac, and on the 21st of October, the left section, under the command of Captain Vaughan, proceeded to Conrad's Ferry, to support Colonel Baker, in the unfortunate battle of Ball's Bluff. In the temporary absence of Captain Vaughan, Lieutenant Bramhall, a New York officer, took one gun, fourteen men and seven horses, over the Potomac, and after severe labor, succeeded in getting it up a steep hill, into position. Here it was fatally assailed by the rebels, and after returning a vigorous fire until all but two of the cannoniers were shot down, the gun had to be abandoned. In February, 1862, the battery advanced on Winchester, and had a severe and fatiguing march.

After the resignation of Captain Vaughan, Lieutenant Walter O. Bartlett, an excellent officer, was appointed to the command, and conducted the battery through the peninsula campaign, doing good service. It engaged the enemy before Yorktown, and on the evacuation of that place proceeded to West Point by water, and thence continued the advance towards Richmond. It was present at the battle of Hanover Court House, as a support, and was under fire at Fair Oaks. It was in position at Peach Orchard, Savage's Station and Malvern Hill, having two or three men wounded at the latter place.

On the resignation of Captain Bartlett, Lieutenant John G. Hazard, who joined the battery at Alexandria, from battery C, August 30th,

1861, was commissioned Captain, and has since held the command. In the battle of Fredericksburg, he fought his battery with great bravery. On the 11th of December, he was in position to the right of the Lacy House, and during the day expended 384 rounds of solid shot upon the enemy's sharpshooters' rifle pits and covers, lining the opposite bank of the river. The next day he crossed over, and on the 13th took an exposed position on an eminence, where he opened upon the enemy, and continued firing with great rapidity for three quarters of an hour, when, by order, he withdrew to the position of the day before in the city. He lost sixteen men, and twelve battery horses. In his report to Captain Morgan, he speaks in warm praise of the bravery and endurance of the men, and of the gallant conduct of Lieutenants Adams, Bloodgood, Perrin, and Milne. The good condition and efficiency of the battery, drew from General Hunt, Chief of Artillery, a highly commendatory letter to Captain Hazard. At Chancellorsville, in the absence of Captain Hazard, on account of sickness, Lieutenant T. F. Brown held the command.

On the 23d of May, 1863, Captain Hazard was appointed Chief of Artillery, of the Second Army Corps, and in the battle of Gettysburg his brigade consisted of Company I, U. S. Artillery, battery A, 4th U. S., batteries A and B, 1st New York, batteries A and B 1st R. I., in all 28 guns. In this sanguinary action, described on page 266, the fire was effective, and the losses in men and horses severe. So, especially, was this the case with the Rhode Island battery A, that it became necessary temporarily to unite it with another. Captain Hazard's horse was twice shot, and his exposure constant during the battle. In the subsequent movements of the Army of the Potomac, Battery B, up to the close of 1863, has handsomely maintained a well earned reputation.

BATTERY C.

(*Mustered into service August 25th*, 1861.)

Captains—William B. Weeden, August 8th, 1861 ; appointed Chief of Artillery on the Peninsula June 13th, 1862 ; resigned July 22d, 1862. Richard Waterman, promoted from First Lieutenant July 25th, 1862.

Lieutenants—John G. Hazard, Richard Waterman, William W. Buckley, promoted to Captain battery D, Oct. 30th, 1862 ; Charles H. Clarke, resigned August 25th, 1862 ; Frederick M. Sackett, wounded at battle of Chancellorsville, Va., May, 1863 ; resigned October 6th, 1863. Charles H. Wilcox, honorably discharged for disability April 10th, 1863 ; Thomas F. Brown, transferred to battery B ; Robert H. Lee, resigned June 1st, 1863 ; Stephen W. Fiske, Reuben H. Rich, Andrew McMillan.

Battery C, after enlistment, went into camp for a short time at "Camp Ames," where it was joined by Captain Weeden. On the 31st of August it broke camp, marched to Providence, and took the cars for Washington, It there occupied Camp Sprague, engaged in daily drill, until October, when it crossed the Potomac, and encamped near Fort Corcoran. The rebels were then hovering around Washington, and occupied Munson's Hill, a commanding eminence near Bailey's Cross Roads, where they threw up an earthwork with abattis, but mounted no guns unless "Quakers." This, and other movements on their part, kept up a lively apprehension of an attack upon the Capital, and perhaps stimulated activity in measures for the defence, as well as for aggressive operations. Troops were constantly passing over Long Bridge and Chain Bridge, into Virginia, and making encampments along the Potomac, from below Alexandria to Langley's, a distance of about fifteen miles, so that before the close of November, an immense army was there gathered, and the safety of Washington ensured.

The battery shortly removed from "Camp Randolph" to Hall's Hill, and thence to Miner's Hill, near by, where it formed "Camp Owen," and passed the winter. The time was spent in acquiring proficiency for service in the field. It was attached to General Morell's brigade, General Fitz John Porter's division of the Army of the Potomac. On the 10th of March, 1862, it moved with the grand army to the Peninsula. Its history, during that and subsequent campaigns, has been so fully related in the preceding pages, that little remains to be said to complete the narrative. After the return of the army from the victory of Gettysburg to the line of the Rappahannock, battery C was assigned a post near Cedar Mountain, in full sight of the enemy's earthworks on the opposite side of the Rapidan, and commanding their position should they attempt to advance. When Lee made his attempt to flank Meade, and gain his rear, the battery fell back with the army, and from the 10th to the 19th of November, was constantly in motion. Lee, disappointed in his purpose, retreated, and the Army of the Potomac re-assumed the position it had recently left. In the advance upon the rebels, and in the successful battle of November 7th, the battery participated. It took position on the right of the road leading to Rappahannock Station, and opened an effective fire upon the enemy, which was kept up nearly two hours. Here two men were wounded, Corporal John Jenkins severely, and private John Seamans, slightly. On the 8th, three pieces crossed the river, and took up position in a fort from which the rebels had been driven. The other three guns, under Lieutenant Fiske, remained near the river on the hither side, to guard a Pontoon bridge. On the 12th, the battery moved forward, and went into camp near Hazle River, where it remained until the 25th, when it advanced with the army across the Rapidan,* and on the 27th again encountered the enemy, for an hour giving and receiving a sharp fire. In this action, Henry Nason, of Valley Falls, R. I., was severely wounded, having both feet taken off. The severity of the weather, the state of the roads, night exposures, and other causes, rendered this campaign of eight days one of unusual fatigue. In the campaigning of twenty-one months since leaving Miner's Hill, the battery has fought in the hottest battles of the war, in which the Army of the

---

*The first section, under Lieutenant McMillan, was detailed to bring up the rear with the 2d brigade, 1st division, 6th corps.

32*

Potomac has been engaged. Its losses in men and horses have been severe. Its varied record bears testimony to the courage and ability of
its successive commanders, and to the bravery of its officers and men.
In the advance by the peninsula against Richmond, it opened the
Artillery fire before Yorktown, and made the first offering of blood
there for the Union.

BATTERY D.

(Mustered into service September 4th, 1861.)

Captains—John Albert Munroe, promoted to Major, October 20th,
1862 ; William W. Buckley, promoted from 1st Lieutenant battery C,
October 30th, 1862.

Lieutenants—George C. Harkness, resigned March 3d, 1863 ; Kirby
Steinhauer ; Henry R. Gladding, mustered out of service, November
30th, 1862 ; William B. Rhodes, from battery G ; Stephen W. Fiske,
promoted to 1st Lieutenant battery C ; Frederic Chase ; Ezra K.
Parker.

Battery D arrived in Washington, September 15th, 1861, when
Captain Munroe assumed command. October 8th, the following
month, it marched to Hall's Hill, Va., and was attached to the division
of Fitz John Porter. October 12th, it reported to General McDowell, ·
at Upton's Hill, Va., and shortly after went into " Camp Dupont,"
where it remained until March 9th, 1862, when it marchd to Fairfax
Court House, and was attached to King's division the corps formation of the army having been organized, General McDowell taking
command of the corps, and General King assuming command of General McDowell's old division.

From Fairfax Court House, it marched to Cloud's Mills, near Alexandria, for embarkation for the Peninsula ; but the plan of operations being changed in some respects, the corps was ordered, March
29th, to Bristow, Va., to which place the battery went. There it remained two weeks, when it removed to Catlett's Station, and thence,
about April 28th, to Falmouth, opposite Fredericksburg, taking part
in the skirmish with Holmes' rebel force who held the city. In the
early part of June it marched to Thoroughfare Gap, Va., Catlett's
Station, Warrington, Gainesville and Haymarket, with McDowell's
corps, in the pursuit after Stonewall Jackson when on his famous
raid up the Shenandoah Valley. It returned to the old camp, opposite Fredericksburg, July 1st ; August 8th, marched from Fredericksburg nearly to the North Anna river, with Gibbon's brigade,
and returned four days after, having had two days' running fight with
Stuart's cavalry. About August 19th, it was ordered to Rappahannock Station, to rejoin McDowell's corps, having been detached from
that corps when it was relieved at Fredericksburg by General Burnside, where it arrived in time to take part in the engagement then going on. Thence it marched to Warrenton ; thence to Sulphur Springs,
taking part in the fight there ; thence back through Warrenton to
Groveton, where, on the evening of August 28th, a very severe engagement occurred, in which battery D took an active part.

In the battle of Bull Run, August 29th and 30th, the battery was
engaged from the commencement of the action to its close, suffering

severely in men and horses. It returned with the army within the defences of Washington; marched into Maryland under General McClellan, attached to the corps of General Hooker; fought at South Mountain and at Antietam. In the latter battle, Captain Munroe was Chief of artillery in Doubleday's division, Hooker's corps, and had the command of thirty-six guns on the right, that did so terrible execution on the enemy's left on the night of September 17th.

The casualties of men, up to August 28th, were very slight, but quite a number of horses were lost. At Groveton, five or six men were wounded severely, four taken prisoners and two missing. Several horses were killed, among which was Captain Monroe's. One caisson was so damaged by a shot from the enemy that it could not be removed, and was blown up to prevent it and its ammunition falling into the hands of the enemy. An exciting circumstance occurred in this action. The battery was ordered to take position on a hill, about three hundred yards from the road, for which it started at a quick trot, but just as it reached the foot, a cavalryman dashed down at a rapid rate, saying that the enemy had a battery going up the same hill on the other side, and a moment more showed them unlimbering their pieces. The battery was taken away at a gallop, behind a clump of woods near by, but before it reached there, received a pretty hot fire.

At Bull Run, during the two days, the battery lost eighteen men killed and wounded. Lieutenant Harkness was also injured. Lieutenant Harkness' horse was wounded; Lieutenant Fiske's horse was wounded and died soon after, and the Captain had two horses shot under him. At South Mountain the battery lost two men missing; at Antietam thirty-nine more were lost in killed, wounded and missing. In this action, the battery lost a large number of horses. From one piece all the horses but one were killed, and all the cannoneers but the gunner and one private either killed or severely wounded. This piece was drawn to the rear by the prolonge. While the prolonge was being attached to this piece, Lieutenant Fiske's horse was shot, and the Captain's horse, upon which he was mounted, received no less than six bullets.

October 20th, 1862, Captain Munroe was commissioned Major, and on the 4th December following was promoted to Lieutenant Colonel. Shortly after his appointment to the rank of Major, he was assigned to the light artillery in and about Washington, north of the Potomac, with directions to organize a camp of instruction for artillery, to which the new batteries from the States might be sent and be fitted for the field. With these instructions, he laid out "Camp Barry," containing about seventy-five acres, and provided with a hospital and stables for 1200 horses. Here a system of instruction in tactics has been established. All the eastern armies are supplied with light artillery from this camp, and a sufficient number of batteries are kept on hand to supply any deficiencies that may occur from loss or otherwise. When batteries in the field become depleted in numbers or broken down, they are sent to Camp Barry to be refitted for service. In various engagements, Colonel Munroe had his garments perforated with bullets, but escaped without wound.

On the 30th October, 1862, Lieutenant William W. Buckley, of battery C, was appointed Captain of battery D, and reached his command just in season to participate in the battle of Fredericksburg, December 13th. He was subsequently assigned with it to Burnside's command in the west, where it has been doing constant service, and has gained an excellent reputation, ranking with the best batteries in that department. Since its organization, about forty officers have been commissioned from it.

BATTERY E.

(Mustered into service September 30th, 1861.)

Captains —George E. Randolph, promoted from 1st Lieutenant, battery C; Chief of artillery in Kearny's division, 1862; Chief of the artillery brigade, with staff, in third army corps of the Potomac, April 17th, 1863.

Lieutenants—Walter O. Bartlett, promoted to Captain of battery B; William Albert Arnold, promoted to Captain of battery A, December 6th, 1862; John K. Bucklyn, severely wounded in battle of Gettysburg, Penn., July 2d, 1863; John A. Perry, appointed Chaplain, January 13th, 1862; Pardon S. Jastram, Assistant Adjutant General on Captain Randolph's staff, artillery brigade, third corps, May, 1863; Israel R. Sheldon; James F. Allen; George C. DeKay, (declined the appointment;) J. Russell Field; Benjamin Freeborn.

Battery E had its encampment at "Camp Greene," and left for Washington early in October, 1861. It remained at "Camp Sprague" until November 5th, when it passed into Virginia, and established a camp near Fort Lyon, southwest of Alexandria, which was named "Camp Webb." At a later day, the camp was moved a short distance east, where stables were erected, and the battery passed the winter. It was now in Heintzelman's division, and not far from his head-quarters. A night reconnoissance to Pohick Church, a distance of about fourteen miles, November 11th, was a first experience of the kind, and as there was an expectation of meeting the enemy, very fairly tested the spirit of the men. At midnight the preparations were made, and at 3 o'clock A. M. the battery was on the move. The cavalry accompanying the expedition had a brush with the rebels, and lost several men. The battery and infantry did not engage, and returned to camp at night, after a fatiguing march over muddy roads. On the 4th of April, 1862, the battery accompanied Hamilton's division (formerly Heintzelman's) to the Peninsula, in the general movement of the army of the Potomac on Richmond. Its work during the four months that succeeded has been elsewhere related. At Yorktown, General Kearny relieved General Hamilton, and thenceforth, until the death of that gallant officer, the battery was closely identified with his movements. The march to Williamsburg, after the evacuation of Yorktown, was one of great fatigue, on account of the bad state of the roads, and though ten or twelve horses were attached to each piece, it was impossible to reach a position in season to support Hooker, as was designed. From the 7th of May to the 4th of

July, the battery was constantly on the alert. It passed through the fiery ordeal of the memorable " seven days" that swung the right wing of the army round to the James river, and closed with the battle of Malvern Hill. In that last engagement, the battery lost one man killed and four wounded. It was next engaged, (after the evacuation of the Peninsula,) with General Hooker at the battle of Bristow's Station, August 27th, driving the enemy and losing two men killed and two wounded. Then came Bull Run battle, number two, losing two men killed and three wounded. Then followed the battle of Chantilly, where the battery made a very destructive fire. Here, Captain Randolph was in command of all the artillery of Kearny's division, consisting of Rhode Island battery E, Bramhall's New York, Clark's New Jersey, Seeley's 4th United States and Livingston's 3d United States.

The hard work of this corps on the Peninsula, and the casualties of Pope's campaign, had greatly reduced its efficiency, and after the battle of Chantilly it was placed in the defences of Washington to recuperate. In October, the battery was at Poolesville, Md., and on the 5th December, at Stafford Court House, Va. Its gallantry in the battles of Fredericksburg, Chancellorsville and Gettysburg, has been described, pages 188, 238, 266. In the advance of the army upon the rebels, November 7th, 1863, it fought at Kelly's Ford with galling effect, as it did again after crossing the Rapidan, and encountering the enemy near Mile Run, November 27th.

After the battle of Chancellorsville, Captain Randolph was appointed to the command of the artillery brigade of the third army corps, having a regular brigade staff, consisting of Assistant Adjutant General, Commissary, Quartermaster, Ordnance officer, Assistant Inspector and Surgeon. Lieutenant Jastram, who commanded the battery at Chancellorsville and fought it with great skill, fills the position of Assistant Adjutant General. In this new and responsible command, Captain Randolph has shown rare executive ability. Since the war begun, he has been twice wounded,—first at Bull Run, July 21st, 1861, and second, at Gettysburg. At Gettysburg, battery E was commanded by Lieutenant John K. Bucklyn, where he was severely wounded. Both there and in the more recent actions of the 7th and 27th November, he displayed the qualities of a brave and efficient officer.

BATTERY F.

(Mustered into service October 29th, 1861.)

Captain—James Belger.

Lieutenants—Charles H. Pope, resigned October 6th, 1862 ; Thomas Simpson, George W. Field, resigned October 6th, 1862 ; William A. Arnold, resigned May 4th, 1863 ; Peter C. Smith, Philip S. Chase, Albert E. Adams.

Battery F was sent to Washington early in November, 1861, and quartered at Camp Sprague, where it received its guns, and Captain

Belger assumed command. After a few weeks, it proceeded to Camp California, near Alexandria, Va. Here it remained until ordered to join the Burnside expedition, when it went to Annapolis, Md , and on the 9th of January, 1862, the men and horses were embarked on board the steamer "George Peabody," and the battery on board the schooner "James Brady. It shared the discomforts and perils of the memorable voyage to Hatteras Inlet, where it landed in a violent storm, from which the men suffered severely. It remained at "Camp Winfield" until February 26th, when it departed for Roanoke Island, and arrived March 2d. On the 11th of the same month it left the Island, and arrived at Newbern on the 14th. From March 20th till May 18th, the company acted as Cavalry, and performed picket duty on roads leading to Newbern. While on picket near this place, March 31st, privates Henry Love and George E. Fuller were wounded, and May 2d, Corporal Benjamin F. Martindale was killed. On the 20th of June, the battery made part of the brilliant military pageant at the State presentation of a sword to General Burnside, and fired the salute on that occasion. It left Newbern July 25th, on a reconnoissance to Trenton and vicinity, and arrived back the 27th. It left again October 29th, and marched to Washington, N. C., where it arrived the next day. It left there on a reconnoissance to Tarboro, engaged the enemy on Little Creek twice the same day, and arrived at Newbern November 12th. It left December 11th on an expedition, engaged the enemy at Whitehall Ferry on the 16th, in which action Corporal George H. Manchester and private John Butterworth were severely wounded, and William Nesbett and James D. Gavett killed. Eight horses were also killed. On the 17th of December, the enemy were engaged at Goldsboro' Railroad Bridge, when Sergeants Alexander Massie and J. A. Gage, and private C. C. Burr were wounded. The battery accompanied General Spinola, in his expedition to raise the siege of Washington, and in an encounter with the enemy, Captain Belger was severely wounded, and for several months was taken off duty.

Among the early losses of the battery by death from sickness and accident, were private William B. Healy, of Providence, Corporal Elisha A. Slocum, of Pawtucket, and Sergeant Benjamin H. Draper, of Providence. Private Healy had an earnest, affectionate nature, and a keen sense of moral and religious obligation. He shared largely the esteem of his commander, and his companions. He died at Roanoke Island, of fever, enduced by severe exposure at Hatteras Inlet, and the effects of climate. He passed away peacefully at the age of eighteen years. His remains were brought home, and interred in the North Burying Ground. Corporal Slocum entered the service with ardent patriotism, and a strong desire for active duty. He was soon prostrated by typhoid fever, terminating in chronic diarrhœa, and after an illness of several weeks at the hospital on Roanoke Island, was brought home to die. He expired July 5th, 1862, aged seventeen years, leaving a large circle of friends to mourn the departure of one whose pure life and Christian resignation gave assurance of ripeness for a happy immortality.

Returning from a night reconnoissance, the company acting as Cavalry, Sergeant Draper received a kick from a horse, which broke his leg badly below the knee. All means that surgical skill could devise were employed to save the limb, but without success, and amputation became necessary. At first the case appeared hopeful, but with a constitution unequal to the shock, he rapidly sank, and on the 27th of May, 1862, departed this life in the 21st year of his age. Sergeant Draper joined the battery at the commencement of its organization, and took an active part in filling up its ranks by enlistments. With strong convictions of duty, he volunteered with the honorable purpose of aiding to restore the harmony of the Union; and endowed with soldierly qualities, his worth was appreciated, and his prospects of advancement promising. His confinement was borne with manly fortitude, and his last hours were sustained by Christian trust. His body rests in Swan Point Cemetery.

> "No stern array in battle's front, of fierce and vengeful foes,
> Can break the holy peace that marks the soldier's last repose."

From January to November, 1863, the battery was much engaged in picket and reconnoissance duties, and has taken a high rank for efficiency. In November it proceeded, by order, to Fortress Monroe.

BATTERY G.

(*Mustered into service December 21st*, 1861.)

Captains—Charles D. Owen, resigned December 24th, 1862; Horace S. Bloodgood, promoted from 1st Lieutenant battery B, December 29th, 1862, resigned April 22d, 1863; George W. Adams, promoted from 1st Lieutenant battery B, January 30th, 1863; transferred from Captain battery I, April 23d, 1863.

Lieutenants—Charles D. Owen, promoted to Captain, December 21st, 1861; Edward H. Sears, resigned November 14th, 1862; Crawford Allen, Jr., wounded at battle of Fredericksburg, Va., May 3d, 1863, promoted to Captain battery H; Elmer L. Cothell; William B. Rhodes, transferred to battery D; Otto L. Torslow; Benjamin E. Kelley, killed at battle of Fredericksburg, May 3d, 1863; James E. Chace; Allen Hoar.

Battery G left Providence for Washington, December 7th, 1861, and went into camp at Camp Sprague, where it remained occupied in drill until January 3d, 1862, when it proceeded to Darnestown, Md., and encamped for the night; and from thence marched to Poolsville, where, on the 8th, the Potomac being frozen over, the pickets on both sides suspending the monotonous business of their respective beats, engaged in the more peaceful and exciting amusement of skating—so closely does the war and peace spirit approximate! In February, the battery was at Edwards' Ferry, where it was visited by Governor Sprague. When, on the 7th February, the joyous news of victory in Tennessee arrived in camp, Lieutenant Sears fired a salute of 34 guns. The encampment was situated in a beautiful grove, about half a mile from the ferry. Here it remained, doing picket duty, until early in March, occasionally exchanging shell compliments with the rebels.

On the 15th of that month it was at Bolivar Heights, having marched by the way of Sandy Hook and Harper's Ferry. From there, it proceeded to Washington to join McClellan's advance on Richmond. March 29th, it left Washington on board a propeller and two schooners, dropped down to Alexandria, and the next day sailed for Fortress Monroe, where it arrived, April 2d. After landing, the battery proceeded up the Peninsula, and encamped seven miles from Yorktown. On the 28th, it was ordered to take position in batteries No. 7 and 8, within one thousand yards of the rebel fortifications, which it did, and at night returned to Camp Winfield Scott. During the siege, it was constantly engaged in picket duty and skirmishes with the enemy. On their abandonment of their stronghold, it followed up with Sedgwick's division to which it was attached, and during the residue of the campaign, shared the dangers and fatigues of his command. During the "seven days" fight, it rendered special service on the retreat, and in one instance, by timely occupying a particular position, prevented an important advantage to the rebels. On withdrawing from the Peninsula, it marched by the way of Yorktown, to Hampton, where it embarked for Alexandria. The guns were sent forward by transport, under charge of Lieutenant Allen. Captain Owen, and Lieutenants Sears, Rhodes and Torslow, followed, on board another, having the horses in care. On the 6th September, the battery was at Arlington Heights. On the 17th, it fought at Antietam, under Captain Owen, with great bravery. On the 6th of October, it was at Bolivar Heights. It left there on the 31st, and crossed the Shenandoah. On the 5th November, it was at Upperville, and moving on, it was in readiness, on the 18th December, to join in the assault on Fredericksburg. In this battle, Captain Owen fought his guns with coolness and spirit.

On the resignation of Captain Owen, December 24th, 1863, Lieutenant George W. Adams, by promotion, succeeded to the command. The part taken by him in the battle of Chancellorsville, is described on page 239. In subsequent service, the battery has maintained its good reputation.

BATTERY H.

(Mustered into service October 14th, 1862.)

Captains—Charles H. J. Hamlin, May 16th, 1862, resigned September 27th, 1862 ; Jeffrey Hazard, promoted from 1st Lieutenant battery A, October 1st, 1862, resigned August 17th, 1863 ; Crawford Allen, Jr., promoted from 1st Lieutenant battery G.

Lieutenants—Clement Webster, did not enter the field, and resigned February 3d, 1863 ; George W. Blair, Charles F. Mason, promoted from battery A, Kirby S. Steinhauer, promoted from Sergeant battery G, assigned to battery D ; Elmer L. Cothill, promoted from Sergeant battery F ; Walter M. Knight, promoted from Q. M. Sergeant battery F ; Samuel G. Colwell.

Battery H was enlisted under Captain Charles H. J. Hamlin, and went into camp near Mashapaug Pond. On proceeding to Washington, October 23d, 1862, it was assigned, October 28th, to "Camp Barry," where it received three-inch rifled guns in place of the "James" pieces with which it left Rhode Island. On the resignation of Captain Hamlin, Captain Jeffrey Hazard was promoted to the command, from 1st Lieutenant of battery A, in which he had seen severe service, and shown undaunted courage. At first the battery suffered, by the desertion of a large number of men from New York, who enlisted for the bounty. In March, 1863, the battery was filled by detached men from the Vermont brigade, General Casey's division, in which division the battery had been since the 23d of January. In March, the battery was ordered from Fairfax Station to Union Mills, on Bull Run. At the time of the battle of Chancellorsville, one section was ordered by General Abercrombie to be taken to Rappahannock Station, where it remained nine days with the 12th Vermont regiment. Upon the return of this section, the whole battery was ordered to Chantilly, where it remained until Hooker's Army passed through to Maryland and Pennsylvania. The time of our nine months detached men had then nearly expired, and the battery was ordered to Washington, where it remained two days, when it was ordered to the defences South of the Potomac, General DeRussey. This battery had fine opportunities for drill and general improvement, but having been retained in the Department of Washington, has never been in any engagement.

The vacancy in the command, made by the resignation of Captain Hazard, was filled by the promotion of Lieutenant Crawford Allen, Jr., from battery G. He was slightly wounded in the battle of Chancellorsville. A correspondent of the Providence Press, writing from Camp Barry, under date of November 30th, says: "Captain Allen, in the time he has been with us, has shown himself quite efficient as a commander, as well as exceedingly popular with the men." In November, 1863, Lieutenant Charles F. Mason, whose gallantry at the battle of Antietam has elsewhere been referred to, was appointed on the Staff of Colonel Tompkins, Chief of the Artillery brigade, 6th Army Corps.

——

TENTH BATTERY.

Three Months Volunteers—Mustered out August 30, 1862.

Captain—Edwin C. Gallup.

Lieutenants—Samuel A. Pierce, Jr., Frank A. Rhodes, Amos D. Smith, Jr., Henry Pearce.

Sergeant Major—Amasa C. Tourtellott.
Quartermaster Sergeant—Asa Lyman.
Hospital Steward—Charles W. Cady.
Sergeants—James S. Davis, Jr., Henry W. Brown, Calvin J. Adams, George W. Payton, Stephen G. Luther, Philip B. Stiness, Jr.
Corporals—John L. Remlinger, Henry L. Guild, Smith F. Phillips, Nathaniel F. Winslow, Jr., Ephraim Greene, John P. Dow, Charles

33

H. Starkey, Alphonso Bennett, Henry A. Boss, Isaac Andrews, James Flate, James M. Harrison, William Almy.

Artificer—Charles J. Noonan.

Bugler—Daniel F. Read.

The Tenth Battery, for three months service, was raised simultaneously with the Ninth and Tenth regiments of three months volunteers, and was recruited under the supervision of Captain Edwin C. Gallup. It left Providence for Washington in May, in three detachments, the first under Lieutenant Samuel A. Pearce, Jr., the second under Lieutenants Frank A. Rhodes and Amos D. Smith, Jr., and the third under Captain Gallup and Quartermaster Sergeant Asa Lyman. On reaching Washington, they proceeded to Tenallytown, and concentrated at "Camp Frieze." The battery lay here, improving its drill, until June 23d, when, in obedience to orders, it moved forward to reinforce General Banks. It marched to Cloud's Mills, and there encamped, waiting further orders. In about a week they came, not to advance, but countermanding those originally given, and directing a return. It therefore countermarched, and made its encampment near Fort Pennsylvania, the headquarters of the Tenth R. I. Volunteers. Here it remained until the expiration of its term of service, when it returned home in company with the Tenth, and shared the welcome that waited their arrival. During its absence it made a proficiency in artillery movements, that excited the surprise, and received the strong approbation of military visitants from Washington. Though not sent to the front, to engage in deadly conflict, the battery formed an important arm of the defence of Washington, at a time when it became necessary to withdraw troops more enured to service from the fortifications around that city, to reinforce the armies in the field. One death only, and that by accident, occurred. Corporal James Flate was run over by a limber, and so badly injured that he died in four hours. He enlisted in New York, as the battery passed through that city. He was faithful in the discharge of his duty, and by his social qualities gained universal favor.

SEVENTH SQUADRON RHODE ISLAND CAVALRY.

Major—AUGUSTUS W. CORLISS.

Adjutant—CHARLES TILLINGHAST.

Assistant Surgeon—H. W. KING.

Quartermaster—GEORGE A. SMITH.

Captains—Christopher Vaughn, Sanford S. Burr.

Lieutenants—John Angell, Samuel A. Lewis, Theodore Kellogg, William H. Stevens.

This body of 165 men was raised for three months service, and sent into the field 28th of June, 1862. It was composed of a company recruited from Dartmouth College and Norwich University, and one company enlisted in Providence. Its services were rendered chiefly in the vicinity of Winchester and Harper's Ferry, in reconnoitering and doing scout duty. It was part of the cavalry force which cut its way out of Harper's Ferry, during the investment of that place by the rebels. It was present on the field of Antietam, ready to go into action should occasion offer for employing its services. During the campaign it lost thirty men taken prisoners. It returned to Providence on the 28th September, and was mustered out of the service. The services performed were creditable to the Squadron and to the State.

GENERAL ISAAC. P. RODMAN.

(*Note to page 150.*)

General Rodman received a musket ball in the left breast, which passed completely through his body. He was conveyed to the house of Dr. Horner, near Hagerstown, where he died, September 29th, 1862, aged forty years, in the presence of his father and his wife, who were with him to comfort his last hours. Before he went to the war, General Rodman was well known to the citizens of Rhode Island, as an active and enterprising manufacturer, of the firm of Samuel Rodman & Sons, of South Kingstown. When the second regiment was raised, he accepted the office of Captain in it. He devoted himself to the study of the military art with the energy he had always brought to his business pursuits. He showed marked bravery and coolness at the battle of Bull Run, July 21st, 1861. Soon after the 4th regiment Rhode Island volunteers was organized, he was appointed Colonel of it, and accompanied Burnside in his expedition to North Carolina. In the battle of Roanoke and in the battle of Newbern, his regiment was distinguished.

In recognition of his eminent services, Colonel Rodman was appointed Brigadier General. The severe labors of the campaign had, by the early summer, so worn upon him that his surgeon and General Burnside both insisted on his going home for rest. He accordingly returned, and spent the summer with his family. His townsmen gave him an enthusiastic reception. Having a great reluctance to anything that might look like display, he refused all requests to appear on public occasions, until the great war meeting was held in Providence, on the 5th of August, when he appealed with great earnestness to his fellow citizens to hasten forward the recruiting. He soon after returned to the army, and took command of a brigade in Burnside's corps. The high esteem in which he was held by his superior officers, is shown by the fact that a division was entrusted to him in the battle of South Mountain, where our forces gained so signal a victory. Besides a wife, daughter of the late Governor Arnold, he left six children to mourn his loss. By his old regiment, the 4th Rhode Island, his death was deeply mourned.

The remains of General Rodman arrived in Providence October 3d, and were received by a guard of honor, and conveyed to the Representatives Hall in the State House, which had been appropriately draped for the occasion. Here they lay in state until the afternoon of the next day, when a solemn and appropriate service was held on the State House Parade. A canopied platform had been erected near the western steps, on which the casket containing the body was placed. Prayer was offered by Rev. Dr. Barnas Sears, a dirge performed by the Band, and brief and impressive addresses made by Governor Sprague, Hon. Henry B. Anthony, Abraham Payne, Esq., Rev. Dr. Sears and Hon. William M. Rodman. Rev. Dr. E. B. Hall pronounced the benediction.

At the close of the service, the remains were escorted through several streets to the cars by the 11th regiment Rhode Island volunteers, the Providence Horse Guards, and a section of battery H. They were conveyed to South Kingstown under escort of the Governor's staff, the Narragansett Guards and the Pettaquamscutt Infantry. On Sunday, 5th October, the final funeral services were performed by Rev. Dr. Barnas Sears, in the presence of an immense concourse. The body was deposited in the family burying ground, on the farm of the Hon. Samuel Rodman, the father of the General. Three volleys of musketry were fired over the grave, and the great company moved tearfully away, but never to forget the christian patriot who fought so valiantly and fell so nobly, defending the honor of his country.*

LIEUTENANT ROBERT H. IVES.

(Note to page 150.)

The remains of Lieutenant Ives were brought to Providence, and funeral services were performed on Wednesday, October 1st, at St. Stephen's Church, at which he was a worshipper and a communicant. Only a month elapsed from the day of his departure from home to the day of his funeral. So brief was his campaign, so sad was its close. Yet not wholly sad; for his example will not be lost. It will call—it does call—to young men of wealth and culture and refinement, to be willing to make the same sacrifice which he made. Few have so much to sacrifice as he. None can offer what they have more modestly or more generously.

* Providence Journal.

GENERAL ISAAC L. STEVENS.

(*Note to page* 142.)

The remains of General Stevens reached Newport, R. I., September 7th, and were conveyed to the residence of his brother-in-law, Rev. Charles T. Brooks. On Wednesday, 10th, they lay in state in the lower room of the State House, from 8 A. M. to 1 o'clock P. M., attended by a detachment of the Newport Old Guard as a guard of honor. The room was appropriately draped with mourning and the national colors. The body, enclosed in a neat casket, was arrayed in full uniform, and the casket covered with flowers. The sword and equipments of the deceased, enclosed in a case, were placed near the head of the casket. The flags of the city, of Fort Adams, and of the shipping in port, were at half mast, and many stores and residences draped in mourning. The obsequies took place at two o'clock P. M. Religious services were held at the house of Rev. Mr. Brooks, where the mourners were assembled, by Rev. Augustus Woodbury, of Providence, who briefly dwelt upon the private virtues of the deceased, and opened to the bereaved family the sources of consolation in the gospel of Christ. The remains were escorted from the State House to the Cemetery by five military companies, formed into a battalion, commanded by Colonel William E. Stedman, of the Newport Artillery. The procession was the largest and most imposing ever gathered on a similar occasion in Newport. At the grave, the military formed a hollow square, and Rev. Mr. Woodbury read passages from the book of Revelation appropriate to the occasion, made a brief address, followed by a prayer and benediction. Three volleys of musketry were then fired over the grave, and the impressive ceremonies closed. General Stevens was a native of Massachusetts. He served with honor in the Mexican war, was one of the commission that surveyed the route for the Pacific Railroad, and had been Governor of Washington Territory. In his civil and military relations, he was distinguished for energy and administrative qualities. He was courageous even to daring, and his attachment to the Union was attested by the sacrifice of his life upon the altar of liberty and law. His noble deeds will live in the pages of history.

PORTSMOUTH GROVE HOSPITAL.

Arrangements having been made with the War Department, for establishing this hospital for sick and wounded soldiers, the first contribution of 1724 patients arrived July 6th, 1862. Active measures were pursued to increase the accommodations, improve the grounds, lay out a cemetery, and enclose the premises with a high, substantial fence. The whole number of buildings is 58, comprising 28 wards for patients, and 30 for mess-house, kitchen, laundry, dry-houses,

33*

hospital store, dispensary, commissary department, officers' quarters, chapel, blacksmith and carpenter's shops, barracks for Hospital Guards, and other necessary purposes. A daily religious evening service is held by the chaplain, who preaches morning and evening on the Sabbath. The chapel building is 80 feet long by 30 broad, and two stories high. The audience room, in the 2d story, will comfortably seat 350 persons, and the walls are decorated with shields, on which are inscribed passages of Scripture. The successive Chaplains have been, Rev. O. S. Prescott, Rev. Silas S. Cummings, and the present encumbent, Rev. Alexander Proudfit. The spiritual labors of these gentlemen have been greatly blest, and the present chaplain finds great encouragement in his work. In the lower story of the chapel is a reading room and a library of 1600 volumes, which are freely used by the men. Every department of the hospital is kept in neatest order, and in the arrangement of its wards for ventilation, is superior to any other government establishment of the same kind and extent, in the United States.

From the opening of the hospital to August 1st, 1863, the number of patients received was 6866. Of these, 414 were Rhode Island men. Deaths in the same time, 124; buried in the hospital cemetery, 101.

List of Past Officers.

Medical Staff.—Surgeons—Francis L. Wheaton, U. S. V. ; D. J. McKibben, U. S. V.; F. P. Ainsworth, U. S. V.

Assistant Surgeons—A. D. Blanchard, U. S. A, II. E. Brown, do.; P. McIlaughton, do.; A. J. Cummings, G. C. Stiebling, Benoni Carpenter, E. Bacon, J. March. U. S. A., A. Cooledge, II. T. Livermore, U. S. A. ; T. Phelps, G. M. Sternberg, do.; II. L. Sheldon, do.; A. E. Dyer, do.; E. Thomas, do.; L. J. Marven, do.; W. F. Hutchinson, do.; E. Flynn, do.; J. R. Ludow, U. S. V.; Francis Greene, do.

Quartermaster—Captain F. J. Crelly, U. S. A.

Chaplains—Rev. O. S. Prescott, Rev. Silas S. Cummings.

List of Present Officers, August 1st, 1863.

Medical Staff—L. A. Edwards, Surgeon U. S. A.; W. F. Cornick, Assistant Surgeon U. S. A.; J. W. Merriam, Assistant Surgeon U. S. V.; J. M. Laing, do.; A. M. Paine, Acting Assistant Surgeon U. S. A.; II. B. Knowles, do.; Ed. Scyffarth, do.; J. W. Cushing, do.; S. Ingalls, do; F. L. Taylor, do.; W. C. Mulford, do.; A. J. Gray, do.; W. T. Thurston, do. The Acting Assistant Surgeons are private Physicians under contract.

Hospital Steward—E. A. Calder, U. S. A.

Chaplain—Rev. Alexander Proudfit, U. S. A.

Quartermaster—Captain Charles E. Russ, U. S. V.

Officers of Hospital Guards, R. I. V., on duty at this post.

Captain C. Blanding, U. S. V. 1st Lieutenant W. C. Chace, wounded at Newbern. 2d Lieutenant John II. Hammond, Sergeant in battery A, in battle of Bull Run, 1861; wounded in battle near Malvern Hill, June 30, 1862.

SOLDIERS' HOME.

The frequent calls made upon the President of the Providence Fifth Ward Relief Association, during the summer of 1862, by invalid soldiers returning to their homes in other States, and the many found at the railroad station, destitute of the means to provide themselves with a night's lodging, suggested to her the utility of establishing a Home where this class could obtain shelter and food, and be otherwise made comfortable until able to resume their journey. The plan was laid before several gentlemen interested in the welfare of discharged volunteers, by whom it was cordially approved. Through the active exertions of a gentleman appointed for the purpose, $2000 were at once raised to commence and carry on the Institution for one year. The State, through Governor Sprague, who warmly favored the movement, granted the use of the Marine Hospital, which was soon neatly fitted up, a Steward and Matron employed, and in October the work begun, under the direction of an organized Board of Managers. Of this Board, Mrs. Edward Carrington was chosen President, Mrs. Dr. Wayland, Vice President, Mrs. William T. Grinnell, Treasurer, and Mrs. A. N. Beckwith, Secretary. Subsequently, Miss Sophie B. Dunnell, of Pawtucket, became Secretary. The professional services of Drs. Collins, N. Miller, Baker, Okie and McKnight were gratuitously given to the Home. At the end of the first year it was closed. During its operations, 750 persons were received into it, for periods varying from a single meal to several weeks, and embracing many wasting away under disease engendered by the exposures of the field, or suffering severely from wounds. Though temporary in its character, the Soldiers' Home deserves to be remembered as having rendered an important service in the work of humanity.

SUPPORT OF SOLDIERS' FAMILIES—BOUNTIES.

(In Providence.)

The course taken by the city of Providence in encouraging enlistments, and in providing for the families and dependents of volunteers and drafted soldiers, has been generous and patriotic. As early as 1861, during the latter part of the year, the City Council appropriated the sum of $8000, for the relief of the families of volunteers, to be expended under the advice and direction of the Mayor. This sum was entrusted to the care and management of Mr. George B. Holmes, and by him judiciously expended in weekly sums of one, two and three dollars, according to the size and needs of the respective families requiring assistance. Additional appropriations of this kind were made from time to time, until the sum expended thus amounted to $11,000.

The first provision made for soldiers and their families in the form of a bounty, was during the summer of 1862, when, to encourage enlistments to fill the quota under the call of the President of the United States for 300,000 men, the City Council, July 14th, authorized the payment of a bounty of $100 to each and every able bodied man, to the number of six hundred, who within thirty days should enlist in any company or regiment raised in Providence by the authority of the Governor of the State. This bounty did not secure the number of recruits requisite to fill the city's quota, and a draft impending, petitions were presented to the Council, asking that bounties of $300 and $500 might be given to men volunteering for nine months, and for the war. The subject was referred to a committee of nine, who, through their chairman, Mr. Reuben A. Guild, presented, August 25th, a lengthy and carefully prepared report, which was adopted. This report recommended the payment to every three years volunteer, of a bounty of $100, and $25 per month to his family, (if he have one, and if not on his written order,) during the first twelve months of his service, provided he did not, in the meanwhile, desert or be dishonorably discharged. On similar conditions the nine months volunteer was to receive $25 per month.

On the 8th of September, 1862, Messrs. Guild, Field and Payton, of the Council, and Alderman Ham were appointed a special committee to report at the next meeting of the Council, what further legislation was necessary for the support of the families of volunteers from the city, and also to report some practical method of disbursing the appropriations made by the City Council, which should come more immediately under their supervision and control. They reported an organization and regulations for a relief committee, which was adopted. The committee consisted of Reuben A. Guild, Chairman ; William J. Cross, Oliver A. Washburne, Jr., Samuel J. Curry, Secretary ; Joseph A. Barker, George W. Payton, G. Burroughs Field, being one councilman from each ward, and Alderman Daniel Paine. Joseph H. Hoyt was appointed Relief Clerk. The families to be aided were divided into three classes, and received weekly two, three and four dollars respectively, according to the number of persons in each.

The entire amount appropriated by the Council from time to time, and expended by the Relief Committee up to the close of 1863, is $300,000. Additional appropriations for the families and dependents of soldiers will probably continue to be made until the Rebellion is crushed out, and the union of the States restored.

LADIES' RELIEF ASSOCIATIONS.

The "Florence Nightingale" Association, in Providence, was a spontaneous organization, that took form the day succeeding the attack on Fort Sumter, and almost its earliest work was to make tunics for the volunteers hurrying to the defence of Washington. In August following, it was organized on a broader scale, and took the name of "The Providence Ladies' Volunteer Relief Association." Its object, as expressed in the constitution, was "to aid in fitting out the Rhode Island Volunteers, and contributing to their confort while absent." Contracts from the government were taken for garments needed by the volunteers, giving to 575 needy needle women the benefit of the employment ; articles were made for the soldiers not furnished by the government, and forwarded to the camps and hospitals. In carrying out the general objects, 29030 garments have been made on contracts from the Quartermaster's department of the State and the United States, and 19,012 for hospital uses. The treasurer has received $13,034,37. Of this $5,338,31 was in payment of contracts, and $7,696,06 from private contributions. $7,510,99 have been paid to the employees, and $5523,38 expended for materials for hospital use, transportation of boxes, &c. The organization was somewhat changed in the spring of 1863, and took the name of the Rhode Island Relief Association, Auxiliary to the Sanitary Commission, and its direct work is in aid of that body, doing such incidental, outside service, as discreet judgment dictates.

The Providence Third Ward Ladies' Relief Association, has been abundant in patriotic works, and has contributed to the army and hospitals, values to the amount of about $5000.

The Providence Fifth Ward Ladies' Relief Association was organized July 25th, 1861, and has been unwearied in its labors. From July 1st, 1861, to December 1st, 1862, it contributed 7755 articles for volunteers in the field, and in hospitals. Numerous letters from officers, soldiers and surgeons, bear testimony to the great value of the services thus rendered.

In Newport, Bristol, Warren, Pawtucket, Woonsocket, and in every other town in the State, similar associations have been industriously engaged in like works. The history of these several organizations reveals a loyalty, as earnest and devoted as that which characterized the women of the Revolution.

SANITARY COMMISSION.

The agency of the United States Sanitary Commission was established in Providence, in October, 1861. Its duties were to receive any articles intended for the relief of the army or navy, and pack and forward them to the places where needed ; and also, to receive all contributions in money and send to the Treasurer. The estimated value of 352 cases thus forwarded is $70,000. Up to March 10th, 1863, $8,318 36 had been expended for hospital articles, freights, &c. Russell M. Larned, Esq., has given his gratuitous services to the agency from his first connection with it.

ALLOTMENT COMMISSION.

This commission was established by the State, in 1862, as a method of enabling Rhode Island volunteers safely to remit their pay to their families. The first State Commissioner was George B. Holmes, Esq., who resigned July 1st, 1863, and was succeeded by Colonel Amos D. Smith, 3d. The Paymasters and Commissioners to receive such sums as the officers and men wish to send home, are Colonel J. T. Pitman, Major William Munroe, who has travelled 18,000 miles in visiting the various regiments and batteries, Daniel D. Lyman and Henry M. Amsbury, Esqs. Cashier, at the office in Providence, Cyrus Dyer, Esq.

The commission has been admirably managed under the administration of the two State Commissioners, and from April, 1862, to the close of 1863, nearly $1,000,000 have been remitted through the visiting commissioners, by the Rhode Island troops. No better commentary upon the excellence of the system can be offered than this fact. Rhode Island was the earliest to organize a safety plan for her soldiers, the essential features of which have since been incorporated into similar agencies in other States.

PROVOST MARSHAL'S DEPARTMENT IN RHODE ISLAND.

On the 24th September, 1862, the War Department issued "General Orders No. 140," organizing a system of Provost Marshals, consisting of one Provost Marshal General, and one or more *special* Provost Marshals for each State. Simeon Draper, Esq., was appointed Provost Marshal General.

For the State of Rhode Island, William E. Hamlin was appointed by the President of the United States, and was afterwards commissioned by the Governor of Rhode Island, with the rank of Major.

Major Hamlin continued in the duties of his office so long as this system was in operation.

In a report made to His Excellency Governor Sprague, on the 17th January, 1863, he states that—

"The duties devolving upon this office are various. They have included the arrest and confinement of deserters and stragglers, and the transportation of them to their respective regiments ; ferreting out cases of fraud upon the Government, and of enticing soldiers to desert, and holding them for trial in the civil courts ; giving certificates of identity and loyalty to our citizens, to enable them, when at Washington, to obtain passes to their friends within the lines of the army ; quelling disturbances in the various barracks of the city ; searching for government property which had been embezzled or stolen, and the prosecution of offenders ; correspondence with Provost Marshals of other States for the return of deserters, and with commanders of regi-

ments and batteries to obtain complete descriptive lists : investigating
the numerous cases of frauds occasioned by the large bounties ; examining into cases of more than one enlistment by the same person, to
ascertain where he belongs ; embarking of regiments and detachments
for their destination ; and, finally, keeping a complete list of all deserters in this State, and of all the arrests made, with the disburse-
ments of rewards and expenses."

During the period of Major Hamlin's official duties as Special Provost Marshal for Rhode Island, he arrested and restored over one
thousand deserters and stragglers to their regiments, about five hundred of whom were deserters. Large amounts of Government property have been captured and restored, and the State of Rhode Island
saved from the loss of many thousands of dollars, by corrupt bounty
swindlers who infested the State, and who by systematic operations devised every conceivable means to accomplish their purposes. Recruits who enlisted in the city of Providence to obtain the bounty of
$4 per week for their families, would, after their being mustered into
the service, ascertain that the recruiting officers had placed them as
enlisting in another town, where a cash bounty was paid down, (instead of a weekly bounty,) the recruiting officer taking the cash bounty, and the soldier obtaining nothing of the town bounties for himself
or family during his service.

Recruiting runners would combine to have the men whom they
enlisted desert, in order to enlist them again in another State. For
this purpose, a party would leave New York in season to meet a detachment going on from Rhode Island. They take state-rooms, and
have an ample supply of clothes,—for gentlemen, sailors, laborers,
&c. After the detachment reaches the New York steamboat, from
Providence, the men, under cover of the darkness, find their way to
the state-rooms, where they are completely metamorphosed. In the
morning, the soldiers are called into line, and six or eight found to be
missing. The boat is searched ; perhaps one of the missing soldiers,
in the disguise of a sailor or a deck hand, assists in the fruitless
search. The detachment leaves for the regiment, and six or eight men
reported deserted.

Again. The same party start to meet another detachment. On this
occasion, to vary the performance, the soldiers go to the state-rooms
and put on citizens clothes *beneath* their uniforms. In the morning
every man is in line and answers to his name, and the detachment
leaves the boat. Meantime, the assistants are not inactive. On
reaching one of the principal thoroughfares, at a given signal by the
assistants, a melee is started in the street, and in the confusion, while
the guards are attempting to quell the disturbance, military jackets
and pants are thrown off from a number of the soldiers, and in *citizens' clothes* they mingle with the crowd, which is the last that is seen
of them. They are reported as deserters.

On one occasion, one entire company of 100 men was raised in ten
days. It was found that the officers who were expecting commissions
had made complete arrangements for the desertion of the entire company. The men were mostly deserters from New York regiments.
On enlisting, the men signed papers making over to the officers $150
of their bounty ($300,) with the understanding, that when the Rhode

Island paymaster paid the State checks in New York, the officers were to give them passes, and they were expected not to return. The men, by this operation, would have $25 each from the general government, and $300 from the State government.

The Provost Marshall arrested the whole company, and selected such deserters from New York regiments as could be identified, who were returned. The company was re-organized by the appointment of new officers, and the State and general Government saved a large sum of money.

The system of special Provost Marshals for the States, continued until the act of Congress passed March 3d, 1863, and called the *Conscription Act*, went into operation.

This act provided for a Provost Marshal General, with the rank of Colonel, and provost marshals for each congressional district, with the rank of *Captains* of Cavalry. The two districts of Rhode Island were represented as follows: The first district Captain William E. Hamlin, and the second district Captain Alfred B. Chadsey. By this act, Boards of Enrollment for each district were created, for the purpose of carrying on the draft. In the first district, William Y. Potter was appointed Commissioner, and Charles G. McKnight, M. D., was appointed Surgeon. In the second district, James H. Coggeshall, Commissioner, and F. H. Peckham, M. D., Surgeon. These appointments were all made by the President of the United States.*

The enrollment for the State of Rhode Island commenced by the two boards of Enrollment on the 1st day of June, and was completed in about three weeks.

The Draft commenced on the 7th day of July, and was completed on the 9th of July.

Reports for examination of drafted men commenced on the 14th of July. More than two months elapsed before the large number drafted could be properly examined. The result of the draft in the first district was as follows:

Whole number drafted	2971
" " required	1980
Of which number went themselves	49
Commuted	323
Substituted for	330
Exempt for disability	897
" " other causes	1142
Absent from the country and in navy	80
Advertised and not reported	150

The number enrolled in the district was 16,466.

Class first subject to the draft	9003
" second, 35 to 45	4563
" third, soldiers in service	2000

---

*The whole number of men composing the Rhode Island regiments, inspected by Johnson Gardner, M. D., up to November 24th, 1863, in all are 7916, of which 1322 are Colored.

Drs. Peckham and McKnight also examined considerable numbers previous to the draft.

Captain Alfred B. Chadsey, of Wickford, R. I., was appointed Provost Marshal of the second district, April 30th, 1863. The draft in this district was made on the 8th, 9th and 10th of July, 1863. Examinations closed September 30th, 1863. The experience in forwarding substitutes and deserters has been similar to that related of the Provost Marshal of the first district.

Number enrolled in second district........................8,400
Whole number drafted......................................1,350
Exempted for disability 423
Exempted for other causes 241
Elected under 4th clause, section 2d, enrollment act........... 15
In service March 3d, 1863................................. 58
Commuted 130
Substitutes accepted at general rendezvous 287
Substitutes accepted, deserted before delivery.............. 61
Drafted men delivered at general rendezvous, 26; detailed for
    service on Block Island, 30 56
Number failed to report, 52; in the navy, 9; at sea, 10........ 71
Died since the draft, 2; discharged by order of the War Depart-
    ment, 1... 3
Required number obtained in 4th sub-district.............. 4
Number of deserters arrested, from June 1st to December 20th,
    1863 183

INVALID CORPS.

The quarters, in Providence, for this corps, are on the Park grounds. They are made the temporary home of recruits and of recovered deserters. The officers in command here, are Lieutenants John B. Blanding and George E. Hall.

BATTLE OF GETTYSBURG.

(*Note to page* 269.)

The Union losses in this battle were 2,834 killed, 13,709 wounded, 6,641 missing. The Federals captured 3 guns, 41 standards, 24,879 small arms, and 13,621 prisoners.

LIST OF OFFICERS.

It was intended to have given a complete list of the officers commissioned in Rhode Island regiments and batteries since the war begun; but the preparation of an accurate one, in season for this volume, has been found impossible. Such a list may appear in another contemplated work.

PENSIONS.

The State has made arrangements to obtain pensions for wounded soldiers, and widows of soldiers having claims to pensions, without cost to the parties. The Commissioner for this purpose is Colonel Joseph S. Pitman. Colonel Pitman served in the Mexican War, and was Lieutenant Colonel of the 1st Rhode Island volunteers in the battle of Bull Run.

CHRISTIAN COMMISSION.

In November, 1863, $6,347 87 were contributed, in Providence, to the Christian Commission, and forwarded by William J. King, Esq.

' CAPTAIN HOWARD GREENE.

Captain Howard Greene, of a Wisconsin regiment, lost his life in the gallant and successful assault on Missionary Ridge, Chattanooga. Captain Greene was a son of Welcome A. Greene, of Providence. He was a graduate of the Providence High School, and is well remembered by his early friends, who mourn his untimely but honorable death. He was married in Nashville, Tenn., in February, 1863.

A spirit spreads its silvery wings,
His heavenly harp attunes its strings,
His guarding angel incense swings
    To lead him to the skies.
Weep! for a soldier dies.

His sun declines while yet 'tis noon ;
His lamp goes out ; but oh, how soon !
From life, bright like a day in June,
    A halo's round him shed.
Weep for a soldier dead !

Weep for a mother left in woe,
For wife whose husband lieth low !
Let all our hearts be chastened now,
    For a mother's darkened life :
Pray for a soldier wife !

'Mid Christmas chimes their boy went home,
From heavenly Christmas ne'er to roam ;
The Christ-child called him for his own,
    His life to him he gives :
Joy, for a soldier lives ! *

* Providence Journal, Dec. 23, 1863.